SEAS...

YESTERDAY'S GONE

SEAN PLATT

DAVID WRIGHT

YESTERDAY'S GONE: SEASON FIVE
(Episodes 25-30)

Copyright © 2011 by Sean Platt & David Wright. All rights reserved
Edited by: Jason Whited jason-whited.com
Email at: jasonhwhited@me.com

This is a work of fiction. Any resemblance to actual persons living or dead, businesses, events, or locales is purely coincidental. The authors have taken great liberties with locales including the creation of fictional towns. Reproduction in whole or part of this publication without express written consent is strictly prohibited.

The authors greatly appreciate you taking the time to read our work. Please consider leaving a review wherever you bought the book, or telling your friends or blog readers about this book to help us spread the word.

Thank you for supporting our work. You rock!

Published by Collective Inkwell
Visit: CollectiveInkwell.Com
First Print Edition August 2016

Layout and design by Collective Inkwell
CollectiveInkwell.Com

* * * *

WARNING: This book is intended for mature audiences. It is a dark book with many disturbing scenes and mature language.

To YOU, the reader.
Thank you for taking a chance on us.
Thank you for your support.
Thank you for the emails.
Thank you for the reviews.
Thank you for reading and joining us on this road.

* * * *

SEASON FIVE
YESTERDAY'S GONE

SEAN PLATT **DAVID WRIGHT**

YESTERDAY'S GONE
::EPISODE 25::
(FIRST EPISODE OF SEASON FIVE)
"THE BEGINNING OF THE END"

CHAPTER 1
LUCA HARDING

Irvine, California
October 2013

Beneath a blue sky baked by an Indian summer sun, astringent chlorine blended with the too-sweet scent of coconut suntan lotion and the happy sounds of careless play coming from the two hundred or so children and adults swimming under Luca, who couldn't feel more out of place.

The water park was thriving with life, and he was teeming with something that could eradicate it all.

Luca stood on the diving platform, staring down at the pool's surface, trying to calm the paralyzing fear that gave his body a tremble and threatened to send him back down the ladder.

Luca had thought that being at the pool was supposed to help test his ability, and that Rose had brought him to such a crowded place because it would be easy to infect and control others.

People's defenses are always low when they're gathered together and distracted by fun.

That's what Rose had said when she was telling Luca where they were going to go, then again once they got there. But after seeing Luca's crushing fear of heights, she had decided it was time for an impromptu lesson in overcoming that fear.

"Come on," a boy called out impatiently from the ladder behind him.

"Jump!" a girl ordered, and added to Luca's already heavy apprehension.

The Darkness inside him spoke. *You'll be safe.*

The Darkness, as the alien had thought of itself, was comfortably nestled in Luca's thoughts, but unlike Rose it had not taken over his body. Luca wasn't a mere puppet or host like most other humans the alien had entered. The alien promised that he was a partner, because *It* found him different than the others. *It* said *It* wanted to work *with* Luca, not just through him. *It* could have easily forced Luca to leap from the edge of the board, but *It* merely advised him instead, knowing that given time Luca would make the right decision.

For that, Luca was thankful. When Rose had forced him to ingest the blue liquid full of alien life just two weeks ago, he had thought it was the end of himself. But it had been the opposite: Luca had been changed by the alien's brother, calling itself The Light. Luca's memories had been replaced with those from another Luca, from this world. The Darkness lifted the veil, scrubbed false memories away, and proved to Luca that his life was a lie.

His parents were not his parents. Nobody could ever understand him, not what he'd already gone through, or what he still had to survive.

No one could understand him as The Darkness did.

"Come on, faggot." The boy behind him was getting louder, petty impatience filling his voice. Luca could feel him, halfway up the ladder, staring holes into the back of his head.

Luca flinched with the word, remembering the kids who'd taunted him at school.

Ignore them, The Darkness said. *Just focus on the water's surface. See that it is only a distance of ten feet, and know it.*

To Luca the board wasn't ten feet above the water. It was five hundred, and thin as a reed, slippery, with a ladder that took an hour to climb. If he hit the water wrong, he'd be dead for sure.

It's a clear drop to the water below, Luca. There is no danger unless you slip. Your desire to retreat is only the fear. You must kill the doubts and whispering fears that will never be true. If you turn around and scramble down that ladder, you're more likely to slip and fall, plunging to the ground and cracking your head like a melon on concrete.

Luca looked down at the water, gleaming bright beneath the sun. He felt dizzy, his stomach churning.

"I can't." Luca turned from the water. He was about to scramble back down the ladder, even though he could crack his head like a melon on concrete.

But the ladder was blocked by the boy who had been yelling at him. He broke the rules and climbed to the top of the ladder before Luca had dived. He was tall, a few years older than Luca, probably around sixteen. The boy's face was big and full of zits, his thick brow was low and angry. He made Luca think of a shovel.

The Darkness said: *Funny how the angriest of people look the least evolved.*

Luca laughed.

"Whatcha laughing at, faggot?" Shovel Face asked.

Luca looked down. Even though The Darkness ran through him, and gave Luca certain gifts, he'd not yet learned to master his new abilities. Part of The Darkness not claiming his body meant that Luca had to tap into these abilities on his own. That's why Rose was helping him. She was like a coach, like when Luca's father who wasn't really his father was teaching him how to fight.

But in the meantime Luca was still vulnerable, and about to get his ass handed to him by a bully at the top of a diving board.

"*Jump*," said a voice in his head.

This time it was Rose, who could tap into Luca's thoughts, seemingly whenever she wanted. Unlike Luca, she was controlled by The Darkness. It was a collective alien with shared memories and experiences, but her Darkness felt different. Better, Luca was certain. His Darkness had changed somehow, evolved for having been in him. Luca wasn't sure how he knew this, whether he was picking up on thoughts from The Darkness or realizing these differences with his own senses.

Luca looked down at the chairs lined up around the pool and found Rose lying back, reclined in a pink-and-blue bathing suit, looking just as carelessly happy as everyone else in the park. She looked up at Luca and smiled.

"OK," he said, both to the jerk and to the voices in his head.

Luca turned and walked from the platform to the ice pack-colored diving board, which bowed slightly beneath his weight. The distance between Luca and the blue water below seemed to somehow expand by another hundred feet. He was staring down from the top of a building into the rippling surface of an inescapable death.

Luca remembered watching the people who had jumped before him. They had bounced on the board then launched into the air. He used his weight to jostle the board.

One, two, th–

Shovel Face screamed, "Boo!"

Startled, Luca turned to look back. He lost his balance and slipped, his leg banging the board hard as he plunged over the side.

Luca screamed on the way down, his stomach hurled down an elevator shaft.

He slammed into the water, his stomach and face smacking the surface and knocking the air from his lungs.

Time turned to goo as Luca plunged deeper into the pool, desperate to touch bottom, propel himself to the surface, and suck some air into his lungs. Panic stabbed his brain and made his limbs do stupid things, screaming inside that he was seconds from dying, sending his legs into kicks and his arms into thrashing.

He'd never reach the surface in time. Luca would drown and no one would miss him, all because of some asshole kid.

His feet hit the bottom, and Luca kicked, thrusting upward toward the refracted sunlight.

He broke the surface, gasping, filling his lungs and feeling like a target for the park's every eye. He turned, desperate to orientate himself and locate Rose. He longed for their hotel, now. Practice was over.

He spotted her, sitting on her lounge chair, leaning forward, looking at Luca, making sure he was OK.

As he started to swim toward her, Luca felt a sudden danger descending a moment before the shadow draped him. He looked up to see Shovel Face diving like a blade straight at him.

Luca tried to move, but wasn't fast enough.

The boy barely missed, instead crashing through the water about two feet away, splashing Luca, getting water in his mouth, and causing him to gasp again.

Shovel Face surfaced through the water with a lunatic's laughter.

Luca glared at him. The boy chuckled, almost like Johnny Thomas, then turned and swam to the pool's side. He pulled himself up and joined another three of his friends, for a total of four assholes laughing and looking at Luca.

He turned away and swam toward Rose, hoping she'd let him practice his infection on Shovel Face.

"What was *that* all about?" Rose asked as he approached.

"I dunno, some jerk who decided he didn't like me." Luca sat in the lounge chair beside her. "Can I infect him first?"

"No," she said, surprising him.

"Why not?"

"Because his guard is already up. He's in adversarial mode, and a far harder person to get into. Start small. Find someone relaxed and having fun. Oblivious."

"And then what? Are we going to bring them back to the hotel?"

"That's not how it works. We are adding to our collective. We leave some of The Darkness inside them. It grows over time, slowly taking over until it's ready to do whatever we need. But you're not leaving anything in anyone today. You're testing to see if you can enter undetected, take over for a bit, then leave."

"OK," said Luca, disappointed.

Though he hadn't been keen on infecting anyone before their trip to the water park, Shovel Face had quickly changed his mind.

Rose had explained that infection was a blessing to humans, and would help to evolve them. Luca wasn't completely onboard but could feel himself warming to the idea. Still, he didn't want to *evolve* Shovel Face.

He wanted to hurt him.

Rose, as if sensing — or perhaps reading — his thoughts, said, "Forget about the boy. Find someone else."

Luca looked around and spotted two girls lying back in chairs near the pool's shallow end. High schoolers, or maybe in college.

"Does it matter how old they are?"

"No one too young. The truly innocent can rarely handle infection, and it would be foolish to draw attention."

"How about those two?" Luca asked, looking at the girls.

Rose smiled. "You picked them because they're hot?"

"No, I dunno why I chose them."

Luca felt his face burn red. It was weird. Though The Darkness inside Rose was neither male nor female, it used Rose's femininity to embarrass Luca during moments such as these. Rose had even caught him looking down her shirt when she leaned over, and had smiled at him in the creepiest way both times. The third time she winked. Fortunately, his Darkness pretended not to notice Luca's occasional arousal around girls.

"They'll do fine." Rose smiled, leaning back in her chair, pretending to read the same book she'd been using as a prop for days.

"What do I do?"

The Darkness inside him answered. *Focus. Can you see them?*

Yes.

Good. Now I want you to really see them.

How?

First, you must unsee them. Stare until they blur.

Luca stared, a brunette and a blonde, both in tiny bikinis that barely covered their oily curves. He couldn't help but stare at their breasts, the thinnest white tan lines peeking out from their straps. He wanted to see more, not less.

The Darkness interrupted his leering. *Maybe you should pick someone else?*

No, I've got this.

Luca shook his head to clear thoughts of oily breasts from his mind, then focused on the girls' faces again.

He stared until they became a blur.

Now he was seeing with his mind instead of his eyes. A switch had been flipped. Then Luca somehow went from his mind to capture their thoughts.

The blonde girl, Ashleigh, was wishing she'd stayed home. Her mom had asked for her help with some flier she had to make for Junior League. Ashleigh had promised to help, but when Brie called she bailed on her mom. Now she felt bad. Worse, Brie wouldn't shut up about all the expensive shit Daddy was buying for her ever since the divorce. "Guilt gifts" she called them.

Why am I friends with this person?

Luca felt odd inside Ashleigh's head — like he was peeking straight into her mind, feeling things she felt, hearing thoughts in her voice, and seeing the movie of her life in flashes of memory. He could see the girl's mom as she pictured her, home and sick in bed. Luca wondered if the girl's mom was truly so ill, or if her guilt was shading the picture.

Luca wanted to dive deeper and see how the girl had last seen her mom, but wasn't sure if he could access specific memories or was only there for the ride, seeing, hearing, and feeling along with Ashleigh.

The Darkness responded. *You are in her head. But you should go with whatever she's thinking. The more you try to direct her thoughts or explore her memories, the more likely she will feel your presence. She won't know what's wrong, but she will sense something, and that will decay your connection. Control requires discretion.*

The longer that Luca stayed in her head, the more connected he felt. The more he liked being inside, exploring her perspective, watching, almost living her memories. He was more than a voyeur. It was like Luca was wearing her body, living the girl's life through her.

In a rush of ten minutes, where his every cell felt fully alive, Luca learned that Ashleigh was an aspiring dancer but had suffered an injury last year that had eliminated her chances for competition. Now she was weighing her options. Ashleigh felt overwhelmed with possibilities, unsure what her next passion was — whether she should continue trying to get into CalArts, or pursue drama instead. And there was always the option for something more practical. Her father was pressuring her to take pharmacology like he had, but Ashleigh would rather wait tables forever.

Luca was intrigued by how different the girl was from how he'd originally seen her. He had thought she was a fun party girl and nothing more, hanging out and laughing with her vapid friend by the pool. But inside she had so much going on, so much internal strife and uncertainty.

The Darkness asked: *You feel the connection is strong?*
Yes.
Good, now I want you to try and get her to do something.
Like what?
Something small, nothing to draw attention or put her in danger. Just something to validate your control.

Luca knew what he *wanted* to make her do. But being inside her head had made him feel a closeness he didn't want to violate, even if it meant not seeing her naked.

How do I get her to do it? Do I say it? Tell her to do something?
Just think it. Imagine you're in control of her body no different from your own. You think, I'd like a drink, then will your body to get you that drink, right? Same thing here.
OK.

Luca pictured the girl sitting straight in her chair.

After he thought it, he saw through her eyes as she sat up.

Look at your friend.

She did.

"Whatcha doin?" Brie asked.

Tell her you're going for a swim.

"I'm going for a swim."

Ashleigh's voice sounded odd, as if doubting the words as they fell from her mouth. Luca felt Ashleigh wonder why she was going to the pool.

The Darkness spoke inside Luca. *She's starting to resist, to sense your presence.*

What do I do?

Ashleigh thought, *do about what?*

The Darkness said: *You're broadcasting your thoughts. Stop it.*

I don't know how.

Ashleigh then thought: *I don't know how to what? What's going on? What's wrong with me?*

Luca felt someone shaking him and was jolted from Ashleigh's head and back into his own. Rose was rattling him by the shoulders to get his attention, but stopped once she saw he was back.

"Why'd you do that?" he asked.

"You were losing her."

"Sorry," Luca said, sad to be gone from Ashleigh's head. After his life's fifteen most intimate minutes with a girl, he felt like he'd known Ashleigh for years.

"It's OK. You did good for your first try. You were able to connect and control. With practice, you'll have it down."

"Can we go home now?"

"No. We'll find a few more people. But first, I want you back on that diving board."

"What? Why? I already went off it."

"Yes, but you're still scared. I want you to smother that fear. You are no longer limited by your human constraints. We can help you be better."

"A better diver?"

"Don't be a smartass. It's not about diving, and you know that. It's about overcoming your weaknesses, killing them if you can."

"It would've been easier if I just let It take over."

Rose smiled. "We can still arrange for that."

He saw her smile for what it was — a threat designed to remind Luca of his place. He was important to the scheme, but only a piece of the puzzle, a bit player in The Darkness's plan for humanity. It had no time to waste on Luca's whims and worries. If he was too scared to conquer a diving board, they'd likely make him a host like Rose.

Whatever remained of Luca would be gone forever.

He couldn't allow that to happen.

"OK, I'll do it." Anger fueled Luca's trip to the board.

He stood in line behind a dark-haired girl with pigtails. She looked around eight years old. There was a tall black kid with red shorts climbing the ladder in front of her.

Pigtails looked up at Luca and smiled sympathetically. "That looked like it hurt."

She must've seen his horrible excuse for a dive.

"Yeah," he said. "It did."

"Your first time diving?"

"Yes. That obvious?"

She smiled, "It's OK, I used to be bad, too. But I got good. You will, too."

"Thanks," Luca said as her turn in line came up and she ascended the ladder. As he waited for the girl to dive, Luca heard the last thing in the world he wanted to hear — Shovel Face laughing as he approached with his friends.

"Hey, faggot," Shovel Face called out.

Luca ignored him, holding his eyes to the ladder.

"Hey, I'm talking to you." Shovel Face lightly shoved him.

Startled, Luca spun around, fists instinctively balling.

Shovel Face looked down and noticed, laughing. "Whatcha gonna do? Hit me?"

The two other kids with him, a fat kid with red skin and a monobrow and a skinny Hispanic with spotty facial hair, laughed along with Shovel Face.

"Just leave me alone," Luca said, wishing he sounded less whiny.

Monobrow said, "Or what?"

Luca ignored them and started to climb the ladder.

"Yeah, I thought so," Monobrow said. "Pussy ass faggot."

Luca wanted to turn around and cut the smug smiles from all their faces. He hated bullies who picked on kids for no reason. He hadn't done anything. They'd spotted him, recognized him as weaker or different from them, and decided to mess with him. It was like those wildlife documentaries he sometimes watched with his dad — *or are those the other Luca's memories?* — where hunters spotted the weakest prey and culled them from the herd.

Of course with nature, the hunters were eating the weak. The circle of life had a purpose. But with bullies, there was no purpose except to make the bullies feel temporarily better about their pathetic lives.

The Darkness chimed in. *Forget them. They'll be irrelevant soon. They are no longer the top of the food chain. You are.* We *are.*

Luca allowed himself a smile as he climbed to the platform. On top, about to step onto the board, he heard the jerks behind him clucking like chickens.

Block them out this time. Just jump.

Luca heard a sound he wished he hadn't — one of the kids quickly ascending the ladder.

Luca looked back to see Shovel Face reaching the top.

"You're not supposed to be up here," Luca said, looking down for the lifeguard on duty — busy chatting with a cluster of girls.

Shovel Face smiled as he stepped onto the platform. "You've got five seconds to jump."

"Or what?"

"I'm gonna throw you off."

Luca's heart raced as Shovel Face's dead eyes narrowed in sincerity.

"One ... " Shovel Face started the countdown.

Luca braced his body.

"Two ... "

Luca carefully took a single step back, looking down to make sure his feet moved from platform to diving board without misstepping.

"Three ... "

Luca turned around and walked to the end of the diving board like a sailor forced to walk the plank.

"Four ... "

Luca looked down just long enough to make sure he was lined up correctly and that no one was beneath him.

"Fi—"

He closed his eyes and jumped.

Luca's second dive was far better than his first. He didn't dive hands first like he saw other people doing, but did manage to avoid a belly flop, keeping his feet pointed down as he sliced through the water.

As Luca's feet touched the pool's bottom he looked up to see two dark shapes growing larger. Shovel Face and one of the others had dived immediately after him.

Luca pushed off the bottom of the pool, hoping the boys wouldn't hit him before he reached the edge.

He broke through the surface and swallowed a deep lungful of air, bracing for impact. The jerks landed milliseconds apart on either side of Luca, sending up giant waves.

He made another attempt for the pool's edge. The last thing he wanted was to stay in the water with sharks.

He made it just inches before hands wrapped his torso and dragged him under the surface.

Luca gasped, swallowing and choking as he kicked off whichever of the two assholes was trying to drown him.

He managed to squirm free and grab some air. He looked around to see where the kids were, his eyes blurred. Monobrow was swimming in front of him, but Luca couldn't see Shovel Face.

He felt movement behind him, but was too late to react before Shovel Face's arms wrapped around his neck and yanked him into a choke hold.

"Where ya goin'? We're just getting started."

Shovel Face shoved Luca back under, squeezing his arms tight around Luca's neck. He couldn't break free.

They're actually trying to drown me!

Luca couldn't believe how quickly they'd escalated from a scare on the diving board to attempted murder.

What kind of monsters are these?

He squirmed, kicked, and flailed, attempting to break free, but Shovel Face held his grip tight.

Luca begged The Darkness to help him.

Kick his knee.

Luca kicked back hard to where he thought the boy's knee might be. He struck, hard and felt something crack.

Shovel Face screamed and let go of Luca.

He didn't bother to look back at Shovel Face, or to search for Monobrow and Jerk Number Three. Luca raced for the side of the pool.

As he neared the edge Luca heard someone behind him, swimming fast. He could still hear Shovel Face crying; it had to be one of the others.

He didn't dare look back.

Luca pulled himself up and out of the pool.

Go to the diving board.

He didn't understand the logic of climbing back up the ladder, but couldn't question The Darkness, who had far superior instincts.

"Hey, faggot!" Monobrow yelled.

Luca ignored him, grabbing rungs and climbing up.

The lifeguard whistled, repeatedly and seemingly shriller each time. Luca didn't look to see if he was whistling at him or just now noticing the injured Shovel Face in the pool.

"Stop right there!" the lifeguard yelled.

Luca paused, halfway up the ladder, and looked down to see Monobrow halted just as he was about to follow Luca onto the ladder.

"He just attacked my friend!" Monobrow said.

The lifeguard looked up at Luca, "Come down."

"No, they tried to drown me!" Luca cried.

He started climbing again, eager to put more distance between himself and Monobrow. While the lifeguard appeared to be around eighteen or nineteen and looked like he could fight, Luca couldn't imagine that he would listen long before chasing Luca up the ladder to extract revenge.

The lifeguard whistled again as if it would bring Luca down, then followed with a stern, "Get down, now."

Luca cried out, "They tried to drown me!"

Luca saw Rose approaching the lifeguard and Monobrow.

The Darkness spoke in Luca's ear: *Go to the diving board, now.*

Luca wasn't sure of *Its* intention, but he listened, stepping away from the ladder, onto the platform, then out to the diving board.

Below, Luca heard Rose ask, "What the hell is going on here?" playing her Adult Card with perfect pitch.

She's buying you time, The Darkness said.

For what?

To do what must be done.

What?

Look down.

Luca looked down and saw the pool crowded with kids, surrounding Shovel Face, looking at him like a car wreck. Some were asking if he could walk, and a couple offered to help him out.

The Darkness spoke: *Now is your chance.*

Chance to do what?

To do what you wanted. Kill him.

Kill him? No. I don't want to get in trouble. I want to go home.

You broke his kneecap. Sometimes the only way out of trouble is to plow through it.

Luca felt an odd vibration coming from the pool. With it the sound of static. No, not static, but the voices — no, thoughts — of every swimmer in the pool.

I'm connected to all of them? How?

Suddenly, there was nothing but silence below, save for Shovel Face crying.

Look down, The Darkness said.

Luca looked down. Everyone in the pool — ranging from young children to adults — was staring up at him blankly.

They're awaiting your command.

Luca looked down and saw that even Rose was staring, as if he'd somehow frozen time and hypnotized the world.

Shovel Face looked around and screamed, "What the hell is going on? What did you do?"

Luca smiled at the jerk's confusion. Even though Shovel Face was a Neanderthal, he could sense that Luca was somehow responsible for whatever was happening. Luca could taste his fear, palpable, sweet like sugar from ten feet above.

Luca stood on the diving board's edge, no longer paralyzed. He wasn't afraid of heights, he was enlivened by his position above them all.

Luca yelled, "I'm gonna give you to the count of five to get out of the pool."

Shovel Face looked up and laughed, though he couldn't mask his fear or confusion.

"One." Luca said.

"Fuck you, freak!" Shovel Face yelled.

"Two."

"You don't scare me."

"Three."

"Whatcha gonna do? There's one of you and hundreds of us!"

"Four."

Shovel Face cried out, "Fuck you!"

"Five," Luca said as a smile crossed his lips.

Go.

As soon as Luca thought what to do, everyone in the pool acted, en masse, closing in around Shovel Face.

"What the fuck?" he yelled, turning, hopping on his one leg as people crept closer, bumping into him.

Someone hit him in the back of the head.

Shovel Face screamed, spinning around to face his attacker.

A woman jumped on his back, opened her mouth wide, and bit down hard on the side of the Neanderthal's cheek, ripping the skin from his Shovel Face.

He screamed as he tried to throw her off.

He went under.

Many more piled on, keeping Shovel Face under, drowning him as they hit, kicked, gouged, and bit into his flesh.

Luca smiled then turned to find Monobrow, standing beside the lifeguard, still staring up at Luca as if awaiting instruction.

Luca turned his attention at the lifeguard, and inserted thoughts into his head.

Go.

The lifeguard snapped into action, kicking Monobrow's feet out from under him and slamming him to the ground before he knew what was happening. The back of Monobrow's skull hit the concrete with a sickening thud.

Though he was dead in an instant, Luca directed the lifeguard to grab both sides of the fat kid's head and repeatedly smash it into the concrete, turning the soup of splashed-up water into ruby goo.

Luca wasn't sure where the Hispanic kid had gone off to, so he searched.

No loose ends.

From below, Rose called out, "Stop!"

All at once, Luca's connection to the crowd was severed.

Screaming started as people reacted to bodies and blood. Luca wasn't sure if they were aware of their involvement, though judging from the residual emotions he didn't think so.

Fear and confusion shrouded the crowd as they rushed to flee the pool.

Suddenly, they all stopped, and everything went still.

What's happening?

"We can't leave this mess," Rose said, her voice in his head.

Luca realized that she was controlling the people in the pool. He'd never seen her exact control over more than one person, not without sending a bit of The Darkness inside them.

Luca looked down in the pool, startled to see everyone go under at the same time as if engaging in some sort of breath-holding contest.

He looked down, and the horror hit him. Men, women, and children. Innocents. Rose was planning to drown them all.

"Stop!" he yelled down.

"No, we can't leave witnesses."

Luca watched as The Darkness's tendrils spiraled from her mouth, found the people still outside the pool, grabbed them, knocking them down, forcing its way into their mouths.

"Stop!" Luca cried out. "You can't kill all these people!"

"I didn't do it, Luca. You did. By losing control."

Luca tried to access his own powers, to intervene, but he wasn't even sure how he'd infiltrated the minds of everyone in the pool to begin with.

Please, stop her, he begged The Darkness.

She's right, The Darkness said. *We can't leave this many witnesses.*

Luca stared down helplessly as the hundreds of lifeless innocents people began to bob in the pool.

He spotted the girl, Ashleigh, whose worry about disappointing her mother he'd shared just moments ago. She was floating, face up, dead eyes wide open, staring at her killer.

Oh my God. I did this.

* * * *

CHAPTER 2
EDWARD KEENAN

Somewhere in Maine

Ed pulled his pickup into the parking lot of Tom's General Store, immediately following the early morning crowd's dispersal. The small lot's only other vehicle was an old Harley whose best days probably predated Woodstock.

Good, Gary's working.

He got out, looking up and down the highway one last time before entering the shop, just to make sure no one was coming. The store was smack dab in the middle of nowhere, scabbed on a long stretch of highway with woodlands and nothing in every direction, the nearest town five miles away.

It had been three weeks since shit hit the fan with an infected Sullivan, and Ed had yet to see anything on the news about himself, dead agents, or the murder of Brent's wife. Still, this offered little comfort.

He still had no idea if Sullivan was alone in his infection and was responsible for the attempts on Ed and Brent's family or if the director, Bolton, had also been compromised.

Either way, Ed was certain that the Guardsmen, and all other agencies, were likely in pursuit — to either find out what happened or to silence them.

Either way, Keenan had to stay off the radar.

Ed was done with the agency, done with the Guardsmen, and on his own with no more resources. No one to turn to, and no one for help. He managed to secure one last safe house in Maine where he was lying low with his daughter, Jade, and Teagan, Becca, Brent, and Ben.

The house was well stocked, but Ed found himself trekking into town every few days for supplies — diapers as Becca was nearing two-years old but still refused the potty every time. They also needed fresh milk and other staples that seemed to run dry no matter how much he stocked.

Ed pulled his black cap low, covering his eyes before raking his fingers through his thick beard and pushing his way through the shop door. The bell rattled against the glass, announcing a visitor to Gary, wherever he was. The store belonged to yesterday, a time before clean shops with minimal stock. This shop was crammed so deep that Ed had to wonder if the owner was a hoarder.

Maybe we should've just bought this store to hide out in.

As Ed walked the aisles, stuffing his plastic tote full of supplies, Gary came out of the back stock room. The clerk was fifty-something years old with long gray hair and a longer mustache, carrying a box filled with cigarette cartons to stock the shelves behind the front counter.

"Hey, Jack," Gary said, greeting Ed with his assumed identity.

"Hey," Ed said, "how's it goin?"

"Same shit, different day." Gary ambled toward Ed, on his way to the front.

Ed didn't care much for the other clerks. They looked at him oddly, as if in suspicion. Gary didn't seem to give a shit. From their few conversations, Ed could tell that Gary had lived a tough life and wouldn't annoy his customers with the wrong sorts of questions.

"How's the wife and kid?"

"Same shit, different day," Ed joked.

"Ha!"

Gary leaned toward Ed and lowered his voice to a whisper. "Had some folks come in asking questions on Sunday, asking if I'd seen a guy, two girls, and two kids. Showed me a picture."

"That so?" Ed asked, wondering if he should drop his basket and reach into his jacket to grab his Walther PPK.

"Yeah," Gary said, looking like he was about to start asking the kinds of questions Ed had hoped that he wouldn't. "Looked familiar."

"Yeah? So, what else did he say?"

"He said they were wanted for some serious shit, but wouldn't tell me what. Asked if I'd seen anyone that fit the description."

Ed kept calm, watching Gary's reactions to mine the man's aim. Gary was good at holding emotions close to his vest.

Is he fishing for information, or wanting me to know that he knows I'm not who I say?

"So, what did you say?" Ed asked, meeting Gary's eyes.

"I told him to get fucked, that's what I said, Goddamned government types always up in people's business." Gary laughed.

Ed smiled, allowing himself to release the slightest sigh of relief.

Gary continued. "Didn't look a thing like anyone I knew. For one, the guy was bald. And he certainly didn't have a beard."

Ed smiled. Gary was *good people*, as Ed's grandpa would've said.

"Well, I better go stock these." He patted the side of box.

"All right," Ed said. "Thank you."

"No problem. You let me know if you need any help dealing with pests."

Ed wasn't sure what kind of help Gary was offering, but smiled and thanked him just the same.

Ed finished shopping, paid in cash, then went out to his truck, acid boiling his stomach. He looked around, searching for anyone camped out with their eyes on the store.

The woods could be crawling with agents, and Ed wouldn't be able to see them.

Gary might not have knowingly sold him out, but there was no way of knowing if the man had managed to mask his initial reaction to the photo. If the agents had seen the slightest trace of recognition they'd be on the store, waiting — and now closing in. Like Ed, they were trained to spot lies even from the best liars.

Ed got in his truck, tension twisting his shoulders into knots at his neck. He turned south on the highway rather than north. He stared into his rearview, then chanced a glance at the sky, searching for any sign of being followed by choppers. Of course, they could be tracking him via satellite, and he'd never know it.

Shit.

Ed wondered if the agents in pursuit were only wanting to talk or if they were like Sullivan, infected by aliens and looking to close open loops that might see them discovered.

After a few miles of nothing but logging trucks and the weathered, battered road beasts that normally swallowed this stretch, Ed turned back toward the safe house.

He considered calling the house to see if everyone was OK, but decided against it. While the line was encrypted and he'd installed voice modulation software on his phone as well as Jade's and Teagan's, Ed didn't want to take a single unnecessary risk, especially if agents were closing in on his location.

They'd need somewhere else to go.

Staying in Maine was too risky.

Problem was, Ed had nowhere to run. He'd burned through his money getting this house and had to assume his connections — forgers, weapons suppliers, and the same money guys he'd been using since his agency days — were all compromised if agents *had* tracked him to Maine.

"Fuck!" Ed slammed his palm into the steering wheel.

He had $6,457 left. He could get some camping gear and equipment then head further north, perhaps into Canada, and do all right. But Ed wasn't sure how well the others would hold up.

Even though Brent and Ed's daughter, Jade, were survivors who could be counted on to weather the tough times, he wasn't so sure about Teagan. She was a child, raising a toddler. Plus Brent had his son, Ben, who was only five.

Ed couldn't be carting children across creation with the government's most dangerous black-ops agents in pursuit.

He wished he had some way of knowing if Bolton was compromised. If not, there was a chance Ed could return to Black Island, forge some sort of truce, and maybe get them to leave his family alone.

But if Bolton, or even people above him (*who knows how deep the alien's tentacles had managed to slither?*) were infected, Ed would be ensuring his death along with all those he had vowed to protect.

**

The half-mile long stretch of dirt leading to Ed's cabin forked from yet another dirt road, blocked by a locked rusty gate that read, *No Trespassers!!!* and looked like it hadn't been used in decades. There was no way you'd find the cabin without explicit directions or previous knowledge. Odds of it being accidentally stumbled upon by agents were virtually impossible.

Hunters were a bigger threat, though hunters in these parts weren't likely to cross the barbed wire or trespassing signs along the property, especially since there was no shortage of game to be had on the neighboring lands.

Ed's truck bounced violently on the bumpy road as the sky opened to dump rain on his final stretch to the cabin, reducing visibility to maybe ten yards, forcing him to a near crawl.

The slower he went, the more eager Ed was to reach the cabin and make sure everyone was OK, even if he didn't yet know how to tell the only family he had that they might be compromised and had to leave just as they were getting settled. He wasn't even sure if he'd tell them of his plan to visit Bolton. Perhaps he'd tell Brent, but Ed was sure Jade would freak out and beg him not to.

That was the last thing he needed. Ed had to keep his head clear and figure out their options.

As he reached the end of the road and the woods thinned to a clearing, Ed noticed a pair of black vans parked in front of the cabin.

Shit!

Ed panicked, not sure if he should back out and make a run for it or get out of the truck and look the piper in his eye. He had to assume that if the agents wanted his friends and family dead, they already were.

Ed paused, still uncertain, and cursed his indecision. He was rusty. Old Ed would know exactly what to do, with a body that moved faster than his mind.

Bright headlights flicked on behind him, likely another black van, barring every thought of retreat.

"Shit." Ed killed the engine and opened his door.

He stepped out of the truck as the cabin's front door flew open. Jade came running out, yelling, "Dad!"

Someone — or two someones — grabbed Ed's arms from behind, injecting him with something before he could turn. He struggled to resist the drug's effects, and the men holding him, as his daughter screamed.

Ed saw a bag being pulled over his head, then nothing.

* * * *

CHAPTER 3
BORICIO WOLFE

Somewhere in BumFuck, South Carolina

If it hadn't been for the asshole playing "Friends in Low Places" for the umpteenth time, Boricio might not have found the strength to stand from the bar and get the hell out of the shithole joint before the jolly band of jerk offs started "singing" the song — *again*.

On the list of worst songs ever made, "Friends in Low Places" had to be Number Fucking One. It was practically an anthem for ignorant hillbilly cousin-fuckers to be blue-ribbon proud of their ignorant hillbilly cousin-fucking ways.

Fuck Garth Brooks for making this piece-of-shit song. Fuck him and fuck his sweat-stained nasty-ass hat.

Boricio stood from his stool and felt the floor swaying beneath him. Despite punishing his liver for three weeks running, not to mention a lifetime of abuse before he met Rose, Boricio was still surprised by his level of inebriation. The world had gone from wavy to what-the-fuck, and that was when anything could happen, and something always did.

Boricio laughed as he made his way to the bathroom, hoping he wouldn't have to smell too much shit as he pissed before leaving.

Halfway to the crapper, some asshole bumped into Boricio, and nearly sent him to the floor.

He managed to stay off his ass, and spun to see what careless asshole had been stupid enough to brush against the devil.

A giant Paul Bunyon-looking fuckstick with a Grizzly Adams beard and a nice big black prison tat of a swastika on his forearm stood there staring at Boricio as if *he* had been the one to bump into him.

Grizzly blurted, "What?"

Boricio looked him up and down, trying not to laugh at an outfit straight out of racist biker central casting or a bad '90s action movie.

Torn acid wash jeans? *Check.*

Black leather jacket spattered with idiot patches? *Check.*

Red bandanna to hide his bald spot? *Check.*

Tattoos that proved how much he hated himself and every other race? *Check. Check. Triple nipple I'll turn you cripple, check!*

Big Billy Badass was trying so hard it made Boricio giggle like a bitch.

"Whatchyou laughing at, boy?"

"Nothin' honey, you just keep rockin' that look."

Grizzly stared at Boricio, open mouthed. Boricio wanted to play more, but still had to squirt.

Boricio turned from Grizzly's stare, giggling on his way to the bathroom and hoping that big didn't mean dumb, and that Grizzly would be smart enough not to bother a man on his way to point Percy at the porcelain.

There was no way he would've looked back, even if he heard the bear charging, but Boricio didn't need to worry. Grizzly was more interested in the hot piece of ass waiting for him to finish — a bleach blonde with an equal number of "I hate my daddy" tattoos, but still young enough that the miles of self-loathing, drug abuse, and whoring had yet to turn her pussy into a pile of rancid lunch meat.

At the door, he turned back to see what he knew he would see — the blonde eyeballing Boricio like she wanted him belly to belly and burying a bone.

Boricio winked, then went into the bathroom. He emptied his eel, then stepped back out and threw his arms around the bar. A song by that cunt Kelly Clarkson came on the jukebox, clearly pissed of a few of the patrons — the song was a few years old, but brand new by shithole bar standards, and not Garth Vader or George Fucking Straight.

As he searched the bar for a reason to stay, Boricio saw Grizzly's blonde coming toward him.

Well, well, well. Lookee here.

The blonde looked Boricio up and down on approach, passing him with a wink and a smile on her way into the lady's room.

Boricio followed her inside, not at all concerned about the restroom's other occupants. Places like this — usually packed like opening day at a glory hole with meth heads, chicks fucked hard on the pain pill du jour, and drunks — women didn't think dick about a dude doing the lumpy batter all over a bitch's back in the stall.

Girls gotta earn their drugs.

Boricio expected a crowded house, but the shit room was empty save for the blonde.

The door swung shut behind Boricio. The blonde looked back, feigning surprise.

"What are *you* doing in here?"

"I think you know." Boricio climbed her body, using his eyes to fill every hole.

"I'm with someone," she said, smiling coyly.

"Yeah, I saw. But we both know he ain't doin' you like you need to get done. Am I right?" Boricio arched an eyebrow and grinned, feeling the liquor swimming inside him.

She stood by the sink and said nothing. Boricio stepped closer. Inches away, he looked down at her swollen tits, beaded with sweat, skin flushing for his touch. Her breath was rapid, and her eyes said she was as starving as him, and for the exact same thing. Hell, he could close his eyes and smell her.

Boricio put his hands on the blonde's hips and pulled her against him.

She leaned in, kissing him hard on the lips like she had cancer and his saliva was her cure.

He wanted to fuck her into a pile right there in the filthy bathroom, make her scream his name and leave her with cum on her tongue when she went to French Grizzly.

But Baby Boricio wasn't cooperating. It wasn't often that he got a case of drunk dick, but he knew not to force shit when it did.

He considered taking her back to his motel and saving her for morning, but the room was maybe six shit stains better than the bathroom, and something told Boricio that the blonde would never taste better than now.

The blonde, realizing Boricio's loss of interest, pulled away.

"What's wrong?"

"Nothin' — just realized I got somewhere to be."

She wrinkled her nose, pushed him away, and clomped out of the bathroom.

Boricio followed, pausing on the sawdust-covered floor as Grizzly passed, likely on his way to the men's room.

He looked at his woman, then at Boricio, slowly adding up two and two in his tiny noggin. He finally got four and yelled at the blonde.

"What the fuck you doin' in there with this pile of shit?"

"He followed me." She pointed an accusing finger at Boricio.

Right, like you didn't want me making cherries jubilee.

"Why the fuck you following my girl?" Grizzly shoved Boricio hard.

He fell back, then paused to size up his enemy.

Boricio was better drunk than most were sober, but that didn't diminish how fuckered he was. Clearly this asshole, and his Neanderthal friends, could kick his dick ass six ways to Sunday. But at the same time, bitches clucked and Boricio didn't. Weren't no way, no how he was backing down now.

Boricio had been on the run for three weeks since The Darkness stole Rose from his soul. Three weeks of getting as far the fuck away from her as possible before this world went to hell like the other one. Three weeks of searching for Mary and Paola, three weeks of failing to find them. Three weeks of nights like this — losing himself down the twin holes of hell — liquor to poison his blood and disposable pussy to help him forget.

Three weeks without the violence Boricio needed. Three weeks without losing himself to the rampage, killing a fucker, especially one who deserved it, and making him choke to death on Boricio's rage.

He met Grizzly's eyes and smiled.

"Bitch was begging, said you're nothing but hair, gut, and stub, and that even with that you only slam her a minute before stubby gets to spittin'—"

Grizzly swung, his ham-sized fist finding Boricio's jaw before he could duck or counter.

A detonation of pain boomed through his jaw.

Boricio stumbled, would've fallen to the ground if he hadn't stumbled back against a wall of tacky framed photos hanging crooked outside the bathrooms.

Blood flooded his mouth.

That fucker better not have knocked out a tooth!

Boricio felt around with his tongue, but didn't have time to check both rows of pearly whites before the fucker was charging toward the second round.

Boricio dropped to the ground, and managed to scramble away just as Grizzly barreled straight into the wall.

Boricio bounced up, looked back at Blondie, who was staring at the two men with a look so jaded she almost seemed bored.

Every drunk in the bar paused their shows for Boricio. Like the blonde, they'd seen this shit play out a thousand times before, but nothing thrilled hill folk like a brawl.

Boricio winked at Blondie.

The giant yelled, "Come on, you fucker!"

"Your GPS now working? I'm right here. And really, is *fucker* the best you got? Now technically, if I'd had another minute or two with your cock cozy that's exactly what I'd be right now, but she smelled like the pussy you get at Goodwill so I passed, and I haven't fucked your mother since yest—"

Grizzly charged and stole Boricio's second punch line.

Boricio saw himself sidestepping the goliath, then rushing him from behind, smacking his hands on the man's ears before going to town. But Boricio was drunk, and Grizzly sent him hard to the floor.

He was a boulder atop Boricio. He managed a few jabs to the giant's ribcage, blows that would've hurt most men, if not broken some bones. But Grizzly was wearing a blue whale's winter coat.

He grunted, reached up, grabbed Boricio's head with both hands, and slammed it hard onto a cushion of sawdust.

Pain splintered Boricio's skull, screaming from the lightning strike through him, white and blinding enough to rob him of everything else.

* * * *

CHAPTER 4
EDWARD KEENAN

Ed woke handcuffed to a bed in a cold gray cell with instantly recognizable glass doors and walls.

Black Island.

The air conditioner whistled through the ceiling and seemed to fuel the feeling that he was deep underground below tons of concrete and steel.

He looked up at the ceiling's many holes to where he knew the cameras were hidden.

"Hey!" he yelled. "I want to speak to Director Bolton!"

The speakers, also on the ceiling, were silent.

He called out again, but still no response.

Ed wondered if he was being monitored, and what the agents had already done to Jade and his friends.

He pulled at his cuffs, but they only rattled against the metal bed frame — solid and soldered into the wall and floor.

Shit.

He sat up and looked around. There were five other cells in the large room. He didn't think he'd ever seen this part of the facility, either the Other Earth's version, or this one's. He wondered if it was new, or somewhere he'd never been. There was a sliding red door with a camera above it at the end of the hall, with a touch screen beside it.

Ed stared at the door, waiting.

After what seemed like an eternity, the door slid open.

A man stepped through, alone, wearing jeans and a long navy shirt. Despite the simple denim and cotton, he looked like he'd just left his tailor's, with everything hanging on his lean frame just so. The man's slightly wavy brown hair was swept back from his forehead, and though he wore no glasses his face seemed almost naked without them. He seemed vaguely familiar, and Ed felt like he should know the man, but couldn't remember ever having met him.

The man stopped in front of Ed's door, pressed his palm against the pad on the outside. The glass door slid open, and the man entered with a smile.

"Who the fuck are you?" Ed asked.

The man's smile didn't even flicker.

"My name is Desmond Armstrong, and I'm here to help. Let me assure you that your friends and family are fine. They are topside, in our housing, safer than anywhere else in the world."

Desmond Armstrong.

The name flashed in his head. Ed had never met Desmond, but he'd dreamed of him after returning to Earth.

"How do I know you?" Ed asked.

"All of us who vanished on October 15 share some collective memories. Perhaps you've seen me in your dreams?"

"Yes," Ed said. "But from what I remember, things didn't turn out so well for you."

"I was killed. But the boy, Luca, returned in another form, like light, and brought me back."

Ed looked the man up and down, trying to get a read on him. He wasn't getting any vibes one way or another, save for the odd familiarity of having seen the man in his dreams.

"So why are you here?" Ed asked.

"I came back to save the world. That's where you come in."

"Me?" Ed held his hands out, palms up. "I'm done saving the world. I just want to rest. I don't know how much you know, or how long you've been here, but the guy running this show, Bolton, wanted me to kill off all of the ten to fifteen survivors, so forgive me if I find it hard to believe that we're sharing common goals."

"Bolton has seen the error of his ways, we've had ... *discussions*," Desmond said with a twinkle in his eye that indicated that he'd likely dressed Bolton down.

Who the hell is this guy? Military?

"Why would Bolton listen to you? You're just a civilian, right?"

"I have The Light inside me, the part of the aliens that wants to save us, rather than murder or absorb us. But there's a darker force out there, gathering strength, searching for vials that contain the alien in its raw form. If The Darkness finds the vials first, then we could have a repeat of what happened on the other world happen right here. But if we find them first, we can use it to destroy The Darkness once and for all. We can stop it."

"We? How?"

"We, those who vanished on October 15, all have a bit of The Light inside us. When Luca brought us back over, some of him came, and stayed, with us. We can use it to find the vials. We can find the people who have the last vials and convince them to hand them over."

"And what then? What are we going to do with the vials?"

"I don't entirely know. But I'm confident that The Light will show us the way."

"Sorry, pal, but I'm not buying the mumbo jumbo and pseudo-religious dark and light shit." Ed meant to rattle the man for a response.

Surprisingly, Desmond held his calm.

He kneeled to Ed's level.

"I'm not going to bullshit you, Mr. Keenan. I don't have all the answers. But I *do* know one thing. If we *don't* get those vials, then you, me, and everyone we love will die at the hands of The Darkness. You and I have both seen what it did to the other Earth. You can be the grizzled cynical bastard that Bolton said you are, or you can do something to save your family."

Ed chewed on the message, then said, "How do I know that The Darkness hasn't already infiltrated Black Island? It got to Sullivan. Hell, how do I know *you're* not infected?"

"Because we've got our very own sniffer, someone who can see The Light and The Darkness."

"Who?"

"Well, I can, for one. But there's also Paola."

"Mary's girl?"

"Yes, she is now The Light."

"What do you mean *is* The Light?"

Desmond explained that Luca had been The Light, but was growing weaker after fighting off The Darkness and sending the other Luca to take his place on this world. He then found Paola in the hospital, in a coma. She needed saving; he needed a home.

"Now she's helping us find the other vials. But she's a kid and helping from here. I need someone I can trust out there, boots on the ground following up on the leads Paola's getting from her visions."

Ed shook his head, trying to stop his world from sounding like bad sci-fi. He wanted to call it crazy, but couldn't dismiss a syllable. He'd seen destruction caused by The Darkness, and how it had murdered a planet.

He didn't trust Black Island to save the world, especially when they couldn't see an enemy in their own damned camp, but Ed felt like Desmond could be trusted. Especially if he'd managed to convince Bolton to let him head this operation.

"So, what do you need me to do?"

"What you do best," Desmond said. "Find people and convince them to do something they might not want to do."

"And my family, friends?"

"They can all stay here on Black Island. They'll be safe."

"OK," Ed said. "I'm in."

* * * *

CHAPTER 5
MARY OLSON

Black Island

Mary sat on the couch, watching as Paola played with Teagan's girl, Becca. Jade sat beside the young mother, looking guarded, and not unlike a gloomy college kid with her bright-blue hair.

Mary couldn't blame her for looking miserable. They'd been dragged here against their will, and she'd yet to see her father, Ed.

Mary wanted to say something to let Jade know things would be OK, that Desmond was there and wouldn't let anything bad happen to her father.

Becca giggled, a deep and almost-hoarse guffaw when Paola tickled her.

Mary watched, feeling a sense of joy swell inside her. It was the most lively she'd seen Paola since she emerged from the coma after Desmond saved them and brought them to the other world before coming to Black Island. According to Desmond, Luca had created the portal to save them, not him. After Paola had woken from her coma, they headed immediately to the island.

Mary continued to watch Paola as the girl smiled at Becca. She even played peek-a-boo with the girl, which might be the most Paola had said since the coma. It seemed like having a younger child around drew Paola out from whatever shell she'd been in.

Dr. Morgan said these things take time.

As if the Black Island doctor could possibly have a clue. They didn't know what had happened to Paola in the chamber or how Luca had come to bring The Light inside her. The Black Island medical staff was as much in the dark as any of them.

Desmond, however, had his theories, and seemed to believe that Paola's recovery and her recent waking visions were all good signs.

Easy for him to say: she's not his daughter.

But if anyone could understand what Paola was going through, it had to be Desmond. He had a bit of The Light inside him, too. He said everyone that Luca saved had The Light inside them, but he seemed more connected than anyone else.

Desmond could see, hear, and do things that Mary sure as hell couldn't. Nothing as powerful as healing people like Luca, but he had made a coin float, and seemed to be excellent at convincing people that his needs were theirs, even more than before. He also seemed smarter. Desmond had always flirted with genius, but The Light seemed to tune his intelligence tighter, as if it took everything good and made it better.

The mere fact that Desmond managed entry into Black Island Research Facility and had convinced Director Bolton to let him (a civilian) head up a search for the vials spoke volumes for just how much The Light had improved Desmond's verbal skills. Or it spoke volumes about how desperate Black Island was to get any sort of help in a war it was losing against an enemy it barely knew, let alone knew how to defeat.

"Do you feel different?" she had asked Desmond one night.

"Of course. I've been changed from The Light. You have too, Mary. We all have. It's inside us all."

Mary did feel stronger, but chalked that up to her many months of training, not some alien DNA or whatever the hell she had coursing through her body. If pressed, Mary would have confessed that she felt nothing special at all.

But that couldn't have kept her from denying the changes in Paola, even before she'd entered the chamber. Her daughter had somehow become a healer, like Luca, and had aged just the same.

Mercifully, Paola had stopped gaining years since their return. Though she'd also healed no one. It was hard for Mary to find comfort in that.

Mary watched Paola talk with Teagan, and thought the same thoughts she'd been threading together all morning: she'd settle for whatever she could when it came to Paola. Mary was just glad to have her daughter back, even if she wasn't exactly the same.

Brent returned from the kitchen, holding a cold Diet Coke in each hand. He offered one to Mary.

"Thanks," she said, taking the Coke as he sat down beside her.

They both looked at Brent's son, Ben, lying on his belly, pushing two trains on the floor, lost in his own little world. Considering that his mother had been murdered in front of him three weeks ago, Mary was surprised that the five-year-old wasn't an utter wreck.

Mary looked at Brent. "How are you holding up?"

"One day at a time." He sipped his drink, eyes on his son. He dropped his voice to a whisper. "It all still feels so surreal. I think the worst is not knowing what will happen next. I mean, how do you tell your children that everything will be all right when you don't know what the hell is going on?"

Mary didn't know Brent that well — they hadn't been together on the other Black Island, or here for long — but he seemed like a good man. And she could tell by the way he watched Ben that he was as fiercely protective of his son as she was of Paola.

"Yeah, tell me about it."

Mary wasn't sure how much he knew of their ordeal, or that Paola was now carrying The Light. She certainly wasn't about to initiate a conversation, especially in front of the kids.

"What do you think'll happen if Ed doesn't play ball?" Brent asked.

Jade looked up, waiting to see what she'd say. Mary pretended not to notice Ed's daughter watching.

"I don't know. But Desmond is a good man. He won't let anyone harm him."

Brent took another sip and said nothing.

The room's air felt heavy, dragged down by Desmond being part of the Black Island Guardsmen. They were getting along, but their world felt temporary.

Brent was right — they didn't know what might happen next. Mary trusted Desmond to keep the wolf far from their door, but knew she was the only person she could ever truly count on to put the wolf down.

* * * *

CHAPTER 6
LUCA HARDING

Luca sat in the passenger seat as Rose drove along the highway on their way out of town before anyone found them.

When he'd asked who was looking, Rose said there were people at Black Island searching, for both them and the vials. And while she didn't think they knew the The Darkness was hiding in her, her shell had allowed a man to escape who *could* tell others: Boricio Wolfe, the Earth version of the man who had once shared an adopted father with Luca. They'd have to be careful, the opposite of his time at the pool.

It was only a matter of time before agents came looking. They had to find somewhere to go — far away.

It was weird to feel like he was in trouble even though Rose hadn't expressed the typical human emotions like anger or disappointment, nor had she scolded the boy. She was a puppet for The Darkness, and whatever was left of the old Rose had either left or gone silent. The Darkness felt *some* emotion, but it wasn't the same as a person's. It was primal, more instinctive, and didn't seem to hold grudges or sulk.

Still, Luca felt horrible for what he'd done. He couldn't get the images of all those dead people out of his head, especially the girl, Ashleigh. He felt like he'd lost a lifelong friend. She shouldn't have died. None of them should have. He'd messed up and let his anger at the bullies consume him. In that way, he wished The Darkness would take over more and help him feel less. To simply do and be.

Rose, as if reading his thoughts, said, "Don't feel bad about the people at the pool. They're animals, really."

"I like animals."

"Why do you care about people so much? They're cruel, unpleasant, and they've not been terribly kind to you."

"I dunno." Luca put his feet up on the dashboard and stared at his new blue Nikes and their neon-yellow laces.

"Well, if it helps at all, know that they've moved on to something better."

"Like heaven?" Luca was surprised to hear Rose suggest such a thing.

"No, I mean that when things die, their energy moves on to become something else."

"Like reincarnation?"

"Not in the way that humans see it, no. You become part of something else — another person, an animal, a plant perhaps. Matter does not die. It changes form and becomes something else. We helped those people move on to a likely less-painful existence."

"Sorry," Luca said, staring out the rain tickled windows. "I don't see it that way."

Rose turned on the wipers and headlights. Luca found it weird how her inner alien knew to do such little things like drive and respond to the weather. He wondered, not for the first time, if there were more of Rose inside her body than he'd felt during their mental connections.

Is it possible that The Darkness inside her is hiding her from me?

Yes, Luca's Darkness said.

It had been a while since he'd heard from his alien. Since the pool.

So there is some part of Rose still alive in her?

Yes, what makes you wonder?

Luca had flashes of the Rose he knew on his home world. The woman who had been in love with his adopted brother, Boricio Bishop.

Why not let her go? You're inside me now. Give Rose her life back. We don't need her.

Do you feel sorry for her? The Darkness asked.

Luca thought about lying, but figured the alien inside his mind might surely sense a lie.

Yes. She was happy before. You've stolen her life.

We've stolen yours, too. You're not complaining.

It's different with me. You aren't forcing me to do anything. You're not taking over my body. Right?

Correct, Luca. You can champion our cause, and help us to usher in a new era for humanity. Working together.

Well, you have me. You should let Rose go.

We still need her, The Darkness said.

Why?

Because it's not easy for a child to travel without suspicion. We need her to help us find the other vials. That is the only way we can win the coming war.

And after we're done with her? Can she go free?

Nobody will be ... free, as you say, Luca. It's time for your species to evolve. Better she stay with us rather than risk losing her to The Chaotic Darkness.

What do you mean Chaotic Darkness?

We are a collective, Luca. We are many; we are one. But as you know, there is The Light, which hopes to destroy us. But there is yet another faction of The Darkness, a part we've lost control of after growing too quickly. This Chaotic Darkness festers in weak minds, urging their owners into violent acts before taking their lives. They threaten our exposure. We must gain control over all of The Darkness, and The Light. Only then can we hope to evolve humanity.

How will we do that?

Once we find the vials we'll be unstoppable. We will consume The Light and all those attempting to halt evolution.

What if we can't get the vials? What if The Light gets them first? What will The Light do with the vials?

The Darkness said, *The Light will find and kill us, along with any humans serving as host. If you want to live, if you want Rose to live, you must help us.*

So I don't have a choice?

Correct, Luca.

* * * *

CHAPTER 7
MARINA HARMON

Three weeks ago

Her father's words echoed in her head as Marina travelled the tunnel's length toward the monastery cellar two blocks from their compound.

"*There's a man there I want you to find, Father Thomas Acevedo. Tell him who you are. He will help you.*"

"*Help me what?*" she'd asked.

"*Save the world.*"

Marina clutched the black metal box close to her chest, knowing that the two vials inside, with their mysterious glowing blue liquid, were more important than anything — from Steven's betrayal and attempted murder, to the world splitting at its seams while Father's ghost rose to warn her that his prophecies were true.

She wasn't a devout believer in the religion he founded, The Church of Original Design, but believed he *was* onto something, and that there were great dangers facing the world.

Marina reached the cellar, a dark-red door barely visible in the dim lights running along the corridor, and was surprised to find no lock. Just a gold-colored metal door handle.

Marina opened the door, still in her pajamas, and found herself in the monastery cellar: long, dark, and piled with old dusty boxes. Concrete walls and wooden beams brought thoughts of her early twenties, and old Parisian churches. A stairway led to another door, this one black with no knob — a deadbolt.

Great. What do I do now? Knock?

Marina felt stupid. She didn't know the first thing about the monastery, even though it was only two blocks away, and shared a tunnel with her compound. She didn't know much about monasteries in general, but couldn't recall ever hearing of a 'father.' They had monks, nuns, and friars to the best of her recollection.

Who the hell is Father Thomas Acevedo?

Is the church Protestant? Catholic? Something New Age I've yet to hear of?

It didn't matter. If her father said to go there and find this man, that was enough for Marina.

She ascended the steps and knocked on the door. The wood was thick and dense. Her knock felt as if it went nowhere.

She waited a minute then knocked again.

The door swung open to a bald man in black robes. He looked around fifty years old. He cast his eyes up and down, but said nothing.

Marina wondered if he'd taken a vow of silence. She felt suddenly stupid for how little she knew of other religions.

"My father sent me. My name is Marina Harmon."

The man looked confused.

"My father is Josh Harmon. He was head of The Church of Original Design. He told me to speak with Father Thomas Acevedo."

The monk's eyes widened in recognition. He swallowed, as if suddenly afraid.

A chill ran through her body. Marina felt like she'd suddenly made a mistake, or maybe Father had in telling her to come here.

The monk nodded then stepped aside, ushering Marina in with his hand.

She followed, clutching the box even tighter to her chest.

The monk led her through the basement, through a long hallway, then up four flights along a narrow stairway that seemed like it might have once been a servant's stairway in a forgotten long ago. The place felt at least a century old and smelled of old wood, though Malibu wasn't known for antiquity.

She continued following until the stairway stopped on what she figured was the third floor: a long hall with a single red door at the end.

The monk pointed, ushering her forward toward the door.

"You're not coming with me?"

The monk shook his head, then started down the stairs.

Marina was equally freaked and confused.

Who are these people?

She approached the hallway's end, slowly, footsteps clomping on the wooden floors no matter how mousy she made them.

Turn around. Go home.

She couldn't go home. Steven would likely be there, waiting to finish her off.

As Marina drew nearer to the door she heard a man humming, perhaps in some sort of prayer.

She didn't want to interrupt, but at the same time didn't know what to do.

She knocked to no response.

The man kept humming.

She knocked again and waited.

Still nothing.

She looked down at the door handle, an ancient-looking knob, glass with no lock.

She reached out and turned it.

The door creaked open to reveal a long narrow room with nothing but a bed, a dresser, a trunk, and another door, which she assumed led to a bathroom. On the floor, facing the open window was a man in a black-hooded robe, on his knees, praying, or singing — Marina wasn't sure which.

As she stepped forward, the wood beneath her creaked.

The humming stopped.

The man sat upright.

Her heart pounded as he slowly turned.

Marina nearly dropped her box when she saw the black thread running through his lips to sew them shut.

* * * *

CHAPTER 8
BORICIO WOLFE

Boricio opened his eyes in the back of a beat-to-hell pickup truck, staring up at the dirty bug-encrusted lights of a gas station overhang that hadn't been cleaned since before Kurt Cobain made himself a buckshot sandwich.

His hands were tied behind his back with what felt like a nylon zip tie.

What the hell are they planning?

Whatever they had in mind, Boricio had no desire to play Honey Boo Boo in their bullshit.

He kept still, not sure if there was anyone in the truck's cabin, wondering if they were all inside the convenience store, loading up on cases of Bud and cans o' chaw, for a night of *Hee Haw* hilarity.

After a few moments void of sound and movements within the truck, Boricio rolled his bones for a better view in the back. No one in sight. He sat up, slowly, and looked around.

Three men inside the gas station — Grizzly plus a pair of gangly fuckers from his personal Nitty Gritty Dirt Band. No sign of Blondie Cumbox.

They were at the counter, either paying for their shit or chatting up the cashier, a woman Boricio could barely see from his angle. He looked around the station and saw woods in every direction. He was somewhere in South Carolina, but Boricio didn't know a dingleberry more than that. They might be planning to drag him into the woods. Killing him there made most sense. They probably had to grab some gas so they didn't get stranded among the trees with a corpse. Or perhaps cousin Jim Bob was getting his banjo restrung so he could play a ditty while they cornholed Boricio.

He stood, feeling exposed, certain they'd see him if he didn't move fast and break free from the ties. Boricio bent over, brought his arms up behind him, then slammed them back hard against his tailbone and snapped the nylon zip ties.

He jumped from the truck, but before Boricio could check to see if the hillbillies had left the keys in the cab, the convenience store bell clanged violently on the door.

Time to skedaddle.

"Hey!" Grizzly yelled as he and the gangly fucks poured out of the store.

Boricio bolted for the field — and the woods just beyond — across the street, running without looking back.

"Hey!" one of them yelled behind him.

As Boricio crossed the wide-open field, feeling exposed, the tree line felt like a mile away, hillbillies hot on his ass.

No way I'm gonna reach the trees!

Their footsteps pounded pavement behind him, then the grass. Boricio could hear them panting like puffy wet pussies, heaving breaths punctuating their pink little pleas.

"Stop runnin'!"

"We ain't gonna hurt ya."

"Come on, we just wanna talk shit out!"

That was beer-battered bullshit, and Boricio knew it. He'd ended plenty of fuckers after swearing he wouldn't. Bert and Ernie could've seen through that shit.

He kept running, hoping he was fast enough.

Just as Boricio got woods adjacent enough to see the escape in his mind, one of the fuckers ran right into his back, tackling him hard at the goal line.

Boricio fell face-first into the wet grass, unable to brace his fall. The ground emptied his chest and had him sucking for air as his tackler, one of the skinny fucks no less, jumped up and pulled a knife on Boricio.

Boricio turned over and was about to stand.

"Stay down, or I'll gut ya."

With his bulging eyes, long skinny neck, and ugly nose, the gangly fuck reminded Boricio of a bird.

Boricio kept gasping for air, heart pounding in his ears as the trinity of cunt hairs closed in around him. They were all far enough from the station that the men could kill him without a witness to dick.

Grizzly looked down and spit on Boricio.

"Gonna talk some shit now, smart ass?"

Boricio darted his eyes among the three men, smiling as he sized them up, weighing options and measuring ways to counter their attacks.

Boricio caught his breath, met Grizzly's eyes, and with exaggerated fatigue said, "OK, ya got me. What do you want?"

"You tried to rape my girlfriend, you fuck. I'm gonna make you pay."

"Oh, please. Your bitch was begging to batter my corn dog, said she was looking forward to having a *real* man play some *cuntry* on her *clitar*."

Grizzly moved forward and drew back his foot, aiming to send Boricio's teeth down his throat.

Boricio threw his arms over his face, bracing for a blow to the elbows instead of his jaw. Boricio countered Grizzly's kick by trapping his right foot and delivering a punch directly above the man's ankle joint, killing his leg so he crumpled in agony to the ground.

Boricio rolled on top of the man, shoved his fingers harder into the man's right ankle, then with his left hand grabbed Grizzly's foot and wrenched it back to effectively hobble him.

As Grizzly writhed in pain, Boricio hopped up from the ground, and eyed the two skinny bastards, Birdman and Nose Ring.

Boricio smiled. "Which one of you wants next?"

Birdman raged forward with his knife.

Few things were as dangerous as a fucker with a knife in your intimate space. Claiming the knife *might* be possible, but maybes weren't aces, and Birdman was as likely to find himself lucky enough to stab Boricio in the arms, or get through to his gut.

Boricio had to stay away from the blade, dodging and weaving until he saw a chance to turn the fucker's face to oatmeal on the road.

He dodged Birdman's first attempt, ducking back as he kept both men in front of him.

Nose Ring might have been armed, but Boricio didn't recall seeing a weapon in the man's hands.

For the moment, Boricio focused only on Birdman. Grizzly woke bears from hibernation — or at least anyone within earshot — with his screams. It was only a matter of time before the gas station attendant heard something and called the police.

Boricio had to get past Birdman, then the fuck out of Dodge. "Come on," he said, "why don't you give up now before someone else gets hurt?"

"Only person gettin' hurt is you." Birdman danced around Boricio like a brain-damaged boxer.

He hadn't seemed threatening at first, but Birdman *did* seem comfortable with the blade, and wasn't making any of the rookie mistakes that most people did.

Boricio had to get in his head and force an error. He could run into the woods and hope the skinny fuck didn't catch him — again. But Boricio wasn't much of a runner.

"You give big daddy over there a reach around whenever he wants it, too?" Boricio pointed to Grizzly, "or do you just fight all of his fights because you're his dumb little bitch?"

"Fuck you." Birdman kept his eyes on Boricio, staring down his every move.

"Come on," Boricio said, "you all know I didn't rape Reese Witherpoon. Your buddy there's just trying to protect his manhood because he can't stand to think his cumbox wanted to dippity-doo-dah with a stranger in the bathroom. No reason for this to get any uglier."

Birdman charged again.

Boricio dodged the slash, raising his elbow to block the attempt. He managed to seize Birdman's wrist and twist the man's hand, and the blade, back on him.

Boricio plunged the knife into his gut, and Birdman fell to the ground, eyes wide in shock. Boricio grabbed the blade and turned on Nose Ring.

Two down, one to go.

Nose Ring turned and took off back toward the station.

Oh no the fuck you don't!

Boricio raced behind him, blade in hand, eager to end another hillbilly's life before he could reach the truck where he would either flee or maybe grab a gun tucked in the glove box.

Nose Ring screamed as he fled. Boricio ran hard — he had to shut the fucker up, and quick. But Nose Ring was surprisingly fast and had a good ten yards on Boricio.

He was close to the convenience store, which may as well have been home base. Every gas station in the world had cameras these days; last thing Boricio needed was to be caught killing a fucker on YouTube. He'd been too careful over the years to get caught finishing off some redneck fuckface at a Stop n' Go.

Boricio pushed himself harder, but couldn't go faster. His body simply wasn't up to the task after weeks of pouring petrol down his throat.

Nose Ring reached the road about twenty steps ahead of Boricio.

If he went toward the station, Boricio was screwed. He'd have to turn and run, head for the woods in another direction or something.

Instead, Nose Ring went for the truck, drawing keys from his pocket as he ran.

He hit the truck's alarm, its angry, ugly, mechanical blurt screaming into the night, and surely alerting the cashier.

Fuck! Now that's two more notches on the killing stick.

Nose Ring reached the truck, threw open the door, and jumped inside.

If he had a gun, Boricio was fucked.

Nose Ring leaned over, toward the glove compartment.

Shit.

Boricio raced faster, near certain he'd sprain something or pull up limp.

He reached the truck as Nose Ring grabbed a pistol from the glove compartment.

Boricio launched himself through the still-open door, jumped on the man, mercilessly attacking with the blade, so fast and frenzied that the asshole was nowhere close to aiming his weapon.

The gun fell to the floorboard as Boricio kept stabbing, screaming, venting three weeks' worth of pent-up anger and turning the fucker to pulp.

For Boricio, time practically stopped as he plunged the blade repeatedly into the man's stomach, his throat, and then into his face, each blow releasing more of the rage that had gathered like a storm inside him for weeks.

Boricio had almost forgotten how good it felt to kill.

Almost.

The last sound he wanted to hear tore him from the moment — a siren.

Boricio turned around and saw two sheriff's cars, lights flashing and casting garish red and blue into the woods.

"Drop the weapon, put your hands on your head, and step back slowly," said a voice over the car's speaker.

A deputy was already out of one of the cars, with a rifle aimed at Boricio.

::EPISODE 26::
(SECOND EPISODE OF SEASON FIVE)
"I KNOW WHY
THE CAGED WOLFE SINGS"

CHAPTER 1
PETER WILLIAMS

Peter Williams sat in the ParkView Elementary School parking lot, staring at the front door, trying to stir his courage and get his ass out of the seat so he could do what had to be done.

Peter still couldn't believe it had come to this.

A year ago everything was perfect. Then, just like that, it all started to crumble. First with the headaches that the doctors couldn't understand. The migraines made him irritable and difficult to deal with, and no amount of pills or booze could get them to leave. At best, they barely dented the splintering pain.

Peter lost his job, then his friends. His wife and daughter right after that, both at once.

Funny how quickly the world turned on you when you lost your job and ability to earn. When you got sick with no relief. The final insult came two weeks ago when he received the restraining order, to stay away from his wife, Josie, and their daughter, Claire.

Something had clicked inside him.

Peter realized that he didn't have to take this anymore.

He was the master of his fate, not his bitch wife or some fucking bullshit court document saying he had to stay a certain number of feet from his own flesh and blood.

Fuck that.

Pain stabbed his brain, again. He reached into the duffel, past the guns, and found pills to dull his roar.

Josie thought she could take his daughter and he'd sit back and take it? Like he'd let some piece of paper keep him from seeing his child — *their* child?

It was originally supposed to be a trial separation, a "breather" from one another. They were supposed to try and put things back together.

But that fucker, Mr. Montgomery, had started working in the classroom beside her. A good-looking guy who seemed like he was used to leather seats. Peter had seen the way his wife had looked at Montgomery when he went to pick up Claire from school for their weekends together.

Peter confronted her. *She* blew up, accused *him* of being crazy. Said she didn't think he should be around their daughter anymore. She didn't *feel safe*.

What the fuck?

Then that asshole, Montgomery, got into it with Peter, coming over, shoving his nose in their family business. Put his hand on Peter, said maybe he should leave before Peter did something he regretted.

Of course he exploded. Who wouldn't have?

Peter decked the asshole fucking his wife. Then when Josie turned on him, yelling at him to leave her lover alone, Peter lost it.

He smacked *her*, letting anger overwhelm him.

A guy smacks his cheating wife one time in twelve years, and suddenly he's a monster who can't see his child?

For the first time it made sense. The headaches weren't a mystery illness. It was his subconscious picking up on his wife cheating with this asshole. He hadn't seen Montgomery until after their separation, but the guy had shared a school with his wife for years. She'd probably been fucking him under Peter's nose for a while.

The headaches showed him what his eyes refused to see.

The headaches said that he'd *allowed* this to happen. Invited a usurper to claim his family.

The only way to kill the headaches was for Peter to man up and take shit into his own hands.

He grabbed the duffel and weapons case, got out of the car, crossing beneath the flagpole, Old Glory whipping in the wind, and headed towards the school's front doors.

It was time to make things right.

* * * *

CHAPTER 2
MARY OLSON

Mary was sitting on the couch, doodling on her tablet, stabbing at creativity — she'd not finished a greeting card in forever — when a scream from the kitchen snapped her attention like a twig underfoot.

She jumped up and ran to find Paola on the ground, having another seizure.

Mary grabbed the pen and pad they kept on the counter for exactly this reason, dropped down beside her daughter, then cradled her head.

"It's OK, I'm here." Mary's mouth went dry.

No matter how many times she saw Paola in this state, the terror never dimmed.

She wasn't sure which was worse, how her daughter's body was shaking, the stiffness of her limbs, or the way Paola's eyes rolled into the back of her head. It all scared the hell out of Mary, even though it had happened five times since their return to Earth.

She'd nearly lost Paola twice to The Darkness. Two too many times for a mother.

Even though the island doctors said she was in perfect health, Mary felt like she was waiting for the inevitable drop of the other shoe. The, "Oh, yeah, one more thing ... " yet to come. Whether that meant The Darkness was on its way to claim her, for Paola to start aging again, or some other unforeseen tragedy, Mary couldn't shake the feeling that they were all on borrowed time, no matter how hard she tried to tell herself that things were finally fine.

Paola's fingers began searching up and down her body for something to write with, and on.

She handed her daughter the pen. Paola snatched it without acknowledgment, and Mary watched it swirl in a pantomime of violent writing.

Mary slipped the writing pad under the pen, straightened the paper, and stared as the ink arced in wide, scribbling strokes, then smaller ones as it grew fluid and words began to form.

The same words over and over:
Peter Williams
Peter Williams
Peter Williams
Peter Williams
Peter Williams
Peter Williams

* * * *

CHAPTER 3
PETER WILLIAMS

Peter stepped through the school's front entrance and approached the front counter where Nancy, the woman who'd worked the front desk forever, looked up and smiled. That expression peeled from her face like fading paint when she saw it was Peter.

"Hello, Mr. Williams. How can I help you?"

Peter kept the duffel hanging loosely from his shoulder strap, and the rifle case hanging behind his back. The duffel was unzipped, but looked closed to the casual observer.

"Hello, Nancy, I'm here to pick up my daughter."

Nancy's frown widened as she looked at her monitor.

"I don't see anything on here about an early release."

"Please," Peter said, "I just need to see her."

"I'm sorry," Nancy said, "I'll need to call your ... *wife*."

The hesitation between "your" and "wife" said it all. Everyone knew that he and Josie were finished. Probably knew that Josie was fucking Mr. Perfect, too.

Everyone knew that Peter was a joke. Hell, they probably laughed at him every day at lunch with his wife telling more stories about her *stupid husband*.

He could feel his nerves showing. Judging Nancy's brow, wrinkling deep as she reached for the phone, she was likelier to call security than Josie.

Peter reached into his bag and pulled out the Colt M1911.

Peter braced himself for that moment, had planned it a million times in his head — the moment between when Nancy saw the gun and when he pulled the trigger. He had steeled himself to be ready, to have the courage to fire if necessary. He'd been worried the whole morning that he'd be unable. That he'd chicken out and maybe run back outside, get in his car, and flee. She'd call the cops, and they'd find him with a self-inflicted shot to the head a few miles from the school, a front-page story quickly relegated to a footnote, an afterthought, his entire life summed up as fate's cruel joke.

But facing the moment, Peter didn't flinch.

He squeezed the trigger. The first two shots missed, but the third, fourth, and fifth found Nancy in the head, chest, and left arm.

She dropped the phone, dead. Her body rolled back with the chair.

Screams erupted from nearby offices behind and to either side of the reception desk.

Peter marched toward his daughter's classroom, taking shots at anyone who dared stand between himself and Claire.

A school resources officer was first to try, aiming a pistol at Peter and yelling for him to put down his gun.

Peter fired three rounds, until he was sure the man was dead. After reloading his Colt, Peter went over, scooped down, and retrieved the officer's gun and dropped it into his duffel.

He shot as he walked, randomly into offices, not intending to kill anyone or caring if he did. He just wanted to keep them down and from even considering trying to stop him.

He continued his assault.

A man's voice came over the intercom. "Attention, teachers, this is a lockdown. Make sure your doors are locked. This is not a drill. I repeat ... "

The man never finished.

Peter found him and blew his brains onto the window, skull fragments and brain matter splattering children's drawings taped to the glass.

Peter kept moving.

As he walked down the main hall, he saw movement through windows. Panicked teachers telling students to get on the floor under their tables.

He passed them, not caring about any classroom except the one he was approaching — Claire's. Second hall on the right and all the way at the end.

Movement behind him. Running.

Peter turned, firing without looking, not about to be taken by surprise.

A redheaded boy, maybe ten, was running in the opposite direction.

One of Peter's shots caught him before he could pull the gun away. Poor kid was running away. Probably coming from the bathroom.

Screams were still climbing in volume.

Peter stopped, looked at the boy lying face down in the hall, crying as blood pooled from his chest. He swallowed, some part of him feeling horrible, but another stronger presence ordered him forward. The longer he waited, the harder it would be to get Claire out of school.

Surely, someone had already called the cops.

Peter aimed his gun at the back of the boy's head, preparing to end his misery.

The trigger caught, jammed.

He tossed the gun aside, reached into his weapon case and pulled out the Colt M4 carbine.

"Please," the boy cried, struggling to turn and face Peter. "Please, mister. Don't kill me."

Peter aimed down the sight, and for a moment was frozen watching the blood pool across the linoleum, unable to think what to do next.

The way the crimson spread reminded him of something he couldn't remember. Something from another time, or ... *perhaps another life.*

His headache stabbed him hard in the brain.

He squeezed his eyes shut, trying to will the pain away.

Peter wanted to grab more pills, but had no seconds to waste.

What the hell was I doing?

He looked down at the kid, forcing his memory.

Oh yeah.

He left the kid to his bleeding, turned on a heel, and kept marching toward Claire's classroom.

The screams had settled. Peter imagined teachers hushing children as the Big Bad Wolf prowled the halls.

Little pig, little pig, let me in.

Peter reached Claire's classroom and peeked in through the window in the door's side.

Dozens of her fourth-graders were huddled under the tables.

What are they doing under their desks? Is there a fire drill?

He couldn't see Claire, and wasn't sure where she sat. There were too many kids all wearing the same-colored uniforms, huddled, faces buried.

He looked up and saw the teacher, behind her desk. Her eyes widened.

He tried the doorknob, surprised to find it locked.

Why would they lock the door in the middle of the day?

He vaguely remembered a man's voice saying something about a lockdown. He was pretty sure his wife had once said they had to keep their doors locked all the time because you never knew when some crazy would come into the school.

He knocked on the door, "Mrs. Kray, it's me, Mr. Williams. I'm here to pick up Claire."

Peter could see her fucking around with her damned iPhone, but she didn't answer.

Why's she making calls in the middle of class? Doesn't she have work to do?

Peter knocked louder.

The fucking bitch is ignoring me!

"Goddammit, open the fucking door!" he screamed, smashing his heel on the wood.

Peter looked down and remembered his rifle.

He raised it and took aim at the doorknob, putting five rounds into the fucker until it was gone.

Children screamed.

Why the hell are kids so damned screamy?

He reached into where the knob had been and yanked the door open.

Kids cowered on the floor, crying, which for a moment confused him. Then Peter realized that *he* was the reason they were crying.

"Don't worry, kids, I'm not gonna shoot anyone. I've just come to pick up my Claire Bear. Claire, honey?"

And then Peter saw her, huddled in the far corner, crying her eyes out, dark pigtails reminding him of her seventh birthday party.

"Come on, honey, it's time to come home."

She stayed in her spot, shaking her head, mouth trembling.

"Come on, honey. We don't have all day."

"Please, Mr. Williams, leave now," the teacher said. "Please ... "

He cut her off with three shots. Only one found her fat mouth. But that was enough.

She fell to the ground. Children screamed.

Their cries only added to his headache. Suddenly, there were thirty blades driving through his skull instead of the one.

"Shut up!" He fired at the chalkboard. "Shut up, shut up, shut up!"

Screams descended to sniffling.

He looked at Claire and smiled. "Come on, honey. Time to go home." He held out his hand.

Claire stood, slowly, tears spilling down her cheeks. "I don't want to go, Daddy."

Goddamn, Josie poisoned her against me. Has her terrified!

"It's time to go, Claire."

She walked forward, so damned slow Peter thought she was stuck in mud.

"Come on," he repeated, lending everything to his smile.

Claire finally reached him and held her shaking hand to his. Then Peter saw the wet spot on her pants.

Jesus Christ, she pissed herself!

Peter tried to bury his surprise. He remembered something the shrinks had said about not making a big deal when a kid pisses themselves, else it could scar them for life.

He closed his hand around her shaking fingers and pulled her along.

"Come on, baby, we're going to go say goodbye to Mommy."

**

Peter found Josie's classroom, peeked inside, and saw his wife huddled on the floor with the other children. He slung the carbine over his shoulder with its strap and clutched Claire's hand with his left as he held the M4 with his right.

The moment she saw him peering through the window, Josie stood and approached the door. She couldn't yet see Claire behind him ... or his weapon.

"What are you doing here?" she yelled through the window.

"Open the door, Claire!"

Peter wasn't sure if it was his tone of voice or her doing the math, but judging from Josie's hand on her open mouth, she just realized that he was the reason for the lockdown.

"What did you do?"

"Open the door; I just want to talk."

She shook her head no, lips pursed.

He stepped aside so she could see that Claire was with him, then brought the pistol from behind his back.

Josie's eyes widened.

She opened the door, stepped outside, and closed it behind her.

"What are you—"

"I just want to talk," he said, aiming the gun at her.

"What are you doing here? You need to give me Claire and go home before you do something you regret."

"Too late."

Josie seemed to notice the duffel, open to a small armory. Perhaps she also saw the rifle slung over his shoulder.

"Oh my God, what did you do?"

"I did what I had to. What you made me do, Josie."

"What are you talking about?" She tried to step past him, reaching out for Claire.

"No!" He shoved the pistol in her face.

Claire cried out, "Daddy, please. Stop!"

"Don't worry, honey. Mommy and Daddy just need to talk some things over, and then we'll go."

"You're not going anywhere with her. Not in this state. Why don't you just give me the guns, Peter?"

"No! I am leaving here with my daughter. There's nothing you, or anyone else, can do to stop me."

Peter heard the sound of a door opening behind him. Josie's eyes went even wider as she shook her head no.

Peter turned to see her lover, Mr. Montgomery, stepping outside with his perfect skin, nice suit, and bright-white teeth.

He turned, aimed his gun at Mr. Perfect.

Montgomery put his hands out, fingers outstretched as if to suggest calm. "Whoa, Peter, what's going on here?"

"I've come to take my daughter back and say goodbye to Josie. Not that it's any of *your* business."

"Please, Daddy," Claire said, "I don't want to go anywhere."

He ignored her.

Mr. Perfect tilted his head and lowered his hands. "I know you're having a rough time, Peter. Why don't we talk this over, see if we can't come to some kind of agreement?"

"Who the fuck are you? What the hell does any of this have to do with you? Oh, yeah — YOU'RE FUCKING MY WIFE!"

"Please," Josie said, "go back in your classroom, Mr. Montgomery."

Mr. Perfect looked up. "But—"

Something clicked in Peter, seeing the love in his eyes. The kind of look that Peter felt for Josie not too long ago. He wasn't just fucking her.

Mr. Perfect was in love.

Peter aimed at his head and shot him twice in the face.

There goes those white teeth.

Josie screamed. Claire slipped from Peter's grip and raced down the hall.

"Claire!" Peter yelled.

His daughter screamed as she ran.

"Come back!" He aimed his pistol — just a shot in the foot to slow her.

He lined up the shot.

Before he could squeeze the trigger, Josie threw herself at Peter, knocking him to the ground, hands on his gun.

"Let go!" He struggled to free himself from Josie's grip before Claire vanished down the hall or into one of the rooms, disappearing before the police showed up and making it impossible to find her.

"Let go, you bitch!" Peter met Josie's eyes as they each struggled for control of the gun.

"No," she said through gritted teeth, using every ounce of her weight and strength to push the gun's barrel back toward him. Her thumbnail dug into Peter's trigger finger, pressing back trying to make him release it.

He could feel her hot breath on his face, their struggle bringing the pistol closer to him.

Their eyes locked, and for a moment he flashed back to when they were dating, how many times he'd been lost inside those blue eyes, wondering what she was thinking, and how he'd lived his life so long without her. With a profound sorrow he realized how few times their eyes had met in their last months together, hell their last two years.

He wasn't sure when the magic died. If it was after he lost the job or before. It just sorta happened. Now Peter realized for what felt like the first time ever she'd never look into his eyes again. Not with anything close to love.

Now there was only fear and hate.

They continued struggling for the gun as he found himself lost in Josie's eyes, trying to find some shard of the love she'd once felt.

The gun went off.

Her eyes went from hate filled to confused. Her mind tried to make sense of the reality that she'd been shot.

"I'm so sorry." Peter swallowed, tears filling his eyes.

He wished he could take back the bullet, and wondered how in the hell it had all come to this.

Oh God, oh God.

Peter tried to talk to her, to let her know he was sorry, but Josie's eyes stayed open, staring into her death.

Hot blood seeped onto his hands, arms, and chest as whatever hope he had of anything — living with Josie, or even with Claire — drained into the void.

It's over.

He got up.

Dropped the gun.

Looked for Claire, but didn't see her.

He had to find her. He couldn't let her live like this, without a mother, and once he killed himself, without a father.

Better to send her to heaven first.

He wouldn't be going with her — if there was a hell, he'd punched his ticket. But no God would send his baby to hell.

Peter grabbed the rifle and glanced down at the open bag full of weapons. He had enough no matter what the day would bring. He would get his daughter, no matter how many people he had to kill.

"Claire! Come here!"

No response.

He could hear her crying and banging on a door down the hall, around the corner.

"Please, let me in!" she cried.

Peter ran toward her. He had to reach her before she got away. Didn't she realize that he was the only one who could help her?

He turned the corner as she ducked into the room.

Peter fired his rifle into the slammed door, shots shattering the window and peppering the wood with holes as the bullets tore through and into the classroom.

Kids screamed.

He wasn't sure if he'd hit them or if they were just unreasonably scared.

He used his rifle's butt to kick away jagged shards of glass still in the doorframe.

Reached inside and opened the door.

Peter pulled the door open, aimed the gun at a heavyset blonde teacher standing in front of Claire.

"Give her to me."

"No!"

He pulled the trigger, hitting her with several shots.

She fell on top of Claire, knocking the girl down and pinning her under the corpse.

Kids raced from the classroom.

"Sorry, honey, but this is for the best," Peter said as he stepped toward her.

Claire screamed, face red, tears streaking her cheeks as she tried to shove the teacher from her body. "No, Daddyyyy! No, please! Please, Daddyyyy!"

Peter hated the sound of her crying. It cut through him as if she were still an infant. A shrill pain like nothing else.

The thought of killing his own child was sickening, but it was the right thing — to end her suffering. After this there would only be a horrible life of misery ahead. How could you come back from your father going on a killing spree and ending your mother?

You couldn't.

He aimed down the rifle at her, closing his eyes. "I'm so sorry, baby."

A voice came from behind them.

A girl's voice: "Please, Mr. Williams, you don't need to do this."

He spun around, stunned. He pulled the trigger without meaning to, but the bullets sailed straight through the girl.

She looked down, and then up at Peter, seemingly as surprised as him.

"Who ... what are you?" he asked, backing away.

The girl looked to be in her early teens. She had long, dark hair and was quite pretty. She was wearing a long, flowing white dress that seemed to radiate some kind of light, even though Peter had never seen anything like it.

"My name is Paola, and I've come to save you."

"There's no saving me, not after what I've done. Please, leave us be."

"Why? So you can kill your daughter?"

"You don't know anything!" Peter fired more shots at the girl. Still the bullets sailed through.

"What the fuck are you?"

She must've been a delusion, further proof of his mental decay.

"You're not here," he said, turning away from the apparition and giving his attention to Claire. She was shaking, lips trembling, begging him not to kill her.

"I'm so sorry, baby. But you'll be with Mommy. I killed her. Don't you want to be with Mommy?"

She shook her head no, and her crying turned into a cracked wail of despair as she realized her mother was dead. Her mouth was open, saliva bubbling from her lips.

Peter flashed back to when she was three-years old and had got bitten by the neighbor's dog. She was rushed to the hospital for stitches on her face.

He looked at the scar turning pink as it did whenever Claire was scared or angry. She wailed, "Please, Daddyyyyy."

He aimed the rifle, wanting to end her suffering before snuffing his own.

He heard the girl's voice louder in his mind.

"You will not kill your daughter!"

He turned to her, "Stay out of my head!"

She stepped toward him, but her steps were more of a floating motion.

"This isn't you," she said, just inches from his face. "You've been infected, and there's a parasite that is breaking you from the inside. It's not you, Peter. Please, put the gun down."

"P-parasite?"

"Have you been getting bad headaches?"

"Yes," he said, stunned. "I have."

"It's the parasite."

"What kind of parasite?"

Peter once heard stories about a type of parasite that infected small animals and took over their motor control.

Or was it insects?

"You mean this isn't my fault?"

Peter couldn't stop the tears pouring down his face. It felt so good for someone to tell him he wasn't a monster, even coated in his wife's sticky blood.

"No, it's not your fault. It's the parasites. Please, stop now and turn yourself in. You can still do the right thing."

A stabbing pain splintered through his skull, bringing a roaring anger alongside it.

"No, you're lying. You're a figment of my imagination."

He turned, aimed at Claire, and put his finger around the trigger.

"Sorry."

His finger froze mid-squeeze.

The stabbing grew more intense as if someone, or something, was slicing his brain into pieces with an icy blade drenched in acid.

Peter clenched his teeth so tight he felt a few break. Blood poured from his mouth.

His body tensed as he felt something sliding through his muscles, going from his chest to his arms and then into his fingers, forcing him to release the trigger and drop the rifle.

He reached into the bag, or his body did, acting against his brain's commands.

He grabbed a pistol, not sure which, and brought it toward his mouth.

No, no, no, no!

"Kill yourself, Mr. Williams. It's the right thing to do," Paola's voice spoke in his head, adding to the intense pain.

No! Get out of my head!

He stared down at Claire, still trying to get out from under the dead teacher, eyes on her father.

He had to resist, had to free Claire from her misery.

His arms refused to obey.

His mouth opened.

He screamed, trying to resist whatever, or whoever, was in control.

The pain in his head was dialed up to a million, so bad he was certain his brain would explode without release.

He put the gun in his mouth.

Peter found freedom from the pain.

He fell to the floor, dimly aware of the world around him, watching Claire scream.

It was the last thing he saw, the final torment he would visit on his daughter.

* * * *

CHAPTER 4
MARY OLSON

As Paola continued to scribble on the paper, Desmond finally arrived at the house, nearly ten minutes after Mary had called.

He ran into the kitchen, fell to his knees beside Mary, and held one of Paola's hands.

"How long?"

"Twelve minutes," Mary said.

He looked down at the pages spread on the floor beneath her. Paola had gone through six sheets so far, writing in giant, messy letters.

He picked up the papers and started sorting through them. "Who is Peter Williams?"

"No idea," Mary said.

Paola started writing faster, bigger letters.

"No, no, no, no."

"Kill yourself Mr. Williams. It's the right thing to do."

Mary swallowed, wondering what sort of horrible thing her daughter was seeing.

The seizures, they had deduced from Paola's vague recollections and the things she'd written matching news reports of recent atrocities, had somehow allowed her to connect with people infected by The Darkness, reporting the things these people were seeing and presumably feeling.

"We need to wake her up."

"No," Desmond said sharply. "We have no idea what harm that might cause her."

Mary looked down at her daughter's shaking, furrowed, sweat-beaded brow, eyes closed tight, tears pouring from them as her hands scribbled something indecipherable, big giant letters, all on the same page.

D

I

E

And then it was over.

The seizures quit in a flicker, just like they started.

The girl's brow relaxed, her hand went limp, dropping the pen. Her head rolled to the side, asleep. Likely exhausted.

Mary exhaled deeply, glad it was over.

Desmond picked up Paola and carried her to the couch. Mary ran ahead to move her tablet out of the way.

Desmond laid her down, then turned to Mary.

"You OK?" He came over and took her into his arms.

It felt so good to have Desmond back. Things weren't quite as cozy and normal as before, but their relationship had been forged in a dead world's chaos. There really hadn't ever been a *normal*.

Mary wondered if there would ever be any sort of *normal* again.

The Darkness had followed them back to this world, was wreaking havoc daily, and yet it seemed like nobody outside of their tiny circle knew what was happening. Nobody, save for the Black Island Guardsmen and presumably a few other government agencies, seemed to be aware of an alien presence.

Mary was shocked that no one had let the information leak, that no civilian had managed to capture any cell phone footage of the black, stringy aliens. They had managed to hide well within humans this time. She wondered if that was a good sign or a bad one. Was the aliens' seeming invisibility a sign of their strength and improved organization or one of vulnerability?

Whatever the case, Mary would do her damnedest to keep Paola safe, and it felt good to have company. While Boricio was God knows where, she could never truly count on him anyway. He had his life to live; she had hers. But Desmond was back, and Mary finally had faith that even if they had to march through fire they'd make it out of hell alive.

He'd always been a confident, if not somewhat mysterious man. He was now more so, and smarter, for his experiences on the dead world. It was as if The Light had prepared him for true leadership. If there was one thing the world needed now, it was someone to guide them, someone who knew how to fight The Darkness.

She just wished Paola didn't have to be part of the fight.

Mary looked down at her daughter, sleeping on the couch, seeming more like a child in slumber than the young woman she'd been forced to become. Mary wasn't ready to let go of her little girl, ready for her daughter's exposure to such horrible things. She couldn't help but fear that while Paola was peeking into the minds of those infected by The Darkness, that the aliens were staring back into hers. She could be in greater danger than even Desmond could appreciate.

As if reading her thoughts, Desmond whispered in her ear.

"She's going to be OK."

"How do we know that?" Mary pulled away from the hug and met Desmond's eyes. "How do we know that The Darkness isn't getting into her head whenever she has one of these seizures?"

"She has The Light inside her. It wouldn't allow such a thing."

"Do you *know* that? Are you an expert on these aliens now? Or is that a guess?"

"Well, it's gut more than anything. It's hard to know what's true of the aliens. Every now and then I get memories that aren't mine, memories of the collective gathered by Luca. I have some of his memories, and some from people I don't know. It's difficult to assemble them with meaning. But there are things I do know, things The Light drip feeds to me as I need to know them. I have to trust my gut or the bit of The Light inside me."

"But you don't *know* she's 100 percent safe, right?"

"You want me to lie to you? You want me to tell you that everything will be OK because we want it to be? You know as well as I do that life has no guarantees. We could defeat the aliens tomorrow and get hit by lightning on the way to the park. No, Mary, there are no 100 percents. Except if we do nothing, *then* there's a 100 percent chance that The Darkness will destroy this Earth as It did the other."

Mary looked down at Paola. "I just wish we could spare her from this."

"We can't control her seizures, Mary. Even if we wanted to. So why not take them for the gift that they are? They will help us find the vials. I can feel it. She's onto something big. I *know* it. You're a hell of a woman, Mary Olson. The strongest, bravest, biggest badass I've ever met. Now you need to let your daughter be strong. Show her the faith you have in her, not your fear for her safety. Trust yourself. And her. Believe also that I'll do everything I can to keep us all safe. Can you do that?"

"Funny," she said. "Before October 15, 2011, I never thought of myself as strong person. Sure, I was an independent businesswoman who managed to survive and thrive as a single mom, but I didn't feel particularly *strong*. I just did what had to be done and coped when things went bad. Even after going through survival training and learning how to handle an assortment of weapons, I never felt particularly *strong*. Yeah, I can handle myself in a fight now, I've killed some aliens, but it's hard to feel *strong* when so much is out of my control. I take one look at Paola having these seizures, knowing there's an alien inside her, and there's not a damned thing I can do. I think strong is an illusion we sell ourselves, but in reality we're not strong at all. We're at these aliens' mercy. To tell ourselves anything different is a lie. We ought not to lie to ourselves and say we're strong, when these things are light years ahead of us in every way that matters."

Desmond pulled Mary back into his arms.

"And that right there is what makes you strong. That you're not complacent. That you recognize the threat. That you're open to training yourself to prepare, to do whatever's necessary."

Desmond hugged her, and while leaning into his strength felt good, Mary wondered if he wasn't *too* optimistic and fearless about their chances. There was a distinction between strength and abandon, and Desmond had already died once at the hands of the aliens. Mary didn't want to see a repeat performance. But there was comfort in having someone who believed in her so strongly, especially when she felt at the edge of falling apart.

Mary embraced him, looking down at her daughter, hoping that Paola was as strong as Desmond believed, and that it would be enough to keep her from The Darkness.

* * * *

CHAPTER 5
MARINA HARMON

Marina stared at Father Thomas Acevedo, unable to turn away from his sewn lips. He lowered his cowl to reveal a thinner, balder, older man than she had imagined: mid-fifties or early sixties.

"Who did this to you?" Marina asked before realizing how stupid it was to query a man with his lips sewn shut.

He reached into his robe, withdrew a notepad and pen, scribbled something, then held it up to her.

"I did. Who are you?"

She thought to ask why, but felt it was too personal a question to ask upon meeting him.

"Marina Harmon. My father was J.L. Harmon. He said that you would help me if I came to you."

Acevedo's eyes widened. He scribbled something else and held it up for Marina.

"Help you with what?"

"These," she said, opening the box.

Acevedo's eyes looked like they might roll from his sockets at the sight of her vials. This wasn't the first time he'd seen them. The man backed away as if she'd just opened a batch of Ebola virus.

"What's wrong?"

Acevedo went to his bed, reached beneath the thin mattress, and pulled out a knife.

Marina backed up, putting herself closer to the door in case he attacked.

He brought the blade to his lips and began to cut the black threads. He cut too fast, the blade slipped and drew blood.

Acevedo kept cutting until the threads no longer bound his lips, even though the ends were still stuck, dangling in blood. He ignored it and words fell too fast from his mouth.

"What are you doing with those? How did you get them?"

Marina wasn't sure how much he knew or how long he'd been locked in the monastery. "My father is dead. You know that right?"

He nodded, still ignoring the dripping blood. She wished he would wipe it away. He looked like one of those crazy homeless people who sometimes harmed themselves outside of the church's compound.

"He came back to me this morning. I don't know how, but he did. He said to guard these with my life, and that you could help me."

"Help you what?"

Acevedo asked as if he knew the answer but was terrified to ask.

"Save the world."

"Oh God, it's true, isn't it?"

"What?"

"*It's* out there, isn't it? I knew it was only a matter of time. I can feel *It*."

"What are you talking about?" Images of the dark thing inside Steven flashed through Marina's mind.

"It goes by many names, but is commonly called The Darkness. It came in those vials from somewhere far away. It came here to destroy us."

"Father said the vials could save us. That you know where the others are."

"Your father entrusted them to a few special people, people he felt wouldn't be corruptible by their power. I'm afraid your father chose wrong."

"Why do you say that?"

"Because he chose me, and I am *not* good. I thought I was. But if I, a man of God, couldn't resist the temptation, what does that say for others?"

"Do you know where the other vials are?"

"Why? What are we going to do, assuming they've not been opened, and assuming these people will turn them over to us?"

Marina said, "I thought you would know what to do."

"You've come to the wrong place. Please, leave, and show no one those vials."

"I can't just leave! I don't know what to do. My father said *you* would help."

"Sorry, I'm not the man your father believed me to be."

Marina looked at the man's spare bedroom, with no personal belongings save for whatever few items he could stuff into the trunk at the foot of his bed. She didn't know much of other religions, but knew an ordinary man didn't sew his lips shut or commit to a monastic life.

She had no clue as to the man's committed sins, but clearly seemed to owe atonement for something.

"Why are you here? Why did you sew your lips shut."

Acevedo looked down, as if ashamed to meet Marina's eyes.

"Please," she said. "I have nowhere else to go. My boyfriend, a man I thought loved me, who led the church alongside me, just tried to kill me. He's got this Darkness you're talking about inside him. If I return to the church, he *will* kill me. And he'll take these vials. Is that what you want?"

He met her eyes, gravely. "No."

"Then please, you must help me."

Acevedo stared at her, his lips a mess of blood and hanging threads. He looked lost and defeated already. She wondered if he *could* help her. Wondered what he'd seen to bring him here, and make him sew his lips shut?

"Fine, I'll help. But you must promise me one thing."

"What's that?"

"Whatever I do, whatever I say, do not give me any of the vials. I cannot be trusted."

"OK," she said nervously, hoping her father wasn't wrong to put his faith in this broken, beaten man.

"So, you'll help me?"

"Under one condition," Acevedo said.

"What's that?"

"You must become pure of temptation. I need to know you're not tainted."

"What do you mean?"

"I means this ... "

Suddenly someone was behind Marina, grabbing her, putting a rag over her mouth. She tried to resist, but the rag was soaked with something that bleached the fight from her body and mind.

* * * *

CHAPTER 6
BORICIO WOLFE

Boricio lay on the top bunk with his hands behind his head — the stingy fucks at Carlson County Correctional Center didn't seem to believe in pillows. How the fuck were they supposed to "correct" criminals when they couldn't even get the bedding right? He was doing his damndest not to show that he was feeling like a cracked-out cat in a cracker box of claustrophobia.

Boricio's cell was a tiny six by eight, with a shitter/sink combo and a pair of bunks with yoga mats for mattresses. Boricio was fortunately alone in his cell for the moment. He couldn't imagine sharing a space so small without his cellmate DOA. And he sure as shit wasn't gonna have some cunt come in and demand the top bunk.

Boricio was *not* a fucking bottom.

He'd been awake for about an hour but hadn't heard dick from the guards or anyone else.

The jail wasn't like that shit on *Oz* where all the prisoners could see one another. Boricio's cell had no bars — just concrete walls, what looked like an unbreakable window, and a locked door with safety glass. He could see another cell across from him, though Boricio didn't know if it was empty or occupied. For that he was thankful. Making friends was the last thing he wanted to do in this shithole.

Boricio had barely slept since the cops picked him up. He'd yet to hear what he was being charged with, though murder seemed high on the list.

The irony was laughable. Of all the murders he'd committed, a number that had to climb high in the hundreds, Boricio had been nicked for what he'd argue was self-defense.

Karma wasn't a bitch. She was a fucking cunt.

He wasn't horribly concerned. Boricio had little doubt that he'd beat the rap. It was self-defense. Sure, he'd chased the fucker down, but he could easily argue that he did so in fear that the hillbilly would get to his gun then come back and shoot him. He could also argue that he wasn't chasing the guy, but rather running to the gas station for help, then the guy said he would shoot him. Boricio wasn't above lying for justice.

Hell, maybe there was even a camera or three that showed the cousin fuckers arriving with Boricio bound in the truck.

And on the off chance that he *was* convicted, well, Boricio would find a way to escape.

He'd go cunt crazy if cooped up too long. Of course, if he *were* convicted, he'd likely be sent to Oz, a place packed with skinheads and other factions that would all have to learn about Team Boricio.

After what seemed like his life's longest morning, a prison guard approached Boricio's cell and peeked through the security glass. He was a pig, fat, late forties, with shoe polish-black hair and a fat gray caterpillar mustache. He also had that slow look that suggested his parents were siblings.

Guard Tard told Boricio to sit on the bed with his back to the wall. He took his sweet time but complied.

Guard Tard stepped inside Boricio's cell and crossed his arms over his ample chest. "So, your name is John Doe, eh?"

Boricio smiled, remembering how much shit the booking officer gave him while taking his prints and purty picture while Boricio refused to say shit. Let 'em look — they wouldn't find dick with Boricio's name. Even his driver's license was a decoy.

"Yeah." Boricio smiled.

"You think you're a real smart ass, eh? Walkin' around like your shit don't stink."

"I'm new, and we've yet to share the pleasure of a proper introduction. I suggest you take it down a notch, hoss." Boricio winked. "That way you'll have less regrets later."

Guard Tard looked as if Boricio had pulled out his pecker and pissed on Old Glory while using the bible to wipe his ass.

"Excuse me, boy?"

"*Boy?*" Boricio laughed. "Do I look like I want a trip to Chuck E. Cheese?"

Guard Tard's face turned bright red.

He reached for his nightstick and stepped toward Boricio, looking hungry for an excuse to whip it from his belt.

Boricio stared at the man without flinching, and smiled. "You touch your sister with that stick? She ask you to shove it up her poop chute, or does she prefer it in her purty little slit?"

Guard Tard responded as predicted — he leaped at Boricio, swinging.

Boricio kicked the man hard, just missing his knee and striking right below it. Rather than breaking his leg as planned, the man merely fell forward, nightstick hitting Boricio twice in the ribs.

Guard Tard raised the stick and swung at his head.

Boricio threw his left arm up to deflect the blow.

Unfortunately, his arm didn't fare as well.

Something cracked. An unholy pain streaked through Boricio's forearm.

He screamed out, surprised by how much pain the fat, fucking retard had managed to inflict.

Guard Tard stopped his attack, eyes wide, realizing he'd gone too far and would have shit to explain.

"Help!" Boricio yelled.

Another guard appeared, a heavyset black dude with a graying beard and thick black glasses. His name badge read: BOYLE.

Boyle yelled at Guard Tard. "What the hell, Sanders?"

Guard Tard withdrew from the cell, whining. "He hit me, sir!"

"Bullshit! He got pissed 'cuz I asked if he fucks his sister with his nightstick."

Boyle looked at Boricio as if to ask: *What? Did you just say what I thought you said?*

Boyle might've smiled. It was hard to focus through the pain.

The guard looked down at Boricio's arm, saw the huge swelling welt.

"Hang tight, I'll get a doc to check you out." He turned to Guard Tard. "You, out here, now."

Guard Tard left with his tail between his legs.

Boricio held his clucking and smiled, hoping the fucker's superiors would turn his ass into burger. He wasn't sure how long his stay in ButtFuck County Lockup would be, but Boricio was no one's bitch to beat on.

Sharks, bears, and Boricio: top of the fucking chain.

* * * *

CHAPTER 7
MARINA HARMON

Marina woke in a dimly lit room not unlike Acevedo's chamber — a bed, dresser, and trunk. An open door revealed a bathroom with a shower.

A single bare light bulb hung from the ceiling. The bare stone walls bore no windows.

Marina stood, her head still dizzy, then went to the door and jiggled the knob, trying to open it.

It was locked.

"Hello?" she yelled.

No response.

"Hey!" she yelled again, louder.

Still no answer.

"Let me out of here!" Marina screamed, wondering what the hell Acevedo had done to her. She vaguely recalled him saying something about her purity, whatever the hell that meant. If the man meant virginity, her dress hadn't been white for a while.

Wait a second. Where's—

She searched the room: trunk, dresser, and under the bed, but couldn't find the vials.

They took the vials!

I knew I shouldn't have trusted him!

"Where are the vials?!" Marina cried out to whoever might be listening. Acevedo *had* to be somewhere nearby.

His taking the vials didn't make sense. He told her not to surrender them under any circumstance — so why would he take them?

Marina paced her cell.

A folded blue paper slid beneath the door.

She picked it up.

It read: *21 days. Training starts tomorrow.*

"What the hell are you talking about?"

No response.

**

The next morning Marina woke to the sound of a bell ringing from above.

She snapped awake and saw an old man standing over her. He, like Acevedo, was wearing robes. He was skinny, bald, and his face and hands, the only areas not concealed by robes, were covered in intricate tattoos with designs she couldn't quite place.

"Who are you?" She sat up in bed, remembering that the note had said that training — whatever that meant — started today.

Is this my trainer?

"My name is Seven. I'm here to strengthen your mind."

"My mind is strong enough, thank you. I'd like to leave."

Marina stood, walking past the man on her way to the door. She grabbed the knob and tried to turn it, but the door was locked.

"Open the damned door."

"It'll open it when you're ready."

"This is stupid! Let me out. People are counting on me. I can't be locked away for three weeks."

"Father Acevedo said you must be ready for what's next. I am here to prepare you, same as I did for him."

"Where are my vials?"

"Locked away safely, don't worry."

"I want them. Now. And I want to talk to Acevedo."

"So, you are not ready to train?"

"No!"

"OK." The old man turned and opened the door with no key.

How the hell did he open the door?

Is someone watching via secret cameras and they opened it from outside?

Marina chased him, not about to let some weirdo in robes keep her in a cell. She reached the doorway, and he spun to face her, deceptively fast. The old man raised his palm, landing it flat on her chest. It didn't hurt, though the look in his eyes and the force with which he moved said that hurt wasn't far from the table.

"Please, Ms. Harmon. Return to your room. Food will be sent shortly."

"I want out," she said, her eyes wetting with tears.

"Your life is in danger right now. You need to be trained in the way."

"I—"

He pressed a pair of fingers to her lips.

She pulled away, not appreciating the old man's touch. She stepped back, and he closed the door. From the other side, he said, "Be ready to train tomorrow."

Marina reached for the doorknob. Locked.

"Damn it!" she yelled, pounding her fists on the door. "I want to talk to Acevedo!!"

No response.

**

Marina woke to the smell of food.

She sat up in bed, with no memory of drifting off. She looked on the floor beside the door and saw a bowl of what looked like chicken noodle soup with steam rising from the broth, a single piece of bread, and a glass of ice water, sweat beading the outside.

She jumped out of bed and tried the doorknob again. Still locked.

Stomach grumbling, Marina brought the tray of food to her bed, sat, and begrudgingly took a bite of the surprisingly fresh bread.

She couldn't remember the last time she'd eaten. Hell, the lack of windows made it so Marina couldn't even tell what time it was now.

"Could at least give me something to read!" she yelled, assuming someone was listening, if not watching.

No response.

**

The next time she woke, Marina found a book on the bed beside her.

The volume looked old: brown, leather-bound, and thin. The spine read: *On Mindful Meditation* by O.M.

Who the hell is O.M.?

She opened the book and began to thumb through the pages. The first few were oddly left blank. No title page or copyright. Nothing.

Marina kept flipping, and was surprised to find that the entire volume was blank.

"Is this some of joke?" she yelled, throwing the book hard at the door.

Marina growled as she dipped her bread into the soup then tore off a chunk with her teeth, glaring at the door.

No response.

**

Marina woke to another bell.

The old man was standing over her, again.

"Are you ready to train?"

"Fuck you."

The man said nothing, turned, and headed toward the door.

"Wait!" she yelled.

Without waiting, he left her alone.

Marina screamed.

"You can't just keep me here! I have a church! A board of directors to answer to! People relying on me for their living! You can't just keep me here!"

No response.

**

Again Marina woke to the scent of soup.

She wasn't sure how many days had passed her. So far, she'd been brought the same meal four times with no regard for time. Apparently, soup wasn't just lunch or dinner, it was her only meal. Still, Marina was just hungry enough to look forward to the broth.

By her estimation, she was nearing the end of her second day being locked in the room. This must be dinner.

The book she'd thrown at the door the day before was back on the bed when she opened her eyes. The pages were still blank.

Marina figured that this was the sort of thing the cult did to new members. A way of slowly breaking her down until she was susceptible to whatever religion they planned to indoctrinate her into. The Church of Original Design had its own methods of doing the same, though not as extreme — until you reached the higher levels and went away to retreats.

They apparently don't know who they're messing with if they think they can convert me.

She finished her soup and continued to stare at the door, wondering when it might open.

Part of her wanted to attack the next person who stepped through the doorway. The old man was fast, but still old. She might be able to knock him down, at least long enough to run out into the hall. But what then?

Would she search the monastery's every room until she found the vials? Even if she managed to find them, Marina doubted she'd do so easily or without interference. And even if she managed to get the vials and was able to leave without incident, she still had no idea how to handle the situation with Steven.

What could she do? Call the police and tell them that he was infected with some kind of alien? She couldn't rely on her security, as he'd been the head. Marina had to assume that her entire team was compromised.

As much as she hated to admit it, Marina needed Acevedo. Her father had sent her to him for a reason, and she had to trust instincts that were proving far less insane than she once thought.

Marina finished her soup and stared at the empty book.

**

She woke to the bell and the old man standing over her.
"Are you ready?" he asked.
"Yes."

* * * *

CHAPTER 8
MARINA HARMON

Three weeks later

As Marina waited for Acevedo in a downstairs chamber, she couldn't help but wonder how the hell she and the Father would get around. Did he have a car? Or did he surrender an old life at the monastery door? Marina felt naked and not just because she was wearing jeans and a shirt that weren't hers. She'd never had a chance to grab her cell, purse, credit cards, or anything when Steven dragged her from bed and locked her in the estate's subterranean crypt.

She'd gone from heading one of the nation's most powerful religions — someone nested firmly in the top one-percent — to no one in hours.

She hated feeling so exposed, so at fate's mercy.

Marina hardly recognized Acevedo when he met her in the chamber. He was wearing jeans, a black shirt, and a matching leather jacket. A gun's butt peeked from beneath the black leather.

A monk, or Father, with a pistol?

He'd also cleaned the blood which dimmed his apparent insanity, even if his brown eyes were still *very* intense. He looked like a cop, or a soldier, on a mission.

"How did your training go?" he asked.

"You mean you don't know?"

"Well, I see that you're here, so obviously you passed. But no, Ondo didn't tell me how you did."

Ondo? Until now, she'd not known his name. The old man had identified himself as Seven, then told her to refer to her as master, something which annoyed her at first, but she played along.

"Well," she said, "I hated the master at first, and hated you and this whole damned whatever the hell you have going on here, too. But, in time, I came to appreciate the training. He taught me to keep my emotions in check, to not give into anger, and to learn patience. Well, to be more patient, anyway."

"Good," Acevedo said. "I couldn't risk entering battle with a weak mind beside me."

"Battle? What is it you've got planned?"

"First, we have to take care of Steven."

"We are?"

"Yes ma'am. You ready?"

Marina stood, still clutching the vials to her chest, glad to have them back. Despite the clarity and calmness the master had given her, she couldn't help the nerves that came with Steven's name.

"What if he has others on his side? I don't know who I can trust. He handpicked our most recent staff. Any, or all of them, could be compromised."

"In more ways than you know. But we'll handle it as it comes." Acevedo led Marina from the chamber, outside into the day's harsh light.

The monastery was fenced in, tucked behind a large garden which hid it from the street. Several monks in brown robes were tending to Camellias, ignoring her and Acevedo as they made their way to the garage.

"You have a car?" Marina forgot that she meant to ask him what 'in more ways than you know' meant.

"Yes ma'am," he chuckled. "You know I'm not a monk, right?"

"I'm not sure what you are."

"That's OK, neither am I most days." Acevedo seemed more at ease than when Marina had first met him. His eyes and movements were still business, but his smile had warmed along with his voice.

Perhaps he also spent some time being trained by the master?

They reached Acevedo's car, a late '70s cherry red Mustang with dark tinted windows, which looked like it could still have a sticker on the windshield.

"What happened?"

"What do you mean?" Acevedo asked.

"You were quiet and scared up there when I showed you the vials. Now you're all ready for 'battle.' Why the change?"

At the passenger side door he met Marina's eyes, his intensity fading.

"I've spent the past two years afraid this day would come. I thought it would happen on October 15, 2011. It didn't, and I began to doubt myself and the prophecy I'd seen."

Great, another person seeing prophecies.

Marina wondered if he was a disciple of her fathers, after all. Maybe the master had been as well?

"When you walked in the door, I was terrified that I wasn't ready. But then I prayed and found the courage to do what must be done. And, of course, I spent some time with the master."

Marina stared at Acevedo, trying to decide if she should ask the question tipping her tongue. She had nothing to lose — she was standing in borrowed clothes with a monk, not a monk, Father who had sewn his lips shut.

"Prayed to who?"

"Are you asking about my faith?" Acevedo asked, smiling. "Still Catholic, ma'am."

"OK. For a moment I thought perhaps you were Church of Original Design."

"Oh, God no. Your father and I were close, but we never agreed on theology."

"Us either," Marina admitted.

"After you." Acevedo held her door.

**

They arrived at the compound to six news vans camped outside the gates.

"What the hell is going on?" Marina asked no one.

Acevedo pulled up to the gate where Clancy, one of the guards, stepped out of the entry shack to meet them.

Acevedo manually rolled down the window. Marina leaned forward so Clancy could see her.

"Ma'am?" he asked, surprised. "Everyone's been looking for you."

"Everyone? You mean Steven?"

Clancy stared at her, then licked his lips. "Oh God, you haven't heard?"

"Heard what?"

"It's best you go in, Ms. Harmon. Mr. Walker is waiting inside."

"Mr. Walker?" she asked, surprised. Walker had been her family's lawyer for three decades.

"Yes, Ma'am, he'll explain everything."

Marina hated the sound of that.

**

Marina stepped into the downstairs media room where Walker was speaking to someone on his cell in terse, bitchy little sentences. She heard no words, only tone. Marina didn't know who Walker was arguing with, or what he was fighting about, but she was sure he was winning.

He turned toward Marina as she stepped through the doorway. He said, "I'll call you back" and a second later slipped the cell inside his pocket.

He quickly crossed the room, arms open wide. "Marina! Where the hell have you been? We thought you were dead."

At six foot six, in his sixties, with a thick head of sandy-colored hair, Walker felt like a grandfather in many ways, a big bear of a grandfather.

He hugged Marina, neither asking about the strange man beside her, nor giving him more than a glance.

"It's a long story," she said. "I'll fill you in, but what's this I'm hearing about Steven?"

"I'm so sorry."

"Sorry for what?" Marina asked, breaking from the hug.

"Steven is dead."

"What?" Marina felt punched in the gut.

"Yes, they found his body at the Camelot, along with the body of a writer, a former cop. A horrible tragedy."

"Oh God."

No wonder the news vans were outside. Steven was her head of security, not a face for the church, but he'd been seen enough in Marina's presence, and had made a name for himself when he punched out a stalking paparazzo. His death was big news for those seeking to damage the church. All eyes would be on her response.

Walker finally looked Acevedo up and down, then turned back to Marina. "Where have you been for the past three weeks? The police, and the media, weren't sure if you were a victim or a perpetrator who took off after killing Steven."

"That's ridiculous!" Marina said.

"Obviously, I've held them off. But if there's something I need to know, Marina, now's the time to tell me."

It took Marina a moment to get what Walker was asking.

"Wait. *You* think I had something to do with this?"

Walker looked stunned. "No, Marina. I'm simply saying that as your lawyer, I need to know what's happening so I can help you and we can get in front of this story before it snowballs."

"I don't know if you'd believe me, Mr. Walker."

"Try me."

"OK, but we'll need to sit."

**

Marina told Walker everything, including the bit about the vials, even though Acevedo flinched at their mention.

After the story, which he seemed to buy despite his questions, Walker pointed to the box beside Marina. "Is that them? These vials?"

"Yes," she said.

"May I?" Walker held out his hand.

"No," Acevedo said sharply, putting his hand on the box, but not picking it up.

"Excuse me." For all of Walker's kindness, he was a man who only heard *yes*.

"With all due respect, Mr. Walker, nobody but the pure of heart can touch these. Being a lawyer, I'm guessing that's not you ... no offense."

Walker looked at Marina. "May I have a word? Alone?"

Acevedo said, "No, you may not."

Marina turned to him, wanting to reprimand him for speaking for her, particularly to a family friend, but that crazy look was back in his eyes. Something told her to stand down, for now.

Acevedo said, "Here's the part of the story Marina didn't tell you, because she doesn't yet know it."

Walker folded his hands across his chest and leaned back in the chair opposite them. "Go on."

"Steven wasn't *Steven*. He was infected by The Darkness."

"Yes, she told me that part. Whatever this *Darkness* is."

"That's just it, sir. You all don't know what it is. Because it's nothing you've ever seen. And it's not just in Steven. The Darkness is an alien race stored in these vials, sent to Earth God knows how long ago. The vials themselves aren't good or bad, Darkness or Light. They're neutral, searching for purpose, seeking to live, whether that means creating new life or destroying what is here. Whether they choose life or death depends on the humans they first bond with. Most of us are impure, and have only the capacity to destroy. So the aliens are now this Darkness, infecting and infesting people with itself, replicating."

"Replicating?" Walker repeated, as if only this most recent revelation were difficult to digest.

"They spread like a diseased parasite, going from host to host, gaining numbers and strength. That's what's happening out there right now. The Darkness is spreading, and we have to stop It, counter It."

Walker's eyebrows arched, as he turned to Marina, "Do you really believe this nonsense?"

Marina looked at Acevedo, trying to come up with one answer to satisfy two men.

"Yes, I believe that something is happening. I'm not sure if it is exactly as Father Acevedo says, I don't know. But I *saw* this Darkness in Steven, felt It as he was trying to murder me. And I saw my father's ghost. He spoke to me, Mr. Walker. He told me how to find my way out of the crypt after Steven locked me in there, and about the monastery. You know me — I've not exactly bought 100 percent into Father's religion. I'm logical, but also not close-minded enough to ignore a very basic truism — the truth is usually what's right in front of you. Unless you have some other explanation, I suggest we listen to Father Acevedo."

Walker unfolded his arms and sighed. Marina wasn't sure if he was starting to believe them. Or was he simply doing his job as her lawyer and absorbing what he needed to give himself, or at least his conscience: plausible deniability while helping to cover up her involvement in a murder?

"What do you need from me?" Walker asked.

Marina looked at Acevedo and requested their next steps.

"There are a total of four more vials unaccounted for. I have one. I also have names for the other keepers. This information is in a secure location. We must go there. We'll need weapons in case we run into trouble, and enough supplies to live off the grid for a while. We'll also need a place that nobody knows about to hunker down. This must be kept quiet. We can assume that people within your church have been compromised. Were I Steven, I would've infected as many top level people as I could. He would have been seeking the vials if he knew your father had some, or perhaps he wanted to use the church to expand the Darkness's hold."

Marina turned to Walker. "Can you help us?"

"Is that all?" Walker's voice was treading sarcasm.

Marina had not the patience nor time for doubt. "Either you can or you can't. Let me know, Mr. Walker, so I can find another way if not."

A light slap on the cheek, just enough to set him straight. Walker would do the right thing. As with her father, sometimes he had to vent his doubt and get prodded in the right direction to feel like he was doing his job. Walker was a good man, or at least he'd always been good to her family. Whether that was due to loyalty, genuine friendship, or billable hours, Marina could never know for sure. But at the moment, he was the closest she had to a trustworthy soul.

"Yes I can help you, of course, Marina. I think we should come up with a story regarding your whereabouts and make sure we're all on the same page before answering any line of questioning. As for the media, I'll hold them off with a press release about how we're still waiting to hear more details from the police and to please respect the church as we grieve a great loss."

"Sounds great, Mr. Walker," Acevedo responded. "Thank you. But I think we should hold off on the police for now. We need the vials and names first."

"If you hold off on talking to the cops for too long, Marina will look suspicious."

"I'd rather she look suspicious than dead. We have no idea where The Darkness went after Steven's murder. It may have jumped into an officer on-scene. Not all of them are able, but the controlling parts of The Darkness can jump from bodies after the death of their hosts."

"How do you know all this?" Marina asked.

"Because The Darkness lives inside me, as well."

"What?" She stood from the couch. "*You're* infected?"

"No," he said, "not so much as I can tell. But I've been around the vials long enough, and exposure is all It needs to change you. How do you think your father became the man he was? How do you think he created some of the science the Church is known for? The Current? The Capacitor? That's alien technology, a gift from the vials. Just the same, I've been cursed with an ability to see things I wish that I couldn't. I can sense The Darkness in others. When I sleep, I feel its dreams. I'm plugged into the hive mind, and get glimpses of what it's doing and what it wants."

"And what *does* it want?" Walker asked.

"Everything."

* * * *

CHAPTER 9
LUCA HARDING

Luca lay in bed, staring at the five vials holding his alien brothers, the blue glow beautiful in the motel room's pre-dawn darkness.

There was something so alluring about the liquid in the glass, it was hard to believe this was the same stuff that, when corrupted, turned black. The same stuff that had destroyed his home world after it failed to take over.

Luca looked at Rose in the other bed, still sleeping.

He fingered the glass, and wondered what would happen if he removed one of the seals.

The Darkness awoke within him and said, *Don't do it.*

Why not?

We need to save these vials for other vessels. The right vessels.

What do you mean?

You are a vessel, Luca. Rose is a host.

What's the difference?

A vessel is someone who helps to shape our species. We must find the right people to give this to. People who can help us evolve humanity.

How will we find these people? How do we know who to give the vials to?

We will know. We are scanning the world now, searching, but we can't spread before finding the other vials. We can't afford to take chances, and fail like before.

Luca kept staring at the azure glow, eyes fixed on the flecks of darkness swirling inside them. He wondered if those specks were there before, or were a response to his holding the vials.

Am I contaminating them?

Luca understood that the liquids were neither good nor bad on their own, which meant that the vial Rose poured down his throat had been turned bad by him.

I'm not a bad person, am I?

No, Luca, you are not. Good and bad are relative, labels humans insist upon one another as a means to categorize and control you, to punish and murder your sisters and brothers. One man's good is another man's evil. Such a primitive species. Something that the coming evolution will change. There will be no good nor bad. There will be no self. There will only be us. We. A collective. Good for one is good for all. Same with the bad.

Luca thought about the boys he killed, the ones who had picked on him. Then all those deaths at the pool.

Certainly those were bad, right?

The Darkness was silent.

Instead, Rose cried out as she woke, eyes wide.

She turned to him. Luca wasn't sure if Rose was awake. She looked very much like the puppet of The Darkness she was.

"She's escaped."

"Who?" Luca asked.

"Marina."

"Who is Marina?"

"She's someone I ... or, rather, Steven ... had gotten close to. Her father had hidden as many as six of the vials.

I had trapped her in her house and planned to return, but then I found you and your vials."

Luca was going to ask who Steven was, then saw in a flash of memory that The Darkness had been in Steven's body, the man who was once Boricio Bishop. Steven died and *It* moved into Rose.

"So what does this all mean?"

"She's working with someone else, a priest, who has also been touched by The Light."

A knot of fear twisted Luca's gut, imagining Marina and the priest's pursuit.

"What do we do?" he asked.

"I'll continue to watch them. But I can't get in her head, or his. And if I try to have someone pursue them now, I'd lose the advantage of surprise once it's time to strike."

"So, what are you going to do?"

"I think it's time we expand."

"Infect more people?" Luca asked.

"No, find more vessels, like you. People who can help us fight The Light, seize the vials and gain the advantage."

"OK," Luca said. "Who can we get?"

"I have a few people in mind. We have five vials now. With these people on our side, The Light can't win even if they manage to get the other six."

Luca felt a chill, and somewhere in the distance heard a dog cry out in the night.

* * * *

CHAPTER 10
EDWARD KEENAN

Las Orillas

Ed sat in the van, staring into the passenger-side mirror at his new Black Island Guardsman partner, Luther, as the giant attempted to make sense of the gas pump's *intricate* instructions.

Luther looked like an offensive lineman, all muscle. Looking at him, you'd think he was jumbo-box-of-rocks dumb. And, as Ed learned on their flight, and subsequent ride from the airport where they were met with an Agency van, you'd be right. Luther was a few fries short of a Happy Meal, and never stopped talking about the dumbest things — TV shows Ed had never heard of, wrestling, and conspiracy theories that were nowhere near plausible. One included Elvis, JFK, and Michael Jackson not only being alive, but secretly puppeteering the world's governments as part of some Illuminati-like cabal.

Ed had nodded around a hundred thousand times in the past six hours, and was wishing like hell he'd been sent on a solo mission.

Luther stared at the gas nozzle, then squeezed the trigger, but judging from his rage face, was having no luck spilling gas into the van.

"Come on!" Luther smacked the pump, then turned to glare at the clerk inside who would have been as likely to hear him from four blocks away. He yelled, "Turn it on!"

Ed sighed, got out of the van, and looked at the giant red "START" button with the white sign above it:

Pay cash inside or insert credit card and press Start.

"Did you put the card in?" Ed asked.

"Yeah, fucker won't start."

"Did you press the start button?"

Luther looked at the big red button, "Oh, this one?"

"Yup."

"Oh," he said, sheepishly grinning. "In Jersey, we didn't pump our own gas. Sorry."

"OK." Ed said as he decided to head into the gas station to kill two birds with one stone: take a piss and get a moment's reprieve from the idiot.

No telling when he'd get a chance to use the bathroom again. From here, they were headed to the Church of Original Design headquarters. They had to find Marina Harmon, or rather the man she was with, a priest, whose name they didn't yet know. Paola had seen him in her "vision," or whatever the hell they were calling it.

"Can I get you anything?" Ed asked Luther.

"Yeah, get me a Coke and some salt-and-vinegar chips."

"I am not getting you salt-and-vinegar chips."

"Why not?"

"Because then I'll have to smell them. Got a second choice?"

Luther frowned and sighed, his heart apparently broken by the loss. "OK, barbecue?" he asked more than said, seeking Ed's approval.

"OK." Ed walked toward the station, wondering how the hell he got paired with the dumbest guy in the Black Island Guard.

Ed had worked with at least four other men who would've been better suited for this mission, but since shit went down with Sullivan, many men had vanished from the island. Ed figured they were either infected, or suspected of helping Sullivan, and were being detained on one of the lower levels.

Whatever the case, God help them if Luther was the best they had left. He had worked in another division of the Guard prior to last week. Ed was guessing it wasn't Research and Development or Applied Sciences. According to Director Bolton, Luther was a damned good fighter. For all he lacked in basic vocabulary, manners, and people skills, Ed figured the guy had to be a one-man army to earn his spot on this mission.

Ed went to the bathroom, then searched a chip aisle that was fully stocked with everything — except barbecue.

After getting some drinks and snacks, Ed returned to the van where Luther was already sitting in the driver's seat. Ed opened the passenger door, climbed inside, and threw the bag of chips at the big man.

"You got me salt and vinegar!" The large man practically squealed.

"They were out of everything else," Ed grumbled as he passed Luther the bottle of Coke then unscrewed his own and took a drink.

"Thanks, sir."

Ed closed the door. "Let's go."

**

Ed was pleasantly surprised to find that Luther stayed quiet, so long as he was shoving food in his mouth. He ate like a buzz saw, but at least he wasn't talking. It was almost enough to make up for the reeking cabin.

Luther polished off the bag, licked his fingers, one by one, savoring the flavor as if these were the best chips God ever saw fit to create.

Ed looked away rather than continue watching the man child making sweet love to his fingers. He looked out the passenger-side window and watched the crammed houses flying by, hoping Luther would think he was lost in thought and maybe leave him be until they reached the church.

"You know," Luther said, "a lot of people say that dance is gay or lame, but I happen to like it."

Ed was intrigued. "Dance?"

"Yeah, dancing. Do you like it?"

"What kind of dancing? Like ballet?"

"Any kind, really. I started watching that *Dancing with the Stars*, and I really liked it. Suddenly, I started watching any kind of dance I could find —Broadway shows, old movies with Fred Astaire and Ginger Rogers, even that *Dance Moms* show."

"Wow," Ed said.

"What?" Luther asked, looking defensive. "I'm not gay."

"Hey, I didn't say you were. And even if you were ... "

"I'm not."

"Again, not saying you are, but even if you *were*, which, again, you're not, I don't care. I'm just surprised that you're into dancing."

"Why, 'cuz I'm big and strong?"

"Well," Ed said, not sure if he was insulting the guy, "that, and you don't seem like you'd be very graceful. No offense."

Luther was silent for a while.

Ed wondered if he was insulted, and almost felt bad. But at the same time he was grateful for the quiet.

As the silence stretched, Ed found himself oddly wanting to know more about Luther.

He had always been good at figuring a person out immediately. He could look at anyone and size them up, knowing their strengths and weaknesses, prejudices and fears, and oftentimes, their sexual fetishes all at a glance. He thought he had Luther pegged, and for the most part, he had. The man's intellectual diet consisted of horrible reality shows, sports, and crackpot radio on the AM stations. But this dance thing was an unexpected wrinkle in an otherwise stupid sandwich. Perhaps there was an artistic type yearning to be freed from his dullard's shell.

Just as Ed was contemplating engaging Luther, his phone rang. It was his daughter, who was back on Black Island with Teagan, Becca, Brent, and Ben.

His heartbeat sped as he answered.

"Jade?"

"Hi, Dad."

"What's wrong?"

"Nothing, I was just wondering why you didn't say goodbye before you left."

Ed never would've left his daughter's side again, except for two things. Desmond had said he could keep her safe, and he had an ability to see the aliens unlike anyone else, except for perhaps Paola. The second reason was that Ed figured if anyone was going to defeat the aliens, it should be him. Truth was, he was the only person he could trust to get the job done. While he'd told his daughter they were going the night before, he didn't want to wake her at the crack of dawn when he headed out with Luther.

"Sorry," he said. "We had to leave early, and I didn't want to wake you. How's everyone?"

"Good. Teagan and Becca are on a play date with Brent and Ben at a small park the Guardsmen put together."

"Good." Ed would've preferred to have Brent over Luther as a traveling companion, but he'd insisted that Desmond keep Brent out of action, along with the girls. "Don't worry, we should be home soon."

"Yeah, I got the note you left on my door. But when is *soon*? A few hours? A few days? A few weeks?"

"I don't know." Ed sighed. "Too early to say. We just got here."

"Where are you at?"

"I'm not sure what I can say. It's probably best not to say anything on the phone. No idea who might be listening."

"Oh come on, Dad, you're working *for* the government. No need to be paranoid."

Clearly she didn't understand that nobody could be trusted these days. Especially other agencies that might be monitoring the phones and that might have someone infected in their ranks.

"Just the same, honey, I can't. So, what do they have you doing? Found a job for you yet?"

She paused. He figured she was wondering whether to continue her previous line of questioning or just now getting the hint that he wanted her to stop discussing Black Island business on an unsecure line.

"They've got me working in the dining hall."

"Doing what?"

"Cooking, for now. Until they learn how bad a cook I am anyway," she laughed. "I was hoping to work in the school, but they already have a teacher, and only a dozen kids here so far."

"Well, if you hate it, talk to Desmond. Tell him I said to find you something in the classroom."

"That's OK, Dad." She was quiet for a moment, then added, "Thank you."

"OK, honey, I've gotta go now."

"OK." She paused. Ed couldn't help but feel like Jade was waiting for him to finish with those three words.

Even though the end of the other world had brought them closer, he couldn't help but feel a residual frost from years of enmity between them.

But they were both trying.

"I love you," he said, rushing through the sentiment.

"I love you too. Be safe."

"You too," he said. "Bye."

Ed hung up the phone and stared out the window. For all of Luther's blathering, he at least seemed to know enough to let Ed stew in his thoughts after he hung up with his daughter.

After ten minutes or so, Luther killed the silence.

"Looks like we're here. And we're not alone."

Ed looked down the street and saw a half-dozen news vans.

"Looks like something's going on."

"Great," Ed said sarcastically.

He was about to tell Luther to find a spot on a side street, but the front gates opened and a red Mustang with tinted windows pulled out.

A voice inside him called out: *It's them.*

Ed wasn't sure if it was a guess, instinct, or something else, but he pointed at the car. "Follow them, Luther."

* * * *

CHAPTER 11
MARY OLSON

Mary wanted to vomit, sitting on the couch with Paola and Desmond, watching news reports of the man who shot up the school yesterday.

She shook her head.

"I can't let you do this anymore," she said to Paola. "This is too much."

Desmond looked at Mary, surprised. "I thought we agreed that this was for the best."

"I know what you said, and I agree with you that yes, we need to do something to stop The Darkness, but this ... this is too much! Paola was inside that murderer's head!"

Calmly, Desmond said, "She was perfectly safe."

"How do you know that? Can you guarantee that The Darkness won't see her and jump into her head the next time this happens, *like it did back at the Drury Inn?*"

"It won't. She has Luca and The Light with her now. They'll protect her."

"You're only guessing." Mary stood, unable to stay seated. "You can't know that!"

Crying, Paola said, "Please, stop fighting."

"We're not fighting, dear." Mary turned from Desmond to Paola. "But we need to discuss this. We need to consider what's really at stake and what other options we have."

"What do you mean *other options?*" Desmond asked. "This is it. The Light is inside Paola, and that's the only thing we have going for us right now. *Your daughter* is the only thing standing between The Darkness and the end of our world. What would you have us do, Mary?"

"Maybe stop using Paola as some sort of psychic alien tuning rod to help you find these damned vials."

"But she's having these seizures anyway. She's seeing these things, connecting with these people, and The Darkness. Do you really want us to ignore her gift?"

"A gift? Is that what you think this is?"

"I'm sorry." Desmond threw up his hands. "That's not what I meant."

"No," said Mary, pointing at Desmond, "it's *exactly* what you meant. You're obsessed with these damned vials, and you don't care what happens to Paola so long as you find them."

"That's bullshit!" Desmond yelled. He stood, eyes enraged.

It was rare to see Desmond so fired up. Mary must have touched a nerve. But she didn't care. She was right, and his head was too far up his ass to see it.

"I love you," he said, "and I love Paola. I would do anything to keep her out of this. Hell, if I could have Luca's soul jump into my body right now, I would."

"Would you?"

"Yes!" Desmond seemed offended by her question.

Mary kneeled next to Paola and held her hands. "Baby, can you talk to Luca?"

Paola, head still in her hands, said, "No."

"Can you try?" Mary asked, feeling that Paola's answer came too fast for an honest attempt.

"I tried!" Paola said, glaring at Mary. "Why can't you listen to me?"

"I *am* listening to you!"

"No, you're both talking about me as if I'm not even here, like I'm not a part of this conversation! Nobody's asked me what I want!"

Mary felt smacked by the obvious, not that it changed how she felt. "Well, no, we didn't ask you, you're right. So, what do *you* want?"

"I want to do this."

"What?" Mary asked.

"Desmond is right, Mom. This is a gift. Luca brought it to me because he thought I was the only person The Light could go into out of everyone he knew. Luca said it had to be someone pure."

"Could he jump into me?" Desmond asked. "Can you ask him? I would gladly take your place, sweetie."

"I can't reach him. He only comes when I'm sleeping, or during the seizures. But he said I was the only one. I think if he could've gone into you, he would've done so when he brought you back."

"That's true," Desmond agreed.

Paola looked up at her mom, eyes welled up, "I know you think of me like I'm your little girl, but it's time to let go. Luca chose me for a reason. For me not to help, when I can, would be selfish. The world is counting on us, and it's not right for you to expect me to follow your fear and do nothing."

Mary sat beside Paola, hugging her, tears rolling down her own cheeks.

"I know, baby, but you will always be my little girl. And I can't stand the thought of something happening to you again. It would kill me."

"Yeah, Mom, but if I *don't* do anything, we'll all die anyway."

"Did Luca say that?" Mary asked.

"He didn't need to. I can see into The Darkness. I know what It wants."

"What's that?" Mary asked, terrified of the answer.

"All of us," she said.

Mary cried as she held Paola tight.

"I'm sorry," she whispered through her cry, both to Paola and looking up at Desmond. "I'm sorry."

"It's OK, Mommy," Paola said. "We'll be OK. I promise."

"Me too." Desmond sat beside Mary and pulled both girls into his arms. "We're not going to fall to The Darkness again, I swear."

* * * *

CHAPTER 12
BORICIO WOLFE

Boricio was in the sorry-ass excuse for a jail cafeteria, standing in line for his slop when a chill started to shake, rattle, and roll right through him.

It started small, just a stick on a snare drum. Then it started to rat-a-tat-tat in the way shit always did when someone was watching him.

Boricio looked around to see who, if anyone's, eyeballs were begging for a gouging.

Nobody in line — three guys in front and several behind — seemed to be paying Boricio a dick tip of attention.

Boricio stepped up to the front and held out his tray as another prisoner, a thin black dude dressed in all white, ladled a wet slop of potatoes beside a slab of gray meat. The dude met Boricio's eyes, then looked away quickly, toward the back of the line, toward a bald Aryan-looking fuckface fresh out high school, with an ugly tattoo on his neck, an idiot's sneer, and the downright stupidity to pretend he wasn't eyeing Boricio.

Boricio wasn't certain, but thought the kitchen dude was giving a warning. Shit and fan were about to bump uglies.

Boricio gave a subtle nod back and looked around for something to use as a weapon. Nothing in sight, Boricio decided he'd wing it. If the Nazi fuck came charging solo, he'd be fine. If he was one of many, an unfortunate number of fuckers might die. He hoped not. A high body count would likely delay his exodus.

Boricio made his way through the line, grabbed a roll from another guy, then crossed to the cafeteria's rear, close to where a pair of prison pigs were standing watch. Boricio sat alone at a long aluminum table bolted to the floor with a connected bench, and kept the room in front of him.

He watched as Hitler Youth made his way to a table with a trinity of lookalike crackers. The fucker was still trying hard to look like he wasn't watching Boricio, but he was as obvious as his ignorance.

Boricio looked past him, also pretending.

Best to lie low, play dumb. Boricio ate, acting like he wouldn't mush the fucker's eyes to goo with his thumbs if the asshole was stupid enough to come at him. Or maybe he'd use his spoon.

Boricio looked down at his metal spoon, seeing it now as a weapon. The guards would run a metal detector wand over them before they were allowed back into their cells. So there was no sneaking the spoon back and filing it down to a shiv.

That didn't mean Hitler Youth didn't have one, or wasn't given one by Guard Tard or some other fucker who saw Boricio as a threat to the delicate ecosystem of BumFuck Oz.

Boricio hadn't seen hide nor hair of Guard Tard since their little altercation. He figured the guy was shuffling papers at a desk or on administrative leave. But Boricio knew better than to think that shit was finished. Beef wasn't settled. If Hitler Youth was gonna take a shot, there was little doubt it was at Guard Tard's behest.

Boricio hoped the pair of pigs didn't have skin in the game. Otherwise, shit would get difficult, at least until he could get one of their sticks.

Boricio finished his meal then waited for the lineup. Waiting to get cleared for a return to his cell, Boricio felt half of the hundred or so prisoners in the cafeteria watching him.

Shit was definitely about to go down.

Boricio wondered if Guard Tard had put a general bounty on his head, reward any motherfucker in the joint who took out the Wolfe. Maybe he offered a few packs of smokes and a tossed salad to the man with the balls to face ye olde Boricio.

He kept his eyes on his plate, tuning his ears, so he could know where the pigs were at all times.

They were about ten feet behind him, standing quietly like soldiers instead of bottom-barrel cops who couldn't be on a real force. And considering the hillbilly hucklefuck town, that said dick about their skills.

Boricio glanced up at the table of Nazis as they started laughing and looking at Boricio more obviously ... the threat looming larger in their eyes.

OK, when you gonna make your move, Hitler Youth?

Suddenly, the lights went out, and the place went pitch black as everyone started shouting nonsense.

Here we go. It's showtime!

Boricio hopped out of his seat and was about to find cover when four arms grabbed his two and yanked them behind his back. The pair of pigs were the only fuckers close enough to nab him.

"It'll all be over real quick," one of the pigs said in his ear as they dragged him to the corner and set up the kill.

Boricio stomped backwards, hard into the top of one of the pig's feet. That little piggy let go.

Boricio's left hand went free as Piggy cried out.

Boricio managed to grab his nightstick, and swiftly brought it straight up hard into the other piggy's face.

That little piggy let go, too, screaming.

Chaos erupted all around, movement, screams full of bass, prisoners shoving.

Boricio dropped to the ground and crawled forward as fast as he could, making his way toward one of the tables to hide under, even though the darkness displayed exactly jack shit.

Boricio was as blind as his enemies.

Someone raced by Boricio and smashed his left hand with their heel. He stifled a scream and prepared for attack, but the person kept running.

Boricio hoisted himself over the bench and scooted his way under the table, heart hammering as he clutched the nightstick, waiting for attack from any and all sides.

The lights returned as quickly as they'd gone out. Another pig's voice boomed through a megaphone.

"On the ground now!"

Boricio held the nightstick as another two piggies came at him, guns drawn.

One yelled, "Let go of the stick!"

Boricio considered his odds of killing both pigs, but once he saw the Head Pig from the other night, the one who prevented Guard Tard from anally raping Boricio with a nightstick, he figured his best move was to fall in line. Head Pig was the closest thing Boricio had to an ally.

Boricio dropped the stick.

The pig whose foot Boricio smashed raced over, retrieved the nightstick, and grabbed Boricio by the back of his collar.

"You're going in the hole."

::EPISODE 27::
(THIRD EPISODE OF SEASON FIVE)
"WHERE'S THE BEEF"

CHAPTER 1
ARTHUR MORGAN

Art had good days and bad days according to the Autumn Manor staff, the quaintly named nursing home where Art found himself following the misfortune of outliving both his children. Art's trouble was that he couldn't remember much of either as he approached his ninety-fourth birthday.

Most days were a confusing palette of grays. Days filled with "activities" to tide him over until the rest of Art's body failed as his mind had long ago.

He sat in the sunroom not feeling particularly social, waiting for the reporter who wanted to get a quote about whatever war the country was currently working its way into.

Art wondered why anyone was coming to him for a quote at all. People had to know his health was failing. But he didn't get visitors often, and wasn't going to turn away someone who genuinely wanted to talk.

Art cleaned his thick eyeglasses as a woman on TV was standing at the scene of a mass school shooting.

People talked about how the world was going to hell, and how the proliferation of guns had suddenly made the world awful. But those people failed to realize that the world had been awful since the beginning.

This country, like most others, was paved in the blood of innocents. This was something that the underclasses in every country throughout time always knew, because they had experienced it firsthand.

Now that violence was encroaching on the white middle and upper classes, people were starting to see the truth — that humans were animals. Worse than animals, really. Animals weren't mindlessly violent.

Humans, however …

Art had borne witness to the worst of humanity, first as a soldier in World War II, then again in Korea. Once exposed to man's evil, whether through war or some random act of violence, it was hard to ever see the world through rose-colored glasses again — a doubly heartbreaking end to innocence because the mourned world never existed.

Art had written thousands of pages about the history of war throughout his twenty-one book career. And not just common, regurgitated history. Art studied the *real* reasons for war. Global conflicts were rarely started for honorable or just reasons. Most were about privileged men in pursuit of power or seeking to maintain what they had. Art had known, prior to his senility, more about war than probably anyone else in the States.

Oddly, he had fans — and detractors — on both sides of the aisle. People on the left *and* the right used Art's writings to bolster their arguments for *and* against war. It was a strange sort of fame, one that he'd never felt particularly comfortable with. He simply saw himself doing his duty to report things as he saw them to those willing to listen and learn.

Art wondered about the reporter's agenda. Was it someone seeking to condemn the current war, or hoping to defend it?

Either way, Art was certain to disappoint the reporter. He rarely gave basic black-and-white answers because everything was gray. Subtleties and nuances were deeply nested in every conflict. Right and wrong were only words. Without all of the facts — and no one *ever* had all of the facts — war was difficult to judge as just or unwarranted.

But a lonely Art had agreed to the interview anyway.

"Do I look OK?" he asked Estelle, the on-duty nurse, and one of his favorites — an attractive Cuban woman who vaguely reminded him of a long-gone girlfriend.

"You look fine, Art. How are you feeling? You up to this?" Her smile made him feel safe.

"Good. Yes, I'm up to this."

An awkward silence hung between them until Art finally found the courage to apologize.

"Sorry about yesterday."

Estelle looked down, just long enough to let him know that he'd hurt her feelings. She looked up and smiled. "It's OK."

Art didn't remember the details. Paul, the nurse on duty earlier, said, "I heard you were naughty yesterday," then proceeded to tell Art that he'd thrown a fit about his lunch, yelled at half the staff, and escalated his curses until he became borderline violent.

Art felt horrible. The last thing he wanted to do was hurt Estelle. She was a sweetheart, never short with him, and always gentle. Estelle listened to his stories and asked questions, unlike most of the others, who would be checking their idiot phones through the entire conversation.

"No," he said to Estelle, "it's not OK. Nobody should have to put up with my shit when I'm having my bad days. Nobody. You're a saint, dear, and don't think for a moment that I don't know and appreciate it. I'm sorry for whatever I said."

Estelle's eyes watered, and Art could tell he was about to make her cry. But he didn't want pity. He just wanted to improve things between them.

Art hated that he couldn't control the anger when it came. Hated more that he couldn't even remember the incidents. It was hard to sincerely apologize for something you couldn't even remember doing, and sincerity was the mother of a decent apology.

Art had never been one to believe in heaven or hell, not with all he'd seen. But that was before his mind had packed its bags. Now he realized that hell was as real as it was eternal and unforgiving.

"Oh, they're here," Estelle said as the receptionist escorted a woman with light-brown hair into the social room.

"Hello, Mr. Morgan, my name is Rose McCallister. I'm a reporter at *The Grunion Sun*. I'd love to pick your brain on a few things for an article I'm writing."

"Sure," Art said. Rose was quite a looker. Young with porcelain skin and a smile that could get anyone talking. He'd learned two things in his life when it came to public relations: never trust a reporter, and never trust a pretty woman who wants to discuss what you know.

Yet there was something about her eyes that held Art instantly captive. He *wanted* to talk to her, and know what she knew. He wanted to tell her anything she was willing to hear.

It was the oddest sensation, but Art felt like he'd known the woman forever and could trust her with anything.

Rose turned toward Estelle. "Can we talk alone?"

"Certainly," Estelle said. She left the room, seeming equally stricken by Rose.

Art was confused.

Estelle normally would've asked Art if he wanted her there, especially given his mood swings and declining memory. She was a good buffer and could prevent him from making a fool of himself or saying something he'd regret. And if he did slip into words that shouldn't be said, Estelle could tell the reporter about his condition and beg them not to quote him. Fortunately, there had been only one incident, and Estelle hadn't begged the reporter so much as threatened to eviscerate him.

Rose looked around, as if trying to find someone within earshot, then leaned closer with a conspiratorial whisper.

"I'm here to help you, Mr. Morgan."

I should've known she wasn't a reporter.

His lips tightened, and Art's heartbeat accelerated as he looked around for someone to call over to get this woman away.

She reached out, put an icy hand on his, which seemed to instantly calm his nerves and shaking hand.

"I'm not going to hurt you, Mr. Morgan. Quite the opposite."

"What are you talking about?"

"I've read your books, sir. You have a brilliant mind when it comes to war."

"Had," he said, "had a brilliant mind. Not quite what it was."

"Yes, I read the feature in *The Economist* about your situation. Which is why I'm here. I think we can help one another."

"Help one another?" Art found his smile. "What do you have in mind?"

"First, let me ask you a question. Would you like your old life back? Your youth? Your vitality? All of your memories?"

"Hey, lady, if you're pitching some snake oil, go peddle your wares elsewhere." Art's smile turned into a laugh full of cracks. "Doctors already said there's nothing that can be done for me. Besides, I've lived long enough. My family, the ones I care about anyway, are all long gone. What's the point of being young again even if you could make it happen?"

"Because nobody wants to die. No one would choose nothingness over life. And I see the glimmer in your eye, Mr. Morgan. I see that you've got quite a bit of fight left inside you."

"See, that's where you're wrong, ma'am. I'm quite tired of fighting. I've seen enough quarreling, enough violence, enough death, to last me five lifetimes. I'm ready to meet my maker — or nothingness if that's all there is. I'm ready to lie down and just be."

Rose shook her head. "You can lie to yourself, but you can't lie to me. I see a tired man, yes, maybe even a discouraged man. But he's not tired of fighting. He's tired of losing. He's tired of not being able to affect change. He's tired of not counting. But what if you could have your health *and* get people listening again?"

Art wanted to tell this woman to leave him alone, stop trying to sell whatever it was she was hocking. He looked around again.

"Where the hell is Estelle?"

Rose leaned in again, put both her freezing hands on his. He wanted to pull his away, but couldn't. His heartbeat sped up, and a shiver ran through him.

He asked, "W-what are you?"

"I *am* the Maker. I am going to change everything in this world. I'm offering you a seat at the table."

"What the hell are you talking about?" Art's blood was boiling in anger, and he felt a twitter from detonation. His body refused to obey him. He couldn't even stir enough anger to yell for someone to get this clown out of here. He was pretty certain that she was somehow holding him down, even if he couldn't figure out how.

What the hell is she doing to me?

"I'm talking about this, Mr. Morgan." Rose released his hands, reached into her purse, and pulled out a glass vial with glowing blue liquid inside.

A hundred thoughts swam through his mind, all screaming danger. For a moment Art was certain the woman was some sort of anti-war protester who had brought a toxin to poison him, to make some kind of misguided political statement.

But just as Art was transfixed by her eyes, he found himself unable to look at anything other than the vial.

"Go ahead," she said, handing it to him.

His hand moved forward, as if with a will of its own.

He touched the vial.

A spark jumped from the vial to his skin. But rather than deflecting his hand, it drew his fingers closer.

The vial was suddenly in his hand, surprisingly warm to the touch. An energy coursed through him, and within seconds Art felt a vitality he hadn't felt since his thirties, perhaps even his twenties.

What is this?

He stared at the vial, watching as the blue liquid seemed to climb up the glass toward the black stopper, as if trying to flee.

Open it, his mind said. At least he *thought* it was his mind.

He heard a swelling of dozens, if not hundreds, of whispers above a low hum. Together, the sounds seemed like music to a forgotten song on the tip of his tongue.

Art longed to hear more.

Rose withdrew the vial.

The energy and wonder that had filled his heart was gone, popped like a bubble.

Art already longed to feel it again. She was like a drug pusher giving him his first hit for free, before she announced the price of his next.

"Please," he said, his trembling fingers outstretched, reaching for it.

"Not here," she said. "Come with me."

"OK." Art stood and followed Rose, willing to go anywhere she wanted if it meant feeling that feeling again.

* * * *

CHAPTER 2
MARINA HARMON

Marina stared out the window into Culver City's filthy, beating heart.

It was charity to say the house had seen better days. The home, with its boarded windows, chipped paint, and weed-strewn lawn, looked like a war zone. Of course, given the neighborhood's general neglect and how many of its citizens faced death on a daily basis, that wasn't far from the truth.

"This is your house?"

"Yes," Acevedo said. "The neighborhood went to hell about ten years ago or so. It used to be beautiful."

"And you stored the most important thing in the world in this dump?"

Acevedo nodded. "Never underestimate the power of hiding in plain sight."

Marina looked up and down the street, saw some thugs standing at the end of the block, wearing oversized clothes that surely covered guns.

She felt guilty for stereotyping young black men, but wasn't naive. It was the neighborhood, not their color.

She told herself she'd feel the same way if it were any other race of young men hanging around looking like thugs. She also realized that anyone living here had to adapt to their surroundings so as not to stand out, and that any kid living here would naturally don a thug's persona. That didn't mean every kid who looked like a thug was one. But at the same time, Marina had to assume they all were, lest she let her guard down.

Marina had lived a lily-white life of comfort and opportunity. She'd done some work in poor communities and had even travelled to Eastern Europe, Africa, and Haiti to do missionary work for the church. But she'd rarely been in neighborhoods like this, let alone truly got to know anyone who lived there.

"You think we're safe?" she asked, fearing that the priest would think her some uptight elitist.

"Nobody's going to mess with us." Acevedo sounded confident. He got out of the car, and Marina joined him. Together they walked toward the house, her trying not to look directly at the thugs, who were definitely scoping them out.

Marina walked quicker, pulling up close to Acevedo, feeling vulnerable, as if everyone in the neighborhood could sense them there, and that she had something of unimaginable power in her jacket pocket, making her a ripe target.

Acevedo unlocked the front door then stepped inside and flipped on a light just inside the doorway.

"Wait a sec," he said, vanishing into the house.

Marina wanted to call out and remind the priest that he shouldn't leave her on the porch too long, but didn't want to sound wimpy.

As she waited, Marina noticed several chipped marks in the door jamb, surely signs of people breaking in. She wondered if they'd made the trip for naught. What if someone had broken in and found the vial and Acevedo's list?

"OK," Acevedo appeared in the doorway. "No squatters."

Marina crossed the threshold into the house and was immediately thrown back by the smell of feces and ... something putrid she couldn't identify.

She saw the walls smeared with feces, blood, and God knew what other kinds of fluids, along with hundreds of words scrawled in pen, pencil, crayon, and even by knife. Words were mostly too small to read without moving closer, but Marina made out a few:

DEATH
NOTHING
VOID
HELP

"What the hell?" she said looking at the place, littered with evidence from countless squatters — food and drink containers, dirty clothing, porno mags, and plenty of paraphernalia from drugs. Large chunks were missing from the walls, as if there had been a party with a sledgehammer. The house looked like the set of a snuff film.

The air was suddenly heavy. Marina felt a mix of strong emotions swirling through her, from euphoria to anguish.

She wanted to leave.

Being in here was too much.

She thought of the master's training, paused, then drew a deep breath and counted to five before exhaling.

"People break in here all the time, no matter what I do. They're drawn to the vial, I suspect. They come in search of something they can sense but not see. Then, driven mad, they tear the house apart, searching but unable to find a thing. Eventually, they lose their minds and leave, or ... "

"Or what?"

"Let's just say the police have pulled many bodies out of here."

"I can feel it," she said, "so much pain. That's the vial?"

"I don't know if it's the vial or residuals — psychic stains, if you will — of those who have suffered here. But yes, it's strong."

"So the vials act in response to what people are feeling, to what they are? Isn't that what you said?"

"Yes."

"So is it possible that your vial may have already been tainted by the people in here? Already turned to Darkness?"

"No," Acevedo said, then after a long pause added, "at least I hope not."

"Great," Marina said with a sense of impending doom. She wasn't sure if the sensation was a response to the situation, a delayed reaction to everything that had already happened, or if she were being infected by the home's haunted emotions.

She tried to think positive thoughts, not let the house change her mood. Marina could see why Acevedo demanded that she complete the training. She couldn't imagine how she would've responded if she'd not been somewhat prepared to combat the overwhelming sense of doom.

Acevedo led Marina to the kitchen. The cabinets were destroyed, ripped from the walls. The sink was torn out. The refrigerator was open, filled with rotting food and what looked like more shit. Walls were broken in many places, paper peeled and hanging low. The floor was scattered with more remnants of squatters, and the linoleum was ripped away to reveal a dry, dirty concrete floor.

Acevedo looked up and smiled.

"It's still here."

She blinked. "It is? Where?"

He pointed to the floor and said, "I'll be right back."

Marina stood in the kitchen as Acevedo went to the car.

Standing there, she felt a humming from the vials in her jacket, as if in response to the one beneath her.

Dig.

Dig.

The thoughts raced through her head so fast she wasn't sure if she'd thought them or if ... the vials had.

The room grew cold while she waited for Acevedo.

Again, Marina felt the stirring of emotions, and they began to seep into her. She found herself wondering what the hell she was doing with the priest.

Who was Marina to think she could save the world?

She couldn't even save herself, let alone see the danger that was lurking inside Steven. What hope did *she* have? What hope did *they* have?

It all felt so futile.

She had to flee the house, clear the dark thoughts from her head.

Where the hell is Acevedo?

Something moved behind her, a dark blur in the living room.

She turned, but it — whatever it was — was already gone.

Her heart like a jackhammer, Marina wanted to run outside, and get the hell out of the house.

The front door opened, and Acevedo stepped back inside holding a concrete saw in his gloved hands, wearing goggles and a mask.

"You might want to stand back. You don't want to breathe any of this dust once I start cutting."

"OK," Marina said, going out to the living room, where the stench of shit and despair was strongest.

As the priest began to cut a hole in the floor and the saw's whirring echoed throughout the house, Marina moved closer to the front door, wanting to just go outside, even if she did wind up with a bunch of thugs throwing their murderous stares on her body.

"Marina," a voice said from behind.

She turned.

Acevedo was still kneeling on the kitchen floor, guiding the saw's blade through the concrete.

"Marina," the voice repeated, a man's voice, slightly familiar, though she didn't recognize it over the noise.

She looked around, and saw the bedroom door in the back of the house swing shut.

She wanted to tell Acevedo, but something stopped her. Instead, Marina approached the bedroom.

"That's it, Marina, come closer."

Everything in her said to turn and run back to the kitchen. But Marina felt a compulsion to see what was inside the room.

Her heart was like thunder, goose bumps raking her flesh as she crept toward the door. Marina reached out slowly for the doorknob, her mind screaming at her to turn around.

She tried to turn the handle.

Locked.

OK, that's it. Turn around and go. Now.

Finally, Marina felt something click inside, and she was able to turn away from the door and walk away.

As she headed back to the kitchen, the sound of Acevedo's saw cut off.

Behind her, she heard the door unlock.

Click

Marina turned, staring at the door.

"Marina," the voice said again, this time sounding muffled, as if coming from the other side of the door.

She turned to look at Acevedo who had turned the saw back on and was cutting again, oblivious to Marina and whoever else might be in the house.

She turned back to the door and walked toward it.

She reached out, turned the knob, and stepped through the doorway into a pitch-black room. Light from the living room should have bled inside but didn't.

The room clutched its darkness like a cloak to disavow nature's laws.

"Come in," the man's voice said from the far corner of the room.

She could barely make out a shape in the darkness, not enough to see who it was.

She wanted to turn and leave.

This is a terrible idea.

Acevedo's saw faded into the background as if it, and he, were becoming impossibly distant and far away.

"Come closer, so I may see you," whispered the man.

Marina's body obeyed.

The door closed behind her.

Click

Marina's every fiber screamed at her to run. She was being tricked by The Darkness, eager to finish the job It had set out to do: kill her.

Yet she couldn't turn away.

Marina had to move closer and see what It had to tell her.

She moved toward the corner.

"You cannot trust him," said the man in the dark.

"Who?"

"The priest. You must make sure he doesn't get the vials."

"Why?"

"You don't really know anything about him, do you?"

"What do you mean?"

The sound of her name cut into the conversation — Acevedo from the other room. "Marina?"

She turned back to the man in the shadows, but he was gone, and she was alone in the darkness.

"Marina?" Acevedo called again, his footsteps approaching the door. He twisted at the handle, but couldn't open it.

"Marina?"

"Coming." She reached out in the darkness, found the lock, twisted it, then opened the door.

"What's going on?" he asked, eyeing Marina suspiciously.

"I was looking around and ... the door just closed and locked itself behind me."

She left out the part about the man in the darkness and his warning, hoping that Acevedo couldn't tell she was withholding.

She looked down and saw a metal box in his hands.

"Is that the vial and the list?"

"Yes," he said, "please, take it. You need to open it."

"Why me?"

"I don't need the temptation."

"OK." Marina opened the box.

Inside was a thick black cloth wrapped around a vial. Marina couldn't see the vial, or its glowing blue liquid, but she could feel it humming, louder as she opened it.

Beside the vial was a piece of folded paper.

She pulled it out and saw three numbers written in her father's handwriting.

"What are these?"

"The names of the other three people who have vials, and their addresses. Written in code."

"I assume you have the key?"

"Yes," he said pointing to his head, "up here. Let me see the list."

He took the paper from Marina and looked it up and down.

"Make sense to you?"

"Yes, and one of these is in town. I suggest we head there first. Let's get out of here. I feel like someone's watching us."

Marina wondered if that's who she saw in the room. The someone watching them. She wanted to tell Acevedo about the person, and the message, but at the same time something in her gut said the voice could be trusted.

Yes, her father had trusted Acevedo enough to give him a vial and a list of the others. And yes, he didn't seem to want any part of the vials, enough to have told her *not* to surrender them.

Yet there was something off about the priest. Being fooled by Steven had taught Marina to acknowledge her instincts. There had been small signs of Steven's *oddness* that she'd gathered from time to time, things she shouldn't have ignored. Marina allowed her love, if she could call it that, to blind her.

She wouldn't be that stupid again.

At the same time, Marina wouldn't blindly trust a voice in the dark.

There was no rush to tell Acevedo anything. She could hold her cards and bide her time until she had reason to trust the priest, or not.

Marina hoped she could trust him.

If not, she had no one else.

* * * *

CHAPTER 3
EDWARD KEENAN

Ed listened through the walls, ear to the long-range Agency microphone's earpiece until the saw's buzzing scream finally abated.

Afterward, he heard Marina talking to the man Paola said was a priest.

Judging from their conversation, they had a list with the names and locations of the other three people holding vials.

"Should we grab them up?" Luther asked.

"He said it's written in code," Ed said. "If we grab him now, he might not give it up."

"I'll make him give it up."

"No, we wait and see. He said one was local, so we follow them some more."

"How many you think they have now?"

"Paola said at least two to start with. So if they picked one up just now and they lead us to one more, at least, then we have four. It's not worth blowing by moving in now."

"You think they know we're here?" Luther asked, having heard the priest say he thought someone was watching.

"I dunno. Maybe they can feel us like Paola feels them."

"All the more reason to grab them now?" Luther suggested, pointing to the pair getting into their car.

Acevedo looked up and down the street, and for a moment his eyes stopped on their van.

"Shit, he made us," Luther said. "Let's move in."

Ed slapped a hand on the man's wrist as he went to key the ignition.

"No, we wait. He can't see anything through the windshield."

"Unless he's like Paola," Luther said.

"We sit still." Ed hated explaining himself to the giant. He wasn't used to questions from people under his rank, and wasn't about to start letting it happen with Luther.

Luther was about to continue arguing, but Ed met his eyes and glared at him.

"I am not repeating myself."

"Yes, sir," Luther said.

They stood down as Marina and the priest climbed into the classic Mustang then headed down the street.

Ed flipped on the tablet, synced to the tracking device he planted on the car while the two were inside the house.

He watched as the beeping dot traveled two blocks. It turned south then east — giving the priest just enough time to ensure he wasn't being tailed.

"OK," Ed said, "now you can follow."

* * * *

CHAPTER 4
BORICIO WOLFE

Boricio woke feeling like he'd been wedged up a giant's asshole.

It wasn't just the smell, Boricio couldn't move his arms ... at all. He shook, trying to break free, but was trapped in a Houdini's worth of FUCKALL.

"Let me out!" Boricio screamed and kicked out, stubbing his toes against the cell door and thrashing against the straitjacket.

Pain shot from his toes to his ankles.

Fuck! Fuck!

The fuckers had taken his shoes. And his clothes, save for the straitjacket. The giant's shit was his own; Boricio was sitting in a homemade pile.

"Goddammit, let me the fuck outta here, you stupid cunts!"

Boricio's heart hammered so fast he thought he might have a heart attack and die — alone in BumFuck County Lockup, buried in a John Doe grave, barely a shit stain to remind the world that Boricio Wolfe had been in it.

The utter confinement made Boricio brew with a fresh batch of rage. It was one thing to be stuck in the cell. That, he could handle. Boricio still had some space and could move around. A shark in a tank was still a fucking shark. And it was one thing to have his hands tied behind his back. A kick in the nuts, but something he could deal with and worm his way out of in time.

But this was different.

The straitjacket was a coffin, pinning him down from all sides, hands secured in front of his chest.

Boricio wanted, no *needed*, to break free of the jacket. He had to move. He felt like he had crabs crawling all over his entire fucking body.

"Let me out!!"

Boricio screamed loud enough to wake his earliest victims, but no one responded to shit. So far as he could tell his cell was small and dark with a floor and walls of concrete.

The only light came from a sliver under the door, cockteasing the world outside.

Boricio screamed again until his throat was raw and tasted of blood.

After what felt like a *fuck you* from forever, a shadow finally moved across the floor and Boricio heard footsteps outside.

He sat straighter. Pain seized his back, but Boricio ignored it, eager to see anyone who might come through the door.

Except the motherfucker who did.

Guard Tard opened the door to blinding light, the man still half-concealed in shadow. But he was quick to talk and surrender himself like a dipshit. No sense of suspense. With turned tables, Boricio would've given the ass crack an HBO of horrors.

"Well, well, well," Guard Tard said, "we've got ourselves a genuine badass here, don't we?"

Boricio let the guard gloat.

"Tell me, *John Doe*, do ya consider yourself a careful man?"

Boricio still said nothing, though he was curious where this bag of cock meat was going.

"Because I get the feeling that you do. You're the kinda guy that lives behind the walls, just outta sight, where ya scamper out to do your sneaky, dirty little deeds unseen, like a goddamned cockroach. Am I right?"

"Yup, you got me all figured out."

"More than you know, pal. More than you know."

Boricio knew the fucker wanted him to beg for an explanation, smiling like a goddamned retard at a petting zoo full of kittens and titties.

But Boricio refused to play ball. He just sat there staring Guard Tard in the eyes instead.

Guard Tard kneeled down, coming to within a few feet of Boricio's face, close enough to smell onion and bologna on his breath, along with a strong whiff of tartar suggesting this man's dental hygiene was about as half-assed as his grammar and attention to nostril hair.

"See, boy, you don't need to use your name for us to find out the best stuff about ya."

Boricio stared straight ahead, pretending not to be a tenth as interested as he suddenly was.

"Even the most careful of killers sometimes leave evidence behind. And you, my cockroach friend, have slipped a few times. Hmm, let's see. We got this motel in California where a former cop and this Church of Original Design guy were found dead. Then we got this case a while back, a pedophile got himself killed and left out in the middle o' nowhere. Any of this ringin' a bell in that little insect brain o' yours?"

"Not even a dinner bell." No one got to Boricio — not ever — but this fucker was. He smiled to bury his rage.

"Don't worry, you don't have to say a word. That's the beautiful thing about DNA evidence. You play dumb all ya want, but we still fuckin' got ya. Rest on that, Smarter Than the Average Bear."

Guard Tard stood up, spun, and slammed the door closed behind him.

Boricio wanted to kick.

Wanted to scream.

Wanted out of the fucking straitjacket.

Wanted to kill something.

But he was stuck in a giant's asshole with a genuine pile of shit.

* * * *

CHAPTER 5
MARINA HARMON

"You want to handle this one?" Acevedo asked as they pulled up to the black iron gate that circled the first house on their list.

The estate was massive, two stories, and situated on a bluff looking down on Hollywood. It wasn't Malibu, but Marina still put the sticker price at three million minimum.

"Sure." Marina got out of the car, then went to the touch screen and camera that stood to greet anyone requesting entrance.

She pressed a call button and was met by a black screen and a man's voice: "Yes?"

"We're here to see Mr. Milton Rosen."

A moment's pause, then, "He's dead."

Marina looked down, embarrassed. "Are you his son? Andrew?"

"Yeah, who are you?"

"It's been a long time, so you may not remember me. My name is Marina Harmon. My father was Josh Harmon, and our fathers were friends. You came out to our house a few times for dinner parties several years ago."

Marina couldn't remember the last time she'd seen Mr. Rosen or his son but was reasonably sure he was a teen at the time, and likely in his early twenties now. She wondered if the kid had inherited everything, or whether it had all gone to his mother. She couldn't even remember if there were a Mrs. Rosen. She barely remembered Mr. Rosen, other than the fact that her dad had played golf with him on occasion, and he was a famous Broadway playwright who'd written some plays her father had rather liked. How the two had become friends, Marina wasn't sure. She didn't think Mr. Rosen had ever been a part of the church.

"So, whadya want?" Andrew asked through the speaker.

"I'd like to talk to you about something."

"Mind telling me what?" He sounded perturbed.

"Not over the speaker. I'd rather we sit down."

"Who's that with you?"

Marina looked back to Acevedo sitting in the passenger seat, looking as annoyed as she felt.

"This is another friend of my father's, Mr. Acevedo."

"I don't know him."

Marina sighed and folded her hands together. "OK, may we still talk to you?"

"You can. He stays outside."

Marina was about to object, but Acevedo said, "It's fine, go ahead."

She rolled her eyes behind their lids and faked her best smile. "OK, then, may *I* come in to talk to you, alone?"

"Yes," the young man said, "alone."

The gate opened.

Marina leaned down into the car and met the priest's eyes. "So, any advice?"

"Ask him if his father left behind a vial of any kind, and then tell him you need it."

"What if he doesn't want to hand it over?"

"Then come back here, and I'll go get it."

"What about these?" Marina patted her pocket where she'd taken his vial and added it to her father's old box. "Do you want me to leave them with you for safekeeping?"

He stared ahead into the house for a moment, as if considering Marina's offer, then shook his head no. "I don't want any part of them."

"OK."

Marina turned and headed through the gates, box of vials shoved into her interior coat pocket. The gates hummed as they swung shut behind her.

She thought again of the warning from the man back at the house. He'd said not to trust Acevedo with the vials, but the priest didn't disagree. It made no sense, unless it was The Darkness trying to wedge its way between them.

The front doors opened before she reached them.

Marina was met by a buzz-cut, stocky man wearing all black with a gun holstered at his side. He held a metal-detecting wand in his hand and told her to stand with her arms out.

"All this to see an old friend?"

Marina wondered why Andrew had a security detail. Perhaps he was famous himself. She recalled him doing some local TV back in the day, but hadn't heard anything about movie roles or some other claim to fame.

"Just doing my job, ma'am," the guard said.

Marina looked around the house. Red carpet, white walls, and matching white modern furniture decorated the living room, stretching from the home's rear where giant windows stared out over the city below.

The kitchen, a mix of black and white, was off to her right, but Marina saw no sign of Andrew. She assumed he was up the spiral stairway, on the second floor.

The guard frisked her, and his hand paused on the box in her coat.

"What's this?" He drew the box from her pocket before she could stop him.

The guard shook the box then went to open it.

"Don't!" Marina reached out to try and retrieve the box.

He pulled it away, glared at Marina, then opened the box and looked inside. "Ah, Mr. Rosen will be quite happy to see these. Come with me."

The guard led her to the stairs.

Shit. Not even a minute into the house before they got the vials. I should've left them with Acevedo.

Marina considered what the guard had said — that Andrew would be "quite happy" to see the vials, which implied an awareness. If so, was that a good thing or a bad thing?

At first she'd taken Andrew's attitude for arrogance, but perhaps he was merely cautious. Maybe he'd seen some of the same dangers that she had and was afraid that someone would be coming for his father's vial.

Marina hoped her father chose right when giving a vial to Milton, and that the man's son would follow in his footsteps.

The upstairs had swapped white and red for cream and chocolate brown. Marina felt a cold chill at her spine, colder and colder the closer they got to the room at the hallway's end.

The guard opened the door to an office with three long, custom-built tables stretching the length of all but one wall.

The tables were clear save for one area, which was crammed with books and three monitors. Andrew was sitting at the spot, with his head in his hands, long brown hair spilling over his fingers. He looked up revealing a thin pale face with dark circles under hollow-looking eyes.

His lips were thin and dry. He looked like he was either on a long bender of drugs or had gone a week without sleep.

He looked up at Marina, but didn't bother to greet her.

The guard walked toward Andrew, handing him the box. "Look what she brought."

Andrew looked at Marina, then down at the box. He opened it. Blue light radiated on his face as he stared at the vials.

"Where did you get these?" His eyes stayed fixed to the vials.

"My father asked me to watch after them."

Andrew smiled as if staring at something he'd been searching forever to find. His eyes teared up.

"Thank you for bringing them here. Are there more?"

"I wasn't bringing them to you. I came to see if you had the one my father left with yours. He has asked me to collect all the vials. It's of prime importance."

Andrew looked up and grinned. "Yeah, I bet he did."

"Seriously," she said, "bad things will happen if I don't get the vials."

Marina wasn't sure how much she should tell him, or how much he'd believe. But something in Andrew's eyes said she wouldn't have to convince him of the vials' importance. He might not know what they are, but he had no doubts about their importance.

"How many more are there?"

"Two more that I know of."

"Where are they?" Andrew asked.

"Um, I don't know. Yet. The information is back at my compound, and that's our next stop. Can you tell me where the vial is, the one your father was holding?"

Andrew smiled again, leaned back in his chair, and met Marina's eyes. "I *bet* you'd like to know."

He eyed her up and down, practically molesting her with his gaze. He reminded her of any number of rich assholes

Marina knew when she was younger, men who thought they owned the world and everyone in it was merely their toys.

"Yes, please. I need to bring it back."

"I'm sorry." He smiled his stupid smile. "That won't happen. You will leave here, return to your weird little cult, and pretend you never came."

"I can't do that. I have to bring the vials back."

"Back to whom? Your father is dead; why do you need these?" He spoke in a singsong, as if enjoying the conversation, and his leverage over Marina, a little too much.

"You don't understand. There are lives at risk."

"Why don't you enlighten me, Miss Harmon? Tell me more."

"The vials contain alien life forms. If they fall into the wrong hands, they can destroy us all."

Andrew's eyes widened, and then his lips curled into an odd expression before he burst out laughing.

"Oh, God, that is rich! I know you all had some loony ideas at the Cult O' Original Design, but Jesus, that's just … wow." Andrew started clapping his hands slowly, then stood and took a bow. "Bravo, ma'am."

"I'm not lying, and this has nothing to do with my religion. My father trusted yours. I'm hoping I can do the same with you. I need those vials."

Marina didn't bother explaining which vials she meant. She'd try to get hers back, then ask for his.

"Sorry, again, Ms. Harmon, but I'm gonna hold onto these for a bit. I already lost my vial to a friend."

"What do you mean?"

"After my dad died a few months ago, I found the vial hidden in a metal lockbox in his bedroom closet. No instructions on what to do or anything. I only knew that touching the vial made me feel good, alive, gave me this rush! I know my dad went on these 'retreats' with these shamans and shit, so I figured this had to be some fly drug that nobody's ever heard of, strong enough to feel it through glass! So I had my friend, who's a chemist of sorts, if you know what I mean, take a look and see if he could replicate it. I haven't heard from him in two weeks, though, so I was pissed off thinking my shit was gone for good, but then ... well, you brought me new bottles! And for that, I thank you."

"They're not some *drug*, Andrew. They're dangerous. We need to find your friend before something bad happens to him, or ... *he* does something terrible."

"I told you, he's not answering his phone."

"Then we need to go to his house and talk to him."

"Heh, you think I didn't send Alfonso here already? Dude has bounced. He is G-O-N-E gone. And now, if you don't mind, I'd like to be left alone with my beautiful blues."

"I'm not leaving them here with you."

The smile fell from Andrew's face. "I don't recall giving you a choice, bitch."

Marina started toward him, ready to smack the arrogant little fucker.

Alfonso shoved a pistol to the back of her head. "Stop where you are, lady."

She did as instructed and held up her hands to prove her compliance. But Marina couldn't give up trying to persuade Andrew.

"These aren't drugs. They're alien life forms. They get inside you and do bad shit."

Andrew laughed, waving a hand in front of his face as he sat back down, examining the vials as if she weren't even there. "Yeah, take that crap back to your cult; I don't need to hear it."

"I'm not lying. Have you seen those bad things happening on the news? That's because of these aliens."

"Yeah, right, and maybe we all ought to pay you fuckers to get our 'current fixed' or whatever the fuck it is you all do. My dad bought into that shit for a while, but I'm not my dad. You're not soaking me for cash, and I'm not some fucking idiot who needs to believe in your brand of make-believe — you feel me?"

Andrew was a typical entitled L.A. brat. A rich kid wanting to talk tough, eager for attention and whatever passed for power in these parts. The only way to deal with punks like him were to get in their faces and be direct. Show them you're fearless, and that you can see through their facades.

"No, I don't *feel* ya. And I'm not leaving here without those vials. If you plan to stop me, Alfonso will have to shoot."

Andrew hopped out of his chair so fast that Marina was taken by surprise, unable to defend herself when his fist slammed into her gut, a second before another crashed against the top of her head.

Marina fell to the ground, doubled over in pain.

Andrew grabbed Alfonso's pistol and started waving it around down at Marina, veins on his scrawny neck bulging, his face crimson with maniacal, entitled rich white boy rage.

"Get the fuck out my house, bitch, before I shoot you myself!"

"You ain't shootin' shit," a voice said from behind Marina and the guard.

Everyone turned. Acevedo fired at Andrew.

Andrew cried out in pain. Marina heard the sound of his pistol dropping, followed by his panicked cries. She turned to see him clutching his left arm, where he'd been shot on his inside forearm.

Acevedo turned his gun on the guard. "He worth dying for?"

The guard shook his head.

"Then get on the ground, on your stomach, arms behind your back."

The guard did as Acevedo instructed, while glaring at the priest.

"Here." Acevedo threw a pair of cuffs at Marina.

She caught the cuffs, surprised that he had them.

"Cuff him." Acevedo started toward Andrew, who'd fallen to the ground and was crying while holding his arm. Blood was spurting fast. Marina was reasonably certain he'd bleed out soon without help.

Marina cuffed the bodyguard as she told Acevedo what Andrew had said about giving the vial to a "chemist."

"Where can I find him?" Acevedo shoved the gun against Andrew's head.

"I need you to call an ambulance!"

"First you tell me where to find this guy."

Andrew cried, "How do I know you'll call an ambulance?"

"I'm a priest," Acevedo said. "Now tell me, or I sit here and watch you bleed to death."

"His name is Beef."

"Beef?" Acevedo asked.

"I don't know his real fucking name. Big, fat redheaded dude."

"Where do I find *Beef?*"

"He lives at 4141 Franklin Avenue, in the hood. But he ain't been there in at least a week."

"Where else might we find this man? He got a job?"

"I dunno, c'mon, man, please call an ambulance."

"First, tell me where we might find him."

"I dunno. He's got some homeys that hang out at Salty's Pool Hall, though. They didn't tell my man anything, but maybe you being a priest and all ... "

"OK." Acevedo nodded, grabbed the vials from the table, closed the box, and handed them to Marina.

"Let's go," he said.

"Wait, I thought you were gonna call me an ambulance!"

Acevedo turned back and fired a shot straight into the man's head. He said, "Oh yeah, I lied," then turned to the guard and shot him too.

Marina screamed, staring at Acevedo, hardly able to believe what he'd done.

"Come on," Acevedo said, removing the cuffs, shockingly casual after two murders. "Let's go find Beef."

He led Marina back to the car. She followed, her stomach churning, horrified to have seen Acevedo shoot both men without needing to. She thought she might retch but somehow found a way to focus, using the master's lessons to drive the panic from her mind.

As she followed the priest, Marina wondered again if she could trust him, or might he shoot her the moment they were holding all the vials?

* * * *

CHAPTER 6
ARTHUR MORGAN

Art sat in the hotel room chair, waiting for the woman, Rose, to return.

She'd headed to the store for food and left him alone with a weird boy with dark hair and piercing-blue eyes sitting on one of the two hotel room beds cross-legged.

"What's your name again, kid?"

"Luca."

"So, is Rose your mom?"

"No, sir."

"Who is she to you, then?"

"She's my aunt," Luca said. "She used to go out with my brother. But then he died. So now she's looking after me."

"You don't have any parents?"

"Nope, they're dead, too," he said so matter-of-factly that Art wondered if the kid was autistic. Art hadn't known many autistic kids during his life — hell, they didn't even have autism, at least not that he'd ever heard of back in his day — but had seen a few on TV. This kid was like those kids, a bit off, maybe void of emotion.

"So, what do you do for fun?"

"Not much these days. I went swimming the other day."

"Oh, how was that?"

"Not too good." Luca looked down at the comforter. "What do *you* do for fun?"

"I'm old; it's a good day when I'm regular."

"Regular what?"

"Never mind, kid." Art laughed. "So, what's the deal with this blue stuff?"

"I can't talk about it."

"Did *she* tell you not to say anything?"

"Yeah."

"Well, I'm considerably older than Ms. Rose, and I say you can tell me. I outrank her, right?"

"Sorry." Luca shook his head.

Art decided to wait. He figured if he allowed some silence to stretch between them, the boy might start talking to ease the discomfort. Unless he *was* autistic, then he might sit like a rock until Rose returned.

After a few minutes of the boy's quiet, Art waved the white flag. "Is it some kind of drug?"

"No, sir."

"Forget this sir, stuff. Call me Art. OK?"

"Yes, s... Art."

"Good, good. So why are you all in a hotel room? Don't you have a home?"

"Not anymore."

"What happened?"

Luca looked down again, his lips pursed.

"Ah, can't talk about that, either, eh?"

Luca nodded.

"Damn, your aunt is one tough broad. I had a wife like that. My first wife, Rina. Tough as nails. She was a great woman, don't get me wrong. But when she set her mind to being a pain in the buttinsky, she was a pain like nobody's business."

Art smiled remembering Rina. Memories flashed before his eyes, things he hadn't thought of in years — the first time they met, one time when they raced home in the rain on a bicycle built for two, then another of them dancing to Benny Goodman at a tiny club in Brooklyn.

He smiled.

"What happened to her?" Luca asked.

"Who? Rina?"

"Yeah."

"Big C. Cancer." He sighed.

"I'm sorry," Luca said. "My brother lost his girlfriend, too."

"You talking about Rose?"

Luca looked like he'd been caught in a fib. Too quickly, he shook his head. "No, another girlfriend. Before Rose."

"Ah." Art nodded, then winked at Luca to let him know he wasn't getting one over on old Art.

Luca looked down again.

If Luca were older, Art would have been more direct, asked the kid why he was lying. But he seemed innocent, and nice enough. And probably *was* autistic. No sense in picking on the boy.

Obviously, there was some weird stuff afoot, why else would this Rose broad come to his nursing home and lure him out with some magical blue liquid? The only thing Art knew for certain is that he *had* to touch it again. He'd know the rest soon enough.

Not only had Art felt more alive in the last hour than he had in the past fifteen years, he was also remembering more than he thought possible. It felt like when you have eye surgery and they remove the gauze from your eyes. You could see more and more with each layer peeled. Art was seeing more of his past playing out in his mind, and the more he saw, the more he wanted to see — the more he wanted to go back in time, and the less he wanted to die.

Of course, with the good came some bad memories that Art had been plenty glad to have forgotten, followed by a fresh coat of memories on the ones he'd wanted to leave behind but never could, like the bodies in Auschwitz, Mauthausen-Gusen, and Warsaw.

But he'd take some of the horrible memories if it meant more Rina.

"Come on, kid, you can tell me what the blue stuff is. Rose is gonna come back soon enough and let me know anyway, right?"

"Yes, but she should be the one to tell you."

"Ah, I get it, she thinks you're too young, right?"

"No. I mean, I don't think so."

"Yeah, that's probably it. She still sees you as her beau's baby brother. She doesn't see the real you, the young man ready to grow up and do his own things in the world. Am I right?"

"It's not like that."

"Then what *is* it like?"

"You wouldn't understand. Nobody would."

"Kid, I've been around the block so many times I wore a path six feet deep. There ain't nothin' you can tell me that I haven't heard, or probably been through myself, a million times or more."

Luca met his eyes and looked like he was ready to spill the beans.

Then the door opened, and Rose entered with two canvas sacks.

"How are you all doing?"

"Great," Art said, winking at Luca.

Luca smiled, "Good. What did you get?"

"I got Oreos and milk for you, buddy. And for Mr. Morgan, I picked up this."

She pulled out a brown-sleeved bag of wine, then removed it and displayed a 2008 Clos Du Val merlot.

Art wasn't a wine aficionado by any means, and hadn't had a drop in at least a decade, but he was fairly certain this was a better-than-decent bottle.

"How'd you know I've been craving wine?"

"I can read your mind, Mr. Morgan."

Art laughed, then stopped when she didn't join him.

"You're pullin' my leg."

"No, sir. And right now you're thinking 'bullshit,' but you don't want to say it because of the kid. You think he reminds you of an old friend back in the day, a boy named Jack Wilson. Am I wrong?"

Art looked back and forth between them. Saw that Luca wasn't laughing either.

"H ... how'd ya do that?"

"Rather than tell you, why don't I show you? But first, your wine."

She popped the bottle and poured some wine into a red plastic cup then passed it across the table. As he reached for the cup, Rose retrieved the vial from her jacket pocket and laid it on the table.

Art felt it calling to him, swore he could hear it, like a barely audible tune. He found himself lost in the blue glow reflected on the table between them.

So soft, so inviting.

I better take a drink.

Art lifted the plastic cup to his lips, took a sip, closing his eyes, remembering many great wines from his past. This one felt all the more delicious for the time that had passed since his last drink.

He kept his eyes closed, savoring the flavor. He loved the raspberry and plum, but his tongue wanted lamb more than it ever had before.

Following his sip, Rose looked down at the vial and picked it up.

Art set down his cup and stared at the vial.

"What is it?"

"The cure."

"For what?"

"For everything." Rose passed the vial.

Art looked down at the vial, warm in his hands. The blue sloshed around even though he was holding it as straight as permitted by his trembling hands. It seemed to respond to Art with movement.

Tiny lights swirled around inside the liquid, moving fast like lightning bugs he once caught in jars as a child.

Art felt the stares from both Luca and Rose.

"What do I do with it?"

"Open the vial," Rose said. "That's all you have to do."

Art put his fingers around the tip of the black stopper and pulled it ever so slightly. The fit was snug enough to keep it from budging.

The liquid began to swirl faster around in the tube, the tiny lights racing as if anticipating his opening the vial. He could swear the vial was vibrating in his hand.

Open us. Open us, Art.

He looked around the room, unsure where the voices had come from, or if they were real. Luca and Rose were quiet, four eyes on him.

He pulled at the stopper again. This time the cap came off with a slight popping sound, not unlike the wine.

The liquid raced faster and began to expand.

Art realized in horror that it was about to boil over the top and possibly onto his hands.

He tried to put the vial down on the table, but didn't want it to spill.

Art cried out, trying to ask for help, but the liquid raced from the vial, up his arm, and into his mouth.

He gagged as the warm liquid shot down his throat, then jumped up from the table and shoved his fingers into his own mouth.

He was overwhelmed, unable to spit or pull the blue stuff out as it seemed to force its way deeper into his mouth.

He fell back in the chair, arms limp, eyes blurring as he saw Luca and Rose stare at him without lifting a finger to help.

They're trying to kill me.

The liquid burned as it rolled down his esophagus and then expanded across his chest.

Art coughed more, but nothing came up. He gasped for air, trying desperately to draw anything other than the blue into his lungs.

He gasped, and then the world went dark.

**

Art woke gasping, this time sucking deep mouthfuls of air into his lungs.

He was no longer in the chair but lying in one of the two beds.

"He's awake." Luca rushed to his side and looked down at him.

Art sat up feeling the oddest sensation. While his lungs still burned, he felt otherwise fine. Better than fine. Energy pulsed through his body. For the first time in decades Art was able to sit up in bed without worrying about pulling something.

He looked around and noticed something else, too.

The world was clearer than it had been in ages.

He reached up for his glasses, but they weren't on his face. He saw them on the table where his wine cup still sat, along with the empty vial.

Art noticed the mirror on the dresser directly across from him. But it wasn't him staring back — well it was him, but younger by at least four decades.

He got up and crossed to the mirror, needing to see closer. He touched his smooth face, no longer cracked with crevices and wrinkles. He couldn't help but smile, breaking into laughter at the wonderfully impossible sight.

"Dear God," he said, "what did you do to me?"

"Welcome to your new life," a voice said.

The voice didn't belong to Rose or Luca. It was like two or three voices, speaking simultaneously, men and women.

But there was no one else in the room.

Are they in my head?

"Yes," the voices said. "We're here, inside you."

* * * *

CHAPTER 7
BORICIO WOLFE

Boricio wasn't sure how long he'd been left alone in the dark like an animal — he'd fallen asleep and had woken a few times since seeing Guard Tard — but it felt like a dozen dick-stained hours without a morsel of food or droplet of water.

Boricio wondered if the people in charge knew where he was, then figured the crooked hogs were running the asylum. He was hungrier than Honey Boo Boo after a half day with nothing from Hostess, and his mouth was dryer than a dead camel's cunt, but it was hard for Boricio to focus on his body's pressing needs when the dull truth kept hitting him like an anvil on the head: *he'd finally been caught.*

Boricio was now tied to the hillbilly murders, the shit that went sideways in the dumpy motel before The Darkness stole his Morning Rose from her body, and the pedophile fuck who had been creeping on Paola.

After more than a decade of killing random innocents who didn't deserve it, Boricio was now getting nicked for murdering the most deserving of fuckers: an irony of bullshit proportions.

You'd think the cops would give me a blue fucking ribbon for doing the shit they don't wanna get caught doing.

Boricio had passed out a few times since Luca had "fixed" him, but hoped his attention to details and steering clear of the law were so ingrained into his rituals that he'd cleaned up after himself before taking an impromptu nap at the most inconvenient of times.

He now sat in BumFuck County Lockup on the hook for who knew how many murders?

How many more will they find?

Boricio had pressed pause on his pursuit of freedom from the straitjacket. His head felt like the Fourth of July from repeatedly bashing it back into the wall behind him, his way of overriding the deep cut of confinement.

He'd never felt further from control.

But fuck if Boricio was about to let anyone see him cry like a bitch.

He stared at the sliver of light bleeding from beneath the door, waiting for a sign that someone might come to smother the darkness and trying to think a way out of his clusterfuck.

A funny thought crossed Boricio's mind: those little bracelets WWJD — What Would Jesus Do?

Boricio cackled, thinking of so many people wearing the bracelets, few acting anything like their Santa in the sky.

He'd never seen anyone run onto a televangelists' stage and expose their hypocrisy. But *that's* what Jesus would've done. He wouldn't be selling overpriced tchotchkes with his name on them.

If Jesus were real, and on Earth today, Boricio was goddamned sure his own believers would nail him to a cross and claim their Lord and Savior was a commie hippie with a vendetta against commerce. And ain't no way on Earth Big

Religion would allow any deity to come before the Almighty Dollar.

Sorry, Hey-Zeus, but we get fuckers doing the shit you would do, and we're plum out of business.

And what would Jesus do if held prisoner after ending a nest of hillbilly knuckle draggers?

There was no FUCKING way Boricio was about to let anyone nail *him* to a cross, strap him to a chair, or set him toe-to-toe with whatever death penalty they handed out in this godforsaken putrid taint of a state.

What would Hey-Zeus Do? No, fuck that, What Would Boricio Do?

Except, for the first time in memory, Boricio didn't know what to do, or what he *could* do. No cavalry was coming to save him. He had no family or people to count on.

Mary and Paola were the closest things he had to friends, but Boricio hadn't heard from them since shit hit the fan at the motel. He'd tried calling Mary and Paola, but their phones only rang. He'd searched the motel, and had even driven to Colorado, but found only nothing.

Boricio assumed that The Darkness got them too. He hoped it killed them quickly rather than claiming their bodies and corrupting their memories.

He tried not to think about them, or Rose. He tried not to tumble down the same abyss of gnarled thoughts that had kept him in search of every next bottle's bottom. Now that Boricio had actual feelings for people, he realized that giving a fuck was one hell of a curse. It was a bowling ball to the baby maker when people you let into your life were suddenly taken away.

Boricio laughed again, staring up into his cell's utter darkness.

God was a cruel fucker if he wasn't a fairy tale, to make people care so much about those he'd pluck from the planet one by one.

This wasn't how things were supposed to be.

Boricio did what he wanted, when he wanted. He killed fuckers in need of a killing and stuffed his stainmaker wherever he wanted — goddamn any asshole who stood in his way.

But as Boricio sat in the darkness, he wondered if this *was* his perfect justice.

He was being made to pay for all the lives he'd destroyed. Not just his victims, but their families. Had Boricio been caught before now, before he'd been "fixed," it wouldn't have mattered. He would've thrived in jail until they put him down.

It would've sucked, but Boricio wouldn't have really felt much of anything at all. He certainly wouldn't be thinking about his friends and the only woman he ever loved being taken from him. Sociopaths can't care. A fixed Boricio could. Worse, he could regret.

And nothing hurt worse than regret.

This was a perfect, almost cosmically planned justice. Make him care, then lock him up tight.

"Fuck you, God," he growled into the void.

**

Boricio woke to the sound of an opening door.

Light flooded his cell, and a blurred shape formed before him.

Is it Guard Tard, or has someone else finally realized I'm in here?

It *was* someone else.

It was the black guard, the one who'd reamed Guard Tard.

Boricio was so happy he wanted to cry.

He tried to remember the man's name, but couldn't. He saw the brass pin on the man's front left pocket.

BOYLE

"Well, hello, Boricio."

How the hell does he know my name?

Boricio's mind reeled as he tried to imagine the circumstances that led to his name's revelation. He hadn't used his real name in forever. Only Rose, Mary, and Paola knew him as Boricio. Anyone else would only know one of his many pseudonyms.

If they know everything, then this is the last yellow brick in the road.

Boyle spoke again.

"I bet you'd like to get out of here, eh? Looks like they're treating you like shit."

The man's eyes went down to the piss and crap carpeting the ground. Boricio wanted to stand and smack the fucker.

How dare you judge me, you cunt!

Boricio said nothing, waiting to discover why the man had come to see him.

"I can get you out of here." He leaned closer, his brown eyes meeting Boricio's.

There was something oddly familiar about his eyes, though Boricio's hammering head wasn't about to tell him what in the hell it might be.

The man spoke again, but this time in a voice that belonged to a woman: *Rose.*

"I can get you out of here, love."

A sledgehammer slammed into Boricio. His heart started beating hard enough to burst from his chest.

"What the fuck?"

"I'm projecting into this shell. I don't have long before he starts to resist and I lose my connection."

Projecting? Into a shell? Fucking alien talk!

"You're not Rose."

"She's still here, Boricio. With us. And you can be with us, be with *her* again. You can be free."

Boricio laughed. "Free? Have Alf controlling my brain? I'd rather rot in here."

"Suit yourself," Rose's voice said as the guard stood and turned around.

"Wait!" Boricio said, surprising himself.

The guard turned back to Boricio. "Yes?"

"What are you doing with her?"

"We're doing something fantastic, Boricio. Something I think you'd approve of." The voice fell to a whisper. "We're evolving humanity."

"Yeah, I saw your 'evolution' on the other planet."

"This is not like that. The Darkness was selfish and messy. In trying to claim the world, we destroyed humanity. Everything devolved into chaos. This time, we're doing things the right way. We will become one with humans, rather than destroying them. We will evolve both species into something *better* than the sum of our parts. Admit it, Boricio, you've felt like a better person since Luca fixed you, right?"

"For all the good that's done. Look where I am now."

"A minor inconvenience if you allow us to help you now."

"I don't want no fucking aliens in my head!"

"You act like we're not in there already."

Boricio stared at the guard or whatever it was, hating it for using his Rose's voice. "The fuck you talkin 'bout, Willis?"

"Luca was the first to be 'infected' by our species, as you all seem to see it. Yet he's not some monster, is he? He saved you. And a part of him is still inside you. A part of *us*."

"Bullshit! And besides, the Boy Wonder is dead now."

"Not the other version of him. He's with us, helping to make this dream a reality. We're not your enemy, Boricio. These, these people in this prison that are treating you like a dog, and all the old thinking humans, *they* are your enemies.

We can make this all go away. You can join us and be truly free for the first time in your life."

Tears welled in Boricio's eyes as he imagined a reunion with Rose. Hearing her voice, even if bastardized from some guard pig's mouth, felt like an invitation to go back in time and spend a few months back when everything was perfect.

God, he wanted to be with her again.

But as Boricio stared at the guard, he couldn't shake the reality. Rose wasn't *Rose*. By any other name she was an alien's marionette.

He remembered staring into her eyes after The Darkness took over. How she had begged him to run.

Boricio couldn't forget the look.

That Rose wouldn't want him to say yes to the guard.

That Rose would tell him to keep running.

"Well?" the guard said. "Do you want to be free?"

"Fuck you, Alf!" Tears streamed down Boricio's face. How dare they use Rose to try and lure him?

"Sorry, you feel that way, love," Rose's voice said.

The guard stood, turned around, and left Boricio alone. Again.

Boricio wailed into the darkness.

* * * *

CHAPTER 8
MARY OLSON

As morning sun creeped through the blinds, Mary rolled over in bed to avoid the light, and bumped into Desmond.

She opened her eyes to find him watching her.

"Stop." Mary covered her mouth, not wanting to blast him with morning breath.

"Stop what?" Desmond smiled in the morning's dim light.

"Stop watching me sleep. It's weird."

"Hey, I didn't think I'd ever see you again. Every new morning beside you is a miracle."

"Oh, please. Do you want to write my greeting cards now?"

"I'm serious."

Mary blushed.

While her ex, Ryan, hadn't been a jerk, she wasn't used to such a saccharine-sweet guy who said the sorts of things no real guy ever said. Ryan had been a gentleman, sure. He held doors open, bought gifts — when he remembered —

and was always respectful. But he was never the kind of guy who flowered Mary with compliments, or flowers.

And yet, *he was* that way with Paola.

Guys were rarely willing to reveal raw emotion to their partners. And yet, they had few qualms saying sweet, silly things to their children.

Perhaps it was a defense mechanism meant to keep them from being hurt by a woman. Mary imagined that guys probably had to grow thick skins, dealing with denial as often as they did. Maybe all that rejection tempered their romantic sides.

Desmond was sweet during their short-lived romance following the events of October 15, 2011. Even so, he had still seemed to bury most of his feelings.

But this Desmond wore his unapologetic heart on his sleeve and didn't care if Mary laughed. It was as if he'd watched the world's chickiest flicks, made it a point to find out what women wanted to hear most, and was going all out with Mary.

She thought of something he'd said the other day, how she "completed him." Like in stupid *Jerry McGuire*. Mary had laughed when he said it, thinking he was just messing with her. But then he asked her what she was laughing about, and insisted that he'd never seen the movie.

She couldn't believe it then, and still couldn't believe he'd never heard the expression now. His utter earnestness only made Mary think he was cornier.

She giggled, remembering his total lack of a clue.

"What?"

"Nothing," she said. "Just not used to people saying such sweet things to me."

"Well, you should be."

The old Mary might've barfed, then smacked the guy who said it and ordered him to stop screwing with her.

But Desmond, she could tell, meant it.

"Ever since Luca brought me back to life, I've decided that I'm not going to let my thoughts die on the vine. If I feel something, I'm going to tell you. I don't want to leave this world with things left unsaid, or regretting what I wasn't brave enough to do."

"That's sweet." Mary traced her fingers along Desmond's strong arms.

He touched her lips with his fingers then ran his thumb down over her chin, staring into her eyes. "Would you rather I keep these things to myself?"

"No."

"Good, because I don't think I could if I wanted." He paused, then, "There's something else I've been wanting to talk about, but I'm not sure how to broach the subject."

Mary knew what he wanted to say before he brought his warm palm to her nervous stomach. "You said you lost our baby, and that the doctors thought it was stress. Of course they couldn't have had any idea what sort of stress you'd really been under."

Mary said nothing, putting her hand on top of Desmond's. She hated talking about their never-born child. Just like she hated contemplating something bad happening to Paola — *again*.

"It's not your fault."

Mary felt a surge of emotion, and was unable to stop the words before they left her mouth.

"I *know* it wasn't my fault, Desmond. I'm not an idiot."

It came off worse than Mary had meant it, but at the same time, she didn't want to take her words back. She wasn't even sure why she was angry at Desmond for wanting to discuss *their* child, but couldn't deny her brewing rage.

She tried to pull her hand away from his, but he grabbed it. "I never said you were an idiot, Mary. And no, you shouldn't feel guilty. But I know a part of you does. That part of you that wants to be Super Mom and protect her family with a lioness's ferocity. And you are that mom, Mary. You are the strongest woman I've ever met. But I know you hate what happened, and feel responsible."

"*You're* going to tell me what *I* feel?" she asked, even though Desmond was entirely right.

Tears began to roll down her cheeks, which only made her angrier.

Mary got out of bed, walked to the adjoining bathroom, and closed the door behind her. If it had had a lock, she would've used it.

She sat on the toilet, peed, then kept sitting, crying and feeling stupid.

After several minutes of weeping and blowing her stupid nose, the door pushed open and Desmond appeared with his understanding expression to infuriate her further.

"We don't have to talk about it if you don't want to," he said. "But you need to forgive yourself."

Mary stared at the tile floor.

Desmond turned to leave.

"You're right."

Mary didn't look to see if he'd turned back around. She could sense him there, waiting for her to continue.

"I did ... I do blame myself. I know it's stupid, and that I *shouldn't*. But who else am I going to blame? Aliens? God? It's not like either gives a shit what I think. And neither can bring our baby back."

"So with no one else to blame, you blamed yourself. It was something you could at least allow yourself to feel. Right?"

Mary nodded. She said, "Jesus, you really need to stop watching so much Dr. Phil," then broke into a much-needed laugh.

Desmond came to Mary, hugging her as she sat on the toilet.

She stood up and followed him back to bed.

"Can we just lie here? It's not that I don't want to talk about it anymore, but I just can't. Not right now."

"Anything you want."

She turned away, allowing him to spoon her and melting into his body and warmth.

Mary had never felt like someone who needed a man to complete her. She did better without Ryan than with him, and had learned plenty in the months since their return from the other world. She had learned how to fight, how to survive, and most importantly, how to protect her daughter. But there was comfort in a strong man beside you, and grace in having someone know you well enough to lie in silence with your truest self.

**

They woke to the sound of Paola at the bedroom door. "You two alive?"

"Yeah!" Mary laughed, looking at the clock: 12:13.

"Oh wow," she whispered to Desmond, then turned back to the closed door. "We'll be out soon. Just had a late night."

"Okaaaay then," Paola said, retreating from the door, probably grossed out at the thought of her mom having sex.

Desmond slipped his hand between Mary's legs and gave her a wicked smile.

She whispered, "No, she's right out there in the living room," and slapped his hand away.

"Oh, come on, she already thinks we're doing something in here."

His hand slid up to her breasts as he leaned in and kissed her neck.

Six minutes later Mary was biting her lip to keep the low moans from rolling out too loudly while Desmond muffled his grunts. Staring into her eyes he panted, "Should I pull out?"

"No," Mary whimpered, pushing her head up from the bed to meet Desmond's lips.

They kissed as he filled her.

* * * *

CHAPTER 9
MARINA HARMON

As Acevedo drove them to Salty's Pool Hall to find the man known as Beef who may or may not still have the vial, Marina found herself staring out the window, trying not to speak her mind.

Better to keep quiet, not let Acevedo know she was becoming increasingly disillusioned with him. Marina thought of the man in the dark's warning, to not trust the priest. It wasn't as if she could invest her belief in a shadow-shrouded man whom she couldn't see, particularly when the threat against them called itself The Darkness.

Yet Marina couldn't get over the truth that Acevedo had shot two men in cold blood.

"Something on your mind?"

Don't say anything. Just tell him you don't feel well.

Marina ignored her inner counsel.

"Why did you kill them?"

"Because they were a threat."

"No, they weren't. Was the guy in cuffs a threat?"

"They both were." Acevedo turned to meet Marina's eyes.

His pupils burned at insanity's edge, yet the rest of him seemed perfectly in control, his voice as calm as his gestures.

"How?"

Acevedo returned his eyes to the road. "Because we need to find the vials. We couldn't risk Andrew warning Beef we were coming."

"He said he hadn't seen him. And you could tell by the way he looked at our vials that he was telling the truth."

"Doesn't matter. We can't take any chances. Retrieving the vials is the only thing that matters right now. Do you understand me?"

"So, what? We're going to go around killing anyone in our way?"

"If need be."

"No, no, no." Marina stared at the priest. "I will not be a party to you murdering innocent people. I won't help you. I didn't sign up for this."

"Neither did I, sister. You think *I wanted* this? Do you think *I wanted* these damned things in my life? I was happy before your father came into my life. I was doing God's work, and making a difference to my congregation. But then he brought this hell into my life and destroyed everything."

"What do you mean?"

Acevedo stared through the windshield, his calm facade finally cracking. Shaking his head, he said, "Forget it."

"No, I want to know."

He turned to her, eyes welling up, jaw clenched, "Well, I don't feel like sharing. Let's just say your father damned us both. And now we're the only ones standing between these aliens and the end of all that we know. So pardon me if I don't get worked up over the loss of some spoiled rich asshole and his bodyguard. It's a small price to keep the world breathing."

Marina stared out the window, lost for words.

This *is a man of God?*

They arrived at Salty's just before dinnertime, and parked outside.

"So, what are we going to do? Go in and ask for Beef?" Marina's first words in a while felt odd on her tongue.

She tried not to laugh at the absurdity her life had become in the last three weeks. She was about to enter some seedy pool hall with a killer priest in search of a "chemist" named Beef so they could find a vial of alien life.

Her personal world had become a surreal parody of what people already believed about her church.

"Pretty much," Acevedo said as he killed the engine and loaded his gun.

"Aren't you worried about police or anything? They're going to trace those bodies to you, right? Hell, there could've been hidden cameras, filming the whole thing!"

This fresh fear terrified Marina; she would be on camera as an accomplice to two executions.

"Oh, my God, they'll see me on the video!"

"Maybe, but I'm sure your fancy lawyer guy can get you out of trouble. He could say I kidnapped you or something. But if we don't tend to these vials, cops will be the least of our worries. Understand?"

She nodded.

"Good, let's go." Acevedo got out of the car.

Marina followed.

Salty's Pool Hall was the sort of place where hope went to die. Its best days looked they had been back before the bar had last changed its decor, or its jukebox selection, judging by the hair metal assault on their ears.

Despite the early hour, people packed the pool hall and filled it with the scent of desperation: people looking to forget, score drugs, or get laid, or perhaps all three.

Acevedo led Marina to the bar. The bartender, a stout guy in his thirties with a friendly, chubby face said, "Hey, what can I get for ya?"

Acevedo slipped a fifty dollar bill onto the bar and slid it toward the bartender.

"Looking for a guy named Beef."

The bartender looked down at the cash, then back at Acevedo and Marina, as if trying to figure out if they were police.

The bartender shook his head. "Don't know anyone by that name."

"Listen," Acevedo smiled, "we both know that you know who I'm talking about. I just need a word with him. Nothing that'll get you in trouble."

The bartender returned his eyes to the money, then shook his head again.

Acevedo reached into his wallet, peeled off another fifty from a thick stack of bills, and laid it on the counter.

"Who's asking?"

"My name is John White, private investigator. Seems Beef has come into some money from a dead relative. I've been asked to find him."

The bartender looked down at the money again, clearly tempted. But then shook his head. "Sorry, can't help you."

Acevedo kept his eyes on the bartender for another long moment, then gave him what looked like an unfortunate nod. He took his money, then approached the jukebox, yanked the cord from the wall, and murdered the music.

The entire room turned toward Acevedo, angry brows and white knuckles wrapped around pool sticks.

"Good, now that I have your attention. My name is John White, and I'm a private detective hired to find someone you all know as Beef. Seems our friend has come into some money from a dead relative. I'd like to find him so I can collect my cut. Whoever helps me first will get a share of my spoils. I'll give you two grand right now, hard cash."

Marina stared at the people in the bar, watching as they considered Acevedo's offer. Hushed whispers rolled through the room. She couldn't believe that he'd turned a hostile crowd receptive, and wondered if anyone would step forward.

Marina supposed it depended on whether Beef was a low-level dealer or someone with power. If he were powerful, she didn't think two thousand dollars would be enough to buy a rat, unless he was a competitor.

"Anyone?" Acevedo asked.

Marina's heart pounded as she waited for someone to step forward, but the crowd remained silent.

Acevedo sighed. "Anyone?" he repeated to the still-silent bar.

Still no response.

Acevedo returned the money to his wallet and headed out of the bar. "All right, your loss."

Marina quickly followed.

Outside in the sunshine, she said, "Wow, you're terrible at this, huh?"

He winked at her, a sly smile creasing the priest's lips.

"What are you up to?"

"Notice anything while we were inside?"

"Like what?"

"The windows are all painted red on the inside, so you can't see the parking lot."

"OK, and your point?"

"Just wait."

Acevedo walked to his car, leaned against the driver's side, pulled a yoyo from his jeans pocket, and started walking the dog.

"A yo-yo?" Marina could barely hide her smile.

"I stopped smoking twenty years ago and needed something to do with my hands."

She burst out laughing, unable to hold it in.

"What?"

"Sorry," she said, "it's just one minute you're doom, gloom, and murder. Now you're playing with a child's toy."

"I'll have you know that yo-yos aren't *just* for children." Acevedo allowed himself to smile.

"Yeah? I suppose you're going to tell me you can do more than walk the dog?"

"As a matter of fact, I can. Want to see?"

She shook her head. "No, that's OK. I'm not seven."

"Hey, it's better than smoking. I'm sure you must have a vice or two. Lemme guess ..." Acevedo looked her up and down. "You don't strike me as someone into marijuana. A bit too high strung."

"*Me* high strung?" Marina laughed. "Oh my God! A few weeks ago, you had your lips sewn shut! And you're calling *me* high strung?"

Acevedo shook his head. "That had nothing to do with my being high strung."

"Then what was it?"

Before Acevedo could answer his eyes grabbed something behind Marina.

She turned and saw a tall and skinny man the shade of flour with a giant head of dark, curly hair leave the bar. He was wearing jeans and a black tee with a skull smoking a blunt on the front, clearly nervous as he headed toward a beat-up green pickup truck. He nodded at them and got inside.

Acevedo said, "He wants us to follow him."

"How do you know that?" Marina asked as they got into the Mustang.

"Because the windows are blacked out. I figured someone would come for the payday if we waited, but they didn't want anyone seeing them."

The Mustang chased the truck from the lot.

Marina tapped her foot on the carpet, trying not to feel as high strung as she was.

A block away, the truck pulled into a gas station and up to a pump. The guy got out and started filling his pickup with gas.

Acevedo pulled up to the opposite pump, then got out and mirrored the lanky man from the other side.

Marina stayed in the car, though Acevedo had rolled his window down so she could hear the two of them talk.

"You wanna know where Beef is?" the guy asked.

"Yes," Acevedo said.

"Who you is?"

"I said, I'm a private investigator, and ... "

"Bullshit, you ain't no P.I. Now tell me who the fuck you is."

Marina couldn't see the man's face, but his voice sounded vaguely threatening.

"I'm a priest," Acevedo said.

The guy started laughing. "No, for reals."

"For *reals*," Acevedo said.

"What you want with Beef?"

"He has something of mine. I'd like it back."

"Like what? Some religious artifact or somethin' ?"

"Something like that," Acevedo said. "So, do you want the money or not?"

"Hell yeah. I just wanna make sure you keep me out of shit."

"I don't even know your name," Acevedo said. "But I will need you to take me to his place. You drive, and I'll follow."

"I dunno, man, he might have people watchin' and shit."

"Well, I'm not trading two thousand dollars for your word."

"Fair enough," the man said. "I'll lead you to his block."

"OK," Acevedo said. "You'll get half now and the other half when I come back."

"I dunno, man. He might not let you leave."

"Then my associate here will give make sure you get your money."

The guy looked down in the window and waved at Marina. He looked mid-thirties, and clueless, though not enough to ignore a probable payday.

They filled their tanks, and Acevedo passed the guy a handful of cash. "Now take me to Beef."

* * * *

CHAPTER 10
EDWARD KEENAN

Ed watched as the red Mustang pulled up beside the green pickup, parked on a quiet cul de sac of middle-class homes built in the eighties.

Luther had parked the van about ninety yards behind them, in the swale of a house with a foreclosure sign in the front yard.

Ed pulled out the long-range microphone and aimed it at the pair of vehicles.

"OK, Beef is in the beige house, right?" the priest said.

"Yep, that's where he's stayin'."

"Thanks. You'll get the rest of the money when I come out."

"No, man, I get the rest of the money now, or I'll blow the horn and get everyone's attention."

"That wasn't the deal," the priest said.

"Fuck the deal. It's a new deal now. I ain't waitin' to see if you come outta there alive."

"Fine," the priest said. "But if he's not in there, I'm going to hunt you down."

Acevedo handed cash to the man in the green truck, then the man left, leaving the priest and Marina alone in the car.

"So," Marina said, "what now?"

"You wait here. I'm going in. If I'm not out in ten minutes, you take the vials and go to the most remote place you can find."

"Then what?"

The priest was quiet for a long moment.

Ed wondered if he'd missed his response.

"Pray," he finally said, then got out of the Mustang and headed toward the house at the end of the block.

"Ten minutes," Luther said. "Now's our chance to get the vials."

Ed nodded. "OK, let's do this real quiet, eh? I'm going to approach the car. You get the van ready to stop her if she makes a run for it. Hopefully, it won't come to that. Last thing we want to do is alert the block."

"And what do we do about this Beef guy and the priest?"

"Once we secure the vials, I'll wait in the car with her. The tint on those windows is pretty damn dark, so he shouldn't expect me. But I want you to train the rifle on him just in case he makes us. Take him out if he tries to run."

"Affirmative," Luther said.

Ed popped out of the vehicle, Glock behind his back, and strolled up the sidewalk toward the Mustang.

He'd been following these two for long enough. They'd nearly gotten themselves killed back at the rich kid's house. Ed had called Black Island to run interference with the local police, calling in favors to squash the investigation before it could start.

Right now nothing in the world was more important than securing the vials.

* * * *

CHAPTER 11
THOMAS ACEVEDO

Acevedo approached the house, turning back to make certain Marina was still waiting. He hoped she'd listen to his advice and take off if things went south, but the car was still there.

It was odd how little terror the moment had left him.

Acevedo had locked himself in the monastery for the last two years, living in fear of what was coming, and what the vials might make him do.

Something clicked inside him when Marina appeared. At first, he was frightened, dreading that the day had finally come. But then, just like that, the fear disappeared. Perhaps it was because he knew that action was his only option. Doing nothing would mean the end of everything. It was easier to be brave with nothing to lose.

That's what Acevedo kept telling himself, standing on Beef's porch, his heart a piston as he waited for someone to open the door.

He had the gun in his right hand, but it wasn't his only weapon. He'd taken one of the vials back when Marina was distracted. *Just in case.*

The alien form in the vial began whispering in his head as it had before he'd locked it under his home's floor two years ago.

"Open me. You won't survive unless you open and drink me."

Acevedo ignored the whispers. He couldn't lose himself to desire. Not now.

"Well then why did you bring me? If you're not going to use me?"

I don't know.

"Yes, you do."

Get out of my head!

More than the temptation, Acevedo hated the alien peeking inside him, peering into his thoughts enough to pull his strings. It had to be worse than drug addiction. His brother, Samuel, died of a heroin overdose in 1979. During one of their many fights over his use, Samuel begged Tommy not to judge him as a sinner, but to try and understand how addiction worked. Heroin wasn't evil. Right and wrong meant nothing when something was *always* in your head, ever present to claim your attention.

"No, Sammy, you're just making a weak man's excuses. You choose to live this lifestyle, to consume these evil drugs. I don't want to hear your damned excuses anymore. I can't stand them. Get clean and stay clean or steer clear of our family."

Those had been Acevedo's final words to his brother. The next morning, he got a call from a cop friend. Sammy's body had been found in an alley, dead of an overdose, heroin kit beside him.

Acevedo had never understood his brother's temptation until the alien seeped inside his thoughts.

Considering what the alien had already made him do, Acevedo had no right to judge anyone, ever again. That's why he'd buried the damned thing.

The front door opened and yanked the priest from his thoughts. He saw a dark apartment with black sheets draping the windows to banish the sun. A large, muscular-looking Hispanic man appeared behind the door. An intimidating scar scraped his left cheek above a mile-long black beard. His large hand rested on a gun holstered in his belt.

"Who are you?" he asked in a thick accent.

Acevedo was quick, his gun in the man's face before he had a chance to draw his weapon.

"Where's Beef?"

"It's OK," a man said behind him, stepping into the doorway's light and wearing a smile. "I've been expecting him."

The man was fat, at least 350 pounds, pale as a ghost, with shaggy, dark-red hair draping his eyes. He was wearing a giant black tee and matching track pants. This had to be Beef.

"You Beef?" Acevedo asked.

"Well, my given name was Eugene, but that doesn't exactly command fear or respect from customers or coworkers, ya know what I'm sayin'? And you are ... the priest?"

Acevedo wanted to ask how he knew his identity, or that he had been on his way, but then felt the answer as a splinter in his mind.

Because the vials told him.

"Then you know why I'm here?" Acevedo stood in the doorway, his gun still trained on the first man.

"Yes, please come inside, I'll show you where the vial is."

"First, he gives me his gun."

The large man surrendered his gun without so much as a grunt, to Acevedo's surprise.

"Here, Padre," the man said, staring into Acevedo's eyes.

This was almost too easy.

"Anyone else in here?" Acevedo asked.

"No, *Father*, just us two." Beef waved Acevedo inside. "Hey, Hector, take a seat on the couch, this won't be long."

Hector did as instructed, again without a whiff of complaint. Acevedo had never seen a tough guy so willingly agree to surrender control to a stranger, gun in his face or not. There was something else happening here, but Acevedo had yet to figure it out.

The alien in his vial was also strangely quiet.

Acevedo followed Beef through the dark house, noticing its immaculate condition. He wondered why they were here. Were they hiding out from the rich kid, or was there something else going on?

Beef led him into a bedroom in the home's rear.

The bedroom was lit in a soft red glow, and sex music played on a stereo. The California King was lumpy. Something lay beneath the thick, white down comforter, writhing as if anticipating the big man's return.

Acevedo felt an uncomfortable chill and wanted to get the hell out of the house before things got any weirder.

"Just one sec, lemme see where I left it." Beef leaned over, shuffling through the nightstand.

Acevedo watched the bed, trying to figure out how many women were under the comforter. It seemed like two, at least. He wondered how many drugs Beef needed to get them in bed. Or did guys like Beef, who presumably had money, drugs, and some amount of power, make getting women — even multiple women — easy?

"Hmm, doesn't seem to be here," Beef said, his back still to Acevedo, looking down into the open nightstand drawer.

The comforter started to rise as someone beneath it sat up.

Acevedo thought to warn whoever was under the sheets, but modesty probably wasn't an issue in Beef's den of depravity.

The comforter fell away revealing two gorgeous women, both nude with long dark hair falling in peek-a-boo strands over perfectly shaped breasts. Acevedo found himself unable to turn or look away.

They turned slowly and looked up at him, staring at him, or rather *through* him, with vacant stares.

"Do you like?" Beef asked, still facing away from Acevedo.

The priest turned to Beef to make sure the man wasn't getting a gun.

In the second it took to turn, the woman threw themselves at Acevedo, all limbs and fingers, dragging him back into bed with the force of a horde.

Someone yanked the gun from Acevedo's hand as the nude women straddled him, holding his arms to the bed.

Acevedo tried to pull away, but they were far stronger than they appeared.

Beef finally turned around, and his smile widened, eyes now all black.

"Oh yeah, I know why I can't find the vial. Because I drank it. Right, girls?"

The women on top of Acevedo answered as one.

"Yes, master."

* * * *

::EPISODE 28::
(FOURTH EPISODE OF SEASON FIVE)
"GONE BABY GONE"

CHAPTER 1
MARINA HARMON

One moment Marina was sitting in the Mustang's driver's seat, watching the house. The next she was staring at the business end of a pistol and the harsh-looking buzz cut behind it.

"Do as I say, and you won't get hurt, Marina Harmon." The man made his way into the car's back seat from the passenger side door.

Marina froze as he entered the car's rear and put the gun to her head. He was fit, looked to be in his early forties, wearing a black jacket over a black shirt, and looked vaguely military.

"Do you have a gun?"

"No." The taste of metal tipped her tongue, and adrenaline surged through her body.

Who is he? What does he want? How does he know my name?

And then it hit her.

Police!

He found the bodies!

Shit.

Marina kept her mouth shut, intent to keep herself from revealing anything the man didn't already know.

"Who are you?"

"My name is Agent Ed Keenan. I'm with Black Island Guard."

"What?"

"We're a division of Homeland Security. I'm here to make sure you don't open those vials."

The vials!

"What vials?"

"I want you to listen very carefully, OK?"

"OK."

"Right now there are four snipers with infrared scopes trained on you. Fail to listen, and they will shoot you in the back of your head. You'll be dead before you know what happened. If you attempt to warn the priest, you'll get a bullet in the back of your skull. If you fail to hand the vials over to me, they will *also* put a bullet in your skull. Nod if you understand."

The man pressed his pistol hard into her head.

Marina swallowed, nodded slowly, and tried to keep herself from breaking down into a blubbering mess of tears.

"Good," he said. "Now hand me the case."

"What are you going to do with them?"

"No talk. Do as I say, or I will shoot you now and take them myself."

"It's on the floor at my feet. I need to bend over."

"Go ahead." He slipped the gun from Marina's head to her spine, pressing again to remind her it was there.

Marina's fingers found the vials, and as she touched the box voices entered her head — intertwined like two people, a man and a woman, talking at once.

No, don't give him the vials. He works for the enemy.

Marina ignored the voices. She had no choice: it wasn't like she could defend a gun to her back, even if armed and able to fight.

"Come on," he said, "hand 'em over."

Marina did as instructed.

He withdrew the slip of paper that had been inside with the vials.

"What's this?"

"I don't know," she said.

He pressed the gun hard into her head again. "No lies, Marina. Again — what is this?"

"The names of the people with the other three vials."

"Three?" Ed asked. "Where's the other one?"

"What are you talking about?"

"There's two in here. I thought you all had three."

"There should be three in there." Marina turned around to look into the case.

The agent kept his gun on her, pulling it back slightly as she moved.

"There are two," he said.

"Shit, he must've taken one into there."

"Why would he do that?"

"I don't know." Marina shook her head. "He went in to get a vial from some guy called Beef. I don't know why he'd bring one into there unless ... *oh no.*"

"Unless what?"

"Unless he plans to use it."

* * * *

CHAPTER 2
ROSE MCCALLISTER

It lay still in Rose's shell on the bed after reaching out to Boricio, who'd been stubborn enough to reject *Its* invitation.

It would try again before moving on and finding another person to join their cause.

It wanted Boricio, but hadn't decided if *It* would infect him and use his shell, or offer one of the vials and invite the man to truly evolve. Boricio was one of the most merciless killers *It* had ever seen. *It*, along with many others, had tried to destroy him, yet the human kept surviving. To have Boricio as part of the collective might be dangerous to *Its* stability. *It* was losing the army of hundreds it had gathered since its bit-by-bit arrival. Humans had proved too difficult to tame through long periods of time.

They were easy to infect and control when weak. But over time, a small something inside them always seemed eager to fight back for control. But how could they fight what they could not understand? So they inevitably snapped into a murderous rampage or ended their misery with a bullet to the brain.

It needed to create a strong group of soldiers prior to *Its* evolution, and control, of the species. Luca was *Its* first. There was something about Boricio — or the Boricio of this world — which The Light had chosen to help.

The Darkness had tried to pluck his doppelgänger from the other world as a counter, but that had failed miserably when Rose, prior to *Its* infecting her, killed Boricio Bishop. *It* had considered leaving Rose's shell and entering Boricio Wolfe's body, but *It* wasn't sure *It* was up to the task.

First, this Boricio's psyche was much stronger than Boricio Bishop's. Second, The Light was stronger in Boricio Wolfe than in Bishop. If *It* entered Boricio's body and failed to take over, that could be the end of all of *Its* plans.

For now, *It* would continue to focus on getting Luca ready to truly evolve into the perfect hybrid of human and alien.

Luca was developing his powers nicely, though he was still a bit too sentimental when it came to humans. *It* would have to break that in the boy, lest his mind weaken to nothing. The collective could have no anemic links.

Now they had a military strategist in the form of the writer, Art. The man was so grateful for his youth, he would do anything to maintain it. His knowledge of human warfare was an invaluable asset in conquering the species.

They still had four more vials, which meant another four people to strengthen their fold.

It closed its eyes and reached out into The Darkness's collective consciousness, filtering the experiences of those It possessed, searching for the right pieces: casting a net then tuning into the thoughts and memories of *Its* many hosts.

It could tap into any of them individually, or the lot all at once, ingesting experience like breath into *Its* body. Sometimes, the process was easier than others. In recent weeks *It* had managed to swell *Its* numbers to nearly a thousand.

But tonight *It* could sense only 658.

It was frustrated to find so many dead connections.

Surely they hadn't all been severed, or *Its* hosts broken.

It would've sensed such a decline in *Its* collective strength. *It* would have picked up on the pain of so many people snapping.

It had felt only a few such cases in recent weeks. And usually *It* could feel the intensity of those who had snapped prior to their break. *It* had even managed to draw a few back from their madness, though by then it was usually too late to get complete control, so *It* usually ordered those to kill themselves before taking out others and drawing unwanted attention.

If they're not dead, then what's happening?

When it came to The Darkness, people were either infected or not. There was no in-between. Those who killed the connection had died following their psychotic breakdowns. There was no cure for infection. No human had yet to return, save for the girl, Paola.

And she was only spared because of the other Luca.

Yet *It* could feel parts of *Itself* out there in the world, unplugged from the collective, somehow there, but not connecting. Were they broken, or somehow refusing connection?

What's happening?

The only thing that made sense was *It* losing control, along with *Its* collective strength. *It* had to accelerate plans.

Suddenly *It* felt something probing back.

It allowed the connection, and was surprised by the source — The Light.

"So, there you are," *It* said to *Its* counter. "I've been wondering where you are. It's been a while."

It tried to lure The Light deeper into *Its* mind, but The Light was too bright, too strong, too wise to fall for such an obvious trick.

The Light was surprisingly strong for a disembodied entity. The boy, Luca, had died on the other world, leaving The Light and the boy fused in some sort of incipient state. But without a host, The Light had been weakened.

And then, as bits of residual memories flowed through the connection, *It* realized the error of *Its* presumptions. The Light was no longer disembodied. It had found a new host, after all — the girl, Paola.

"Where are you?" *It* asked.

The Light had tried not to tell *It*, but was unable to mask Paola's thoughts quickly enough.

Black Island.

It now knew *Its* enemy's location.

Even better, the island harbored four infected humans, that neither she nor the humans knew of.

It smiled in the darkness.

Perhaps the war would end sooner than planned.

* * * *

CHAPTER 3
MARY OLSON

Mary had never had a job with a company picnic, but had been to enough of Ryan's to loathe them. She hated sitting with coworkers and their families, pretending to ignore the obvious politicking as employees jockeyed for raises, promotions, and ideal schedules that didn't exist.

She remembered sitting with Ryan as he detailed the nasty things that someone had done behind his back. Then the very asshole he was telling her about would greet them, and Ryan would offer an enthusiastic hello with a wide, phony smile. Mary was always forced to do the same.

She hated when Ryan put her in that position.

"You can't tell me what monsters these people are right before I meet them, then expect me to be all nice. Now I come off like some cold bitch," she'd said several times in many different ways. It was one thing for him, as he could mask his dislike for the people. But Mary had never done well at hiding her feelings.

Ryan would always apologize, but too late, with the damage already done.

Mary found it sadly fitting in a full-circle sort of way. Here she was again, this time on Black Island with people she didn't know in what felt like the world's most uncomfortable company picnic.

A shame, because the park, on the southwestern tip overlooking the mainland, was gorgeous.

They were at one of two dozen picnic tables under a wooden pavilion, where the men all crowded in front of a row of grills to show off their skills.

Most of the hundred or so attendees of the island "eat n' greet" for nonessential personnel and their families were at the other tables. Mary and her flock sat by themselves like the black sheep she felt like they were.

Desmond was working on some urgent business or another. Mary sat with Paola by her side, and what she'd come to regard as her new family: Brent, Ben, Jade, Teagan, and Becca.

She tried to focus on Paola and her table, but couldn't ignore stares that screamed, *You don't belong here.*

Mary was used to living in places she didn't *belong.* She had lived among blue bloods behind a gate in Warson Woods, a single mom making her living as an artist — a dubious job judging from regular neighborhood stares. Yet Mary had managed to make a few friends and find her tribe, including Desmond.

She'd do the same here in time, she hoped, though making friends on Black Island seemed an even taller task than it had in Warson Woods. She wasn't sure if the island wives' looks were because they were civilians and civilians were never welcome, or if people hated them for another reason.

Mary was reasonably certain that the island's inhabitants, save for a few, were jealous of the speed in which Desmond claimed his position of power. He was officially an advisor at the facility, but it was clear that Director Bolton, the man in charge, greatly respected his advice.

Desmond came from the other world and convinced them of the alien threat, and the importance of finding the vials. He persuaded them to let Ed Keenan help, even though the man was considered a traitor before they'd discovered Sullivan's infection. Desmond had brought Paola, a child, to help them find the vials.

Their search had yet to bear fruit. Mary could feel a certain contingent hoping it wouldn't, praying for their failure and a return to the way things were before. Back before the world seemed less certain, when they still had their defined roles and niblets of power.

Desmond didn't get involved in such politics nor did he bitch about these things to Mary. While she had heard nothing directly, she wasn't stupid. Mary knew what welcome felt like, and *this* wasn't it.

She sat at her table, trying to make the best of things.

Jade, sitting to her left, leaned in.

"You getting the same vibe I am?"

"What's that?" Mary wondered if her discomfort was obvious.

"These people freaking hate us," Jade said just above a whisper. "Look how they're looking at us. Check out that redheaded over there giving us the stink eye. Yeah, fuck you, too, lady."

Mary laughed as the woman turned. She was a good six tables away, so there was no way she heard Jade, but it was funny to imagine she had.

Jade Keenan, a young college girl with purple hair and a pierced eyebrow, looked like she was comfortable as the black sheep. She was sweet once you got to know her, despite her don't-fuck-with-me attitude. From their few exchanges, Mary could tell that things were strained between Jade and her father.

"Yeah," Mary said, "I was thinking the same thing."

"I think they're jealous."

"Yeah?"

"Yeah, look at 'em, they're all military and scientists used to running the show. But we all showed up and are more or less doing it now. They fucking hate us. We upset their stupid Stepford utopia."

Mary laughed again, this time loud enough to draw attention from the nearby attendees.

Jade was right. The men, along with the few female scientists at the island, were all dressed as if on their way to work, and the wives as if going to church. Mary had on a loose blouse and tight jeans, which felt only slightly better than Jade's ripped leather pants and black Misfits tee.

Teagan, in her staid blue dress, might have fit in with the island's people if she hadn't been a teen mom.

Brent leaned over. "What are you two laughing about?"

"Laughing at the sheep here," Jade said, making a "bah" sound loud enough for others to hear.

"What sheep?" Ben asked, looking around like the innocent five-year-old he was, searching for literal sheep.

"There's no sheep, buddy," Brent said laughing.

"Why did Aunt Jade say to look at the sheep?"

Mary laughed as Ben's volume got louder and Brent's face turned red, trying to hush his son and deflect attention.

"She's just joking," Brent said to Ben.

Ben looked at Jade. "Aren't jokes supposed to be funny?"

"Ouch," Jade said, "schooled by a five-year-old."

"I'm five and a half!" Ben said, outraged that someone would dare to snip months from his age.

Mary smiled, remembering when Paola was that age and how she'd wanted nothing more than to be older than she was. Now, following everything that had happened she seemed content to be herself: perhaps the single good thing to have come of the past two years.

Mary watched as Paola pinched Ben's cheeks and acted normal.

Normal was good.

Hell, normal was great.

But Mary also knew that any moment Paola could slip into another seizure and start seeing things again. She hoped it didn't happen here, in front of everyone. She wasn't embarrassed but didn't need these people, or the few kids close to Paola's age, making fun of her daughter.

Mary was sure she'd get violent if another adult said shit.

Watching Paola, it was hard not to consider that she had someone else, or *something* else, living inside her. The thing calling itself The Light, as Mary understood it, was Luca's soul, blended with the good alien that had infected the boy.

Mary wanted her daughter back to normal, wanted the alien, and the boy, out of Paola. But at the same time, she knew their presence was the only thing saving her. Without them, Mary might not have Paola.

She'd settle for this as long as she had to, until they figured something out.

Though *what* that something was, Mary had no idea.

To Paola's credit, the girl was handling this all better than Mary would have. Mary was pretty certain if *she'd* felt like someone else was inside *her* head, she'd go nuts trying to claw it out.

"Burgers and wieners are up," said one of the men closest to the grills.

Mary and the group stood then waited in line. Farthest from the grills, they were also last.

There was more food than they could possibly eat. Everyone was supposed to bring something. Mary and Paola had baked six dozen oatmeal and chocolate chip cookies the night before. Someone else had made cupcakes. There were a ton of brownies sitting on a plate at the end of the table.

Mary figured the island was too square for the sort of brownies she wanted most.

Her stomach growled as the scent of grilled meat hitched a ride on the wind. It had been a long time since she'd had a decent burger, and she couldn't wait to sink her teeth into one.

As the line inched forward, Mary caught the redheaded woman eyeballing her, snickering with a friend, an older blonde with an uptight ponytail.

"Ignore the bitches," Jade whispered in her ear.

"Why are they even looking at us?" Mary asked.

"Her name is Rita. She's married to Ned Wilson, that bald douche bag at the grill who Dez pretty much replaced as Bolton's right-hand man."

Mary looked at the bald man, in his forties, standing behind the grill, piling two burgers onto the plate for a waiting woman.

"He was Bolton's second in charge?" Mary winced. "And now he's here at a nonessential employee picnic? Ouch."

"Yeah," Jade said. "My dad said he's a real screw-up. He's the reason for the whole thing with that Sullivan guy getting infected without anyone even knowing."

"So he was a scapegoat?" Brent asked.

Jade said, "I dunno if he was a scapegoat or really to blame. My dad said he's an idiot, though, so maybe both."

Brent asked, "And Ed *told you* all this? He's never been the most gossipy of guys."

"He only told me because I said the guy's wife had given me dirty looks one day in the cafeteria. He explained why."

"Great," Mary said, "so she hates us all."

Ben, holding his dad's hand, asked too loudly, "Who hates us?"

Mary laughed, and pursed her lips.

"Nobody, buddy. I was just ... joking," she pinched his nose, and he giggled.

Making their way down the line, Mary grabbed a hamburger and some potato salad, saving space for a cupcake.

Paola's plate looked naked with only a few potato chips.

"Aren't you hungry?" Mary asked.

Paola looked bothered, not meeting her mom's eyes, and shook her head no.

Mary wondered if she'd noticed the nasty women ahead of them in line.

Bitches.

As they approached the front, Mary saw that the cupcakes were nearly gone, along with the brownies. Not a single one of her cookies had been touched.

What the hell?

Mary's skin began to sizzle. Nobody, at all, had taken a single cookie. That wasn't an accident.

She turned to see Rita and her blonde friend sitting at a table, laughing as they pretended not to eyeball Mary.

"No, Mom," Paola said, grabbing her arm.

Mary looked down at her daughter.

"Don't go over there."

Mary looked down, surprised her daughter was reading her emotions so well.

"What's wrong?" Jade asked.

"Nobody's touched my cookies," Mary said. "Not a single one."

"Those cunts," Jade said, before putting her hand over her mouth and adding, "I'm sorry."

"No, you nailed it," Mary said. "And don't worry about Paola, she's heard it all. You've nothin' on our friend, Boricio!"

Jade said, "Come on, let's just eat. Ignore them."

Mary looked down, grabbed four of her cookies, two of each kind, then headed back to the table with Paola in tow.

As they sat, still waiting for the rest of the group to join, Paola whispered, "They hate us."

"Who hates us?"

"Everyone."

"Did you hear them say something?"

"I heard them thinking it," Paola said. "Or rather, Luca heard, and he told me."

A chill slithered through Mary.

"He's talking to you now?"

"Yes."

"How long has he been talking to you?"

"He just started."

"What else did he have to say?"

"He said that The Darkness is coming."

"What?"

Paola swallowed then repeated, "He said that The Darkness is coming."

* * * *

CHAPTER 4
THOMAS ACEVEDO

Acevedo struggled against the women's weight as they held him down.

Beef patted his pockets, searching.

"Where are they?"

"What?" Acevedo asked, hoping the man wouldn't pat down his ankle where he had tucked the vial away.

"You know what, the vials!" Beef's voice brayed in an array of blended voices. Acevedo wasn't sure if the man was using the many voices at once as a play on a possessed man, or if the alien were simply channeling voices in its collective — those of the already infected.

"Out in the car," Acevedo answered.

Beef stared at Acevedo as if the man were considering infecting him, or trying to read his mind.

He can't read your mind, said the alien in Acevedo's head who'd been whispering ever since he slipped the vial into his sock. "He's too strained controlling the women. You must distract him."

How?

Get him to the car.
He'll hurt Marina.
No, he won't. You can stop him.

"I swear, they're out in the car. I'll go with you, if you want."

"Why would you leave them out in the car?"

"They're with my friend. I'll go out with you and hand them over."

Beef stared at the priest. "But I thought you came to get them from me. Why you so eager now to hand them over, Padre?"

"I'm not, but now that you've opened one of the vials there's no point in trying to control anything."

"That's your first correct assumption."

"Just please," Acevedo said, "spare us."

Beef smiled. Nodding, he leaned over, picked up Acevedo's pistol, then trained it on him.

"Funny," Beef said, "a priest with a gun. What happened to *Thou shalt not kill?*"

"I'm not a priest anymore."

"Finally saw that your Christ abandoned you?"

"Something like that."

Beef stared down the pistol's sight at Acevedo like the caged prey he was.

"Tell me, why do you want the vials? What do you hope to accomplish?"

"I saw what you're going to do to the world."

"Did you now?"

"Yes, the vials showed me."

"And what did you think you would do if you got the other vials? Stop us?"

"I don't know," Acevedo lied. "I just don't want to see the world destroyed."

"Oh, we're not about to destroy the world. The *world* will be fine. You animals, however ... "

Beef brought the gun closer to Acevedo's head.

"Please. I'll give you the other vials. I'll walk you out to the car."

"I don't need your help." Beef looked down the sight, taking aim.

A bright flash filled the room, followed by thunder.

Gunshots erupted. Beef's body jerked helter-skelter, riddled with gunshots before thudding like a collapsed piano to the ground.

* * * *

CHAPTER 5
MARY OLSON

"What do you mean The Darkness is coming?"

"The Light told me that it's coming. We're in danger."

"When?" Mary looked around for any obvious signs of danger. She had six rounds in a Springfield 1911 Ultra Compact in her small-of-the-back holster. She wished she'd thought to bring extra magazines. Six rounds were fine for a small threat, a person or two, but would do little against the infected, or the aliens.

She had to get back to their cabin, and the assault rifles inside. And she had to reach Desmond.

She grabbed the cell in her pocket and called him.

"Something's wrong," she said when he picked up.

"What is it?"

"I don't know. Paola said 'The Darkness is coming.'"

"Coming where?"

"Here. She said we're in danger."

"Impossible." Desmond cleared his throat. "We've got this island on lockdown. Nobody comes onto the island without getting screened by me."

"Maybe they're already here?"

"I've checked everyone."

"Maybe you can't sense it as well as you think?"

Desmond was silent, save for a deep sigh. "Maybe she saw the infected in the secured level. Is that possible?"

"We have infected here?" Mary asked.

"Of course," Desmond said. "But there's no way they can get out. It's a secure level below seven other levels of the facility, with too many checkpoints and fail-safes for them to escape. Trust me."

Mary looked around the picnic: the warm sun, the nice gentle breeze wafting off the ocean, the chirping of kids laughing and enjoying themselves. The world was at odds with her feelings, and the certainty that danger was near.

"Relax," Desmond said, "everything is fine. We have it all under control. May I talk to her?"

Mary handed the phone to Paola. "Dez wants to talk to you."

"OK," Paola said, taking the phone. "Hi."

Desmond was faint as Paola tried to hold the phone so they could both hear, without putting it on speaker.

"What exactly did The Light tell you?"

Paola said, "That The Darkness is coming."

"And?" Desmond asked. "Is that it? Did it say when, where, or in what form?"

"Nothing else. But I'm pretty sure he meant it was coming to the island."

"Why do you think that? Did he *say* the island? Could he have been referring to the things that are happening out there on the mainland?"

"I dunno," Paola said. "It felt like he meant the island."

"What do you think, sweetheart? Do you *feel like* we're in danger here?"

Paola paused. "I dunno."

Mary took the phone, trying not to let mounting agitation show in her tone.

"Paola felt what she felt. I don't think we should question it."

"What would you have me do, Mary? Run and tell Bolton that Paola *thinks* we're in danger? Then what? Lock everyone away in their own cells in the research facility?"

"I don't know," Mary said. "Don't talk to me like I'm stupid."

"I didn't say you were. But we can't jump on the heels of some vague threat."

"You trust Paola to help you find the vials, but you won't trust her when she says there's a threat to the island?"

"I didn't say that. We'll double check our security protocols, and suspend ferries onto and off the island until I can be there to check all the passengers myself. How's that?"

Mary sighed. "Sorry, I just hate not knowing what's next. Feeling like there's some threat out there and we have to sit here and wait for an attack. I'm tired of living like this, Dez. I thought the island would be safe."

"It is, Mary. I promise. You and Paola are safer here than anywhere else in the world. Do you trust me?"

She sighed, imagining Desmond's earnest eyes boring into hers. How could she say no to such a kind, sweet man, who had done everything he could to protect her and Paola since that fateful October night when they were flushed into another world? She had to trust the instincts that had already led them this far. It wasn't as if *she* had any concrete idea of what was coming or a better way to protect them against The Darkness.

"Yes," she said. "I trust you."

"OK, I need to get back to work. Call me if anything happens. Or if Paola has any more visions. Anything at all. OK? I love you."

"I love you, too." Mary ended the call.

"Well?" Paola said, looking into her mother's eyes.

"I guess he's got it under control."

Paola looked down, clearly hoping for a better answer.

But Mary had none. She had to trust Desmond's instincts, even if hers were shredding her gut.

* * * *

CHAPTER 6
THOMAS ACEVEDO

Acevedo looked up to see a giant of a man in all black standing with an assault rifle aimed at Beef's fallen body.

The man seemed more like he'd been sent by special ops than from a rival cartel. Acevedo wondered if he was part of a drug bust or if the government had grown wise to the vials' existence.

The women screamed, launching themselves at the gunman, fingers open like claws eager to tear him apart.

The big man's eyes went wide, seemingly surprised by the women's ferocity, likely unaware that they were infected with an alien species.

The big man slammed his rifle's butt into the first woman's face, sending her to the ground in a heap. The second woman was too quick, grabbing the rifle with both hands and wrenching it from his.

Rather than fire, she swung it like a bat, hitting the big man across the face and knocking him to the ground. She tossed the rifle back, where it landed at Acevedo's feet, and approached him slowly, like an animal stalking prey.

A low growl rolled from her throat, just under some sort of alien clicking.

The large man looked up at her, seemingly frozen, mesmerized more than frightened. The alien was likely seizing control of his limbs, rendering him incapable of fighting back.

Acevedo considered his options.

If he didn't intervene, she might tear the man apart.

Acevedo didn't know who in the hell the gunman was, or if he was a threat, but the giant had saved his life, so the priest owed him the same.

Besides, if Acevedo did nothing, there was a damned good chance she'd seize control of the man and give the alien another puppet for attack.

Acevedo grabbed the rifle and aimed at the infected woman, squeezing the trigger twice, the semiautomatic fire tearing her head and back to shreds. As she fell to the ground, twitching, Acevedo turned the gun onto the first woman.

She started to stand, but Acevedo fired a few rounds into the back of her skull, then aimed the gun on the big man just starting to get back up.

Is he already infected?

Acevedo's heart pounded as the giant stared at him with the same glassy eyes he'd been giving the woman.

Acevedo asked, "Who are you?"

"Luther Wahl, with Homeland Security." Confusion faded from his face. He put his hands in the air as if to show he wasn't about to reach for his sidearm or any of the fancy-looking grenades attached to his belt.

"State your business," Acevedo said, still trying to determine if the man was under alien control.

"We're here to get the vials, and I suggest you put the rifle down as we have the place surrounded."

"Bullshit," Acevedo said.

"Your lady friend, Marina Harmon, is already in custody."

Shit.

"Get down!" Luther yelled, eyes bulging wide.

Acevedo heard something, like the sound of water pooling, behind him. He spun back, firing the rifle into a thick, black liquid-like substance rising from Beef's fallen body. The liquid seemed to be assembling itself into some sort of form.

The Darkness.

Acevedo had seen it in his dreams, in the visions, but this was his first time seeing it face to … icy black void.

It was abhorrent, the antithesis of life, of goodness. It was worse than evil. Worse than the devil. It was nothing — an emptiness desperate to grow, stretch its tendrils, and absorb all that it could.

But no, it was more than nothing. *Nothing* held no intelligence, but The Darkness had a cold, calculated intellect, far greater than his own. He could feel it peering into his soul, picking him apart, searching for any weakness to exploit.

Feeling the alien's mental prods sent a chill through his core. And for the first time, Acevedo wondered if he had what it took to battle what had to be stopped at all costs.

He was paralyzed, standing in the bedroom staring, as The Darkness gathered its mass above Beef's corpse, floating above his body as if suspended by dozens of slowly undulating wind currents.

"Come on!" the big man yelled, pulling Acevedo by the shirt tail, backward and through the bedroom doorway.

As they fell back into the hallway, The Darkness shot a large, ropey black appendage almost blindly over them, knocking a hole through the plaster above the door frame.

"Go!" Luther shoved Acevedo toward the living room.

The priest's mind was chaos in a blur, his eyes still drawing The Darkness in its raw form, still trying to process what he had seen, as the big man pushed him forward and out the front door into the brightness of a lying blue sky.

"Down!" Luther yelled, shoving Acevedo down and falling atop his body, crushing him against the rifle still in his hands, now pressing into his chest.

Behind them an explosion, likely from one or more of Luther's grenades.

The sound and heat washed over them, along with a dying alien scream that sliced through Acevedo's soul.

* * * *

CHAPTER 7
EDWARD KEENAN

After updating Director Bolton of the operation's status, Ed leaned against the van, waiting for Agent Harrison of Homeland Security's Los Angeles field office to finish talking with reporters outside the cordoned off area at the end of the block.

Several agents in biological suits were securing every house to ensure that the block held nothing left of the alien threat.

So far, it seemed to be contained, though it was impossible to know if the man calling himself Beef had infected others elsewhere in the week or so since he came in possession of the vial.

Harrison finally finished with the reporters and headed over, sucking his cigarette to a nub.

Harrison was in his fifties, a seasoned vet who seemed to know his shit and how to do his job — an unfortunate rarity in agency types.

Harrison said, "OK, reporters are handled. They're running with the homegrown terror cell angle, for now.

Residents are cooperating because they want to be sure their street is safe and free from the 'chemical weapons.' So, where you headed?"

"To get the rest of these damned vials."

"So how long were you guys at Black Island going to keep us in the dark about the real shit going on?"

"Sorry, not my choice," Ed said. "Need to know and all that shit."

Harrison smiled. "Gotcha. Director Bolton has updated us, so feel free to reach out to me if you need anything or want more people on this. I've got some great agents who can help you."

"Thanks. For now, we'll keep it small as we can. I think we might be able to put an end to this before risking this thing getting too big." Ed walked around the van and got inside.

Luther was sitting in the driver's seat, shaking his head no, meaning he had yet to convince the priest and woman to help them.

Ed sighed and turned back to Acevedo and Marina, sitting in the van's rear, each cuffed to a bar along the side of their seat.

"So, you're still not cooperating?" Ed asked.

Marina said, "I want to talk to my lawyer."

"That's nice and all, but you see, you're not involved in some random crime. This is a matter of national security, and as such, you have no rights. None. Zero. Zilch. You have no right to remain silent. You have no right to an attorney. You have only one option, to cooperate."

"You can't just keep us detained," Acevedo argued.

"Ah, but we can, Father. And we will. Now I believe my partner here explained the stakes, right? That this is a matter of utmost urgency, correct?"

Neither spoke.

Ed continued, "I want to know how you're involved in this, and I want the names on this list translated." Ed had already sent a photo of the paper and its code to the agency's code breakers, but had yet to hear back.

Acevedo said, "We're not helping the government to get a hold of the vials. God only knows what you all will do with them."

Ed laughed. "What *we'll* do with them? These vials are out there and this thing is infecting God knows how many people, and you're worried about what *we'll* do? Not to highlight the obvious, but you do realize that you'd both be corpses, or worse, if my partner and I hadn't come along and saved your sorry asses? I've *seen* what these things can do, firsthand."

Acevedo looked down, saying nothing. Clearly he had some trust issues with the government. He needed persuasion, and time was thin.

Ed hopped into the back of the van to join them, and pulled out his Glock.

Marina's eyes widened. "What are you doing?"

Ed looked up at the priest, who seemed to be barring the fear from his face.

"Here's the deal. You're going to help us find and secure the remaining vials. In return, you'll get your freedom back with no charges filed."

"Charges?" Marina interrupted, "we didn't do anything!"

"We both know that doesn't matter," Ed said. "So, as I was saying, you'll help us, and we'll pretend like none of this ever happened. Or we could open door number two, and see what's behind it."

They both looked at Ed with a mix of curiosity and fear, exactly like he wanted.

Ed turned to Luther. "Oh, man, I love when they pick door number two."

Luther said nothing, perhaps uncertain of his role in the performance.

Ed took the gun and pressed it against Marina's leg, hard until she winced.

"Door number two isn't something you want to open. I know Mr. Acevedo here is a tough customer, but I'll bet he wouldn't want to see *someone else* get unnecessarily hurt."

"Are you threatening me?" Marina glared at Ed. "Are you saying you're going to hurt me if he doesn't give you the information? What kind of thug are you?"

"The kind that will do whatever it takes to protect his country."

"Yeah, real patriotic," Marina said, "threatening innocent civilians."

"I do what has to be done. And in my book, you're hardly innocent. Not when you choose to harbor evidence that will truly help people."

"Yeah, whatever helps you sleep at night," Marina said. "Your kind of 'patriotism' is exactly the kind of overreach that scares us from cooperating. You don't think twice about threatening people to get what you want; what the hell are you going to do once you get the vials and have some real power?"

Ed punched Marina hard in the mouth.

She fell back, crying out in shock and an eruption of pain.

The priest was quick, kicking out with his feet and knocking Ed backward.

Still cuffed to the seat, Acevedo was restrained when he attempted a follow-up move.

Ed was back on his feet, gun aimed at Marina's head. She continued to glare at him, the kind of woman who wasn't used to taking orders. Ed respected her brazen nature but couldn't let that respect prevent him from doing what the situation required.

He hoped Acevedo wouldn't call his bluff. Because Ed *was* prepared to shoot her, if that's what it took.

And while Marina was right (Ed *was* a government thug) it didn't mean he took pleasure in hurting others, particularly a woman.

"You're a monster," Acevedo said.

Ed met his eyes and held them. "You're damned right, Father. I am. Now, are you going to tell me what I need to know or do I have to prove just how monstrous I can be?"

The priest inhaled and exhaled, nostrils flaring as he glared at Ed.

"Fine," he said. "I'll tell you."

* * * *

CHAPTER 8
BORICIO WOLFE

Boricio woke cold and naked with the certainty that someone was watching.

His eyes flicked open, though Boricio kept his body still so as not to alert any fuckers who might be waiting for his rise n' shine.

As his mental haze slowly faded, Boricio was surprised to find that he was no longer in the cell, or even inside. He was out in the woods, with a frigid morning fog gluing itself to the ground like a cunt hair clinging to wax.

What the hell? How did I wind up here?

Fuckers better not be wanting to play Hillbilly Cornhole.

Boricio's last clear memory was a plate of food being slid into his cell. Hard bread and some sort of cold crap that looked like chum slopped out from a can. Boricio was just hungry enough to eat the shit he wouldn't have served to a dying mongrel, but couldn't help picturing that gaggle of guards buttering his bread and barf slop with their baby gravy, chasing squirts with slapped asses like the merry band of butt ticklers they were.

They must've drugged me.
But why would the fuck would they set me free?

Boricio wondered if Rose, or the alien squatting in her body, had been involved. Had she taken over one of the prison pigs and set him free?

If so, had she also infected him?

Boricio didn't feel like there were any aliens inside his head, but would he know if there were? He wondered, not for the first time, if Rose knew her body had been hijacked. Or was the alien somehow able to fool her into believing that all the bullshit belonged to her? He remembered when the alien had first entered her body, how she'd told him to run. She knew what was happening and that if he didn't run she'd attack him as the alien's puppet.

Sometimes Boricio wished he'd had the courage to kill her and spare Rose a life as a host for some fucking parasite. He found it ironic that the one time he should have killed someone, he couldn't. It was like a sex addict going to a hooker without getting a hard-on.

If I could've done what I should've done, she'd at least be at peace.

Boricio again wondered if Rose was behind his escape and if she could've possibly infected him.

There's no fucking way I wouldn't know if some fucking goo monster was up in my head.

Boricio wondered if he'd been inoculated against an alien infection when Luca had gone inside him. The Boy Wonder had turned out to have been infected by the good aliens, after all. Boricio wondered if the prison guards — if Rose *had* infected them — had brought him out here, tried to infect him, then realized they couldn't and left him alone.

But Boricio didn't feel alone.

Someone, or *something*, was watching.

He listened, trying to make out any sounds that might surrender his spy. Whoever it was they were too quiet to be one of the lettuce-licking yokels who'd locked his ass up.

Boricio risked turning his head an inch, and heard a twig snap behind him.

He turned, fists clenched, ready to strike out, but was surprised at what he saw — a fox, lying on its belly, its paw caught in a snare trap, a rope noose around the animal's front left paw, tied to a tree a few feet away.

The fox whined as Boricio sat up, golden eyes watching him, frightened. The fox was either too tired or drugged to growl.

Or maybe it recognizes that we're not too different.

Boricio moved toward the animal, admiring its silky red coat, and the streaks of deep black along its ears and paws. A beautiful creature and from what Boricio knew, a gifted predator.

"Sorry, boy," Boricio said, assuming it was a boy fox, he sure the hell wasn't about to go checking for spuds. "I know how you feel."

Boricio examined the rope, a thin yellow line around the creature's paw, which was wet from chewing in attempt to escape.

It was a simple noose construction, and Boricio figured he could pull it off — if the fox let him.

"All right, Brer Fox, I'm about to *proclimate* your emancipation, but you bite me and I'll have to snap your neck like a Pez dispenser. *Capisce?*"

The fox whined, brow furrowing as it looked at Boricio, its tail moving slightly back and forth.

"I'll take that as an aye-aye, Captain," Boricio said as he moved his hands closer to the fox. He figured foxes probably sensed fear like dogs, so he kept his movements slow and deliberate, showing no nerves as he set his hands near the animal's razor-sharp teeth.

The fox winced, then vented a low growl as Boricio touched its leg. Boricio could feel its hot breath on his arm.

"Now, now," Boricio said, "you agreed to let me help you. Don't worry, I'm not gonna eat you, wear your coat, or fuck you like some of these hillbillies might get to doin'. I'm setting you free, as you should be."

The fox continued to watch him, but the growl faded.

Boricio found where the knot slid around the rope and pulled, loosening the noose enough to slide it off the fox's leg.

"OK," Boricio said. "Here we go, nice and slow."

He lowered the noose, opening it more as he reached the fox's thick wide paw, then pulled it off.

The fox stood, its ears at full alert as it looked around, then bolted off.

"What? No thanks?"

The fox reached the thickening tree line and was about to disappear when a gunshot boomed like thunder.

Boricio watched in horror as the fox fell to the ground.

What the fuck?

Boricio spun around, seeing nothing but woods in every direction.

In front of him, Boricio heard the sound of hillbillies hooting and hollering. It sounded like a dozen, maybe more.

"The hunt is on!" someone yelled in front of a cackle.

Hunt? What the fuck are they talking about?

Then, Guard Tard's familiar drawl: "You better run, boy. You is next!"

Another shot, though Boricio wasn't sure where it landed.

Not needing to be told twice, Boricio ran.

* * * *

CHAPTER 9
MARY OLSON

Mary woke to her child screaming. The clock read 2:15 a.m.

Even though in all likelihood, Paola was having another seizure, Mary's first instinct screamed danger, so she grabbed the shotgun beside the bed and raced from the bedroom.

No one in the hall.

Paola's door was closed.

Mary burst through the door, hoping it was only a seizure.

But her daughter wasn't in the room.

Instead, there were two large men wearing blue Black Island Research Facility overalls. Behind them, the window was wide open, curtains blowing in the cold ocean breeze.

The men's eyes were dark, their mouths agape, faces not at all responding to Mary's gun. While their bodies were not decomposed or changed in any visible way, she could somehow sense their infection.

"Where the fuck is she?" Mary screamed.

Both men rushed her at once.

Mary shot the first in the gut and sent him to the ground. As he fell, she turned the gun toward the other man, but not fast enough.

The man grabbed the shotgun and whipped it from Mary's hands with surprising speed and powerful force.

He tossed the gun to the ground and reached for her throat.

Desmond bolted through the doorway, pistol in hand, and fired point blank at the man's face, shooting twice, not taking any chances. As the second man dropped, Mary pointed out the window, "She's gone!"

Mary grabbed the shotgun and raced out the window.

"Paola!" she screamed repeatedly, turning in the loneliest of circles, desperate for any sign at all of her daughter.

Cabin lights lit up, shadows falling across windows as the island's civilian residents looked to see what was going on. Mary scanned the windows, searching for anything that would lead her to Paola.

This can't be happening!

Desmond followed her outside, on his phone, barking urgently into the receiver.

Mary cried out, "Paola!!" and listened, hoping her daughter was still close enough (or alive) to answer.

Desmond, now off the phone, set a hand on Mary's shoulder. "Don't worry, we'll find her."

"She told us The Darkness was coming!" Mary spat. "She told us, and we — no, you — ignored her."

"I've got all available Guardsmen on this. We're on an island, Mary. There are only two ways off, and we've both docks on lockdown."

"They could've taken a rowboat for all we know!"

"There are two choppers on the way. There's no way they could reach the mainland before we caught them."

"I can't believe this is happening again." Mary shook her head. "We were supposed to be safe!"

"We'll find her," Desmond repeated.

Mary didn't want to hear anything from Desmond. He said they'd be safe, and they weren't. His words were empty and his promises hollow. She could count on no one but herself — same as it ever was.

Mary brushed by Desmond, back into the house, and threw on her black pants, boots, shirt, and jacket. She holstered a Glock to her hip, grabbed a few magazines, and shoved them in her pocket, along with a box of shells.

"What are you doing?" Desmond asked.

"What's it look like? I'm going to find my daughter." Mary marched toward the front door, stopping to grab a heavy black flashlight that doubled as a baton.

"I've got my people out. We should stay here in case she comes back."

Mary spun around and met Desmond's eyes. "Do you really expect me to *sit here* while my daughter's out there with those ... *things?*"

Desmond looked lost for words. "No. Of course not. I'll come with you."

Desmond was still in his pajamas, and Mary wasn't about to wait for him to get dressed and ready. "I have my phone. You can come and find me."

Mary slammed the front door then marched down the dirt road between the cabins. Guardsmen appeared at people's doors, knocking, asking residents what they'd seen. She held no hope on someone seeing anything worth a damn. These things worked in the shadows, invisible to everyone — but Paola.

Maybe that's why they'd come after her.

They knew she could see them coming, and that made her a threat.

"Wait up!" Mary heard a man calling.

She turned, expecting Desmond, but instead saw Brent, dressed in jeans and a T-shirt, holding a pistol. Jade was trotting behind him, in black leather pants and a matching shirt, flashlight in her hand and a gun on her hip.

"We heard someone took Paola. We'll help you find her," Brent said, catching up.

"What about Ben?"

"I left him with Teagan."

Mary glanced up the dirt road and saw truck lights slicing the night to the east and south. Docks to the mainland were on the island's south side. Another dock serving the ferry to Paddock Island was on the east end.

Both seemed like improbable places for the infected to take Paola, because they were on lockdown. That left the island's west and north ends, the darker forested parts, left unaccounted for.

Desmond finally caught up with the huddle, holding a shotgun with a mounted light in one hand and his phone in the other.

"I just spoke to Bolton. He issued an emergency order to everyone in the facility. They'll all be joining the search. We'll find her, Mary."

"OK, I think we should split up." Mary swallowed. "Are you two OK to go on your own, either north or west?"

Brent said, "Yeah, we're good."

"Yeah," Jade nodded. "We'll take the west end, unless you want it."

"That's fine," Mary said. "We'll take the north end. And be careful, I think these people are infected — working with the aliens."

Desmond said, "Be careful out there. I'll let the Guard know not to go shooting civilians, but if you run into Guardsmen, don't raise your guns."

Mary turned to him, "What if the Guardsmen are infected? The two men who broke into the house were wearing facility coveralls. How do we know they didn't infect Guardsmen, too?"

"It's not likely," Desmond shook his head, "but do keep a look out for suspicious behavior ... from anyone."

"Gotcha," Jade said, and headed off.

"Good luck." Brent turned to follow Jade.

Mary looked north into the dark woods and wished she could feel something, anything from Paola that might tell Mary if she were alive. Usually, she could feel her daughter, much the same way some twins were said to sense one another, or know when the other was suffering. Mary had that bond with Paola. She could often tell what her daughter was thinking, even if she was nowhere nearby. Mary could also tell when something was wrong.

But now, she felt nothing but a black vacuum where her child had been.

She headed north, shining her light into the trees, with Desmond beside her, flashing his alongside.

"We're going to find her," he said, as if repetition might make it so.

"We don't even know if she's alive."

"If they meant to kill her, don't you think they would've just done so and left her there for us to find?"

Mary hadn't considered that. Perhaps. But it also begged another question. "So if they don't want to hurt her, what *do* they want with her?"

A stretched silence, then Desmond said, "I don't know."

Mary wanted to yell at him some more, blame Desmond for not listening to Paola's warning. She wanted someone to wag a finger at besides herself. But she had only herself to blame. Desmond wasn't the boss of her. She could have demanded a ferry to the mainland. She could have left, but chose not to.

That was on her.

Mary prayed that her mistake wouldn't cost Paola her life.

* * * *

CHAPTER 10
BORICIO WOLFE

Boricio scrambled through the underbrush like an animal, ignoring the branches, brambles, rocks, and other sharp bits of debris that kept tearing into his naked flesh like a bitch in heat.

The hunters were close behind.

How close, Boricio wasn't sure. He didn't dare look back.

He could hear their footsteps like galloping thunder behind him, along with the hillbilly hoots and hollers of fevered excitement. In his head he heard the sound of a half-wit strumming his banjo.

Boricio kept running, eyes darting across the landscape, searching for any possible advantage. He'd spotted a few large branches that looked like they could serve as a bo staff for close combat, but they were either too far out of reach or it would take too long to drop or wrest them from the underbrush.

He couldn't stop.

Had to keep going.

Every time Boricio considered slowing down or reaching for something, the noises behind him grew louder — closer.

He kept running.

His chest burned like fire. His heart was an engine on the verge of blowing.

After days in a straitjacket, and without much sobriety prior, Boricio was surprised that his body was able to chug. His pursuers were more Special Olympics than Special Forces, but they had guns and if the dead fox was any evidence, the tater ticklers knew how to use them.

He'd managed to stay ahead, but Boricio wasn't sure how long his luck would hold. They knew the woods better than he did. And the mere fact that they freed him for a hunt meant they were confident in their ability to track him.

And what then?

How many other prisoners had they brought out to the woods for their redneck reindeer games? There had to be a trail of paperwork. You couldn't just go into a jail and vanish forever, *could you?*

Boricio had thought himself a ghost, but they had evidence tying him to crimes outside their little neck of the woods. Someone somewhere with indoor plumbing had to be looking for Boricio. The guards had to know that. They couldn't just lose a prisoner as notorious as Boricio Fucking Wolfe without having to answer some questions.

But these guys struck Boricio as Idiot, USA's bottom rung, so maybe they didn't think past the longest toe on their ugly bare feet. Or perhaps they never made any official inquiries to let people know they had a gen-yoo-wine serial killer in lockup.

Maybe they wanted to keep this little treat for themselves.

Which meant he had to keep running.

As Boricio kept moving south, which he judged by the location of moss on the trees, he heard rushing water ahead.

That could be his break, assuming the body of water wasn't too large to cross. Maybe he could pretend that he had, then double back on the fuckers and go north.

Too soon to tell, so Boricio kept running, trying to lay distance between himself and his hunters. As long as he kept moving, Boricio figured he was likely safe from a bullet. You couldn't run and quick scope in real life. That was *Call of Duty* bullshit for sure.

However, if they came to a clearing or a large enough hill where the hunters would have the advantage of stopping and lining up their shots with his movement, he was fucked with a capital F.

The sound of water grew louder as he approached a steep incline that ran as far as Boricio could see in either direction.

As much as it promised to slow him, he'd have to ascend the steep hill. As he reached the peak, Boricio saw the stream of water rushing downward, heading east through trees so thick he couldn't tell where the slope leveled off.

Boricio had no idea how steep the hill was, and didn't have time to worry.

Without thinking twice he jumped into the river, hoping the rapids would carry him down the hill like a giant slide. But the water was moving fast, shoving him underwater as it carried him down the hillside.

The world disappeared under the surface. Boricio ignored the creeping panic, knowing he couldn't flee the current without a clear head.

He gasped for the air as he broke the surface, his body bobbing up and down, head going back under water and hitting something hard — *a rock, a log?*

Above Boricio, the world went dark light dark light as the canopy of trees thinned and thickened, adding to his confusion. He fought to maintain his senses as pain spread from the side of his head and threatened to overwhelm him. He had to be bleeding.

The river continued to carry Boricio while he gobbled air, gulping as much as he could between dunks, his body rocked up and down, side to side along the river as it wound around the hill and through the woodlands.

Water roared as he continued downstream. Between dunks, Boricio's eyes caught something he wished he hadn't seen — a deep drop.

He was rushing toward a waterfall.

Boricio braced himself as he closed in on the drop, hoping that the water was deep, that he wouldn't hit rocks, and that this was his chance for escape. There was no way in hell the hunters could catch him unless they all jumped in the river, and he doubted they'd do that.

Boricio went under again, then back up, gasping for air as the drop came.

Freedom!

The river below looked deep, with no visible rocks.

Holy shit, this might work!

If I don't break my neck in the fall.

As he reached the drop, crippling pain splintered his back. Boricio had been shot in the spine.

The drop came, and the world fell out from beneath him.

**

When Boricio came to on the side of the river bank, facedown in the mud, he felt only cold. A deep and bitter chill that bit so hard into Boricio's bones that it might as well have been freezing him from the inside out.

Boricio could feel nothing else.

His entire body was numb, as if the gunshot weren't even there.

Did it sever my spine?

He panicked, trying to will his body into motion, and pull himself along the bank to safety.

Oh Fuck. Come on, move!

Boricio stared at his arms, like noodles before him, useless vestiges weighing him down.

From somewhere, a country accent shouted, "There he is!"

Oh shit.

Footsteps drew closer, alongside laughter.

Boricio couldn't even turn to see his enemy approaching. He was a fucking vegetable, about to be slaughtered by a swarm of cousin fuckers.

No, no, no!

Suddenly his body was flipped over to face the sky, even though he barely felt the hand grabbing his hair and yanking him over.

Guard Tard stood above Boricio, smiling like he'd won the fair's prize pig and couldn't wait to get it home and fuck it into a banshee's squealing.

"I'll give this to ya, boy, you were a helluva hunt! Right, guys?"

The men shouted unintelligibly together as they circled Boricio's body. He opened his mouth to say something and was horrified when no words would come.

Am I Silent Fucking Bob?

"Well," Guard Tard said, kneeling down, pulling a blade from his belt, "should we gut him and let him bleed out slow, or put a bullet in his head?"

Guard Tard ran the blade over Boricio's stomach, but Boricio felt only the faintest trace. Hell, he could've stabbed him already and Boricio might not have felt it.

He couldn't believe that *this* was how it would end. He thought of Rose, wishing he'd taken her offer. If only to see her again, spend a few minutes together, even if an alien was pulling the strings. There had to be some part of his Morning Rose still inside, some part he could spend a few final moments enjoying. Anything was better than this.

Boricio thought back on how many lives he'd ended. How many he'd hunted without mercy.

Perhaps this was fitting.

But fuck it if it felt right.

Luca fixed me! That was the old Boricio! I ain't killed anyone undeserving since.

If there was a God, which Boricio thought as likely as MC Hammer having another hit, then He was surely laughing now. Fix him up enough to make him care, then kill him for his sins.

"I got an idea," Guard Tard said, "how about we all shoot him at once. Sort of a twenty-one gun salute, minus some guns."

Boricio recognized some of the hillbillies as pigs from the prison. Others were maybe friends or coworkers from different shifts. Each seemed to like the idea. They gathered around Boricio, all taking aim with their rifles.

Guard Tard said, "Any last words?"

Boricio tried to open his mouth, but couldn't feel his lips to know if he had managed to open his mouth.

He wanted to say *Fuck you, cunt* and go out in style, but couldn't say shit and might have been drooling for all he knew.

"No?" Guard Tard laughed. "All righty then, on the count of three."

"One ... "

Boricio closed his eyes, refusing to give them the pleasure of being the last thing he saw.

He remembered the first time he'd seen Rose on Paddock Island, on a Sunday morning at a restaurant called Schooner or Later.

Wait, no, that's not how we met. We met at that bar. It was night.

Yet he was seeing her clear as day, in a memory that felt as real as any.

And then he realized. It wasn't his memory. He was somehow remembering something that happened to that other Boricio — Boricio Bishop.

What the fuck? How can I have his memories?

"Two ... "

Memories flooded, none of them his. The old man, Will, who had adopted the other Boricio, along with the other Luca.

Then he heard the boy's voice: *Do you want to live, Boricio?*

Boricio opened his eyes and saw every gun aimed at his body. The hunters appeared frozen, a collective second from squeezing the trigger.

"Do you want to live?" Luca repeated, his voice coming from Guard Tard's tobacco stained mouth.

Lightning flashed across the sky, and rain fell, though Boricio could barely feel it pelting his body.

Boricio tried to say yes that he wanted to leave, but his mouth refused to move.

Damn it, work!

"It's OK," Luca said. "I heard you think it."

Guard Tard raised his rifle and shot one of the hunters in the head.

None of the hunters reacted, all still frozen, even as the rain fell fast around them to prove that time still poured into the future.

Guard Tard shot the rest of the men. When his rifle was empty of ammo, he reached for a pistol and finished them off.

As corpses rained around him, Guard Tard bent over and gathered Boricio into his arms.

I can't feel anything!

"It's OK," Luca said from the man's mouth. "We'll fix you up."

The Boy Wonder carried Boricio out of the woods.

* * * *

CHAPTER 11
BRENT FOSTER

As the wind picked up and cold rain began to pelt them, Brent was starting to wonder if searching the island's west side was a waste of time. There was nothing out here but too many trees. And no sign of Paola.

But given that nobody else was searching this area, Brent decided this was the best place to look. If someone had taken Paola and was lying low, what better place to do so than in the middle of the dark woods?

Their narrow dirt path seemed to be thinning, bringing the swaying skeletal branches closer to their bodies. Flashlights battled the surrounding blackness, but did little to pierce it. The icy rain only made visibility worse.

Something reached out in the darkness and scratched at Brent's face.

He threw an arm up in defense, the one with the heavy flashlight, relieved to just see a branch and not something alien reaching out to grab him.

Brent shoved the branch aside and turned his face downward, covering it with an arm.

"Careful of the branches, nearly poked my eyes out." Brent turned back to Jade who had been walking beside him but was now behind as the dwindling path left little room for more than congestion.

"OK," Jade shouted over the howling wind.

They walked a bit farther, and Brent figured they had to be close to the shore, even though he saw no sign of the sea or lights from the mainland beyond.

How big is this damned island?

It, like its counterpart on the other world, seemed so small on the ferry ride over. But the island felt like Dr. Who's TARDIS upon arrival, deceptively larger than it seemed. That wasn't even counting the sprawling research facility that descended God knew how many levels underground.

The path abruptly ended.

Brent ran his light over the thick wall of trees ahead and around, searching for a fork in the path he might have missed. But it seemed to end, as if unfinished.

"Shit, that was a waste of time." Brent turned back to Jade and shined his light at her waist so he could see her face without turning her temporarily blind. "Think we should turn back?"

She pushed strands of wet purple hair from her eyes and looked around, flashing her beam into the woods ahead. "There!" Her eyes widened. "What's that?"

Brent turned toward her discovery. In the distance, light grabbed what looked to be some sort of barely visible structure.

"What is it?" she asked.

"Hell if I know."

"Let's go." Jade pushed past Brent and marched into the woods, fearless like her father.

Brent followed, burying a creeping unease, a whisper inside him somehow (illogically) certain that they were tromping toward their deaths.

While Jade was only about ten years younger than Brent, and not at all a child, he couldn't help but feel some sense of obligation to look out for her, to protect her from harm. Ed had asked him to do just that.

Don't let my daughter get into any shit.

Ed may as well have asked Brent to keep the sun from shining in their sky.

Jade was fiercely independent, living as if she had something to prove. It was in her stature, in the way she took to their survival and gun training, and, like her father, in her eyes.

When Brent first heard that Paola was missing, from one of the Guardsmen on the radio, he went to Jade and Teagan's cabin, hoping they would look after Ben while he helped Mary search for her daughter. Jade had insisted on coming, even though Brent had argued otherwise.

She refused his feeble attempts to stop her, and insisted that four eyes were better than two.

Brent surrendered. Jade wasn't his daughter, and it wasn't his place to order her around. Trying made him feel like a jerk.

Now, as they were out in the woods on "monster island" and inching toward some decrepit lair, Brent wished he'd told Jade to stay behind. Ed would kill him if something happened to his daughter, if the aliens didn't end him first.

They drew nearer to the small clearing, and the structure sharpened into view. Jade stopped in her tracks, clicking her light off. Brent killed his, too. He stared ahead at the back side of an ancient-looking, two-story wooden house, half swallowed by wild weeds and vegetation.

Brent's heart raced as he considered his next move. Something felt wrong.

Wind whistled louder, and rain pounded harder, now stinging Brent's face and eyes.

He leaned in close, putting his mouth next to Jade's ear and doing his best not to shout. "Let's look around the front."

They stayed in the trees, navigating in the inky-black darkness, slowly making their way toward the home's front.

Light flickered from behind a sheer curtain in an upstairs window.

Someone's in there!

Brent wiped wet hair from his eyes and looked at Jade to see that she'd noticed the window as well. She drew the gun from her holster, ready to race inside.

"Wait." Brent put his hand out to stop her from moving forward. "We should call this in."

"*Call it in?* If someone is in there with Paola, then every second counts."

Brent argued. "If they wanted to kill her, I think they would've done it already."

"There are things worse than death," Jade said, her eyes firm.

Brent wasn't sure if she meant the girl was in danger of sexual assault or alien infection. Either way, he thought it would be best if they waited for backup.

"We can't go in there alone," Brent said. "If something happens to us, she's screwed. We're all screwed. We need to call it in and see how close they are. We might not have to wait long."

Jade looked at the house again, sighing in protest. "Fine, call it in. But if they're not here in a few minutes, I'm going in — *with or without you.*"

* * * *

CHAPTER 12
MARY OLSON

"We're going to find her," Desmond repeated as they walked the shoreline, flashlights sweeping for any sign of Paola in the stormy darkness.

Three choppers growled from above, spotlights probing the rolling ocean between island and mainland for any sign of boats that the kidnappers might be using. According to Desmond, the choppers were outfitted with thermal viewers to spot heat signatures on land or sea. Anyone attempting to leave the island would light up on the choppers' screens.

"We're going to find her," Desmond repeated a bit louder over the wind.

Mary ignored him.

Discussion was pointless, and his reassurances meant nothing — empty as a wish in a well. Hope meant little, or maybe nothing in a world cruel enough to take her husband, unborn child, and now her daughter — *again*.

Action was all that mattered — doing what had to be done to find Paola. They had to keep looking. They had to find her.

Desmond's phone chirped, though Mary couldn't hear it above the pounding rain. She watched as he brought the glowing face of the phone to his ear.

Mary moved closer, hoping (wishing) for news — good news — about Paola.

"Where are you?" Desmond said. "Wait, never mind, I can track your phone."

He pulled the phone away, swiped the screen three times, and raised a map of the island populated with hundreds of bright-blue dots. He highlighted Brent Foster from a list of names on the left, then pressed it.

A red dot lit up on the island's west side, near the shore and what looked to be a blue block.

"OK, I've got you on my screen," Desmond said after returning the phone to his face. "Stay put. I'm sending backup immediately. Don't do anything until they get there. Understand?"

Brent offered a faraway "Yes," then Desmond killed the call and turned to Mary.

"Did they find her?" Mary asked, daring to voice her hope.

"Hold on," Desmond said, then barked orders to Guardsmen over the whipping wind and pelting rain.

He dropped the phone in his jacket pocket and turned to Mary. "I don't know. They found an old house on the island. Brent said there's a light on inside."

Mary's heart began to race. "What else did he say?"

"Nothing. I told him to wait. I'm sending Guardsmen over, and someone is coming to pick us up."

A black jeep rolled up before Desmond finished his sentence. Desmond gestured toward the vehicle, then followed Mary into the back seat.

Desmond nodded at the pair of unfamiliar Guardsmen up front. The jeep skidded as it turned, then bounced along the bumpy dirt road toward coordinates already loaded into the GPS.

"What is this place?" Desmond asked.

The passenger, an older man with salt-and-pepper beard and matching short, curly hair said, "The old Wilson home, belonging to one of the original owners of the island back in the early 1900s. Black Island considered tearing it down, but I guess someone had a soft spot for history and decided to leave it."

"Does anyone live there?" Mary asked, thinking a caretaker would explain the light.

"Oh God, no. The place should be torn down. It's decrepit and spooky as Satan's bachelor pad."

"Great," Mary said.

Desmond squeezed her hand. "Don't worry."

They hit a bump, jostling them hard. Mary didn't care. All she wanted was to reach the house and find Paola safe inside.

* * * *

CHAPTER 13
BRENT FOSTER

Jade paced in the rain while waiting for the Guardsmen. "What the hell is taking them so long?"

"They'll be here." Brent wished she'd stay in one spot. Jade was making him jumpier than he already was.

"Would you stand still? Someone might see us if you keep moving."

She looked at him. It was too dark to tell if she had rolled her eyes, but Brent figured she probably had. Jade finally stopped pacing, then moved closer.

"Every minute we sit here—" she started to say.

"Is another minute she's safe," Brent interrupted. "We go in there, we're more likely to do harm. Let's leave it to the trained professionals."

"Would you say that if it was Ben in there?"

The girl had a point.

"I don't know," Brent admitted. "But Desmond said to stand down. And he's with Mary. I think we should respect their wishes. She's Mary's daughter, not mine … or yours."

Jade pursed her lips, then resumed pacing.

A shape appeared in the window.

Brent grabbed Jade and yanked her down into the brush, hard on her knees, beside him.

"Look!" Brent pointed at the window and the black shape behind it, pulling the curtain aside and stepping closer to the glass.

"Can you see?" he asked her.

"Only that it's a guy."

"Stay down," Brent whispered.

Lights flooded the first floor, and a second dark shape appeared in the downstairs window, also staring out into the night.

Brent sank lower to the ground, water and mud soaking his pants and shirt, hoping that he and Jade were invisible. They were crouched so low he could barely see through the brush and the land's slight rising.

"Shit," Jade ducked lower, practically lying on the ground. "Someone's coming outside."

Brent dared to peer above the brush, and saw the front door swing shut. His eyes found a man, already outside, approaching with a rifle raised.

A bullet whizzed past, so close, Brent could hear it zip by before slamming into the ground behind them.

Jade lifted her Glock and fired.

Brent scrambled to his knees, raising his own weapon to fire at the man.

Both shots missed.

The man, still cloaked in shadows, fired again.

Brent wasn't sure where the bullets went, but wasn't about to stick around for discovery. He emptied his gun into the darkness as Jade did the same.

One of them dropped their enemy to the ground.

Brent reloaded, looking over to see if Jade was OK.

She seemed to be, sprinting toward the house, about twenty yards from their spot in the brush.

Brent scanned the darkness for the first man, to make sure he was still facedown in the mud.

Brent put another bullet in the back of his skull, then turned his attention toward the house and the dark shape in the second-floor window.

The man was no longer there.

Shit!

Brent was about to call out for Jade, but the front door swung back open before he could. A tall man in blue coveralls stepped out, shoving Paola in front of him, gun to the girl's head, holding her so close that any shot was too risky to take.

"Put your guns down, or I'll kill her!" The man's voice was eerily calm, revealing none of the panic a pair of guns should invite.

"Fuck you," Jade said. "You put yours down."

"I'll kill her!"

Paola's mouth was taped shut by a layer of electrical tape wrapped around her jaw and dark hair.

"No you won't," Jade said, sounding oddly like a seasoned hostage negotiator, "or you would've already."

Don't piss off the kidnapper!

The man pressed the pistol into the side of Paola's head. Judging from the way she winced, the man was definitely hurting her, and likely getting more desperate. If Brent and Jade didn't listen, they might back the man into a corner where his only way out was to kill the girl and then himself.

"Put the gun down," Brent said to Jade, bending at the waist to lower his own.

"No," Jade said, "he won't do shit."

"Please." Brent tried to find Jade's eyes, hoping to talk some sense into her. She was wrong on this, just as she was wrong to charge into the house. But she was too stubborn to recognize a man at the end of his rope.

"Mary said he's infected. He won't kill the girl. They want her for something else, but they're not gonna kill her."

Brent looked at the man. Yes, he might be infected and working under direction from The Darkness, but he was still desperate and scared. Maybe he had enough control of his senses to be reasoned with. Brent remembered how his friend, Luis, had retained his senses enough to try and talk Brent into leaving him behind even after his infection. This man was talking with them. Clearly, he wasn't at the crazed stage people reached just before they lost all control.

"Can't you see?" Brent spoke just loud enough for Jade to hear. "He's scared. He's going to hurt her. We have to do this his way."

Jade finally turned and met Brent's eyes. "Fine, we'll—"

Then she went down.

A shot to the head.

Brent screamed, barely turning in time to see the man training his gun on Brent.

He fired. Brent dropped to the ground and rolled back toward the brush. The man continued to fire.

Bullets tore into the ground around him. Brent scrambled toward the closest cover, the bushes they'd been hiding in a few moments before, his body moving faster than his reeling mind, praying that Jade was OK.

Lights from a chopper above blinded Brent, then two pairs of headlights added to the glow.

Brent stayed on the ground, hoping the vehicles would stop before running him over.

They did, just barely.

The cavalry had come.

He hoped they'd come in time.

* * * *

CHAPTER 14
MARY OLSON

Mary bounded out of the jeep, gun in hand, raised at the man standing with Paola at his mercy.

"Let her go!" she screamed, marching forward.

Mary saw Jade on the ground with her glazed eyes to the sky, the front of her skull missing from the left side.

Mary's stomach dropped.

She turned her gaze back on the man, hoping like hell he wouldn't kill another tonight.

"Please," Mary said, "don't hurt her. She's just a little girl."

Paola's mouth was taped shut, her eyes wide with panic, staring at her mom, silently pleading for help, black, soaking hair in strands over her face.

The gunman stood frozen, eyes darting back and forth among Mary, Desmond, and the other four Guardsmen now staring down at him with weapons drawn. Brent joined in the standoff, his gun drawn on the man, too.

The bounty of guns pointed at the man terrified Mary, amplifying the odds that someone would start something that would end in too many deaths.

Please, please, God, get us out of this one.

Please don't let Paola get shot.

Please, God, I beg you, spare my daughter.

"You have one chance to get out of this alive," Desmond said, voice confident, assertive. "Give us the girl, and we'll help you."

"Help me what?" the man said to Desmond, while staring oddly at Mary.

"We know this isn't you wanting to do this," Desmond said. "Something is making you do this. There's a voice in your head, telling you to do this, isn't there?"

The man's eyes went from scary to scared. "You hear it, too?"

"Yes," Desmond said. "It's The Darkness. It's got hold of you, but we can get it out of your head if you let us."

"You can?" The man's face cracked, as if near tears.

Mary stared at her daughter, hoping Paola could pick up on her thoughts, and hoping she believed them — even if Mary wasn't sure she did.

It's going to be OK.

We're going to get you out of this.

Just be calm.

Desmond continued. "It's not your fault, Jerry. We can get it out of your head. And you get you back to your life. Back to your wife and child."

Mary was impressed that Desmond knew so much about the guy. She wondered if he worked directly under Desmond, or if Desmond's memory was simply that good.

"I can have my life back?" The man's face twisted as if he were waging a battle inside himself.

"Yes," Desmond said. "I swear. Just give us the girl."

The man kept staring at Mary, his face twisted and anguished.

Then it went blank. He stared at Mary, neutral, with no emotion.

Did he win back control?

Mary's heart swelled with hope. She was about to get her little girl back. The nightmare was almost over.

Just a few more sec...

The man's eyes stayed locked onto Mary's as he slowly shook his head.

Why is he shaking his head?

The man fired his pistol point blank into the side of Paola's face.

Mary screamed as the Guardsmen opened fire and brought the man down.

Mary raced to her daughter, praying that somehow Paola had survived.

But as she dropped down next to her girl, Mary realized that God wasn't answering prayers tonight.

* * * *

::EPISODE 29::
(FIFTH EPISODE OF SEASON FIVE)
"RISE AND SHINE"

CHAPTER 1
MARINA HARMON

Marina glared at the agent, Ed Keenan, as her jaw pulsated in pain. She couldn't believe he'd just punched her, and threatened to kill her if Acevedo didn't translate the list of names.

She'd heard horror stories of reckless government thugs harassing church members, but had never seen someone so flagrantly stomp all over her liberties.

Marina wished she wasn't cuffed, so she could take a shot back at the agent. She didn't think she could take him on — he was a paid government thug, after all — but she would have liked to have some form of revenge, perhaps scratch an eye out or worse.

Acevedo buckled to the threat against her, and offered a pair of names.

Marina had never heard of the first name, Kerri Sampson. The second, however, was so surprising that even Keenan did a double take.

"Max Torrino," Acevedo said translating the code.

"Wait, the Max Torrino? The movie star?" Keenan asked.

"Yes." Acevedo nodded. "Surely you knew he was a Designer."

Keenan shook his head. "I don't follow the gossip rags. But I've seen his movies."

Max Torrino wasn't just Hollywood's biggest and best box office bet — a young actor admired for both his serious and action-heavy roles — he was also the church's brightest star. Some might say Torrino was even bigger than the church, and had been rather critical of it, or specifically Marina, following her father's death. Thankfully, he'd so far kept his criticisms within the inner circle and had leaked nothing to the press.

Keenan seemed to pick up on Marina's consternation.

"What is it? Can you get a hold of him? Is Torrino still with the church?"

"I can't really comment on something like that; it's privileged information." Marina looked down, wishing the list had harbored any other name.

"I'm not asking you to tell me how much he donated, what secret level of the cult he is, or whatever other bullshit you all discuss behind closed doors. I just need to know if you can get us in a room."

"I don't know," Marina admitted. "We're not exactly on the best of terms."

Keenan's eyebrows arched. "Go on."

Marina sighed, then explained that she had never cared all that much for the pampered actor. Her father had discovered Torrino as a newcomer and had helped the actor kick drugs and overcome some emotional issues — all well documented in the actor's biography, as if the church had written his IMDB page. But as her father's health had deteriorated and Marina took a more active role in the church, Torrino had taken exception to some of her ideas, such as doing more work with impoverished children.

"But I thought the church was known for its altruistic efforts?" Acevedo interjected.

Marina wasn't sure if Acevedo was truly that ignorant of the church's reputation or whether he was secretly delighting in her admissions.

"This is nothing on my father. I don't think he intended it this way, but the people beneath him seemed more interested in helping those they could hold some power over — celebrities, addicts connected to wealthy families, and politicians. Other than the token gestures and tax write-offs, the church rarely helped anyone without getting something in return. I fought hard to change this, to make it so the church was truly helping people in need — people who didn't provide the church with a steady income or help them win additional influence."

"And Max Torrino didn't like this?" Keenan asked.

"He'd never say so publicly, but I've heard from others that he thought I was 'bringing down the church by introducing unclean elements.' Seems that if you're an addict not connected or in Hollywood, you're weak and a threat to the fabric of the church."

"Wow," Acevedo said.

"Yeah, so he's been sniping about me to anyone in the church who will listen, but has never had the guts to say anything directly to me."

Keenan asked, "Do you think he'd agree to meet with you?"

"Why can't you just storm into his house and put a gun to his head, maybe punch him?" Marina met Keenan's eyes and smiled.

He ignored her bait. "We'd prefer to handle it quietly, without an army of lawyers making things difficult. If we can get a face-to-face between you and him, it might help us avoid any blowback."

Marina sighed. "I might make things *more difficult*."

Keenan stared at the van floor as if it might offer a helpful suggestion.

An idea popped into Marina's head — Veronica Barrow.

Veronica wasn't just a longtime friend, she was also Torrino's agent. If anyone could arrange a meeting between them, it would be her. Marina would likely have to grovel at His Majesty's feet, but what choice did she have? If Torrino really had one of the vials, they needed to get it.

But Marina wondered how long she and Acevedo, or hell, she alone, would play ball with the government. Could she trust them with the vials? Not likely. And the brutish behavior from Keenan and Steroid Case in the driver's seat didn't exactly warm her to their cause.

Marina would go along with them, for now, but only because she had no other options. She wondered if Acevedo was thinking the same thing. She couldn't help but think he was. He'd rolled over too easily. Yes, Keenan had punched her, and he'd threatened her with a gun, but still, he couldn't think the agent would actually pull the trigger, could he?

"So," Keenan said, "can you get us a meeting?"

"Well, first we have to assume he's even here. He spends half his time in Paris, or one of his other homes out of the country. I have no idea where he is at this very moment."

"Well, can you find out?" Keenan asked.

"Can I have my phone so I can call my friend, Veronica? If anyone can get us in to see Max, it would be her."

Keenan fished her phone from his pants pocket, then slipped the phone into her right hand, the one not cuffed to the seat.

"Don't call anyone else or tip her off to our reason for meeting."

Marina rolled her eyes, sighing as she dialed Veronica.

**

Marina didn't know what sorts of things Veronica had said to grease the wheels, but she'd managed to land them a same-day (and virtually unheard of) meeting with Torrino at his palatial estate.

Torrino had bought his LA mansion for $24 million three years before her father's death, then spent another $6 million on renovation. The Montecito estate was just under fourteen thousand square feet and modeled after a Northern European mountain home. The estate had eight bedrooms, a dozen full and six half-baths, a 2,800-bottle wine cellar, two indoor swimming pools, an atrium, a thirty-six-seat movie theater, and a par-six golf course. Marina's estate had different versions of all the same things, and still she found Torrino's home ostentatious.

Before the meeting they had to get Keenan into some clothes other than his black government thug duds.

They stopped at T. Baker's Fine Menswear, one of the nicer men's clothing shops along the way, and managed to find a decent charcoal suit that fit relatively well off the rack, even if it was short on the cuffs and tight around Keenan's muscular arms.

Luther parked the van just outside Torrino's estate, where he waited with Acevedo while Marina and Keenan drove up to the guard's gate in a late-model Infiniti.

Luther had outfitted them both with hidden microphones and earpieces so he could track the conversation. A block away, several field agents were on standby in case things went horribly awry. Marina wasn't sure if they were Guardsmen, Homeland Security, or something else. But she hoped they didn't get involved. Escalation would give the government a near certainty of getting the vials.

Marina was too smart to believe that she or Acevedo could ever return to a normal life after that.

Whether the government did something awful with the vials to the world as they knew it, or killed them for silence, the longer she stayed with Keenan the more Marina felt her old world slipping away.

After driving nearly a half mile, they came to the end of the drive, where a valet took their Infiniti. As they stepped toward the house, Marina silently prayed to her father.

Please, help me. I don't know what to do. Please give me the wisdom to know the right path, and the courage to take it.

They were met at the front door by an older woman in a red dress. Her smile and perfect teeth couldn't hide the contempt in her icy-brown eyes. Marina remembered the woman's picture from the church's dossier on Torrino. Her name was Viv Schwartz, Torrino's right-hand woman and an old family friend. There was a rumor that he'd been sleeping with her since he was a teenager, even though he'd also been rumored to have bedded half of Hollywood's young starlets.

"Hello, Marina," Viv said through her teeth.

"Hello, Vivian." Marina kissed her on the cheek.

"And this is?" Viv looked Keenan up and down, her eyes obviously liking what they saw.

"This is Mr. Edwards," Marina lied, "my new head of security."

"Ah," Viv frowned, though her Botoxed forehead showed no wrinkles. "I'm sorry to hear about Steven. Absolutely tragic."

"Yes," Marina agreed, "such a waste."

"Just this way." Viv led them through the living room.

After walking down a long, warmly lit hallway, they stepped through two sliding glass doors leading to a large circular room. The room's front half was made of stone walls and columns, giving the space an old, earthy look. Beyond that room terracottas and browns surrendered to modern glass walls and steel support beams running up to a high-pitched, glass-domed roof that looked nothing like the Old World estate outside.

In the center a perfect circle glistened, ten feet deep of brilliant-blue water. Lying on a raft, wearing just shorts and shades, body glistening with oil, was movie star, Max Torrino, lounging without a care in the world.

As they made their way along the wooden deck toward the pool, Viv cleared her throat for Torrino's attention.

"Ah," he said, taking off the shades and sitting up on the raft, "Marina! How are you?"

Torrino hopped off the raft, dove underwater, swam to the side of his pool, and ascended the steps, smiling his billion-dollar smile. He was young, perfectly sculpted, and had blue eyes that women, and a fair share of gay men, swooned over. While Marina definitely found him attractive, his personality, his *true* personality, was toxic enough to make him repugnant.

"I'm good." Marina shook his hand.

Torrino didn't acknowledge Keenan, which didn't surprise Marina at all. Keenan was seen as *the help*, and therefore unworthy of acknowledgment. Before she'd come up in the church, Torrino had viewed her in the same dismissive way.

"So, what brings you to Montecito?" Torrino walked to one of the lounge chairs along the pool's side, grabbed a thick white towel, and began to dry himself.

"Is it possible to speak in private?"

Marina didn't need to look at Viv to know the woman was fixing her with a polar-cap stare.

Torrino's face faltered for a moment before he returned the movie star smile to his face. "Sure, we can talk alone. Come on, I'll show you my new office."

He finished drying off, grabbed a robe from the bar in the back of the room, then led them through another pair of sliding glass doors along a hallway also decorated with giant slabs of stone.

The estate, downstairs at least, was a beautiful blend of past and present. The furniture was mostly custom, except for the Louise Bradley, Fleming & Howland, and Parnian pieces that Marina hated herself for admiring.

They headed up the stairs, then down a long hallway toward the west side of the house where they stopped in front of a pair of large ebony wooden doors carved with ornate flourishes.

Torrino opened the door and entered first. Marina followed into a room the size of two of her master bedrooms sandwiched together.

If downstairs was past meets present, Torrino's upstairs office was future modern, with black metals blended with rich dark woods, a plush crimson carpet, and five Bang & Olufsen monitors mounted on the walls. One of the monitors — not much more than a sheet of glass surrounded by steel piping— showed a 24/7 cable news channel feed while the other four monitors, two on the back wall and one on each side, all showed what looked to be glowing purple lava flowing into black before melting into other colors. Marina wasn't sure if it was supposed to be art or some sort of screensaver.

She had expected to see movie posters of Torrino's many hits, or perhaps his two Oscars prominently featured but was surprised that the room was absent of any declarations of his stardom. Instead, a long recessed bookcase ate the bottom half of the back wall, though Marina couldn't decode a single title from where she stood. She wondered if Torrino had actually read any of the books, or if they were only for show.

As Keenan trailed her, Torrino put a hand on Ed's chest and looked at Marina. "I thought you wanted to talk alone."

"It's OK," she said to Keenan, hoping he'd not cause a scene ... yet.

Keenan nodded, stepped outside the door, and said, "I'll be right out here."

Torrino closed the door on Keenan's face, then led Marina toward a massive desk in the room's center — empty save for a silver laptop with two chairs on either side of it.

This is his meeting space, cold, dark, fancy. Just like him.

Torrino sat with his back to the rear wall, and Marina sat opposite him.

He folded his hands in front of him, smiling. "So, what do you want, Marina Harmon?"

She wasn't sure which way to go: slow and smooth talk him into giving her what she wanted or short and direct, hoping to earn his respect. Torrino was too used to the Hollywood game, and was far better at it than Marina could ever hope to be. Feeding his ego would backfire, and likely piss him off.

"I know you're busy," she said, "so I'll cut to the chase. I need the vial my father gave you."

"The vial?" Torrino feigned ignorance fast enough to fool probably anybody else. But not Marina.

"Yes, the vial my father asked you to hold onto. I need it."

"Ah," he said, "the vial. Wow, it's been so long. I'd almost forgotten about that old thing."

Torrino maintained eye contact even as his face went through the motions of trying to con her. Marina could tell he was fishing for a reaction, perhaps trying to judge the vial's true value — if he didn't already know.

She said nothing, waiting for him to nudge the conversation.

Torrino leaned back in his chair, crossing his fingers on the desk, also saying nothing. He could barely conceal the smile playing at the corners of his mouth. He was enjoying this moment too much for Marina's comfort. She wondered how much crow he expected her to chew on, and what he'd demand in exchange?

"Tell me," he said, "why do you want the vial?"

"My father asked me to get it."

"Really?" Torrino said, thick eyebrows arching, his smile spreading wider. "Because I specifically remember him asking me to hold onto it shortly before he died. He said he couldn't trust anyone else. Including you."

Marina was surprised by his directness. She figured they'd dance around the issue a while longer, perhaps he'd maintain a false sincerity throughout the meeting. But no, Torrino was laying his cards on the table.

"Yes, well he's since asked me to get the vials."

"*Vials?*" Torrino said, seeming genuinely surprised. "So there's more than one? How many are there?"

"I'm not at liberty to say."

A small laugh, then, "No, of course not. Yet you expect me to hand mine over."

"Yes, Mr. Torrino."

"Tell me, Marina, when exactly did your father ask you to get the vials? And why didn't he put something in his will regarding this supposed wish?"

"He asked me a few weeks ago."

Torrino broke into a laugh, not bothering to hide his disbelief or contempt. "A few weeks, you say?"

"Yes, he came back and said that we're all in danger, and that I had to collect the vials."

"And do what with them? What kind of danger?"

Both Acevedo and Keenan had said to tell Torrino nothing. He was too big, with too many connections. Any hope of containing the story — the real story, not the media-hyped, random-acts-of-violence story — would be dead if they told one of the top five movie stars in the world.

She shook her head.

"Ah, *not at liberty to say*, right?"

Marina nodded.

"I always felt like this vial was something very powerful. Something from the Great All-Seeing. But your father wouldn't confirm it. I think perhaps he thought I might open the vial if he did. And he was right, I might have. But I wanted to prove myself to him, prove that he was right to trust in me. So I never opened it. But man, it was sooo hard not to. Just being near the vial makes me feel so damned alive!"

Torrino slapped his chest to punctuate his virility. "A lot of people laugh at us, laugh at our beliefs, even though they don't know half of what we truly believe. But I *never* doubted your father, Marina. Never. Can you say the same?"

"No, you're right." She shook her head. "I did have my doubts. But I think that strengthens my faith."

"Yeah," he said with a light laugh. Marina wasn't sure if Torrino was agreeing with her, or calling bullshit.

"Please," she said, "I wouldn't ask you for the vial, but my father said I had to get them, and that the world was counting on me to do this ... *for him.*"

Torrino ran a hand through his still-wet hair and massaged his temples as if agonizing over her request. Marina could practically smell his refusal.

He stood and circled his desk, then paused to Marina's left, just inches away, looking down at her as he leaned his ass against the desk's corner. Marina's eyes drifted down his sculpted abs, stopping at the large bulge in his shorts.

She looked back up, too quickly, at his eyes.

He smiled.

Smug bastard!

He crossed his hands over his chest, casually, not bothering to hide his erection. It took a certain bravado to sit and insult someone sitting eye level with your balls. She could easily hurt him for the way he was treating her, but he knew she wouldn't. He reveled in that knowledge, letting his cock stick straight out, daring her to hit him or move away.

"You know, I always liked you." Torrino stared down the front of Marina's shirt at her cleavage.

She didn't bother to adjust, refusing to surrender in any way.

"And," he continued, "I think your father wanted you and me to be together. He tried talking me into dating you a few times, but I always felt like it might be too weird. He thought of me like a son, you know?"

"Yes," Marina said, wondering where he was going.

"He took me under his wing after my first movie, when everyone was calling me the next big thing. Stardom had already gone to my head, and though I didn't know it I was vulnerable, in with a bad crowd, and soon strung out on too many drugs. My agent was a Don King of corruption, and I had an army of hangers-on all dragging me down. They were, as your father said, 'suffocating my star.'"

He continued. "But your father saw me as more than a flash in the pan. He saw my potential and helped mold me into the man I am today."

"You've done very well for yourself," Marina said, sincerely. "I know he was proud of you."

"Yes, yes he was. He was a far better father than my own deadbeat piece of shit, that's for sure. Josh Harmon was the father I *deserved*."

Marina nodded. "He was a good man."

"Yes," Torrino agreed. "And he was a far better father than you deserved."

Marina stifled her anger. Still, she could feel her cheeks burning. If she didn't need the vial, she would've stood and slapped Torrino across the face, or maybe kneed him in the groin.

Instead she kept her mouth shut, choking on crow.

He continued, not daring to let up. "You were always such a cunt."

Torrino kept his eyes on her the entire time, like a monster toying with prey.

Marina knew for a fact that he'd been violent with a few ex-girlfriends; it was all in the dossiers that the church kept on anyone with power. The same dossier asserting that without the church's programs, Torrino would be a raging sociopath. *Whoops, too late.* It was the sort of thing Marina could've leaked to the press if she were a petty person, but she'd only play that card if she had to.

For now, she kept saying nothing.

"Your father didn't deserve you either. You were, or rather *are*, a cancer in the church. There are people looking to have you removed, especially after this whole stink with your former head of security dying under mysterious circumstances. You know this, right?"

Marina didn't have a chance to answer before Torrino barreled forward.

"Tell me, did he do it?"

"Who? Did what?"

"Your new head of security, this agro guy you came in with. You hired, or promoted him rather quickly, eh? So soon after your lover's death. So, is this your new man? Is he the one that did that to your face? Or was it Steven? Ah, I get it. Steven punched you, and this new guy killed Steven. That sound right? I bet Papa would be proud, you fucking whore."

Whore?!

Marina stood, her face on fire and heart pounding out of her chest.

Torrino held his position as she stood, just inches from Marina. She had to push the chair back in order not to bump into him. He seemed like he expected her to fall back, afraid.

She'd stand her ground, screw him.

He was about an inch shorter than her, maybe two, and it thrilled her to know that he noticed. Marina tried to stand straighter as she bore down on Torrino, hoping her strength was making his cock flaccid like the tiny man he was.

"I always knew you hated women."

"Not all women, just whores like you who don't know their place."

"My place?" she said, getting in his face. "My *place?!*"

"Yeah," he said, refusing to back down, eyes red, glaring into hers. "When your father died, you were supposed to go off and enjoy his money, let one of the other leaders take over the day-to-day operations, repair some of the damage you were already starting to do. But *nooo*, you had to go whole hog with your plans to sully the church and turn it into some bullshit liberal charity, throwing money to fucking mongrels who don't work for a thing."

"Oh, wow, so a womanizer *and* a racist, elitist scumbag? Wow, real class act, buddy."

Torrino stood his ground, fogging Marina's face with his breath. "You know they laugh at you, right? All the church leaders think you're a fucking disgrace to the organization! You'd never have this job if your father hadn't given it to you."

Marina shook her head, nearly as fast as her racing heart. Her leg was shaking; she hated confrontations like these, but damned if she would let this asshole treat her like he treated everyone else with the misfortune of living in a lower station.

She inched ever closer, putting her face inches from his.

"You wanna know something, Max? My father didn't love you. He didn't even respect you. He felt sorry for you. He pitied you. Because you were a nothing when he met you, and you're a nothing now. All the money in the world won't make you a tenth of the man my father was."

"Yeah, well I guess he respected me more than he did you, or he would've given you the vial and not me. Now, if you'll excuse me, cunt, I've gotta get back to my tan."

Torrino started to walk past her, his smug grin like a kick to her gut.

"No!" she said, "you *will* give me that vial!"

Marina reached out to grab Torrino's shoulder and turn him around.

He spun fast and ferocious, like a predator, punching Marina hard in the jaw, where Keenan had punched her before. Her face exploded in pain.

She fell back, her head hitting the desk, hard.

Marina cried out as she sank to the carpet, feeling dizzy, weak, like the world was blurring, darkening at the edges of her vision.

Torrino looked down at her with disgusted rage, before kicking Marina in the ribs. Pain tore through her body. She cried out with the one word she was able to form.

"*Help!*"

* * * *

CHAPTER 2
EDWARD KEENAN

Ed stood outside Torrino's office, pacing, eavesdropping on the conversation via the earpiece connected to Marina's mic as the actor's steroid case, the bodyguard with a buzz cut and no neck, guarded the door like Ed might decide to rush into the room.

Ed had every intention of letting Marina try to get the vials first, as he didn't need the shit storm he'd get from his superiors if things went south with Max Torrino.

But then shit went south anyway.

Ed had his gun in the bodyguard's face the moment Marina screamed.

The bodyguard froze, hand reaching for the pistol inside his black jacket.

"Is he worth dying for?" Keenan asked.

The bodyguard's eyes widened, frightened to die. He shook his head no.

"Good, take your gun out, by the barrel, then hand it over nice and slow," Ed ordered. "I'm with Homeland Security. We have this place surrounded."

The bodyguard did as instructed. Ed grabbed the man's Colt Python and barked, "Open the door!"

Behind the door, Marina let out another cry as the guard followed orders.

Keenan followed the man into the room and saw Torrino about to kick Marina.

"Freeze!" Ed yelled, aiming his gun at the movie star. It was almost surreal pointing a gun at a man whom Ed had seen in countless action movies as the guy who always outsmarted his enemies. Pulling a gun on Torrino in a movie was the quickest way to get your ass handed to you.

But this wasn't a movie, and Ed was no more afraid of Max Torrino than he was the boogeyman.

Torrino turned, eyes wild, hair mussed, stunned that someone was stopping him.

"Get away from her!" Keenan said, "Homeland Security."

"Homeland Security? What the hell is this about?"

"Get in your chair," Ed said. Then, pointing to the guard, added, "You get in the corner and keep your hands in the air. Lower them or turn around, and I'll shoot you. Understand?"

The bodyguard nodded.

Ed watched as Torrino went to his seat. Ed then turned and locked the doors to the office.

"Hands on your desk, palms down," he snapped. "Move 'em, and I'll shoot you."

Torrino sighed as he put his hands on the table, rolling his eyes.

Ed bent down and looked at Marina. She seemed woozy, her jaw screaming red where Torrino had apparently punched her. He felt a sting of guilt as he looked at her jaw, seeing one bruise shading another.

"You OK?" he asked.

She tried to stand, eyes tearing, pissed and wanting to go after Torrino.

"You sit down a minute," Ed said. "I've got this."

Ed helped Marina stand, set her in a chair opposite Torrino, then turned to the celebrity. "So, you're a big Hollywood tough guy, eh? Hitting women?"

"Fuck you," Torrino sneered. "I want my lawyer."

Outside the office door, Ed heard Torrino's assistant yell, "I've called the police, Mr. Torrino. They'll be here shortly. I suggest you all leave here before they arrive."

"We *are* the police!," Ed growled back. "I'm with Homeland Security. Now shut your mouth and get your ass downstairs."

Ed wished he could see the woman's face. She'd been such a bitch when they arrived, as arrogant as Mr. Hollywood himself.

"I want my lawyer," Torrino repeated, glaring up at Ed.

"Oh, you didn't hear me? I said I'm with Homeland Security. You *have no rights*. Here's what you're going to do. You're going to cooperate and give us the vial before I have this place crawling with agents and leading you out your front door in cuffs."

"You can't arrest me. Mr. Harmon gave me the vial. It's mine. And besides, it's not even here. It's in a safe deposit box at the bank."

"Bullshit," Marina said, surprising Ed. "I can tell he's lying. He wouldn't trust it in a bank. It's here, somewhere. No way he leaves it out of sight. He wouldn't trust anyone."

Ed saw something creep across Torrino's face — a look that confirmed Marina's accusation. She'd figured him out, and he didn't like it.

Torrino shook his head, "I'm not handing it over. Do whatever you want, you're not getting shit."

"Oh, you'll hand it over." Keenan leaned forward and sneered into his phony Hollywood smile.

Ed saw movement in the corner, the bodyguard's right arm creeping down.

Ed fired a shot into the monitor behind the man on the adjoining wall. "Keep your hands up!"

The guard jumped when the monitor screen shattered, then did as he was told.

"Fuck!" Torrino screamed, starting to stand. "Do you know how much that costs?!"

Ed shoved the gun in his face and barked, "Sit down!"

"Do you know who I am?" Torrino yelled, his face turning beet red. "Do you know what I can do to you? To *both* of you?"

"Yeah, you're a guy who gets paid a lot of money to play pretend and shoot bad guys and fuck starlets. And oh yeah, you're a lot shorter in person. And you like to hurt women. *Yeah*, I know who you are. But all I care about is that vial. So you're going to lead me to it and hand it over, or else."

"Why the hell do you even want it?" Torrino whined.

"It's a matter of national security, and you, sir, are impeding our attempts to preserve said security. That makes you a terrorist, son."

"I want to know why you need it."

Keenan was tired of playing patty cake with this bastard, but figured the man was clinging to his fragile ego and needed a win, something he could cling to. If that meant trading the vial for some information, Keenan had no problem throwing the mongrel some scraps.

"Have you seen the violence on TV? The mass shootings at the mall, at the school, that woman who tried to bite a child's face off? These people have been infected with what's inside the vial. It's a highly dangerous biological weapon."

"Bullshit," Torrino said. "No way Josh Harmon would have a biological weapon, or give it to me, or anyone else, to hold onto."

"It's complicated," Ed said, "but believe me — if we don't get the vials back into custody, millions of people will die."

Torrino stared at them, his grin finally fading as he seemed to consider Ed's words. He looked at Marina, and something twisted in his face, an anger he couldn't dismiss. He shook his head no.

"I want my lawyer."

Marina shouted, "He's telling you the truth, Max! Innocent people will die if we don't hand over the vials. Do you want to be responsible for that?"

"I'm *not* responsible. Whatever happens happens, it's what's meant to be. As the Great All-Seeing intended."

"You can't be that heartless," Marina said. "You're willing to let innocent men, women, and children die because of what? Some stupid belief that the Great All-Seeing won't let bad shit happen?"

"It won't happen to me, or any of the other enlightened. *We'll* be fine. It's all ordained. Perhaps the world needs a proper flushing."

Ed shook his head. "You can't be serious. Are you stupid? I mean, I know you Hollywood types will believe anything, but this is some world-class high school misfit nihilism shit here."

"Why should I care about anyone else? You think I don't know what people think of me, think of *us*, Marina? They laugh at our religion, mock our beliefs, and they thought your father was a fraud. But it looks like he'll have the last laugh, eh? No, I'm tired of being everyone's dancing monkey. Fuck humanity, and fuck you, too, Marina. You can die with the rest of the unenlightened flotsam."

Torrino grinned his big, stupid Hollywood smile, like he was sitting on a talk show host's couch, discussing his latest flick, oblivious as he was evil.

Ed had had enough.

He reached into the loop on his belt, fingered the handle of his black carbon blade, and whipped it out, slicing across Torrino's left cheek.

Torrino screamed, fingers up as the flap of skin fell open and blood began to gush down his face and onto his neck.

Keenan glanced over at the guard who stared back with terrified eyes. Keenan pointed his gun at him and said, "Staaay." The man turned back around.

In his ear, Keenan heard Luther ask, "What did you do?"

"Don't worry. What's the situation with the cops?"

"The agency is taking care of it. We're good."

Keenan smiled, and leaned closer to Torrino. "My man just said the cops are getting sent home. That means we have all night to give your plastic surgeon the biggest hard-on of his life. Now you might not give a shit about most people, and that doesn't surprise me at all, but as long as there are people, you'll care about your appearances. And as long as there are people around to watch your stupid movies, you wanna be making as much money as you can, right? So here's the deal, *Max*. When I'm done with you, the only role you're gonna be able to land is a remake of *The Elephant Man*. Do I make myself clear?"

"You're fucking crazy!" Torrino held the flap of flesh to his cheek, as if it might mend itself back if pressed hard or long enough.

"You're right," Ed said, "I am crazy because I *love* my job. Especially when I get to put little bitches like you who *play* tough guys on the big screen in *your place*."

Ed turned and winked at Marina.

She smiled.

"So, what's it gonna be?" Ed asked. "The vial, or round two of Stabby Pokey?"

Torrino nodded yes, tears in his eyes.

Sometimes, Ed really did love his job.

* * * *

CHAPTER 3
MARY OLSON

Mary stared up at her bedroom's darkness. She could feel hot sun outside the drawn curtains, trying to pour light into her room, but wanted nothing of it, nor the people in her cabin — Brent, Teagan, Ben, and Becca.

She could hear them outside, discussing Jade's death and how they couldn't tell Ed that his daughter was gone because Bolton had killed all communication between the island and the mainland. It was wrong — that the people in charge were choosing operational security over Ed's rights as a parent.

There were also whispers about Mary. She couldn't make out much of it, other than how horrible everyone felt about her losing Paola.

Every now and then someone would come to the door, gently knocking to check on her needs. Mary said no thank you each time, wanting nothing more than to be left alone.

But Desmond had asked them to stay while he was back at the facility working to get the situation under control. The island was on lockdown. No ferries in or out. No shipments from the mainland. Civilians were told to stay in their cabins while the Guardsmen scoured the island for infected and Desmond inspected everyone.

It was all meaningless to Mary.

Paola was dead, murdered right in front of her.

Mary was trapped in a vortex of vicious thoughts. Waves of memory collided, too many things she'd not thought of in years. She flashed back to the first time her baby had stared up into her eyes; then to the time when Paola had drawn something for Mary, eager to be like her mommy and make cards; and then back to a rainy Saturday morning when she, Ryan, and Paola let morning turn into afternoon without leaving their bed, watching cartoons on TV. Such a silly little thing, that one moment of inactivity would be among Mary's most cherished moments. A sign of happier times when the family was together. Alone, those memories were heartbreaking. But then they blended with darker thoughts — the imagined memories for her daughter's future that could now never be. Paola's first job, her first boyfriend, going to college, doing something she loved for a living, perhaps exploring the world. Her life erased in a flash by some alien entity bent on humanity's destruction.

And for what?

Why had they targeted humans?

Why were they so hell bent on using Mary's daughter as a pawn?

It wasn't just the aliens. Even the horrible people at The Sanctuary had tormented them for no reason other than some *top-of-the-food-chain* bullshit.

Mary wanted to scream. Wanted to punch things. Hell, she wanted to shoot something.

But screams invited company. And whom would she shoot? The man who murdered her daughter had been shot dead the moment he pulled his trigger.

Mary had no target for her wrath, no well to pour her grief. Nothing to fill her soul's wretched void.

She turned over, squeezing her pillow as tightly as she could, and screamed into it.

* * * *

CHAPTER 4
BORICIO WOLFE

Boricio woke to a world of blurry pain.

He tried to move, but couldn't.

He panicked, looking around, barely able to move his head, trying to suss out his situation.

Boricio was in a bed, in what had to be a hotel room. A nice hotel, from what he could see in his limited view.

The last thing Boricio remembered was being in a motel while Rose, Mary, and Paola had gone off to see that weird-ass cult chick from the Church of Original Design.

What the hell happened?

Was I in an accident?

"Hello?" he called out, barely able to push breath into voice.

He turned, coughing blood violently onto the bed.

Boricio tried moving his fingers, his hands, his toes, anything, but his body couldn't hear him. The more he focused, the more tired he felt.

Boricio noticed a tube running from his hand back to an IV bag hanging from a pole beside the bed. A peek under the covers would probably show a catheter moving piss from his prick to a bag beneath the bed. But there were no wires or machines, so far as he could tell, meaning that despite the medical equipment Boricio wasn't in a hospital.

He drifted off, exhausted.

When Boricio woke, he had a bit more strength to his voice. He called out, "Hey!" And then, "Hello?!"

* * * *

CHAPTER 5
LUCA HARDING

Luca sat at the foot of their occupied summer home's stairs, wondering when Boricio would finally wake up.

The house belonged to a man named Parker Davison, founder of P.K. Davison Industries, a multinational company with its fingers in a bit of everything, including, Rose said, elections across the country. Davison was seventy-five years old and had been on the verge of suicide a few months ago when *Steven* befriended, infected, and ushered him into the Church of Original Design.

Rose had turned to Davison before getting Boricio out of jail, requesting his summer home in Highland Park — with sweeping views of the San Gabriel Mountains — to use as their new headquarters. It was better than a hotel, as they didn't have to worry about suspicious staffers, and Davison rarely used the house himself, so they didn't have to worry about *him* being around either.

The home was two stories and well kept for a place so rarely used. Most of the furniture was made of dark wood and looked cozy, reminding Luca of his mom and the magazines she used to read.

Luca was spending a lot of time alone as Rose was getting Art accustomed to the alien inside him. She was also often busy meditating, during which time she was reaching out to other elements of The Darkness, trying to strengthen its core and prevent its weakest members from doing anything rash that would draw suspicion from the government agents searching for them.

Sitting in the house alone, Luca couldn't help but think about his parents, and his sister, Anna. Not just his real family, who had died in a car accident years ago, but the other Luca's mom and dad, the ones who had been raising him unaware that their real son had evolved into something else, his place taken by a child impostor from another world.

Luca also felt horrible that he had to run away after he killed the bullies. His family had to be worried sick about their son, never knowing they were worried about, or perhaps even mourning, a fraud. Their real son had become something they couldn't comprehend.

He imagined them sitting up at night, sick with worry, wondering if their son would ever come home.

Luca wanted to call them, to let them know he was OK. It was the least he could do.

But Rose had refused to let him. She said they couldn't risk the police tracing the call and coming to get him. After all, Luca was wanted for murder.

It would ruin their plans to secure the vials if he were in custody. Even worse, the moment someone realized that Luca had The Darkness inside him, his family would be doomed. They would be picked up then shipped off to Black Island or some other secret experimental place. They could be murdered into silence.

No one could know about The Darkness. The government wouldn't allow it, Rose explained. And the government had killed far greater numbers to keep lesser secrets.

Still, Luca longed to call home. And it surprised him to realize that it wasn't just to ease their minds, but a hollow part of Luca missed them. He knew they weren't *really* his family, but he'd lived with them since his arrival, and had come to love them as if they were his. After spending so long with the silence in his head, Luca was desperate for the sound of their voices.

The Darkness spoke inside his head: *You know you can't call them.*

I know. I just miss them.

It's odd how your species can be so disconnected from one another and yet remain so bonded. Why is that?

I dunno.

When we evolve the species, all will be connected. Things such as misunderstanding, violence, and war will all be relegated to the past. You will all truly be one with each other. When you wonder how your family is, you'll be able to reach out in your head and know. What you're feeling now is the result of mankind struggling to be something more — to be part of a whole. In time, we will make that happen, Luca. In time, all will be one.

So, what will happen when we evolve? I mean, are we no longer ourselves?

Self is an odd human construct. A need to identify as something more than what you are. It's as silly as each part of your body wanting to declare itself a different being. What if your finger tomorrow wanted to go off and be its own person, perhaps change its name? I know it's hard to understand in your current form, but there is an elegant beauty to all being one.

But I like being myself. I like the way my father would tell corny jokes. I liked the way Mom would make me feel special. And I loved Anna.

When they evolve, do they stop being who they are? And what happens to me? Am I like I am now, which is kinda like me but with someone else inside? Or will I change again?

Do you feel like yourself now?

Yes. But I'm not alone in my head. You're always there. I get the feeling that when you and Rose do whatever it is you're planning, the part of me that's here will go away and it'll just be you. Is that true?

You will still be you, but not.

That doesn't make sense. Will my parents and sister still be themselves? Or will they see themselves as The Darkness?

Evolution will leave us no need for names. We think as one. I know this is difficult to understand, but once you've evolved, all will make sense and nothing will seem scary. This is a learning experience for our species as well as yours. I see nothing in our collective memories to suggest that we've ever evolved a species in quite this way.

So, this might not work? This could end just as badly as it did on the other world? Everything could be gone?

We will not allow that to happen again. We will make this work. The Darkness on the other world was misguided, seeking only to destroy and consume the land. But that can't work without exhausting both humans and our own species. We must find a more sustainable way. And together, Luca, we will.

Art entered through the front door, carrying four grocery bags, two per hand.

"Wanna give me a hand?"

"OK," Luca said, glad to be pulled from the depressing conversation in his head and happy for distraction.

After Luca helped him unpack the groceries Art asked if he'd like to help him make chicken fried rice.

Luca helped Art with lunch, wondering what kinds of conversations the old man was having with The Darkness in *his* head. How comfortable was he with this whole notion of evolving humanity? Before now, Luca hadn't dared ask.

He didn't feel safe, especially with Rose always around. The Darkness controlled her, but Luca couldn't help feeling that her Darkness was a different strain. It didn't feel the same as the alien that coursed through his blood. In fact, Luca wondered if his own Darkness was all that dark. It wasn't forcing him to do evil things, and seemed to have regard for his feelings. It felt more like a neutral presence than something out to demolish humanity.

Luca wondered if perhaps that was his way of rationalizing the things that were happening inside him.

Of course nobody wants to be the bad guy. But maybe bad guys don't see themselves as all that bad.

Don't think so much about it, Luca, The Darkness answered in his head.

Where's Rose?

The Darkness answered. *She is in her room, reaching out to others.*

So, she's busy. Too busy to monitor our conversations?

Why?

Luca didn't need to answer The Darkness. It was a step ahead of his thoughts, warning him away from the conversation. But Luca didn't listen.

He looked up at Art and asked, "How do you feel about our mission?"

Art was slicing chicken breasts on the wooden cutting board. He looked up, "What do you mean?"

"You know we're trying to evolve the species. And Rose came to you because of some book you wrote about Genghis Khan, because you said the man was actually good for humanity overall, right?"

"Yes."

"So, how do you feel about that? How do you feel with this alien in your head? Does it talk to you?"

"Yes, it does. It was odd at first to feel my innermost thoughts exposed, but I quickly grew used to it. You learn not to care when someone is so accepting of your every flaw. You get over your ego."

Luca didn't want to get into a debate on self versus collective, though he was curious if Art shared his concerns about surrendering his identity to the alien.

Art continued. "But then I started seeing my situation — our situation — as an opportunity. I have this thing inside my head that knows so much more than I ever could. What a blessing it is to converse with an alien species! And while its own memory as a species is spotty, it has the collective memory of all that it has absorbed or infected on both worlds. I've been tapping into the minds of scholars and psychopaths alike, mining a true understanding of our peoples' full breadth of differences and similarities."

"And?" Luca pressed, "How do you feel about our mission?"

"I think that mankind will destroy itself if we *don't* intervene. We have a moral obligation to evolve our species. Now I have a question for you, young man."

"Yes?"

"What do you know about that man upstairs?"

"Boricio?"

"Yes." Art's face wrinkled in a grimace.

"I've seen some of what others remember of him. And I have some of my own memories of another version of him. He was my brother on the other world. We were both adopted by the same man, Will Bishop."

"Yes," Art said. "I've seen the memories, too."

"OK, so what is it you're really asking me, Mr. Morgan?"

"I like you, kid," Art chuckled. "You don't beat around the bush."

Luca smiled.

Art said, "I'm wondering why Rose chose to give the vials to *him*? He is a horrible, wretched example of humanity. A true monster."

"Some would say the same thing about Genghis Khan, right?"

"Yes, but Genghis Khan had a vision, and improved the lives of others."

"Those he didn't kill?" Luca countered, dipping into The Darkness's collective memories concerning the military leader.

"History has many examples of people who through fate or choice have been on the wrong side of war. But make no mistake, Khan wasn't a cold-blooded murderer killing victims at random. He was leading people against barbarians who would've been stuck in the Dark Ages forever had he not come along. The world needed him to advance humanity. Just as the world needs us now."

"OK, and you think Boricio isn't worthy?"

"No, I do not. He is a fine killing machine, I'll give you that. His unflinching ability to do what must be done is a rare trait that will serve us well against our enemies. But I believe that Rose should infect and control him so we can do what must be done. She shouldn't give him a vial."

"What's the harm in giving him a vial?"

"As I understand it, The Darkness responds to those it comes into contact with. We shape it and whether it's used as a tool for creation or destruction. You and I are good people, Luca. Not perfect, of course, but more good than bad. We see humanity as something worth saving, and that turns The Darkness into something more like Light."

"But we're not Light," Luca said. "The Light doesn't want to evolve humanity, does it? Rose said it wants to destroy us, that it wants to erase itself from this world so there isn't a threat."

"No, we're not The Light. But we can be something in between. We are the greater good that must inflict itself upon the world in order to save humans from themselves. Introducing a man like Boricio is a sure recipe for disaster.

That monster is chaos. Unleashing a more powerful version of him is tantamount to handing a child a nuclear missile with a big red launch button that says PRESS ME. Don't you agree?"

"I dunno," Luca shrugged. "I haven't even talked to him yet. I know he's helped a lot of people, and that the other Luca fixed the thing inside him that made him so bad."

"Can you ever really fix evil, Luca?" Art slid the chicken into the wok with the already cooked rice and started slicing onions.

"I dunno." Luca watched Art add eggs, spices, and soy sauce into the wok, wondering why the alien inside him was silent.

Why are you so quiet? What do you think about Boricio? Should we give him a vial?

I think there is an equal case for either side.

Some help you are. I thought you could give some mathematical answer or something about the odds of this blowing up in our face.

I could, but Boricio is too wild a variable.

Luca went to check on the rice. Before he reached it, a scream erupted upstairs — Boricio.

"Hey!" Boricio shouted. "Hello?!"

Art yanked the wok from the fire and bounded up the stairs far faster than a man his age, should be able to move, even with decades removed. Luca followed.

Art opened the door to reveal Boricio in bed, sheets pulled up to his waist, flesh on his chest purple and rotten with stitches where Rose had sewn the wounds along his chest and face. He was paralyzed from the neck down, his face warped with frustration.

* * * *

CHAPTER 6
BORICIO WOLFE

The door burst open, and an old man entered, looking down at Boricio. Behind him, Boricio was surprised to see Luca in the doorway, looking afraid to come in.

"Luca?" Boricio asked, confused, wondering why he was back to being young. "Where are Rose and the girls? They OK? How'd you get here?"

The old man wrinkled his nose at Boricio. "I'll be right back," he said with no emotion, then pushed Luca out the door.

"Oh, come the fuck on!" Boricio shouted, coughing bloody phlegm.

He was pissed that he couldn't remember dick about shit, and hoped that everyone was OK. They must have been ambushed by one of them crazy alien fuckers. That's the only thing that made sense. Someone got the drop on old Boricio, and shot him from behind.

Then why the hell ain't I in a hospital?

Boricio looked around the room. As best he could see with his limited motion, he was in someone's house.

Maybe this is Luca's place? Maybe that old man is his grandpa?

But why not bring me to a hospital? And how the hell did Luca find me? I ain't seen him since we got back.

A horrifying thought slithered into Boricio's mind: Perhaps he'd already been to a hospital. Maybe he'd been in a coma and resigned to hospice care at home. What if the old man was some sort of nurse or doctor?

"Luca!" Boricio shouted, hard enough to invite more coughing and blood.

The bedroom door opened to Rose.

"Oh, Morning Rose!" Boricio said, tears wetting his eyes, grateful to see her OK. "I thought something happened to you."

Rose came to his side, looking down at Boricio with a tentative smile. "Everything's fine," she said, running a hand through his hair.

Boricio flinched at her touch, his head pounding hard enough that her brush felt like a wallop.

"I'm sorry," Rose said. "How are you feeling?"

"How's it look like I'm feelin'?" he said, harsher than he meant. "I'm sorry. I'm just ... so confused. What happened? Where the hell are we?"

"You were attacked by some police," she said.

"Cuntstables did this shit to me? What the hell? *Why?*"

Boricio wondered if his past had been pursuing long enough to finally catch him. Had some cop linked him to any number of old murders, maybe an innocent from the old days, or more recently, from a fucker who was begging karma to claim him? He hoped not. The last thing he wanted was for Rose to know who the real Boricio was. She was an angel. The sweetest woman he'd ever known. There was no way someone so pure could stay with a monster like him.

"I don't know," she said.

"How did I wind up here? And ... where the fuck am I?"

"One of the officers saved you, brought you to us at the hotel, but then left before we could ask any questions. You were in a coma, but we got you help. You're recovering. As for where we are, we're home, at a friend of mine's. A writer named Arthur Morgan. He lives in the area and said we could stay here until you're better. I'm afraid to fly you in this condition, not until we have another doctor check on you."

"Why the hell am I in some dude's house instead of a hospital?" Nothing made sense, and everything felt like a nail in his head.

Boricio cringed.

Rose went to the dresser and returned with a hypodermic.

"Here, this'll make you better."

"Whoa, whoa, what's in there? And when did you become Florence Fucking Nightingale?"

Rose laughed. "I'm perfectly capable of taking care of you, sweetie."

She slid the needle into Boricio's arm, though he couldn't feel a thing, and pressed the plunger until whatever medicine Rose was administering entered his bloodstream.

"I'm so confused," Boricio said. "Why are ... "

Words escaped him as a pleasant warmth spread through his head. Pain ebbed, replaced by a surging tide of emotions — joy, love, and happiness that his Rose was here taking care of him.

Sadness came next, and Boricio felt horrible for being a vegetable while she was forced to take care of him.

"I'm so sorry this happened," he said, staring into her deep-green eyes.

"Don't be silly. It wasn't your fault. I don't know why it happened."

"Am I paralyzed?"

"Yes, but the doctor said it's only temporary."

"Really?" A wave of relief soothed his sorrow. Boricio broke into tears, thanking her more, feeling drunk like a fool but not giving a fuck.

Boricio felt like he was forgetting something, but his emotions were jumbled like shit in a hoarder's closet, and he was so happy to be with Rose everything else seemed too small to matter.

Boricio remembered what he'd been wondering before Rose came into the room. "Where are Mary and Paola? Are they OK?"

"Yes," she said. "They had to go home, but they send their love."

"How long have I been ... like this?"

"You really should get some sleep." She leaned forward and kissed him.

Though Rose wasn't wearing her usual perfume, she had a scent all her own. Boricio deeply inhaled as her hair fell across her cheek.

"Thank you, so much, sweetie," he said. "I ... "

**

Boricio woke to darkness, with no memory of falling asleep.

He vaguely remembered Rose giving him some medicine and some jumbled words after that. But the world was still so confusing. Best he could tell, someone attacked him, and for some reason Rose was keeping him out of the hospital.

Boricio wondered if it had been an alien. He remembered some infected fuckers at the one hotel. Maybe some aliens infected the police. Why they wanted him, he had no idea. He tried to remember if he'd told Rose about the aliens, but couldn't recall.

Maybe Mary had spilled the pintos, and that's why they were living a fugitive's life in some stranger's house.

That still didn't explain why Luca was with them.

Boricio looked at the clock beside his bed: 5:07 a.m. He longed for the morning sun and maybe some answers that would come when he could talk to Rose, or even Luca again.

More than answers, though, Boricio just wanted to see Rose again. He felt as if he'd been away from her forever. He wondered how long he'd been in a coma. How long he'd been paralyzed.

Boricio felt a horrible claustrophobia, unable to feel or move his limbs. The feeling felt oddly familiar, though that didn't make any sense.

He wondered if this was karma paying him back for years lived as a murder machine. Boricio didn't believe in karma, God, or any other hoodoo voodoo bullshit. That didn't mean his past couldn't have finally caught up. Ironic since now he was intent on doing the right thing. Had he gone his merry way, killing and fucking anything that crossed his path, karma might've kept lagging behind. Now, fixed by Luca and domesticated by Rose, Boricio was an easy target.

For the first time in Boricio's life he had people to care for. People he loved — if such a thing were possible. Not just Rose, but Mary, Paola, and even the Boy Wonder. They were a part of his fucked-as-shit family. And as good as it was to have friends, for the first time in his life, as Boricio lay helpless in bed absolutely helpless, that reality made him anxious.

For the first time he also feel guilt and shame for his past. Not the murders so much as the rapes. He prayed that Rose would never find out, that Paola wouldn't ever peek inside his mind and see what he'd really been. She knew he was a monster, but Boricio didn't want her, or Mary, or Rose to know just how monstrous he'd been.

Hell, he even felt bad about some of the murders. Not all of them. Plenty of fuckers had deserved to die. But there were some, innocents who just happened to be in the wrong place at the wrong time.

He flashed on something — an image of a girl he'd beheaded.

Another flash — her father, finding Boricio, angry at him, wanting revenge.

What the hell? I don't remember that.

Must be the drugs fucking with my head.

Lots of shit, still so fuzzy. Like he'd been dreaming for a long time and was awoken too early, still trying to untangle dream from reality.

He thought of Rose again and was so thankful that she was here with him, to help him through this. But even as he felt good, Boricio felt an unease he couldn't explain — a fear that didn't make sense.

Darkness is coming.

What the hell does that mean?

Love, for all the good it could do, was a weakness. And he was already weak enough, his body frozen in bed.

Boricio had to get better. Not just to get out off the fucking mattress, but so he could go back to protecting those he loved.

Yet, as he lay in the stillness of predawn, listening to the clock hum beside the bed and staring at its blue digital face, he couldn't help but feel that love had somehow left him frail. Boricio wondered if now he wasn't man enough to keep his *family* safe.

* * * *

CHAPTER 7
MARINA HARMON

"How are you doing?" Father Acevedo asked from the bucket seat across from Marina in the back of the van as Luther drove north toward the final vial.

"OK." She tried to smile, even though her ribs, jaw, and head were all throbbing, competing for which part of her body could claim the most pain.

"That should never have happened," he said, not even trying to whisper.

Marina looked up to see Keenan meet her eyes in the rearview, then he looked straight, staring at the road and into the setting sun.

"It's OK," she said, "we got the vial. And Keenan did beat the hell out of Max Torrino."

Acevedo sighed. "Well at least one good thing came out of it."

They'd been driving for about four hours, mostly in silence, neither she nor Acevedo happy to be hostages. Marina felt like the priest was hatching some plan. While she didn't know him well, Marina was familiar enough with Acevedo to be reasonably sure he had no intent to surrender. He'd given in, telling the agents where the vials were to keep Marina from harm, but she knew a temporary arrangement when she saw one. Acevedo wasn't going to let the agents take the vials.

Though the more Marina considered it, the better the idea seemed.

While Keenan had threatened to hurt her if they didn't cooperate and she wasn't about to add the agent to her Christmas card list, he *had* saved her from Torrino and had seemed personally offended that the movie star had hurt her. And it hadn't seemed like some macho-man-defending-a-woman sorta thing. Maybe a little, but there was definitely something else, too. Keenan seemed as outraged by entitled assholes as Marina was, particularly ones who abuse their power. There also seemed to be a genuine kindness just under his gruff exterior. He seemed like someone who had spent a long slice of his life battling assholes.

Marina wasn't sure how she could mine so much from their limited exchanges, yet could feel it nonetheless. Keenan *wasn't* a bad guy, even if half the pain in her jaw was from his punch.

Luther, on the other hand, Marina had yet to get a feel for. He seemed all muscle and little brains, but it was tough to glean much from his silence.

She looked back up at Acevedo, who was staring down at his handcuffs as if trying to figure a way to break free.

They were both cuffed to bars at seat level on either side of the van. The black metal appeared impossible to break without special equipment. There was a lock, which Marina figured a better criminal mind than hers could probably pick. She wondered if Acevedo had fashioned some sort of MacGyver way out, and was merely waiting for the right moment to break free.

She wished they weren't so close to the two agents. Any attempts at conversation would be easily overheard, otherwise she'd try to persuade the priest from his plot, whatever it might be. She'd tell him that maybe the government ought to have the vials, so they could fight these damned aliens in ways that they couldn't.

Sure, the government couldn't be trusted on most things, but what other options did they have? It wasn't like she and Acevedo had a plan or the ability to save the world, despite her father's ghost, or whatever it was, urging her to do so. Marina had nearly been beaten to death by a short, pampered movie star. What hope did she have of waging war against the infected, or the aliens lying in wait to swallow the world?

Acevedo kept staring, the dark circles under his eyes blending with the van's shadows to give him an almost sinister appearance.

* * * *

CHAPTER 8
EDWARD KEENAN

The last name on their list was a woman named Kerri Sampson, an impressionist painter who was semi-well known among art circles before retiring to run an RV camp along a lake at the foot of the Santa Lucia mountains.

Marina wasn't sure how her father had known the woman — he'd never expressed an interest in paintings to her. Marina also didn't recognize the woman as a church member. Nor did the agency dig up anything that might suggest why the woman might be trusted with the vials.

Keenan was also entering the situation blind, but it had to go better than securing the other vials had.

Luther exited the dark highway and made a left onto a darker dirt road where a sign read: *New Moon Lake Recreational Vehicle Campgrounds.*

The van jostled as they drove through the dark woods. Ed surveyed the area, seeing lights from a handful of RVs among the trees as they passed. A sign with an arrow pointing ahead read: OFFICE.

Ed hoped the office was still open and that's where he'd find Sampson. If not, her address was listed at the camp site, but how the hell he'd find her among the forty or so campers spread out in the woods, Ed had no idea. He didn't want to go door-to-door and risk someone alerting Sampson that the feds were looking for her. If the woman knew what she had in the vial, and it stood to reason that she knew it was something special even if not exactly what, then Sampson could become a ghost, impossible to track.

Keenan noticed a building ahead, the only permanent structure aside from a few pavilions and bathrooms. It was blue and wooden with the word OFFICE on a black sign over the front door. Beneath the sign, two windows and a light on inside.

"Pull up to the parking spot," Keenan said, figuring the direct route was least suspicious.

"Wait here," he said to Luther.

The woods were alive with a symphony of insects, birds, and frogs as Keenan hopped out of the van and stepped out into the cool night air.

An old Pepsi machine's light flickered on and off promising liquid refreshment for a few quarters on his way to the office. He spotted a woman in her late fifties with an auburn bob and big brown glasses through the window, sitting at a desk, tapping away on a laptop.

He recognized the woman from her file's driver's license photo — Kerri Sampson.

So far, so good.

As Ed reached the front door, he saw Sampson look up from her desk, suspicious at this newcomer arriving after dark.

He opened the door, tinkling a bell as he entered.

"Good evening," she said, standing, eying Ed up and down. He'd changed from the suit back to his Guardsman gear. "How can I help you?"

"My name is Edward Keenan, with Homeland Security. I need to talk to you about the vial given to you by J.L. Harmon."

The door closed behind him, again tinkling the bell.

Ed saw the truth in her eyes: Sampson knew exactly what he was talking about.

"What about it?"

"I understand that Mr. Harmon trusted you to hold onto the vial. Did he tell you what it contained?"

"No, he just made me promise not to open it until the right time, and assured me that I'd know when that was."

"So you've never opened it?"

"No," Sampson said, concern clear on her face. She seemed so much easier to deal with than the prior two custodians. Ed was thankful that some people still believed in actually helping the authorities, rather than viewing them all as the bad guys.

"Good," Ed said. "It's a lethal material, and we need to get it from you."

"Oh gosh, what is it?"

Ed noticed a small TV sitting on top of a filing cabinet, streaming CNN's coverage of the school shooting.

He pointed at the screen. "You've been seeing all the recent violence on the news, right?"

"Yes. It's so awful. So glad we're here in the middle of nowhere."

"Yeah, this is a good place to be," Ed agreed, hoping to foster a calm rapport. "Nice campgrounds."

"Thank you. So, um, what does the vial have to do with the news?"

"Seems this isn't the only vial. There are quite a few out there, and they're causing horrible things to happen."

"Oh my. Is it like some sort of toxin?"

"Worse than you can imagine."

"Why would Mr. Harmon have them? Why would he want me to open it?"

"How did you know Mr. Harmon?"

Sampson looked down, her first bit of hesitancy.

"Don't worry, you're not in any trouble, Ms. Sampson. We just need the vial, then we'll be on our way. We're trying to get as many as we can before things get worse."

"Josh was a friend. We met in Narcotics Anonymous many years ago."

Keenan nodded, letting her continue.

"We were friends ... *good friends*, if you catch my meaning, for a while. It was great while it lasted, but then he got into that weird religious stuff."

"So you weren't a member of his church?"

"Oh gosh, no," she said. "I always knew Josh was a bit off, but who among us isn't a little weird? But it got worse over time, and he started talking about all these dreams he was having, and this New Age pseudo-religious stuff. I tried not to be critical, and even let him try and convince me of what he was talking about, but I just couldn't buy into it. And I think when you're with someone you ought to be honest about everything. So I broke it off."

"Ah," Keenan nodded.

"A few years ago, Josh appeared on my doorstep. No call, nothing. He gave me the vial and said I was one of a few people he could truly trust. After all, I'd been honest with him rather than lie to maintain our relationship. So apparently, I had earned his trust. He wouldn't tell me what was in the vial. He just made me promise not to open it until it was time. When I asked how I'd know when the time was, he said I wouldn't have any doubt, then he left, promising to call so we could catch up soon. But Josh never called."

Keenan nodded. "And you're *sure* you never opened the vial?"

"Oh Lord, no," Sampson said, seeming in no way insulted by Keenan repeating the query. "I didn't know what it was. Part of me thought it was some figment of his religion — like holy water, or something Josh thought was important but wasn't really. But I have to tell you, the longer I've had that thing, the weirder it's felt. I even have dreams about it — like it *wants* me to open it. I thought maybe I was going nuts. I was tempted to throw it in the trash, but there was this little voice in the back of my head that remembered when Josh was a sweet, normal guy. Haunted by something, but sweet. I could never bring myself to toss it."

"Where is it now?"

"It's in my camper. Hold on, just let me save this document. I'll take you there."

"Thank you, Ms. Sampson. We appreciate your cooperation."

Sampson saved her doc then led Ed out of the office.

"I'm a ways down the path," she said. "I usually ride my bike to the office, but today I had a flat with no time to fix it. Would you like to walk with me, or — ?"

Sampson looked at the van.

"We'll give you a ride, Ms. Sampson."

"Thank you."

Ed opened the side door, waved his hand, directing Sampson to one of the back seats.

She stepped into the van, looked at Marina and Acevedo, and must've noticed their cuffs. She turned to Keenan. "Don't worry, they won't bite," he said, then closed the door.

They drove down a long path in silence, took a couple of turns at Ms. Sampson's direction, and found themselves at a clearing with four campers along the lake, each surrounded by about five hundred feet of yard. It seemed like a nice place to retire from the rat race. Keenan couldn't wait until he could retire from this life, settle somewhere with Jade, and maybe Teagan and Becca if they wanted to come along. Hell, he'd even bring Brent and Ben, make it one big hippie commune.

Ed stifled a laugh at the thought of them all living in the woods then stepped out of the van and let Ms. Sampson out.

"Right this way." She led Ed past her small garden, festooned with whimsically painted bird feeders, garden gnomes, and a few dream catchers hanging from the branches of a small tree.

Sampson opened her front door, which Ed was surprised to see wasn't locked. *Man, she must really trust her neighbors.* He couldn't decide if it was nice to live in that sort of community or if she was simply too naive to realize that you could never *truly* trust anyone.

"Just this way."

Keenan closed the front door behind him as Ms. Sampson flicked on lights to illuminate a small, but well-decorated space.

"It's just inside my bedroom," Sampson said making her way down the small hall.

Ed followed, even though she seemed like she wanted him to wait in the living room. Sampson had seemed cooperative so far, but he couldn't take the chance that she might sneak into the room, grab the vial, then open it. She didn't seem like one of the cult kooks in Harmon's church, but that didn't mean she wasn't. Hell, Harmon's daughter, Marina, seemed like a perfectly reasonable, normal person, not at all someone who would buy into J.L. Harmon's homespun bullshit. You never could tell who was cuckoo for Cocoa Puffs.

Sampson clicked on her bedroom light and gasped.

Ed, immediately behind her, shotgun in hand, saw two people, a man and woman in their mid-forties standing in her bedroom, blank eyed and slack jawed.

"Carol? Kevin? What are you doing in here?"

"Give us the vials," her apparent neighbors said together in voices that belonged to neither of them — the voices of hundreds braying through their mouths.

The Darkness was here.

* * *

CHAPTER 9
MARINA HARMON

Marina stared at Acevedo, wondering what his mind might be concocting. Part of her was hoping he wasn't going to do anything. Another part longed for an escape plan.

He was staring at his handcuffs, as they were parked in front of the woman's camper with time for action evaporating. Soon, Keenan would come out with the final vial, then one of three things would happen: Keenan and Luther would bring them somewhere safe as they'd promised, the agents would send them to some secret prison for God knows how long, or the agents would simply kill them and dump them in the middle of nowhere.

Luther, sitting up front, was impatiently bouncing his leg like he had to use the bathroom.

Or maybe he's itching to kill us.

Acevedo looked up, eyes wide. "Something's wrong."

"What's that?" Luther asked.

"Something bad is about to happen. I can feel it."

Marina's heart began to pound as she wondered what Acevedo was up to. Was this his move? If so, what was he hoping to do? He was selling his anxiety well. His eyes were going back and forth, like he was trying to see through the van's walls into the darkness. And if he wasn't faking, what was he sensing?

Luther turned in his seat, looking back at Acevedo, and grabbed one of the two shotguns resting in a rack in front of the van's center console.

"What the hell are you talking about?"

"We're in danger. You need to tell Keenan to get out of there. Now."

Luther's brow furrowed.

Gunshots erupted from inside the camper.

Luther turned and hopped out of the van, shotgun in hand, slamming the door closed behind him.

"What's happening?" Marina asked Acevedo.

The priest shook his head. "It's coming."

"Who is coming?"

"It!"

Marina heard an odd animal-like clicking coming from outside the van, though it didn't sound like any animal she'd ever heard before. And it wasn't a single clicking, it sounded like several, surrounding them.

Her heart raced in anticipation of the unimaginable.

Something thumped the van's side, hard, as if a wild animal had barreled into it. The van shook violently in the wake of the crash.

Startled, Marina let out a yelp.

She looked up front to the van's only windows but could only see Kerri Sampson's camper in the dark, along with the tangled shadows behind lit curtains, suggesting something awful inside.

Acevedo pulled hard on his cuffs, frantic as something kept slamming the van.

"No," he said to himself. "Focus."

"What is it?" Marina asked.

Acevedo closed his eyes, continuing to stare at his cuffs, just as he'd been doing through much of their trip.

What the hell? Does he think he's a Jedi?

More thumps, this time harder, and from both sides, rattling the van as if it were between giants playing kick the can.

Marina wasn't sure what was outside in the night, but her mind flooded with images of black, fluid-like creatures descending on the van from all sides — The Darkness, the same Darkness that had infiltrated Steven.

The driver's side window imploded.

Marina screamed, pulling at her handcuffs, hard, trying to slide out, near certain that if she tugged any harder, she'd tear her left hand off at the wrist.

She looked over at Acevedo, still staring at his cuffs as if trying to will them open.

Something black appeared in the left corner of her vision. Marina turned to look and saw thick black, ropy strands circling their way into the van's driver side, as if searching for something.

The vials!

She pulled harder on her cuffs, heart thumping so fast Marina wasn't sure it could go faster without exploding, killing her in an instant.

The clicking grew louder, not just outside but inside — as if coming from the alien's ropy appendages.

It must be using some sort of radar mechanism to locate the vials — or us.

The strands encircled one another, melding, growing thicker and certainly more formidable. Its tip, now one instead of many, turned to them, that awful clicking filling the van.

Marina screamed as it seemed to see them.

The van shuddered as the aliens pounded the sides, their pelting echoing off the walls, blending with the clicking to create a chaotic chorus of madness and nightmare.

The Darkness grew closer, the appendage inching toward Marina.

She looked at Acevedo. His eyes were closed, as if he were meditating, like that might prevent the creatures from tearing them apart.

She screamed, "Father!"

His eyes opened.

Acevedo's cuff fell from his wrist. How he'd managed to open them, Marina couldn't tell.

He bolted forward in the cabin, dived to the floor, and rolled between the middle seats, beneath the writhing black tentacle.

Acevedo grabbed the second shotgun from the rack, turned it upward, and fired at the alien's slick black flesh.

The Darkness reeled back, its broken tentacle retreating as screams erupted from all sides outside the van.

Acevedo looked up, met her eyes, seemingly as surprised as she was that he managed to momentarily scare the creature back.

He did it!

Marina thought Acevedo would take the gun and perhaps go rescue Keenan and Luther. Instead, he turned, looked in the glove compartment for the vials, nodded, then turned back to Marina.

"We're getting out of here."

"What?" she yelled.

"What about the agents?"

"They're on their own." He threw the van in reverse. Dark, ropy strands appeared in the front window while Acevedo raced backwards. "This is our chance."

"Our chance for what?"

Acevedo kept the van in reverse as The Darkness raced after them like rippling fields of black wheat in an angry wind.

"Our chance to finish what we started."

Acevedo slammed on the breaks, and began to spin the van around.

The black tentacles began to close in.

The van's tires struggled to find purchase in the dirt as the tentacles closed in from behind. While she couldn't see them, Marina could hear their awful clicking growing louder.

Dozens would reach out in seconds, and likely race around the van and through the broken front window to overtake Acevedo and Marina.

"Come on, you cocksucker!" the priest said, pumping hard on the accelerator.

The van kicked forward and then found speed.

Marina listened as The Darkness shrieked and clicked.

Sounds grew mercifully distant as Acevedo put the pedal to the floor and raced forward into the night.

Marina was glad to be away from the aliens but couldn't help feeling guilty for leaving the agents to die.

Acevedo, seemingly to sense her consternation, said, "There's nothing we could've done."

He was right. She wouldn't know how to fight something like The Darkness even if her left hand wasn't still cuffed to the seat.

"Just be glad we made it out alive." He looked in the rearview and sighed with relief.

Marina couldn't share it fully. Though she'd escaped the agents and the aliens, she had yet to escape Acevedo.

And as she stared at the priest, Marina couldn't help but wonder if she was in worse hands now than before.

* * * *

CHAPTER 10
EDWARD KEENAN

Ed fired two shots, one for each of the infected, right into their chests.

Ms. Sampson screamed, turning toward Ed, eyes glaring. "You shot them!"

Ed heard the aliens' sick clicking coming from outside.

The Darkness appeared, seeping through the bedroom's broken window — not more infected humans, but dozens of tendrils from Its true alien form.

"Get down!" Ed shoved Sampson to the ground, lifted his shotgun, and fired into the largest mass where most of the tendrils seemed to diverge.

The tendrils vented a scream and scurried back out the window.

Ed heard chaos outside — more clicking, screams, and thumps against the van. This was an assault. The Darkness had somehow found them here and was going after the vials.

"Luther!" he shouted into his jacket mic, hoping the agent was still alive.

Ms. Sampson peered up from behind her fingers and cried, "What was that?"

"That's what's in the vials. Now where did you put it?"

Two shotgun blasts exploded in the living room.

Ed turned to see Luther standing over another pair of infected corpses.

"All clear in the living room," Luther said.

Ed heard movement behind him, followed by the sound of Sampson choking.

He turned to see The Darkness that had been in her neighbors forcing itself into Sampson's mouth, infecting her.

She cried out, hands scraping at her lips, trying to pull at what was essentially a liquid form, like trying to stop a waterfall with a fishing net.

"Damn it!" Ed raised the shotgun and blasted Sampson in her head.

Luther stared down at the woman's corpse, eyes wide, then looked up and raised his gun at Ed, or something behind him.

Ed dropped to the ground. Luther fired three more shots at a mass of writhing Darkness.

Luther connected, but not enough.

The Darkness broke into four separate branches. Two limbs were slapped by the blasts and fell onto the bed in wet chunks of oozing blackness. The other two kept moving, like tentacles, melding into a single razored limb that shot forward straight into Luther's gut.

It tore through him, slicing into Luther then spreading through his body before Ed could do anything.

Luther's face filled with panic then pain. "Get out!" he screamed, dropping his gun and clawing at the tentacle.

Ed wasn't sure if Luther was warning him to get out before the alien took over or begging the alien to leave his body.

Either way, Ed barely had time to raise his shotgun before Luther's intense eyes were on him. He swung one of his massive limbs at Ed, knocking him back onto the bed, and sending the shotgun from his hand.

Luther leaped, landing on top of Ed and pinning him to the bed. Luther, now even stronger because of the alien form coursing through him, grabbed Ed's jaw with one hand while prying his mouth open with the other.

"Let us in," hundreds of voices said in unison. The black liquid flowed as if weightless from Luther's maw towards Ed's parted mouth.

"No!" Ed scratched, squirmed, and kicked, trying to free himself from Luther's grasp.

He couldn't budge the behemoth.

Ed could barely move his head. Luther held Ed's mouth open and let the black, wiry tendrils hanging from his mouth creep closer.

The Darkness was inches from Ed's mouth, squirming like worms eager to burrow into his body.

Ed bit hard on Luther's fingers. The taste of hot iron flooded Ed's mouth, but the big man held tight.

Tendrils poured down Keenan's throat.

But then as quickly as they entered, they pulled themselves out, as if Ed's mouth was infected with something repugnant.

The Darkness fled back into Luther's throat. He released Ed with one hand, only to punch him in the gut with the other.

Ed gasped, then fell to the floor on top of Ms. Sampson's corpse. He glanced up at the big man, wishing he could get the alien out without murdering him but knew of no way to cure the infected. Ed continued to lie there as Luther turned away from him, searching the room, clicking as he did.

He's looking for the vial.

Ed wished the woman had found the vial before he had to bring her down. As it was, he had no clue where to find the damned thing. Her bedroom was lined with bookcases, two dressers, and a closet stuffed with boxes.

Ed had an idea: he could continue to stay down and play dead or injured and wait for Luther to find the vial, assuming The Darkness had some special ability to sense it.

Ed closed his eyes, lying on the floor beside the bleeding corpse, playing dead as Luther stomped around the bedroom, making that horrible clicking, searching for what The Darkness had come for.

Ed wondered how The Darkness had found them. How It had known he was here for the vials. Perhaps It had Its own version of Paola It was using to search for the missing vials.

Luther ripped the closet door from its track and threw it aside where it banged into a bookcase, knocking it to the floor.

Not one for subtlety, that one.

Luther ripped at boxes in the closet, grunting. A shotgun blast exploded outside. Ed hoped that Luther had given Marina and Acevedo a gun before leaving them alone in the van. Otherwise, he'd have more bodies on his hands, and more aliens to fight off outside.

Luther continued tearing through boxes as Ed impatiently waited.

To play possum while all hell was breaking loose outside was gutting him. He needed to get up, go outside, secure the other vials, and protect Marina and Acevedo.

But if he got up before Luther found the vial, he might never get the last one.

He couldn't risk moving. Yet.

Luther will find the vial soon.

Luther suddenly stopped throwing boxes.

For a moment, Ed thought perhaps Luther was onto him, and was coming back to finish him off.

Ed risked opening an eye to see Luther still facing the closet, holding a small black wooden box in his massive hands. He lifted the lid and cast his face in the vial's blue glow.

Yes! He found it.

Luther closed the box, turned, and looked down at Ed.

Ed closed his eyes, hoping The Darkness wasn't running some sort of body scan. Ed figured the alien inside his partner was capable of telling the difference between a dead human and one playing possum.

Outside, the van's tires were kicking up dirt.

Shit!

Luther ran from the room, drawn by the fleeing van.

Ed popped up, grabbed the shotgun, and followed his partner out of the room.

No time for regrets or second thoughts. Ed raised the barrel and fired into the back of Luther's skull, sending him dead to the ground.

Ed grabbed the box with the vial, and searched the camper through the open front door.

There were no infected, just waves of Darkness in its raw form pursuing the van down the dirt road.

Ed hoped that Luther had freed their prisoners before leaving them. Otherwise, God only knew who was driving the van, or what happened to the priest, Marina, and, of course, the other vials.

Ed couldn't stick around to find out — he had to get out of there before The Darkness realized he had a vial and it returned to salvage whatever victory it could on this night.

Ed raced out of the RV and along the path toward a camper, bright in the distance. In front of the camper, a Harley.

Ed hoped he wouldn't have to kill anyone else to get it.

* * * *

CHAPTER 11
MARINA HARMON

They'd been driving for nearly an hour before Acevedo finally pulled into a gas station on the side of the highway.

He crawled into the van's rear and looked down at Marina's cuffs. "I can't find another key, so you'll have to sit tight until I can find something to pick those."

"What do you mean? Why don't you use your Jedi mind power or whatever the hell you did to get out of yours?"

"I could try, but it might take forever. It'd be easier to get a paper clip or soda can to make a shim, then work on it that way."

"How the hell *did* you do that?"

"I told you the vials have an effect on you over time. I noticed some abilities the longer I held onto the vials — moving stuff with my mind, hearing people's thoughts. Nothing big, and it's off and on, but I got lucky back there, I guess."

"So is there anything *I* can do?"

"I don't know. You tell me. I mean, you said you didn't even know about the vials until recently, right? Maybe you weren't close enough for them to exercise any influence over you."

"I don't know. I don't feel anything. So, what's the plan now? What are we going to do? We have four vials instead of six, right? That guy drank the one, and we didn't wait around for Keenan to come out with the other. Is that enough?"

"It'll have to be for now."

"So, what are you planning? Do you think maybe we ought to give them to the government?"

Acevedo laughed, then stopped when he saw in Marina's eyes that it was a serious suggestion.

"Wait? You really want me to hand the vials over to them? You know what they'd do with this kind of power, don't you?"

"I don't know, maybe fight The Darkness and win?"

"You really think that? You, of all people, I would've thought you'd know better than to trust the government. All the trouble they put your father through because of the church."

"He invited plenty of those problems on himself, and we both know it," Marina argued. "Besides, Keenan saved my life and didn't have to. Hell, you would've been dead if Luther hadn't saved you back at Beef's house. And you just left them behind. What kind of priest leaves innocent people to die?"

"*Innocent?*" Acevedo laughed. "Need I remind you that that innocent G-man put a gun to you and punched you in the face to coerce us to cooperate with him? I think someone here's getting a case of Stockholm Syndrome, identifying too closely with the bad guys."

Marina shook her head. "I'm not identifying with anyone. But at least they had a plan. They knew what to do. They have resources. We only have us. And in case you missed it back there, I'm not exactly a fighter."

"How do you know they have plans? Did they tell you about them when I wasn't listening? Did they tell you what they were going to do other than *get the vials?*"

"No. But neither have you. You're acting like God will personally give you directions or something."

Acevedo met Marina's eyes, no longer laughing, his harboring a sadness that Marina wasn't sure she wanted to understand.

"I have a plan," he said, "and I know what I need to do."

"What?"

"I have to find the vessel and kill it."

"The vessel?"

"Yes, The Darkness is hiding inside a human. I've seen him before, and the vials will show me where he is."

"You've seen him before? Who is he?" Marina asked. "Do we have a name?"

"Yes," Acevedo said. "I've been dreaming about him since I got the vial. His name is Luca Harding."

* * * *

CHAPTER 12
BRENT FOSTER

Brent stared at the TV's clock: *10:30 p.m.*
When the hell is Desmond coming home?
It was late, and Brent wanted to get Ben home and to bed. He was pretty sure Teagan wanted to get home, too. They'd promised Desmond that they'd stay with Mary. But that was late last night. He hadn't counted on Desmond staying at the facility all day.

Sure, there was a ton to get done, and Desmond was pretty much the island's number two, just under Director Bolton, so he had plenty on his shoulders. Still, Mary had just lost her daughter. And while they weren't married, Desmond and Mary were a couple, and the closest thing Desmond had to family — so why the hell wasn't he here in her time of need?

Ben was sleeping in Paola's bed, with Teagan's little girl sleeping beside him.

Brent hoped Desmond would return before Mary emerged from her room. He wasn't sure how she would react to their kids sleeping in her daughter's room so soon after her death.

Brent looked at Teagan passed out but sitting up beside him on the couch, her neck at an awkward and uncomfortable-looking angle. She'd not only lost her closest friend on the island but also her roommate. Still, she didn't have the luxury of wallowing. Grief was expensive when a young child was counting on you, so she seemed to be shoving her response deep down, as low as it would go.

Brent could relate. He'd barely had time to process his wife's death before they'd hit the road with Ed and crew.

Holding it together, maintaining a strong facade, was tough, and sometimes felt impossible.

That wasn't to say Brent didn't grieve for Gina, but it was usually in the dead of night, while alone in his bed. But he, like Teagan, had to stay strong. Ben was counting on him. The five-year-old had been surprisingly resilient, sometimes making it an entire day without crying for his mom, wondering when she'd come home.

While Brent thought his son had understood death after he explained that Mommy had gone to heaven, the boy sometimes seemed to forget that his mother was dead. It was worst when Ben was tired and cranky. He'd cry, "I want Mommy."

Times like that threatened to crack Brent's brittle facade to nothing.

Listening to Ben cry for his dead mother, wondering when she'd return, was a cold blade to his gut. But Brent had to stay strong for his son. Had to guide him through the grief, even if he barely knew how to navigate the lonely waters himself.

He looked at his cell phone, hoping to see a signal. Nothing.

He had to reach Ed and let him know about Jade.

But the island was still on lockdown.

The front door clicked unlocked, and Desmond finally came home.

"I'm sorry." Desmond inside with a face filled with apology. "Everything at the facility is insane."

"No problem," Brent lied, standing to meet Desmond in the kitchen, hoping that Teagan wouldn't wake.

Desmond went to the fridge and pulled out two bottles of Heineken. "Want one?"

"I'm good," Brent said.

Desmond popped the cap and took a long swig.

"So," Desmond asked, "how's Mary holding up?"

"She hasn't come out of her room."

"At all?"

"No. We went to her door a few times, but she just kept saying that she wanted to sleep. Teagan went in a couple of times to leave food and drinks. She said that Mary's back was to the door, and she couldn't tell if she was asleep or not. So she set them on her nightstand. She went back a few times, but the food and drinks were always untouched."

"Jesus." Desmond sighed then finished his beer with four long swallows.

Desmond offered the second bottle to Brent again. After he said no thanks, Desmond asked, "You sure?" then popped it open and started gulping.

Brent didn't think Desmond was much of a drinker. Maybe it was the stress.

"So," Brent asked, "what's the latest on the outbreak, or whatever they're calling it?"

"They're calling it 'Incident 1151,' officially, between you and me, which doesn't sound scary at all, eh?" Desmond let out an odd laugh, as if stress was pinching every last nerve.

Brent suddenly felt stupid. He'd not considered how hard Paola's death might be hitting Desmond. The girl was like a daughter to him, Brent figured, and Desmond had yet to grieve. Work was calling, and he had to secure their safety.

Brent felt selfish and guilty for wondering where in the hell he was earlier. Desmond obviously wanted to get home to Mary and process what happened. But he had a duty to keep the island secure, so his own needs, and Mary's, had to come second.

Brent said, "I'm so sorry about Paola."

"Thanks," Desmond said as he finished off the second beer. "And thanks for hanging out today, or rather, tonight."

"Ben and Becca are in Paola's room. I hope that's OK. It was getting late, and ... "

"Yeah, don't worry about it, man. Thanks for helping. How is she doing?" Desmond nodded at Teagan, still asleep on the couch.

"She's being strong, but I'm worried about sending her back to her place alone."

"They can stay here," Desmond offered.

"I don't want to burden you all. Plus, I was going to invite them to stay with Ben and me for a while. Unless you think Mary needs us to hang around more?"

"Actually, about that ... I was going to ask if you can all stay through the night. I have to go back and take care of a few loose ends. If the kids are sleeping, no need to wake them up just to bring 'em back to your place, right? I have some inflatable beds in my office; you and Teagan can bunk in there or bring the beds into Paola's room — it's pretty big. *If* you can stay, that is."

Brent surprised himself. Ten minutes ago he was annoyed and couldn't wait to get home. Now he felt eager to help Desmond and the others however he could. Maybe in helping others get through their grief he could better process his own. They'd been through hell together, and while he'd lost the love of his life and Ben had lost his mother, he had to focus on what they still had left — for as long as they still had it.

"Yeah, we can stay. Just one thing," Brent said as he reached for his cell, "how long is the island on lockdown? I can't get a signal, and I really think someone should call Ed to let him know about Jade."

Desmond's eyes narrowed on Brent. "I'm not sure how long Bolton will keep us on lockdown. He wants to make sure that if there are any more infected they won't be able to contact anyone they might be working with off island."

"Working with? What do you mean?"

"We have reason to believe there are certain people, not infected, trying to undermine our efforts."

"Like *terrorists?*" Brent asked.

"That's as good a word as any."

"Who?"

"We're not sure. But there are some alien vials out in the wild, and someone has released a few already. We're trying to contain it, and that's what Keenan's doing now. He's doing vital work out there. And as much as I agree that he has a right to know about his daughter, he's one of the only people who can get these vials before it's too late."

"Yeah," Brent said, not sure how to frame the next part of his argument without seeming insensitive, "but weren't you using Paola to find the vials? I would think that without her, you might as well bring Ed back here."

"He has a couple of the vials and should be able to use those to help him find the others. From my understanding, these vials *want* to be together. Once you have some, they will lead you to the others. And we need to make sure we get them before the enemy."

"So you're not going to tell him that his daughter is dead?"

"It's not my decision. This is straight from Director Bolton. But as heartless as it may seem, I tend to agree. Tell me, Brent, you know Ed best of all. How do you think he'd react if we told him about Jade? Do *you* think he would finish his job, or rush back here, demanding answers, wanting to beat down everyone who failed to protect his child?"

Desmond had a point. As dedicated as Ed was to his job, he was only helping out to ensure Jade's safety, and perhaps to a lesser extent Teagan, Becca, Brent, and Ben. But with his daughter gone, there was little to entice him.

Brent said, "Yeah, I think he'd come back here immediately, and heads would roll."

Desmond nodded, putting a hand on Brent's shoulder, "So you see how tough a position I'm in?"

"Yeah, I get it. It just sucks so much. He's going to hate us for not telling him."

"Maybe, for a bit. But in the long run I'm sure he'll understand. Hell, I think he'd do the same thing if things were reversed. I don't know him that well, but from all I've heard, Ed was one hell of an agent."

"Yeah," Brent said, nodding, as he stared at Teagan's sleeping form. It was still so odd to not see Jade beside her.

Not odd — wrong.

"OK," Desmond said, "I'm going to slip out before Mary wakes up. I should be back in an hour or so, but you never know. We're still processing people we picked up on the island that are potentially infected. And unfortunately, I'm the only person left that can sense if they are."

"You didn't bring any of that tech over from the other world when you jumped back here? I remember they had these wands to show infection."

"No, I didn't think to, and a lot of that stuff was destroyed with the facility. There's not much left. Now it's pretty much just me."

"Well, thanks," Brent said, "for working so tirelessly. I know you'd rather be here consoling Mary."

Desmond nodded, staring at Mary's closed door. "Yeah, it's tough. Which is why I need to get going before I say to hell with it and go and lie down next to her for the night."

Desmond left, taking a third bottle of Heineken on his way.

Brent wondered again if Desmond was an alcoholic. Not that he would tell the man to slow down or say anything at all. So long as it helped him get through this, Brent figured no harm, no foul.

He went into Desmond's office and found the inflatable mattresses along with a battery-operated pump. He filled two, then thought about bringing them into Paola's room, but didn't want to wake the kids — or it could be hours before anyone got any sleep again.

He dragged the beds, along with blankets and pillows, into the living room then went to the couch and tapped Teagan on the shoulder.

She wouldn't wake up.

Man, she must be wiped out.

Brent considered letting her stay where she was, but was near certain she'd wake with an awfully sore neck if he did. He reached beneath her, her body warm, scooped her up, then laid her gently on the bed.

She stirred as he set her down and looked up at him. "What's going on? Where's Becca?"

"She's sleeping in Paola's room with Ben. She's fine. Desmond asked if we could stay the night, so I got us these beds. Relax, I'll wake you up if Becca needs you."

"OK," Teagan said, eyes delirious before she closed them again. "Thank you."

Brent covered her with a blanket, then turned off all the living room lights, leaving the TV muted on Disney Junior, in case Ben woke up and came out looking for him.

Brent lay down on the other mattress beside Teagan's and watched her sleeping bathed in the TV's dim-blue light.

Teagan looked so peaceful in her sleep, more like the teenager she was, rather than the young single mother and survivor of an apocalypse on the other world that had aged her waking self.

If only we could all go to sleep and wake in a world before this all happened. Have things return to the way they were.

Brent thought of Gina. How much he would give to wake up beside her, and have his family whole.

He closed his eyes, trying to stifle the black thoughts and wishful thinking before they brought tears. But he couldn't.

Teagan's voice surprised him.

"Are you OK?"

He looked up, and was going to lie with a *yes*. He had to be more like Desmond, wear his strongest face to get them through this.

But Brent's mouth ignored his brain.

"No," he said.

"Me neither."

She moved closer to Brent, and for a moment he was startled, thinking she might kiss him or something — which would have been a hundred kinds of wrong.

She wrapped her arms around his body and hugged him, crying into his chest.

"I miss them so much," she said. "Paola, Jade, and Ed."

Brent was confused then remembered that she'd been in a relationship with the other Keenan, who had sacrificed himself to save them on the other world. It must've been tough for Teagan to be around this other version of Jade's father, who didn't have that same attachment to her.

Brent felt stupid for not seeing the obvious sooner, and perhaps helping her through it. Though he wasn't sure what he could do or say. He didn't know her nearly as well as Ed or Jade.

But as they lay side by side, holding one another through their tears, Brent realized perhaps this was enough for now — to simply be there for each other.

* * * *

CHAPTER 13
DESMOND ARMSTRONG

Desmond watched as numbers on the elevator's panel ascended and the box dropped lower.

On the seventh floor, the elevator stopped.

Desmond pressed two buttons, seven and zero, then the elevator lurched, descending again to the unmarked eighth level.

He placed his hand on the panel. The doors slid open, accepting his palm print.

Outside the elevator, Desmond came to a set of double sliding doors, guarded by a Guardsman holding an AR-15.

"Good evening, sir," the Guardsman said.

"Good evening, Proctor." Desmond raised his face to the retinal scanner to the right of the double doors, waited for the second scan, then the doors slid open.

Desmond stepped through the doors then headed down the hall, passing several chambers filled with specimen for the scientists' experiments on The Darkness.

The hall ended in a fork that went left and right. Desmond took the left hall, a long corridor with black metal doors rather than cells. He stopped at the end of the hall in front of a white door with another retinal scanner, this one keyed for his entrance alone.

He brought his eyes to the scanner, and the door slid open.

Desmond stepped inside the cavernous room, which housed eight reinforced, unbreakable glass captivity cells, all dark and empty — save for one.

He approached the cell and looked down at the sleeping figure on the mat, covered by a blue blanket.

He pressed buttons on the touch screen beside the cell door and turned on the light. Another press of a button brought the microphones and speakers to life.

"Time to wake up," he said.

The figure moved, and the blanket fell.

The girl looked back at Desmond, confused.

"Hello, Paola."

* * * *

::EPISODE 30::
(SIXTH AND FINAL EPISODE OF SEASON FIVE)
"IN YOUR DARKEST HOUR"

CHAPTER 1
FATHER THOMAS ACEVEDO

October 9, 2011

Acevedo sat low in his car, watching from the parking lot as children frolicked and laughed in the playground. He hoped nobody noticed him.

A priest hanging out in front a playground — there was a time when most people wouldn't have thought twice. Nowadays, with the rampant abuse by adults and supposed men and women of God, he'd be tarred and feathered before getting a chance to explain his intentions.

Not that his real reason would be viewed with more sympathy. No one would believe or understand him, even if he tried to explain why he was there and what he was about to do.

Where is he?

Acevedo had yet to see the person he'd come searching for. The boy he'd dreamed of nearly every night for the past few months. The boy who his dreams insisted would be in the park.

Perhaps his dreams were wrong, and the boy who promised the apocalypse didn't exist.

God, he hoped so — even if that meant Acevedo had lost his mind. Hell, sometimes it felt like he *was* losing it.

He couldn't remember the last time he'd slept more than an hour during the past month. It was difficult to sleep through the nightmares. The dreams that said the world would end at 11:15 p.m. on October 14.

Acevedo wished he'd never accepted the vials from Joshua Harmon back in January when the Church of Original Design's leader had asked him to guard them, saying he had but a few people he could truly trust.

Until then, Acevedo had never given much credence to the things others had said about Harmon and his cult.

They'd had many conversations in the few years since they'd met, spirited philosophical and theological debates, but Harmon had never seemed the least bit like an opportunist or scammer like so many people seemed to think that he was. Did he believe in a false God? Yes, so far as Acevedo was concerned, but Harmon truly believed in his religion, and that made him different from so many of the charlatans and TV preachers who pretended to believe when their true faith was in the Almighty Dollar.

Though Acevedo had never doubted God as he knew Him, he *had* wrestled with the notion that he could be wrong — that perhaps some other faith had it right. It was difficult to condemn other religions or their followers.

That said, Acevedo didn't think Harmon's God was anything close to what He truly was. Still, he respected the man's faith and his charitable actions. Harmon was by all accounts, a good man. And not the least bit crazy.

At least that's what Acevedo had thought prior to Harmon telling him that the vial contained another life force, something closer to God than we could fathom, and that he had to protect it at all costs and never allow anyone "impure" to open it.

Acevedo had accepted the vial, along with a coded list of other recipients that Harmon had entrusted him with, because what else was he going to do? Harmon had seemed like he was genuinely afraid to let it fall into the wrong hands. Acevedo entertained the man's delusions a bit, no harm done.

But as months passed, and the vial spoke to Acevedo in dreams, he wondered if Harmon's madness was contagious.

Or ... was Harmon actually onto something?

Acevedo had dreamed that the boy would be here by now. It was 5:15 p.m. on Sunday afternoon. In his dream he'd looked at his watch, saw that the time was 5:00 p.m., then saw the boy with his sister and mom on the playground.

Fifteen minutes later, and he'd yet to see the child or his family.

Yeah, maybe I ought not to put so much faith in dreams.

He keyed the ignition and turned his head to make sure he was clear to back out of his parking spot. As Acevedo looked back, he spotted a digital clock across the street, in front of a bank. The time read 4:59 p.m. As he watched it went to 5:00.

Acevedo looked at his wrist, then his phone, which also read 5:00. His watch was fast.

He turned back to the park and saw the boy.

His heart sank.

He killed the engine and sat, watching.

The boy looked around eight years old. His sister a bit younger. They ran to the swings together. Their mother, an attractive woman with long, flowing brown hair, sat on a bench, sipping a cup of ice coffee. She set the drink down and fumbled with her phone.

Acevedo turned his eyes to the boy.

He didn't look at all like the harbinger of the apocalypse that Acevedo had seen in his dreams. The boy was smiling, playing nicely with his sister, not at all a jerk like so many others kids could be to a younger sibling, especially one of the opposite sex.

This is crazy. I should leave, right now. Even if the dreams are right, who am I to stop the apocalypse? If it's God's will, so be it.

But what if He is calling me to intervene? What if He is using the vials to call me?

God had made odder requests.

Acevedo had long believed there was a reason for his faith, some greater good being served. It wasn't enough to deliver sermons on Sunday. And while he'd done his share of charitable works — community outreach, feeding the homeless, raising money for children in crisis, and countless other things — Acevedo had always felt another purpose. To serve as God's soldier in the war between good and evil.

But the vial isn't God's. Perhaps He is testing me?

Acevedo's head hurt as he tried to reconcile what he felt versus what he was seeing — evidence of the his dreams' reality. If the boy was real, then the damage he would unleash upon the world was likely real as well.

Isn't it?

"Why would you have me do this, Lord?" Acevedo stared at the gun on the seat beside him. "I need some sign."

Acevedo slipped the gun into his brown leather jacket, worn loose over a light-blue polo, and got out of the car.

One test left: He had to find out the boy's name, to see if it was the same as in his dream. Proof that there was something greater than Acevedo's imagination at play.

He closed the car door behind him and walked slowly toward the park, heart beating harder than he wanted.

A cool breeze blew through his hair as children's laughter made him nostalgic for his youth — the rare times he'd been happy, before his father's drinking had ripped the family asunder.

As Acevedo approached the swings, he fished the black leash and stack of papers from his interior jacket pocket and approached a woman and a young girl standing at a picnic table. The woman was helping the small girl unknot her shoe laces.

"Excuse me." Acevedo held up one of the *Missing Dog* flyers he printed yesterday using some photo of a husky from the Internet. "Have you seen my dog? I was walking him in the park this morning, and he got away."

The woman studied the paper, then the leash, and filled her face with apology. "I'm sorry, no, I haven't seen him."

"OK. Can you call the number at the bottom of the page if you do?"

"Yeah," the woman said, taking the paper and showing her daughter when the girl asked to see. "Good luck."

"Thanks."

Acevedo made his way to a few other parents and children, waiting for the moment the boy's mother would spot him. If she saw him speaking to others, she probably wouldn't think much of him approaching her children.

Acevedo spoke to the other parents and children, the gun gaining weight in his pocket. He felt unreasonably certain that the bulge would be spotted by someone. He had not yet dreamed of what would come next for today. He'd opened his eyes to the real world after seeing the boy on the playground. There was no telling what would happen next, and the thought of how many things could go wrong soured his stomach and beaded his forehead with sweat.

But he had to play it cool and make his way to the boy on the swings.

As Acevedo drew closer, the boy's mother finally ended her call and headed toward her children. Perhaps she'd sensed the danger, or had seen him making rounds and wanted to be there when the stranger with the papers and leash finally arrived. She pushed her daughter on the swing.

"Higher!" the girl shrieked, her laughter infectious.

Even though it hurt Acevedo's odds of doing what he had to do, the priest was glad to see that she wasn't yet another absent parent spending more time with her eyes glued to her phone than her children.

He made a point of talking to one more person, a pizza-faced boy of around thirteen, sitting at a table, screwing around with his skateboard's wheels while secretly admiring a huddle of girls at one of the other tables.

"Hey, man, you seen this dog?" Acevedo held up the paper.

The kid, with bright-blue hair hanging in his face, shook his head, "nah, man ... sorry."

"Thank you."

Acevedo turned and steeled himself to approach the boy from his dreams — the harbinger of worldwide destruction.

The kid's mom looked at him sternly, as if sensing his motives. Or perhaps she thought he was a pedophile hunting for prey.

"Hi," he said, meeting her eyes, pretending he wasn't even aware of her children, "have you seen my dog?"

Acevedo handed a paper to the mom. She looked at it as the boy dug his feet into the dirt to stop his swing. He looked up. "Can I see?"

The boy looked at the paper, then at Acevedo. "What's his name?"

The priest looked down, realizing that he hadn't even put a name below the dog's picture. He cursed himself for his stupidity, surprised that the boy was the first person to ask.

Acevedo thought, then said, "Luke."

"As in Skywalker?" the boy asked with a smile.

"Yes," Acevedo said, returning his grin. "Me and my son are big *Star Wars* fans."

"So's my Dad. That's why he named me Luca. My mom wouldn't let him name me Luke."

Luca. It is him.

The gun weighed a thousand pounds in his pocket.

Kill him now, before the fourteenth!

Acevedo held his smile. The mother's eyes caught him by surprise. She was staring, not smiling — as if she could pull the plans from his mind. As if her maternal senses saw through the gauze of his guise.

Luca said, "No, I haven't seen him, mister."

"How about you?" Acevedo showed the daughter.

He could feel their mother's eyes like hot lasers. His heart raced, thinking about how to best shoot the boy. Shoot his mother first, so she couldn't protect him, or just shoot the boy in the head, and then run?

But as the little girl said no, she hadn't seen the dog either, Acevedo felt a blade of guilt twist so deeply into his gut he could hardly bring himself to raise his eyes to the mother.

A proverbial devil and angel were battling for the priest's mind.

I can't kill her child in front of her.

YOU MUST. IT IS THE ONLY WAY.

No. We don't know for certain. I could be nuts!

YEAH, BUT HE HAS THE SAME NAME. IT IS HIM! HOW ELSE CAN YOU EXPLAIN THE DREAMS? THAT YOU DREAMED HIS NAME?

I don't know.

YOU DO KNOW. YOU HAVE BEEN GIVEN A GIFT. THOSE WHO HEAR THE WORD OF GOD, HIS INSTRUCTIONS FOR US, ARE BLESSED. IT IS NOT FOR US TO WONDER WHY HE ASKS WHAT HE DOES. WE

CANNOT KNOW HIS WILL, BUT WE MUST ACT UPON OUR DUTY TO FOLLOW HIS WORD.

This isn't His word. God would never ask this.

OH?

That argument had crumbled with Abraham, and all that God has asked of his children since.

Acevedo's sweaty palm reached into his jacket, fondling the butt as his other hand clutched the papers and leash.

DO IT!

The priest looked up into the mother's cold eyes and saw something other than the harshness of a mother protecting her young. He saw a kindness, as if some part of her saw what he was about to do, and was reaching into his heart, begging him not to.

It was so subtle, and perhaps he was imagining it, but there was something in the mother's eyes, her crooked smile, and the way she put her hands on her boy's shoulder that crushed Acevedo's heart and ripped the will from inside him.

"OK," he said with a sigh, "thank you."

Acevedo didn't hand them a flyer. He wouldn't want them to call the number and fall deeper into his lie.

He turned and walked away.

The mother called out, "Good luck finding Luke."

Acevedo couldn't turn back, tears already flooding his eyes.

He'd failed to act. He'd ignored the word of God.

And because of it, the world might perish in days.

* * * *

CHAPTER 2
MARINA HARMON

Marina sat in the van's rear, still cuffed, wondering when Acevedo would stop somewhere and pick up a pair of bolt cutters or perhaps try some of that telekinesis he'd used to free himself. The longer he waited, saying they had to reach Luca, the more she felt like a prisoner.

"So," she said, "tell me more about this Luca Harding you're going to kill."

Acevedo found Marina's eyes in the rearview. "What do you want to know?"

"Who is he? How do you know he's the vessel?"

"I already told you. I dreamed it. As for who he is, he looks like an ordinary boy."

"A *boy*? How old?"

"Around ten, I think. I don't know."

"You're going to kill a ten-year-old? Based on some dream?"

"It's not just a dream!" Acevedo snapped, glaring back at her angrily.

"How do you know it's not *just* a dream?"

"The same way your father knew, perhaps. Or the same way your father came back and gave you messages? I don't know how or why, only that God has chosen to tell me for a reason. He must want me to act."

Marina couldn't believe the priest was about to kill a boy, based on a dream.

"How do you know the boy is the vessel? How did you even come to dream about him?"

"Well, at first I thought maybe I was losing my mind, dreaming of some kid I never saw before. This kid was holding vials, same as the one given to me by your father, and I kept seeing the date October 14 over and over. As the date drew nearer, the dreams changed. The boy opened the vials and unleashed evil upon the world. A voice in my head said I had to stop him."

"By which you mean kill him?"

"Yes," Acevedo said, staring at Marina in the mirror again, "but don't think I didn't wrestle with it. Or I just dreamed up some nonsense and planned to find and kill him. First, I tested my dreams to see if he was real. I had dreamed that he'd be at a park on the Sunday before the fourteenth. I went there and saw him. I went up to him, to find out his name. The kid's name was Luca, same as I'd dreamed. Then I *knew* it wasn't just a dream. I had a gun, and was going to shoot him, but for some reason, when I looked at his innocent face, then into his mother's eyes, I lost my nerve."

Acevedo drew a deep breath and continued.

"I went home, and questioned everything. I thought about the vials and wondered if they weren't making me crazy like your father seemed the last time I saw him. I met with your father, and told him about the boy. I asked him what I should do."

"What did he say?" A chill ran through Marina.

"He said I should listen to the vial. Of course, back then I didn't think it was the vial talking. I thought it was God.

So I tried to ignore the voice, but every night my dreams grew more intense. The voice got louder, more insistent, ordering me to find the boy and kill him. The dreams told me that this would all happen on October 14 at 11:15 p.m. Despite the dreams, I still wasn't sure I could kill him. He was a child, after all. So I sneaked into his house, which was difficult because the boy's father was still awake. He was working in his office and didn't even see me as I crept down the hall toward the boy's bedroom."

Marina's chill grew colder as Acevedo spoke faster.

"I stood over his bed, gun in hand, waiting with my eyes on the clock. As 11:14 came up on my watch, which I had made sure was running true, I trained the gun on his head. I stared at him, waiting for something to happen, my finger trembling against the trigger. My heart was beating so damned loud, and that minute seemed to take an hour. The entire time I kept asking myself if I could really do it. Could I shoot a child to save the world? But as the minute stretched on, I began to doubt myself. Started to think that maybe I *was* going crazy. Maybe your father's vials were doing something, because by all accounts this was a normal kid, sleeping in his bed. As the seconds ticked down, I felt this awful feeling like I'd become some sort of crazy monster. Then it happened."

"What?" Marina asked from the edge of her seat.

"He vanished."

"Vanished?"

"Yes, he vanished. Poof, just gone. There were these dark swirls around where his body had been, and I was so scared that I nearly shot at them, at the empty bed. I ran from the room, from the house, and went home, certain I'd damned the world. But then, after a few days, when nothing happened, I thought maybe I'd dreamed it all. Or had lost my mind. I even started watching the news to see if he was reported missing, but not a peep about the boy. So I took a chance and drove past the house again a few times, just to see what was happening. Then I saw him, playing in the front yard with his sister, and his father on the porch. And I decided the vial was messing with my head and I had to do something about it, so I locked myself away."

"So why do you think he's dangerous now?"

"Because I saw him in my dreams again, and he's not alone. He's with others who are infected, and they're planning something big. I need to stop him."

Acevedo's dark eyes returned to the mirror. "Do you think I'm crazy?"

"I don't know what to think. We've seen so much. But you also said the vials have a corruptive force on anyone who isn't pure, right? What if the vials are trying to get you to do something awful?"

"I thought that for a while, myself. I mean, I don't *want* to kill a child, whether he's infected or not. But there's the aliens' brilliance. They find someone innocuous to burrow into, someone that nobody would suspect, like a child. But we can't see Luca as a little boy. We must see him as the threat he is."

Marina said nothing. Acevedo kept driving. After a while, she broke the silence.

"And what happens after you kill him? Did your dreams, the vials or whatever, tell you what happens next?"

"No. I just hope that God gives me the strength to finish the job this time."

Marina looked down at her cuffed hand, tugging to no avail. Even if she escaped, Marina wasn't even sure if Acevedo was wrong in killing the boy. The aliens' attack on the van had changed everything. It was hard to deny a threat that was trying to murder you.

Still, Marina couldn't help but wonder if Acevedo was on the wrong path, his thoughts twisted by the very vials they were collecting.

* * * *

CHAPTER 3
PAOLA OLSON

Paola woke to see Desmond staring down at her from the other side of the glass.

Her head was dizzy. The last thing she remembered was going to bed.

"How did I get here?" she asked, starting to sit up.

Paola's head pounded as she moved too fast. She stopped short of standing from the mat.

"What's going on? Where am I?"

"You're in the facility," Desmond said, matter-of-factly, missing his usual delicate tone.

Something was wrong.

"Where's my mom?"

"She couldn't make it. We had to put you here for your own safety."

"What are you talking about?"

"You don't remember?"

Paola shook her head, trying to sort through cloudy thoughts. "No. Remember what?"

"Oh, you did something very bad," Desmond said. "You're here for your own good. To make sure you can't hurt any of the others."

She stood up, tears welling in her eyes as she approached the glass door. "I hurt someone? Who?"

Desmond turned his head sideways, looking at her oddly enough to click something inside her.

"That's not Desmond," The Light said.

She met his eyes, and saw that The Light inside her was right. There was something festering inside him — The Darkness.

"You're not Desmond."

"Ah, so you *were* on to me. I had a feeling, so I had to take some preemptive action. I hope you don't take it personally."

"I want out!"

"Perhaps, in time." Desmond smiled. "For now, I need you here, where I can keep an eye on you and you won't endanger my plans."

"What plans?" Paola asked, angrier by the second.

"I just want to finish what I started on the other world."

Darkness spreading across the land, roaming monstrosities, killer tornadoes, and bodies stacked in rows flashed through Paola's mind.

"You won't take this world."

"I won't?" Desmond smiled wider. "And who's going to stop me? You? The so-called Light? Rather pompous of you to call yourself The Light, don't you think? High and mighty, behaving as if your wants are different than mine."

Paola's mouth moved, but she wasn't driving the words. It was The Light, leaving her voice. "I'm not seeking to destroy. I seek to create."

"I'm creating, too."

"I saw what you created on the other world."

"No, it's different now. I've learned. *We've* learned our lesson. We're looking to do something different this time. We're not seeking to destroy humanity, not all of it, anyway. They have their place in our paradigm. As will you, your mother, and friends, if you *choose*."

"What is it you're planning?" Paola took control of her voice.

Desmond smiled, seeming pleased by his thoughts. "Oh, something grand, my dear. Something this world has been waiting for, even if they didn't know it. Something your people have needed for so long — order. A new order."

Desmond turned to leave.

Paola called out, "Why did you come here? What do you want from me?"

"Just your cooperation, dear. I'll come to you when I'm ready."

"And if I don't cooperate?"

Desmond turned, leaned both hands on the glass door, and looked down at Paola.

"Do you really want to know?"

His dead eyes insisted she didn't.

* * * *

CHAPTER 4
BORICIO WOLFE

Boricio woke in a small dark room, sitting on a cold concrete floor, arms bound in front of him in a straitjacket.

What the fuck?

He squirmed in the jacket, trying to break free, but he could barely move his arms.

Boricio screamed, "Rose!"

Where the fuck is she?

Where am I?

Nothing seemed right.

His head was spinning, his stomach an acid marsh. He felt like he'd drunk a gallon of that green shit he'd found on the other world, the rich fuck's shaman shakes. The only thing missing was the hallucinations.

No sooner had Boricio thought of the nightmarish things he'd seen than he heard footsteps outside the door.

A sliver of light bled into the darkness, a shadow creeping across the center as someone — or *something* — came closer to the door.

"Little pig, little pig, let me in," the voice said from the other side.

The voice made no sense. It was Boricio's, taunting him in a singsong and sending a chill through his soul.

His heart raced as footsteps retreated from the door, and then returned, seeming to drag something — something metal from the sounds of it.

"Little pig, little pig, let me in," his doppelgänger repeated, then responded to himself in a twisted falsetto. "Not by the hair of our chinny chin chins."

A bang on the door.

Boricio's body tensed, his nerves frayed.

"Open up, little piggy!"

Boricio tried to move but couldn't. Tried to speak, to tell his alter ego that he was stuck in a fucking straitjacket, but his mouth had gone numb.

The doorknob began to violently jiggle, obviously locked.

"I said open up!!" Boricio's twin screamed from the other side.

Boricio's heart galloped faster.

He had to get up, and out of the jacket, as the something on the other side of the door wouldn't just walk away.

No, it was coming back.

Footsteps faded from the door again. Boricio counted maybe twenty paces.

The footsteps stopped.

And then his twin ran toward the door, footfalls echoing through the cell, and Boricio's head, like thousands of buffalo tromping across the plains.

The ground shook.

Footsteps grew louder.

The walls wiggled and floundered, threatening to jostle loose from the floor.

Something hit the door with the force of thunder. Splinters of wood flew from the door and lacerated Boricio's face.

He closed his eyes to protect them.

Footsteps again backed away from the door as his twin grabbed another running start.

More light seeped through a zigzagging crack in the door's center and reminded Boricio of lightning.

As the footsteps rolled forward again, the door, the light shook in a constant blur. His eyes couldn't turn from the blurred jag.

Boricio braced for impact.

The blade of an ax slammed into the door.

A large wedge of wood broke away along the crevice. Blinding light poured inside.

Boricio closed his eyes again, the light like a migraine.

"Go away!" he cried out, feeling he had to be in some kind of fucked-up nightmare and maybe it would bend to his will if he demanded it.

Boricio heard the doorknob being fumbled with, this time from the inside, and opened his eyes to see a man's hand reaching through.

The door swung open, and a shadow draped him.

Boricio looked up to see himself, naked, covered in blood. Then it wasn't him, but rather a retarded fat fuck wearing a prison guard's uniform.

The guard drawled, "Hey, boy, you ready for some real fun?" then lifted the axe and brought it down.

Boricio woke with a scream, back in his bed, unable to move, sweat slicking every inch of his body.

The door flew open.

Rose appeared, wearing the same blue dress he'd seen her in last time.

"Are you OK?" She rushed to his side and ran a hand through his sweaty mop.

"Yeah, yeah, I had this crazy fucking nightmare."

"What was it?" Her eyes met his.

Something about her gaze instantly soothed him — sent the nightmare to the recesses of Boricio's memory, gone and almost forgotten already.

"It's OK," she said, kissing him on the cheek.

As she started to pull away, their eyes met. Rose leaned back in, kissing Boricio softly on the lips. For a moment, the kiss felt like a warm, familiar jacket, yet fresh and unfamiliar.

Normally, all Rose had to do was kiss Boricio to get his missile on countdown, but fuck if his nethers registered shit.

He let out a deep sigh.

"What's wrong?"

"I still can't feel anything."

"How's your headache?"

"Better. I've had worse."

"So, that's something."

"Thanks," he said with half a laugh.

Rose pulled a chair beside the bed, then reached out and held Boricio's left hand.

He thought for a moment that he could feel it. But when he closed his eyes, to see if he still felt her touch, he didn't. It was a phantom feeling.

"I can't feel your hand."

"Can I tell you a story?"

"Well, it's not like I've got anywhere to go. And you do know how to spin one helluva yarn."

"Thanks," she said, smiling. "When I was nine, my grandma was dying of cancer, and we spent a lot of time visiting her in the hospital. But nobody in the family wanted to tell me she was actually dying. They kept saying she was sick, but that she'd get better. They didn't think I could take it. I could tell they were lying, though, because of the way people always got quiet around me, and all the red eyes and runny noses. Things were bad."

Boricio wished he could squeeze her hand.

"Anyway, all the times I had to go to the hospital the nurses wouldn't let me in to see Grams. I'm not sure if they said I was too young or what, but I had to sit downstairs in the main lobby where I passed my time with Judy Blume."

"Oh, yeah," Boricio said, "she was one of my favorites. I loved *Tales of a Fourth Grade Fuck-Up.*"

"She was one of my favorites, too," Rose said, missing the joke.

"So, one day, my Mom came down to the lobby and whispered to me to hurry and come with her. I grabbed my book and followed. She told me to stand behind her and stay out of sight. She said to act like I belonged, and that if anyone were to look at me I should barely acknowledge them, just nod, and move on. So I did."

"Hell, yeah," Boricio nodded. "That's how I always do."

"So, she brought me into see my grandma. Grams asked that my mom leave us alone for a minute. So my mom went to get a soda or something, and Grams looked me in the eye and admitted she was dying."

"Shit," Boricio muttered.

"Yeah, it was heavy. She said she thought I was old enough to know, and that she'd be dead soon anyway, so she'd rather we had our chances to say goodbye now rather than her dying and my wishing I'd known. So I kissed her, cried on her chest for a while before my mom came back. Mom knew immediately that Grams had told me, but neither of us said a word. Grams took my hand and said that even though she wouldn't be here any longer she'd always be here. She pointed at my heart. And then, just like that, she died."

Rose's eyes welled up as if she were remembering this memory for the first time in years. Maybe she was.

"Wow, thanks for the snuff film, I liked the play by play," Boricio joked, trying to lighten the mood. "Shit, here I am paralyzed, but I guess it could be worse."

"That wasn't the point," Rose said, seeming distant.

"I'm sorry," Boricio said, "what was the point?"

"Well, even though you can't feel my hand touching yours, I hope you can feel me in your heart."

Boricio smiled, "Well, sheesh, I didn't know you were gonna get all Hallmark, Morning Rose."

"I just want you to know I'm here for you, and that I promise you'll get better."

Boricio wanted to ask Rose how she could possibly know something like that, but he wasn't about to give her best intentions a golden shower. Besides, as shitty as he felt, he did feel that things would be OK. Because when the chips were down, Team Boricio never surrendered or left a play on the table. You kept playing dropping cards until you left the house with your sphincter bleeding.

"I love you, Rose."

She whispered, "I love you, too," then kissed Boricio again on the mouth.

* * * *

CHAPTER 5
LUCA HARDING

Luca wasn't supposed to be listening, but he couldn't help it.

He lay in bed in the room below Boricio's, concentrating on the space between them, focusing on sounds until they formed in his head and he heard Rose telling Boricio about her grandmother.

Why is she doing this to him?

She's trying to get inside his head more. Makes it easier to control him, The Darkness responded in Luca's mind. *She may be searching for ways to shape his memories, to make him forget more. If she can erase some of the worst of his past, she may be able to turn him into something she can use.*

Is she going to give him a vial or infect him?

She still wants to give him the vial.

And what do you think?

I think what you want me to think.

That's not what I asked. What do you think?

I think it won't matter. Art has something else planned.

What do you mean?

I've been looking in his head. The Darkness in him is making alternate plans — to infect Boricio. To remove the vial from the equation.

He can do that? I thought she could see into our thoughts. Or at least his.

She's getting weaker. Rose is starting to surface more. Especially now as she was telling the story about her grandmother. Art senses it, along with a chance to take control, and steer the course back to where it was.

Which is what?

Toward your species' evolution.

And what do you think about that?

This was the first time Luca dared to ask The Darkness anything that might alert *It*, or Rose, to his misgivings about her plans.

I think what you want me to think.

Really?

Luca wondered if *It* was trying to trick him into admitting something he'd been trying not to think about. If he revealed his thoughts, would he be marked a traitor? Would Rose, or now Art, infect him and consume his body and soul?

The Darkness answered, reading his thoughts, and fears. *I'm not sure their plan is the right way forward.*

Luca felt a tingling through his body at the prospect that The Darkness might agree, and wondered if he had somehow won *It* over.

I am not The Darkness in your interpretation of the word, Luca. I am neither Light nor Darkness. I am something in between. I am not even an I, but a we.

Gray?

If you must assign a color, that is fine.

What do you think we should do with the vials?

I don't know. But I no longer think you should attempt to evolve your species.

Why?

Because The Darkness on Black Island is growing stronger. It has found our agents there and killed them. It wants something different from Rose, something far less friendly to your species. This will end badly for all — humans and us alike.

Does Rose know this?

Yes, but she doesn't see the threat as clearly as we do. Art does. And he's making other plans.

Plans to what?

Join them. He outed our spies there in exchange for freedom to join them when the time comes.

He's betraying us?

He sees a weakness in Rose, in that she still feels for Boricio. She's tainted too much by her humanity.

I thought Art was like us.

He's nothing like us. He's seen too much, done too much, and the vial has twisted that inside him. He is playing kind, but you cannot trust him.

What do I do? Should I tell her?

No. First, you must heal Boricio.

Heal him? How? With a vial?

No. With your Light.

* * * *

CHAPTER 6
BORICIO WOLFE

Boricio woke to the sound of nervous footsteps.

He opened his eyes, relieved to see Luca standing in the dimly lit bedroom, rather than someone looking to murder him.

"Hey, Boy Wonder, what's up?" Boricio asked, still groggy and feeling the effects of whatever drugs they were piping through his IV bag.

"Shh," Luca said, a finger to his lips. His eyes were wide, nervous.

"What's wrong?" The hairs on the back of Boricio's neck stood at attention.

"We can't let them hear us."

"Who's *them?*"

"Art and Rose."

"Why not?"

"They're not who they say they are."

"Whatchyou talkin' bout, Willis?"

"I don't know how to say this, Boricio. Not without making you mad."

"Out with it," Boricio said, getting annoyed. He hated when people couldn't spit out whatever the fuck they were tryin' to say, pip-squeaks included. Fuck, life is only so long, and most people spent way too many hours stammering ways to couch their words rather than lettin' shit fly where it may.

Luca met his eyes and swallowed.

"They're aliens."

Boricio said nothing, waiting to see if Luca would crack into a "Nah, I'm just fuckin' with ya" smile.

The boy wasn't smiling.

"What do you mean?"

"You really don't remember, do you?"

"No, kid, and you're about to piss me off if you don't just fucking fill the spittoon."

"I can do better," Luca said.

"Yeah? Whatcha gonna do, show me a video? Put on a play? Just out with it."

"I can heal you. And with it, the memories will return."

"You can *heal me*? You mean make me walk again?"

"Yes."

"How?"

"You don't remember how the other Luca healed you, do you?"

"I know he 'fixed me,' but ... "

A memory flashed back — how Luca had healed him, and other people, aging each time until he was old.

"Oh shit, I do remember, but it's all foggy. Did you age?"

"He did, yes."

"Well, you gonna get a bunch of hair on your balls if you heal me now?"

"We don't have a choice. Not unless you wanna be infected, too."

"No, I don't wanna be fucking infected, boy. But I don't want you hurting yourself. Why don't you go get Rose, and we can talk this out."

"You don't believe me, do you? Rose isn't Rose."

"Of course she is," Boricio said. His head was pounding, and he felt more confused than ever. He tried to remember the old man's name, but couldn't. "That old fucker, yeah, I can believe *he* might be infected. But not Rose. I'd know it if she was."

"No," Luca shook his head, "you wouldn't. *It's* good at hiding *Itself*."

"Bullshit." Boricio wondered why this little shit was fucking with him. "You're not even the same Luca I know. Maybe *you're* the one who's infected?"

Luca was shaking, looking back at the door as if he heard someone coming down the hall.

"I have to do this now," he said. "Can I heal you?"

"I want to talk to Rose," Boricio said.

"I'm sorry," Luca said and reached out for Boricio.

* * * *

CHAPTER 7
PAOLA OLSON

Paola couldn't tell if it was day or night from deep beneath the island's surface.

She'd never felt so far from her mom.

She wondered where her mother thought she was. Desmond must've told her some lie to cover her absence. But what had he said? That she was missing? That she was sick and locked in the facility?

Horror found her.

What if he'd killed her?

Paola shook her head, refusing to give that thought more space to grow. Her mother couldn't be dead. Paola would know it. Of that much she was certain.

Paola wished she could reach out to her mom and tell her the truth — where she was and that she was OK, for now.

But as Paola closed her eyes and tried to reach out to her mom, like The Light told her to do, she found nothing but interference.

Maybe she is dead?

No! No, she's not.

Frustrated, she kicked at the glass wall, and screamed.

Paola wondered if the ceiling's tiny holes held cameras, speakers, or some sort of hole to vent poisonous gas.

If there were cameras, was Desmond watching now?

Paola couldn't believe that she'd been so stupid. That she'd not noticed Desmond's infection. She wondered if he'd been infected all along, when he came and saved them. Or was it more recent? If it had been all along, why come and save them in the first place? Why not just let her and Mom die in the hospital? It was the perfect time to do so.

In Luca's voice The Light said, *Because he wanted to use you to find the vials.*

Sometimes The Light spoke to Paola in her voice. Other times, it sounded like Luca. She liked it better when The Light sounded like him. She liked to think that a bit of Luca was with her. It made her feel less alone.

What do I do now? I can't reach out to my mother. He's got me in here, and nobody knows.

Reach out to another of them. We're all connected. Everyone I pulled back to this world has a bit of me, a bit of us in all of them. Try someone else, someone who can transmit your message and let your mother know where you are.

Paola found a slight smile as she thought of the perfect person.

* * * *

CHAPTER 8
BRENT FOSTER

Brent was in Times Square with Luis, standing off against a horde of aliens. They were on top of the cars, firing weapons blindly into the encroaching mass of infected and black, shape-shifting aliens.

"Come on, you fuckers!" Luis screamed like Rambo, holding a massive machine gun that looked like it could bring down a tank.

Brent was too terrified to scream anything. He kept firing his rifle, barely denting the onslaught.

Darkness overcame them.

He was then in a warehouse with Keenan and Lisa, the Black Mountain Guardsman he hadn't seen since they were all on Black Island. They were at a card table, playing poker while gunfire erupted outside.

He found it odd that no one seemed the least bit concerned with the fighting around them. But then, just like that, some part of Brent knew he was in a dream. The same dream he'd had so many times before.

"Are you alive?" he asked Lisa.

She looked at him and said nothing.

So far as Brent knew, Black Mountain was something that didn't even exist on this Earth. Perhaps she wasn't one of the people Luca brought over, or brought back. She was a native of that world. Maybe she was still there, if anything could've survived. Or perhaps Luca brought her back to Earth with the rest of them.

If so, Brent didn't know her last name or how he'd find her — assuming she *wanted* to be found. Maybe she was wandering around the country like some crazy person, trying to convince people of what she saw. Hell, maybe she was locked in an asylum.

Or maybe the government had her locked up to quiet her mouth.

Ed looked at Brent, brow furrowed, "Well?"

"Well, what?" Brent stared down at his cards. "It's your turn."

"No, I'm waiting for you to tell me."

"Tell you what?"

"About Jade. How is she?"

This part of the dream was new.

Brent didn't know what to say. He couldn't lie to Ed, even in a dream.

"She's ... " he started.

Gunfire ended outside and brought a knock at the door. The warehouse had turned into Brent's tiny living room back in Manhattan.

Brent stood, curious. The knock and change of locale was also new to the dream.

Lisa grabbed a blade from the table and was off her feet, asking, "Who is it?"

Ed grabbed his shotgun but remained seated, one eye on Brent.

A girl's voice came from behind the door. "It's me, Paola. I need to talk to Brent. Please, Brent, open the door."

"I don't trust her." Lisa looked back at Brent. "Isn't she dead?"

Brent stood and grabbed his gun from the table.

"You sure you wanna open that door?" Lisa asked.

"Please." Paola sounded urgent, seeming so real against the dream's artifice.

Brent approached the door, reached out, twisted the knob, and opened it.

Paola was standing before him, but she wasn't in the hallway outside his apartment. The door opened into a dark glass cell.

"Where are we?" Brent closed the door closed behind him, shutting off from Ed and Lisa to seal himself in Paola's cell.

"We're on the facility's eighth level, and I have so much to tell you."

Brent looked at Paola, confused. "Am I dreaming?"

She shook her head. "Not anymore."

**

Brent woke in the darkness, cold, terrified, and trembling on Mary's living room floor. He looked over and saw Teagan stirring in the darkness beside him.

"What's wrong?" she asked.

"Paola's alive."

* * * *

CHAPTER 9
MARY OLSON

The darkness held a comfortable silence, and an icy chill that Mary felt tempted to curl into for the rest of her miserable forever.

Mary wasn't sure how long she'd been lying in bed or how much of that time had been spent sleeping rather than staring into the gloaming that pressed on her lungs and left her so short of breath she could barely muster the will to want.

She reached out and sipped from one of the water bottles that Teagan had set on her nightstand. Mary could smell food there as well. The scent of roasted garlic made her stomach growl, but even with her body empty and her stomach chewing Mary from the inside out the thought of eating made her want to vomit. She thought she smelled sugar and cinnamon, perhaps a snickerdoodle. That made it worse.

She looked at the clock: *4:15 a.m.*

Mary wondered why Desmond wasn't beside her. She thought she'd heard him come home, but he could have had to go back. Work seemed to own him lately. She wondered if Brent, Teagan, and the kids were still there.

Mary felt an overwhelming guilt for burying herself in the room and avoiding contact with the world. It had been steadily creeping, but now the tragedy threatened to swallow her whole. They'd lost someone, too — their friend and Ed's daughter, Jade. She had no right to hoard all the grief.

OK, Mary, time to stop feeling sorry for yourself. Get out of bed and do something other than this.

She undressed, turned on the shower to scalding, then stepped inside and put her head under the piping-hot water.

Pulsating water massaged Mary's scalp and felt good on her skin, thawing the chill that had settled into her marrow, slowly bringing her back to life.

She sank to the shower floor, and let the warmth rain on her body, through her hair, down her back, all over every inch of her skin.

After her shower, Mary flicked a switch and turned on the overhead lights and looked at the plate of food on the nightstand. An apple, a sandwich that must've had garlic, and a small saucer with two cookies. It reminded Mary of the times during summer vacation when Paola would make her lunch and bring it to her office. Like Paola, Teagan always tried to overperform in the kitchen.

She smiled at the memory, and at Teagan's sweetness.

Mary dressed in jeans and a charcoal tee, then crossed the room, sat on the bed and tore into the apple. It was crisp and sweet. Like the warm shower, it seemed to waken her.

Mary spun her head toward a soft knock at the door.

"Yes?" She wondered who else was up with the dawn.

"Can I come in?" Brent whispered to keep the house sleeping.

"Yes, of course."

Brent stepped into the room, his hair a mess, eyes exhausted and hollow. He looked like *he* could use a shower.

He shut the door softly behind him and turned back to Mary, seeming as if he had something urgent to say.

"What's wrong?" Mary stood and set the apple next to the saucer.

"I'm not sure how to say this, so I'm just going to come out and say it and hope you don't think I'm crazy."

"What?" Anxiety rose to stab Mary in the gut.

"I don't think Paola is dead."

"What?" she asked, confused, and feeling as if Brent had just punched her in the stomach.

"Please, just hear me out. I had a dream, and in it Paola said she was being held on the facility's eighth level."

Mary stared at Brent, wondering why he'd raise her hopes then burn them by saying it was only a dream. "She died in front of me, Brent. I saw it with my own two eyes."

Mary wondered if maybe Brent had snapped himself. He'd lost his wife, and Jade, and was trying to keep his shit together and be there for both Teagan and the kids. Maybe denial had bested him.

He shook his head. "I know it sounds crazy. But she also told me to give you a message, something that would prove I was telling you the truth."

"What?" Despite her fighting it, a blossom of hope bloomed inside her.

"Paola told me about Hammy the Hamster, and how when she was in kindergarten she was afraid to go to school, so each day you put a drawing in her lunchbox of a hamster you called Hammy, who would give her a new message each day. Sometimes Hammy said, 'I love you,' and other times you'd have Hammy doing something funny like getting stuck in a toilet paper roll, with his little tail sticking out the back end."

Mary felt as if the world had been ripped from beneath her — again. She fell back on the bed, only realizing she was sitting after she was.

"What? How?" were all she could manage, though Mary had a million brewing questions. "I saw her die. Who is holding her in the facility?"

A name flashed in Mary's mind before Brent could answer, a name she was ashamed to even consider.

Then he confirmed it.

"Desmond."

Mary stared at him, barely able to breathe. Words were impossible.

Brent sat beside her on the bed as Mary gasped for air, her heart racing, fairly certain she was having a panic attack.

"Relax." Brent set a hand on her back, rubbing it as if Mary were a child. "We'll get through this."

She closed her eyes, focusing on her breath until she was able to stop gasping for air. She found a deep breath then held it as if it could keep her floating in an ocean of insanity.

Calmly, Brent said, "Paola is OK, that's all that matters. We'll find a way to get her out of there and take care of this."

Mary had a million more questions, such as how the hell they could break her daughter out of a top secret government installation? Why did Desmond do this? And whom *did* she see die?

But she had to focus on her breathing, in, count to five, then out, long exhale.

Once slightly calmer, Mary launched her questions, too many at once, bombarding Brent like a reporter at a press conference assailing a senator.

"Paola wasn't sure why he'd done it. And she didn't know anything about the girl we saw die. My guess it was an alien. Desmond's infected. She thinks he probably has been since his return. Now he's controlling The Darkness, and planning something big. Paola was standing in his way, so he's keeping her hidden underground."

Mary's lone bite of apple rolled in the acid and started to rise. She raced to the bathroom, landed on her knees in front of the toilet, and retched up the only thing she'd swallowed other than spit in God knew how long.

How could I not have seen it?

I trusted him.

I loved him.

I ... slept with him ... with It!

Her skin felt clammy, and itchy, corrupted by the alien's touch. Mary wondered if he'd somehow infected her with The Darkness as well.

A horrifying thought surged to the front of her mind, demanding her full attention.

Oh God, no.

She retched again, this time nothing but water.

"Oh God," she said, over and over.

Brent opened the door. "What?"

Mary shook her head, wiping vomit from her chin, and stood. She went to the sink and started to wash, unable to meet Brent's eyes in the reflection.

She couldn't tell him what she was thinking. Voicing the thought might make it come true.

Mary had to steer her mind back to Paola, and figuring a way to get her daughter back. The last thing she could think about now was that the thing posing as Desmond may have gotten her pregnant.

* * * *

CHAPTER 10
BORICIO WOLFE

Boricio screamed as flames licked his insides.

Luca had laid both of his hands on Boricio's arm. The fire had started there, then spread outward in every direction, waking numb flesh in its path. At first, the fire hurt. But then it felt strangely ... *good*.

Luca was shaking, too, his whole body trembling so fast it was barely more than a blur.

But Boricio couldn't tend to the boy, not while his brain was getting beaten by a barrage of memories shaking him free of the fog and confusion that had settled on him since waking up paralyzed.

Boricio watched as hundreds of memories unspooled at once, playing like a dozen screaming IMAX screens, with none of them making a cumdrop of sense ... at first. But then shit started to click into place, and Boricio was putting two and two together like he had a goddamned Beautiful Mind.

Boricio remembered everything.

Remembered Guard Tard, the prison, the weeks of running away, and then the cause of his running — the horror that had happened to his Morning Rose. The alien infecting her.

Fire slowly receded, and time seemed to drip back to normal. The Boy Wonder slipped away from Boricio's bed and collapsed, spent on the floor.

Rose stepped through the door and looked down at Luca. "What's going on?"

The boy had aged nearly a decade, a ball's hair over twenty. Luca didn't seem to realize what had happened just yet, looking down at his Hulked-out outfit, pawing his body in confusion.

Luca looked up at Rose. "I healed him."

She turned to Boricio, but it wasn't his Morning Rose. And it *hadn't* been.

Some motherfucker had been pretending, wearing her body like it was goddamned Halloween.

It had lied to him.

Had made him feel safe. Loved.

Boricio wanted to do more than kill it. He wanted to destroy it down to the molecule, dig a ditch, and shit on its remains.

He looked down at Luca. "Can you give us a second, Hulk Junior?"

Luca, still clearly dazed, looked up at Boricio, then nodded and left the room.

The door closed, and Boricio sat up, moving his body for the first time since his arrival. His muscles were stiff, and pain prickled like a village of tiny needles, but at least he could move. Like the Boy Wonder said, he'd been healed, and now he remembered.

Boricio looked at the soon-to-be-dead thing pretending to be his Morning Rose, looking at him with her artificial loving eyes, and that sad smile she sometimes had when he fell into one his darker moods that he couldn't explain.

"You're healed." She tried to smile, but Boricio saw right through it. He flinched and pulled back on her way to a hug.

"*You* ... stay the fuck away from me."

She stopped, her eyes wide. "What's wrong, honey?"

Boricio swallowed, trying to keep his rage from making him do something stupid.

He cast his eyes around the room, taking inventory of all the shit he could use to send this monster into oblivion. He could gouge *Its* eyes and puncture *Its* throat with the pen on his nightstand. A brush on the dresser could be snapped in half and used as a blade. He could shatter the mirror and use its shards to slice the alien wide.

But the fucker didn't deserve anything so pleasant, and Boricio longed to take his time, snaking his fingers into *Its* throat, then choking the fucker dead with his bare hands.

"I remember," he said staring into the alien's widening eyes.

He leaped on the creature, hands around *Its* neck, falling on top of it, straddling Rose's body, staring into her eyes as he choked the impostor.

"Wait!" Rose's voice cried out in a rasping gasp.

Boricio loosened his grip, just enough to tease it with mercy. "What?"

"I'm still in here, Boricio! It's me, Rose!"

"Bullshit!" Boricio screamed, squeezing tighter.

"I am!" it insisted again. "We're both in here. Just like with Luca. We can coexist with them, Boricio."

"Stop it!" He pushed his fingers harder into her flesh, not wanting to know what the hell she, *It*, meant about Luca.

Rose's eyes welled with tears as she vented an anemic, "Please."

Boricio closed his eyes.

He couldn't look his old Rose in the eyes as he killed her.

No, not a her, It!

He kept squeezing, tight, telling himself that his Morning Rose would prefer death to this corruption of body and soul.

But even as Boricio thought it, a large part of him longed for his Rose so much to maybe believe there *was* something left of her in the puppet. Maybe the alien was telling the truth. And maybe she could have her body back again.

No.

There's nothing left of my Rosebud.

Don't believe its lies.

She tried to say something.

"Die," he said, squeezing his eyes shut, despite their will to open. "Fucking die."

"Stop!" a voice yelled.

Boricio looked up, saw the old man, Art, aiming a shotgun at his head. "Get off of her."

Boricio looked down at Rose's face, her crying eyes, and couldn't help but feel like a monster. Another part of him felt like he was being worked by the alien, being made to feel guilty. Using his love for her against him.

"Let go of her or I *will* kill you," Art said.

Boricio let go, slowly, then stood, eyes on the old fucker, trying to figure the best way to get his gun.

The thing that wasn't Rose stood, swallowing, wiping tears from her eyes, still playing victim.

Art turned to It. "What do you want me to do? Shoot him?"

"No," It said. "Please, leave us alone."

"He just tried to kill you."

"I said leave us!"

Art shrank back like a dog being scolded then gave *It* the shotgun.

It took the weapon, training it on Boricio until the door shut and they were back to being alone.

It lowered the gun, meeting his eyes.

"I don't want to kill you."

"Well, I *do* want to kill you," Boricio said. No reason to pretend, or try and outsmart an alien. This would only end with one of them dying.

"I wasn't lying when I said she's in here."

"So, who am I talking to now, Rose or the alien? You said 'she's in here,' meaning you were pretending to be her before."

"No, now we are one. She and I. But the Rose you love is still in here. We've done nothing to her."

"Yeah, is that so? Well, how about you just get out of her body. Find someone else to live in."

"I'm afraid we can't do that. But I have another proposal. Why don't *you* join us?"

"Yeah, I don't think so." He chuckled. "Boricio is the quarterback, and he aint' throwing for Team Nasty-Ass Alien Goo!"

Not Rose smiled. Boricio wasn't sure if it was some part of *her* smiling or if the alien was a condescending cunt. Boricio had had enough artificial mirth, of fuckers looking down at him like he was half-retard. People always thought they were better than him and smiled when, in fact, they were writing him off.

But nobody writes Boricio off. No. Body.

"Please, Boricio, don't you want more than this? I know you. I know you're so much better than most of these filthy, lazy, and supremely ignorant humans. You realized this early. That's why you culled them from the planet."

"OK, you can stop blowing smoke up my dirthole, because I wasn't doing anyone no favors by killin' folks.

That was all about me. No need to shine shit and tell me it's gold."

"Perhaps, but still you know what I say is true. We can change humanity, once and for all, evolve it into what it was meant to be."

"What the fuck are you talking about?" Boricio asked, eager to bitch slap the foreplay and get back to killing this fucking thing.

"All species evolve. Humans evolved. We, our species, are evolving. We can evolve together, create something new from the best of our species."

"I saw what your species did on ole Bizarro Earth, so forgive me if that don't exactly sound like a roomful of titties."

"We have changed. Though I should warn you that there is another force out there, trying to do what we did to that other world."

"What do you mean 'another force?'"

"Our species is a collective, operating as one. But we've since split, parts of us wanting to seize power for itself, disagreeing with our notions of how to evolve your species. They want to enslave most of you, use you as nothing more than fuel."

"Let me get this straight, E.T. — you're claiming to be this great, advanced alien species working as a collective and wanting to evolve us. Yet your own fucking species is subject to the same whims as ours, wanting to gobble more than its share of the pie?"

"I never said we were perfect. But *together* we can be as close as possible. We can offer you power, Boricio. We can cure your kind's diseases. We can allow you to live forever. Just say yes."

He looked at the shotgun, again trained on him.

"So join the Dark Side or die, right, Darth?"

He met *Its* eyes, but *Not Rose* refused to flinch.

It nodded.

Boricio clenched his fists, glared *It* in the eyes, and said, "I got an idea. How 'bout we play of game of rock, paper, you're dead. You first!"

* * * *

CHAPTER 11
THOMAS ACEVEDO

"You're really going to do this?" Marina asked, pestering him as if he had chosen his path, or worse, was deluded.

"The vessel has to die. There is no other way." Acevedo continued loading up on weapons from the agents' van. He had an assault rifle, a pistol, and four of the weird-looking grenades, which he hoped were explosive. Once Acevedo ended the vessel, he'd have to burn the alien before it could leave the host and infect another. There were two more in there with the vessel, Acevedo had seen in his vision. One, a woman named Rose, who was strong and maybe the smartest of the aliens. Then there was an old man, Art, who was still new to infection and had not yet worked out his abilities. He would be the easiest to kill, and Rose the toughest. Luca was probably the most powerful, even if he didn't yet know it. But if Acevedo only had a single shot, he'd have to take out the boy. He was the one in the dreams, after all.

It all revolved around Luca.

Without Luca, the prophecy failed, and the world would be safe. At least, that's what his visions kept swearing.

Yeah, but what if the visions aren't real? What if he is just a boy?

Acevedo shook his head to silence the doubt he couldn't afford. That was why Marina couldn't come with him. Sure, he could use the backup, but couldn't afford to have her doubts as infection.

He had to stay strong and keep his mind clear of the alien influence.

Marina, still cuffed to the back seat, begged, "At least set me free before you go. If something happens to you, I'm screwed."

"I don't have anything to set you free."

"Use that mind thing you did on yours."

"Sorry, Marina. I don't have time. But don't worry, I will return."

"But what if you *don't* come back? I'll be stuck here with no way to get help. If one of our enemies doesn't kill me, the sun will bake me once it gets hotter."

Acevedo crawled into the back, close enough to assure her, but not so close that she might be able to strike out in anger. "Listen, Marina. I promise I'll be back. And if not, well, you'll have bigger things to worry about than a hot van."

"Please," she cried out as Acevedo slid open the side panel door and hopped out into dawn.

He looked back at Marina and shushed her with a finger to his lips. "I'll be back in twenty minutes or less."

The priest softly closed the door, despite her begging.

He looked down the street where Luca and the others were staying, assuming his visions were true.

A low fog clung to the ground, obscuring all but the closest two houses, giving him an advantage upon entry. Of course, if they sensed him and were dreaming of him as he had been of them, the advantage was theirs. Marina would die in the van.

But Acevedo couldn't worry about her now.

He had to find and kill Luca Harding.

* * * *

CHAPTER 12
LUCA HARDING

Luca stared at himself in the mirror, mouth agape, barely able to believe the changes.

It looked like he'd aged nearly a decade.

And yet Luca felt only partly surprised. because some of the other Luca's memories, as well as memories of the people the other Luca had saved, were swirling through his head more frequently. They weren't solid enough that he could make sense of them and assemble a narrative of everything that happened to each of the survivors, but he saw the other Luca age in the memories, both from the boy's viewpoint as well as others'. He also saw the other Luca die, shot by his friend, Will, and then return. The other version of himself had continued to age until he seemed ancient.

Is this what's going to happen to me? Will I get older each time I do this?

Possibly, The Darkness said inside him, not exactly a comfort. "But perhaps we can change that. I am working on a way to halt the aging within your body's chemistry. Perhaps I can return your youth."

No. I don't want to be young any more. I need to be older, bigger, stronger. I need to be ready for what's coming.

Art stood beside him in the bathroom, unable to stop staring either. He seemed caught somewhere between awe at the change and disappointment in what he'd done.

Luca wondered if Art was onto him — if he knew of his betrayal. And if so, would he try to kill him?

"Why did you heal him, kid?"

Luca didn't shrink from the old man's stare.

"Because it wasn't right."

"What wasn't right?"

"To lie to him like that. To use his love for Rose to trick him into joining us. I know you wanted to either infect him or kill him."

Art's fuzzy eyebrows rose. "And how do you know that?"

"Because I'm not as dumb as people think. I pay attention."

"Hey, kid, I never said you were dumb. Far from it. And I'll agree that yes, I didn't want to give Boricio a vial, but that's because I'm concerned for our safety."

Luca was about to call Art on all of his lies. To let the old man know he wasn't fooling him.

But Luca's Darkness said to keep his mouth shut. "Sometimes it's better to play a bit dumber than you are if you want people to make mistakes."

Luca decided to play along with Art, even if playing nice to a liar made him sick to his stomach. "I understand, Mr. Art. You were looking out for us. And I'm sorry to go behind your back like I did. But Boricio is like a brother to me. Or at least the other version of him was. He is capable of goodness. I've seen it."

Art looked at Luca as if gears were turning in his head, trying to decide how to best deal with the boy. Luca considered using The Darkness to spy on Art's thoughts, then reconsidered. Though he couldn't be certain, Luca was pretty sure if he tried to read Art's mind while looking at the man, he would figure Luca out. Art would know he'd been made, and at that point would have nothing to lose by killing the boy, or all of them.

Art smiled and put a hand on Luca's shoulder. "Why don't we see if we can find you some clothes that'll fit, eh?"

"Thank you," Luca said.

Art led him down the hall to one of the guest rooms he'd not yet been in. The room was smaller than the others, filled with racks like you'd see in a store, with clothes hanging in neat rows.

"What's all this?"

"Rose asked me to gather clothes. Different sizes and sexes to fit our growing group, since some of the people, like myself, may not have had time to pack their bags before leaving their old lives."

"Wow, she really thought ahead." Luca looked at the variety and sizes.

Art pulled out a black hoodie and some dark-blue jeans. Both looked like they belonged to a college kid.

"Wanna try these on?" Art asked holding them up.

They looked too large and baggy, but it was better than a shirt that made him look like the Incredible Hulk without the big green muscles.

"OK."

Art handed him the clothes and a belt. "You might need this."

"What about shoes? Did you get shoes?"

Art sighed. "That's one thing I didn't have time to pick up yet. Plus, we figured the people would probably have shoes. We *do* have underwear, though. Check the dresser, and you'll probably find a pack. I'd say you look like a men's small, maybe medium? There are some socks in there, too, that should fit you."

"Thanks," Luca repeated.

He looked down at his feet, still bare from when he was sleeping. They were larger and had a few tufts of dark hair, mostly on the toes.

Art left the room so that Luca could change.

He stripped from his shredded apparel and couldn't help but notice that among the areas to grow — both size and hair — was downstairs. Luca felt a flush of embarrassment, like he was looking at someone else naked, and quickly put on a pair of well-fitting red boxers.

He slid on the jeans, which were too baggy and longer than his size, then slid on a belt. He slipped the notch through the last hole, which pulled the belt as tight as it would go. It wasn't a perfect fit, but would do for the moment. Luca rolled up his pant legs, making light-blue cuffs that reminded him of how his dad had dressed for a Halloween party when he said he was going as some guy from the '50s that Luca had never heard of.

Luca wondered which father that was, his or the other Luca's. He couldn't place the memory in time, so he couldn't be certain if it was before or after the car accident that took his family from him.

He slid on the black hoodie, also baggy, just like most older kids seemed to wear them. Luca didn't feel *too* stupid as he stared in the mirror at the late-teen, early-twenties version of himself.

Luca lifted the jacket to see his abs, admiring his physique. He wasn't built, but there was definitely more muscle than he remembered having in his younger self. He wondered how strong he could get if he started lifting weights, and how long it would take to get into good fighting shape.

The past few weeks had shown him that he no longer had time for a childhood. He had to prepare for what was coming by getting as smart and strong as possible. While Luca supposed some might lament the loss of a decade, those people weren't children, and didn't know how badly most kids wanted to be adults. And those people didn't know that a war unlike any other was already on its way.

It was time to put his childhood in the closet where it belonged, and Luca was fine with that.

Suddenly, a gunshot thundered downstairs.

* * * *

CHAPTER 13
EDWARD KEENAN

Ed followed the tracker to his van parked on a suburban street in Highland Park.

He killed the stolen motorcycle's engine and pulled the Mossberg from his back, where he'd slid the shotgun between his shirt and jacket like a makeshift scabbard.

Fog was hanging too low and thick to spot the van. But Ed could see it blipping on his Guardsman watch's interface as he approached, gun drawn.

His heart raced as he moved closer, hoping that whoever was inside, whoever had taken the van, wasn't also lying in wait to attack him. He needed to take care of whoever took the van, secure the vials, and make sure that Acevedo and Marina were safe.

But the closer he got to the van and saw its dark shape taking form in the fog, he grew ever more certain that he was about to discover a bloodbath. He'd find Acevedo and Marina slaughtered, and the perpetrator gone. Ed hoped that whoever took the van didn't know about the vials, and they were still safely hidden in the glove compartment. If not, then he'd need to figure out another way to find the vials. Maybe call back to Black Island and see if Paola could help.

Ed was about ten feet from the van when he saw through the broken windshield that no one was in the front seats.

OK, let's check the back.

He stepped softly in front of the van, shotgun drawn, and peered through to the rear.

He could see a figure in the back seat, cloaked in shadows.

He tapped the gun on the van's hood and said, "Come out with your hands up!"

Silence.

His heart beat faster as he circled to try and get a better look.

"This is Homeland Security. Step out of the van with your hands up!"

A woman's voice: "Agent Keenan?"

"Marina?" he asked, surprised.

"Yeah, I'm still cuffed to the back seat! Can you let me out?"

Ed couldn't believe she was still alive.

He tried the driver's side door and found it locked, then used his shotgun's butt to break the driver's side window, then reached in and unlocked the door.

He slid into the van, flicked on the rear light, and was further surprised to find Marina alone.

"Where's the preacher?"

"He took off when the shit hit the fan. I'm so sorry. I asked him not to leave you and Luther, but he wouldn't listen. He's obsessed with getting the other four vials."

"Other four?"

"He said he had a vision, and that some woman had the other four and was using them to build an army led by some kid. He's down the street now, intending to kill the kid so he can prevent whatever it is he dreamed about."

"A kid? Did he tell you a name?"

"Luca," she said. "Do you know him?"

Ed sighed. This was getting deeper than he wanted. "I need you to show me which house."

"I don't know." Marina shook her head. "He didn't tell me."

Ed checked the ignition, hoping that Acevedo had left the keys in it so he could turn on the van and check the GPS. No such luck.

Ed grabbed the phone from his pocket and dialed the local Homeland Security headquarters, hoping that someone would be able to pull the GPS's most recent coordinates.

As Ed waited for his routing to the special agent in charge, he reached into his pocket, grabbed the handcuff keys, and released Marina.

"I'm going to set you free. I want you to wait behind this house here until I return. If I don't come back, get the hell out of here and don't look back."

Ed grabbed an AR-15 from a hidden compartment in the van floor, along with a couple of incendiary grenades. He loaded up on ammo, shoved his shotgun into the storage space, and hopped out of the van.

Agent Harrison finally answered.

"I need your help," Ed said. "I need you to get a lockdown team here ASAP. And paramedics."

* * * *

CHAPTER 14
BORICIO WOLFE

Boricio leaped at the alien, betting *It* wouldn't fire the shotgun.

His risky gamble paid off. Boricio dropped, feet sliding forward, hands grabbing the gun as his feet met Rose's and knocked her forward.

She toppled on top of him, and the shotgun.

Their faces were inches apart. Something stopped Boricio cold. He wasn't sure if it was the look in her eyes, her familiar scent, or her lips (which he felt suddenly desperate to kiss), but something stripped his urge to kill quicker than a bucket of water dousing a fire.

"Boricio," she said, "please. It doesn't have to be this way."

Maybe she was right. Maybe it didn't.

Boricio suddenly wondered if he *could* kill her. Even though he'd nearly choked her to death just moments ago, he couldn't help but feel sickened by such a sour thought. Perhaps he could figure something else out. He wasn't sure *what*, but something to buy time until he could get the alien out of her body and into someone else's.

Then it hit him, a new thought that should've been old by now. Boricio looked into her eyes. "Leave her alone. Jump into my body."

It stared at him.

Rose's voice cracked, "No, Boricio ... don't."

"Leave her alone, and my body's yours. We can talk about this whole evolution thing then. It's either that or I kill you both right here and now."

"Are you sure?" *It* asked.

Tears welled in Rose's eyes, as if the human still inside her was devastated that Boricio would sacrifice his body for hers. In that moment, he realized that the alien was telling the truth. And if Rose was still in there, that meant he would still be in his own body, too. No alien stood a Pluto-as-a-planet's chance of evicting Boricio from his own body for good. He would find a way to kick that fucker out. But for now, this was his only chance to save Rose.

"Yes!" Boricio opened his mouth wide, "take me."

Dark swirling tendrils began to peek out of Rose's parted mouth.

One, two, then many, like tiny snakes slithering out past her tongue, checking to see if the coast was clear.

Every fiber of his being screamed inside.

Are you fucking crazy?!

What the fuck are you doing, Boricio?!

He ignored them all, keeping his eyes locked onto Rose's. "I love you," he said.

"I love you," she cried as the alien snaked toward his open mouth.

A gunshot erupted downstairs.

Tendrils zipped back into Rose's mouth as if evading a sprung trap, and she leaped up, looking at the door.

"Downstairs!" She opened the door and rushed out of the room as Boricio lay stunned.

He stared at the open door, watching as Rose vanished from sight.

Seconds later, another gunshot.

Rose screamed.

Boricio's heart pounded in his throat as hell and chaos held hands. He bolted up and into the hall, stopping when he saw an old man ascending the stairs, aiming a shotgun at Rose and opening fire.

Buckshot hit her in the chest and sent Rose flying backward.

She fell back before Boricio could leap and break her fall. Her head slammed against the floor.

Boricio dropped to the ground, ignoring the old man at the end of the hall even as he approached Boricio with his shotgun aimed.

Boricio stared into Rose's wide-open eyes staring up. Her eyes found his, though they seemed to be having trouble locking on.

Her mouth opened to say something, then stayed wide as if frozen. Her eyes stared straight up, past him.

Her chest was rising and falling quickly, rapid breaths as she gasped for air.

Boricio wondered if the blast had punctured her lungs.

He glanced down, and couldn't bear to look at the pellet wounds pocking the left side of her chest, bleeding out into her shirt's fabric.

"You're going to be OK, baby, you're going to be OK."

Rose stared straight up, not at Boricio, but past him as her chest stopped moving.

No!

No!

Boricio stared helplessly at Rose, wishing he could pull the pellets from her chest, and breathe life back into her body, but he didn't know what to do.

He cradled her head in his hands, his fingers streaking blood across her porcelain skin.

"No, no, don't go."

He heard the old man's breathing as he stepped closer, leveling his gun at Boricio.

He looked up, both wanting to kill the fucker and wanting to die.

A series of rapid-fire shots — not the shotgun — rang through the house.

Boricio watched as the old man fell forward, the back of his head a busted melon.

Footsteps bounded up the stairs.

Boricio looked up to see Ed Keenan, standing with an AR-15.

"You've gotta help Rose," Boricio begged, looking down at her empty husk.

He spun around, looking for Luca, desperate to turn truth into lie. "Luca! You've gotta heal her!"

Keenan turned and looked down the stairs, then back at Boricio.

"What?" Boricio asked.

He stood, went to the stairs and saw Luca lying at the bottom, face down, blood pooling out under his body.

"Noooo!!" Boricio screamed.

* * * *

CHAPTER 15
EDWARD KEENAN

As Boricio bounded down the steps toward Luca, Ed leaned over and checked Rose's pulse. Her mouth was dangling open, something inside it.

Ed gasped as he realized what it was — the infected, trying to slither out from its host.

He grabbed one of his belt's incendiary grenades, pulled the pin, dropped it on the ground, then rolled her over on top of it.

Ed turned back toward the stairs and raced down them, three at a time until he was at the bottom with Boricio and Luca.

"Get down!" he said ducking down, covering the back of his head with his palms.

The grenade exploded with a loud shriek upstairs. Ed turned to see Rose's charred body in pieces, splattered on the walls. The alien should have been incinerated in the explosion. He saw no sign of *It* attempting to leave what was left of Rose's body.

Ears ringing, Keenan heard something behind him. He turned to see Boricio screaming. Seconds later, he swung at Ed and hit him hard in the jaw.

Ed fell back, using his momentum to roll out of Boricio's way as the man swung again, this time missing.

Ed raised the AR-15 at Boricio and barked, "Back down!"

"You killed her!" Boricio screamed, his words sounding underwater despite his scream thanks to Ed's still-ringing ears.

"She was already dead. I killed the alien!"

"She was in there!" Boricio cried out, face twisted in anguish.

Ed kept the rifle on him until the man seemed like he wouldn't chance another swing. Boricio's face fell from rage to utter devastation. He fell against the wall and slid down beside Luca's corpse.

Ed stared straight ahead at the living room.

Upstairs, fire began to spread along the walls.

"Where are the vials?" Ed asked.

Boricio shook his head. "I don't know."

Ed thought about trying to convince Boricio to help him, but the man was too far gone, staring at the wall.

Suddenly, a gasping below drew their attention.

Luca!

Boricio was alert again, bounding downstairs. He dropped to the boy's side and turned him over.

Luca coughed up blood, though his eyes were still closed. Ed noticed the shotgun wound had hit Luca's shoulder, potentially high enough to miss his vital organs, though the boy had lost a bucket of blood.

Ed got on his phone and called Agent Harrison. "I need those paramedics STAT!"

Ed grabbed a towel from the upstairs bathroom and showed Boricio how to keep it pressed on Luca's wound.

"You got it?" he asked Boricio. "I need to get upstairs and find the vials."

"Yeah," Boricio grunted, putting pressure on Luca's wound and saying, "You're gonna be OK, little man. You're gonna be OK."

* * * *

CHAPTER 16
MARY OLSON

Mary was sprawled on the couch, pretending to numb herself with TV when Desmond came home just after dawn.

He crossed the room to Mary, leaned in, and planted a kiss on her cheek. She could barely stifle her revulsion.

Desmond pulled away, looked at Mary as though she had one missing tooth, then looked around the living room. "Where'd everyone go?"

"I told them to go home and get some rest. I don't think they slept too well last night."

"Damn," Desmond said. "I specifically asked Brent to stay with you."

"It's OK, honey, I'm fine."

"Fine? No, you shouldn't be alone at a time like this."

"Well, maybe you should've stayed instead of working last night," Mary said, putting him on the defensive to get his mind off of Brent, and into the argument he might expect her to have.

"I'm sorry." Desmond sat on the couch beside her, put his hands on her shoulders, and began to massage them. "Wow, you're tense."

Mary wondered how much Desmond could pick up by proximity. Could he read her thoughts? If not, he could probably read her anxiety. Mary couldn't pretend she wasn't terrified. She simply — or not so simply — had to redirect her fear toward something that Desmond would logically buy. Or play the grief angle hard ... but not too hard.

She shook her head, eyes still on the TV. "I can't believe she's gone. No matter how hard I try not to blame myself, I keep thinking we should've left the island when Paola said The Darkness was coming. But *noooo*, I didn't listen. Paola knew we were in danger, and I ignored her."

"No," Desmond soothed, "you can't blame yourself. Paola chose to stay here, to help us find the vials. You actually told her we should leave, and *she* insisted that we stay."

Mary pulled away from Desmond, not hiding her anger. "Are you saying it's her fault because she chose to stay here? She's a child, Dez! She looks to me to make the ultimate decision, and *I* failed. I should've put my foot down and insist that we go."

Mary buried her face in her palms, mining genuine tears for Paola's predicament.

Desmond ran a hand through her hair. "You didn't do anything wrong."

"No," Mary said, glaring at Desmond. "Stop it. Stop trying to tell me I'm not to blame. I'm responsible for my child. No one else."

She put her face back in her hands, fingers squeezing her scalp tight, milking her frustration for Desmond.

She wanted to make him uncomfortable enough to leave the room. Mary wasn't sure she could stay in the living room with him for hours if he chose to sit by her side trying to console her. She could put on a front and lie through her teeth, pretending that she wasn't disgusted by the alien posing as her lover, but it would only be so long before cracks would start showing. Before Mary would surrender to her rising tide of rage.

She continued to sit with her head in her hands, feeling Desmond beside her on the couch, staring.

Mary wondered if he was probing her mind.

She tried to focus all of her thoughts and rage at herself. Anger was a strong emotion, and she hoped it masked the fear beneath it, the fear of the alien posing as Desmond.

He leaned back on the couch, releasing a sigh.

Shit, he's never going to leave.

"So," she asked, head still in her hands, "what's next? Did you find all of the infected?"

"I think so, but we're working on some leads going back to the mainland. There's some missing staff at the facility. I have Homeland Security going to their houses, looking to bring them in for questioning."

"What about the vials? How's that going? Now that you don't have Paola."

Mary said it with a hint of accusation, a dash of intended guilt to make Desmond more uncomfortable. Her attempts were based on a human's expected response, not an alien's. She had no idea if any of this was working to make it want to leave. A man would be exhausted, but the aliens might not need sleep. Though, Mary had seen Desmond sleep plenty.

Unless he's faking it.

She hoped not. In order for her plan to work, as convoluted as it was, she needed Desmond to sleep and give her a chance at grabbing the upper hand.

She'd gone through her scheme a hundred times in her head but actively tried not to consider things now, lest he pick up on her thoughts.

Part of Mary wished she had simply executed the monster when *It* entered the house. She still would've had the element of surprise. But there was also a strong chance that his guard would be up, too. He had no idea what she knew, and coming home, he might be suspicious of her and prepared for her actions.

Best to lure him into a false sense of security.

Mary waited for him to respond to her comment about his using Paola. Either intentionally, or because he wasn't that adept at reading between the lines, he didn't.

She decided to drive the point home directly. "You know who else I blame for all this?"

"Who?"

"You." Mary looked up and met Desmond's eyes. "You made Paola *want* to help you. You fed into her desire to be helpful, and her need to feel special. You knew she looked up to you like a father ever since Ryan died. *You* made her want to stay here, not me."

Mary glared at Desmond, using her hate as a hammer. It was all she could do to keep from pounding the nail into her plan, knowing that would only build a disaster. He was full of adrenaline, ready to fight because she'd pushed him hard.

Perhaps too hard, Mary thought as he silently stared.

Her heart began to race as fear fueled it.

Don't let him sense the fear. Just the anger. Just the anger.

She glared harder.

Desmond continued to stare at Mary, void of expression. Now that she thought about it, he'd given her that same blank look several times in the past few weeks. She felt stupid for not seeing his deception sooner.

As Desmond kept staring, Mary tried to push back the fears racing through her mind: The Darkness creeping from his mouth and enveloping her; him drawing his gun and blowing her head from her shoulders; or perhaps he'd tear off his face to reveal some sort of hideous black, gelatinous creature beneath.

Stop thinking about it! He's going to see my fear!

Mary was certain she was busted. Desmond's eyes seemed to read her every thought.

She had to do something, and fast.

Mary closed her eyes, then launched herself at Desmond, swinging her fists, hitting him, but not too hard, in the chest and face, crying dramatically like someone's baby mama on reality TV.

"I hate you!" she cried, "it's all your fault!"

Mary kept her eyes closed because she was terrified that if she met his again, he'd see right through her, or she'd lose enough nerve to falter her facade. She cried louder, maybe loud enough for their closest neighbors to hear.

His hands grabbed hers, firm, but not too hard. He pushed them back toward her chest, "Mary!" he yelled, trying to end her emotional outburst before it threatened to draw unwanted attention.

"Mary!" he yelled again, shaking her.

She finally stopped crying out, though tears streamed down her face. Mary met his eyes, waiting to see what he'd say.

Either he was buying her act, or this was the end.

She looked down, as if embarrassed by her reaction, still letting tears flow, her fists in tight balls.

"You're right," he said. "I'm sorry. I just wanted to protect you both, protect the island, and hell, the world, from these damned things. I just don't want to see what happened over there happen here. And maybe I let that cloud my judgment."

"*Maybe?*" Mary repeated, her tone dripping with accusation, keeping him backpedaling.

"OK, not *maybe*. Definitely. I *definitely* let it cloud my judgment. But I thought I could protect you, both of you."

Desmond moved closer, his eyes wearing the sweetness she remembered so well. Hell, his expression was so genuine, she almost bought it. For the first time, Mary wondered if maybe Brent's dream was wrong.

No. He told me about the Hammy the Hamster. I have to stay strong.

Desmond continued, his voice low and saccharine as he wrapped an arm around Mary, then found her chin with his hand.

"You and Paola are my family, Mary. I would never intentionally do anything to harm either of you. I thought I could protect you both, and I was wrong. I am so sorry, Mary. I wish I could bring Paola back. I wish I could take her place, please know that."

Mary closed her eyes, his words seeming so genuine they cut through to her heart. She wished she could believe him, and that somehow that would bring him — the real Desmond — back. But at the same time believing him meant that Paola was dead, and that was a trade that Mary wasn't willing to make.

Desmond pulled her close and kissed her softly on the lips.

Fear, sadness, and rage coursed through her system, threatening to sever Mary's tether to sanity. She wanted to scream. Wanted to tear into his flesh. Wanted to collapse.

I have to hold on. Have to be strong.

Mary closed her eyes, pretending that the man at her mouth was the same man who died. Pretending that the bastard wasn't holding her daughter prisoner underground. Pretending that she didn't plan to murder him the moment she could.

Mary wrapped her arms around him, pulling him closer and deeper into the kiss.

"I'm sorry," she said. "I know you love us. And that you're trying to do your best. I know that, baby."

She looked in his eyes, surprised to find that he was crying, too.

If this was an act, Mary hated him all the more for his lack of heart and sickening guile.

How dare he use my daughter's memory so manipulatively?

She reached up, wiping tears from his eyes. "I think we're both just exhausted."

"Maybe," he said.

"Can you nap with me?" she asked, "or do you need to get back to work?"

"Yeah, I can take a nap."

Good.

**

Desmond was snoring.

They'd been lying down for half an hour when he seemed to finally sleep.

If they can.

It was now or never.

Mary got out of bed as she normally did on her way to the bathroom. Her feet hit the cold tile, then she softly closed the door behind her.

She waited a second at the door, her ear to the wood, heart pounding loud enough to hear it.

When Mary heard no sign of Desmond, she crouched low and opened the cabinet beneath the sink.

It was full of toilet paper, feminine products, and stuff that Desmond didn't normally bother with so long as the dispenser held a roll.

She pulled away a box of feminine pads, then pulled out the second box beneath it where Mary kept the gun.

She grabbed the pistol, the very Glock she'd trained with for months. Mary had been a decent shot from the start, but training wasn't about making your shots. It was about teaching your body to act reflexively and instinctively in tense situations. It was about removing all thoughts from the equation when you were most likely to tense into a mistake.

Mary still hated how she'd gotten scared when she and Boricio were attacked in the parking lot, how she'd stayed back while he battled the infected. She'd told herself countless times that she stayed back because Boricio had ordered her to, and that when push came to shove, you tended to listen to Boricio, especially when he was doing what he did best.

But ever since that moment, Mary had felt like she'd let him, and herself, down by not rising to the challenge.

She vowed to never let that happen again. While she hadn't had time to train much since arriving at Black Island, Mary had rehearsed all that she'd been taught mentally on repeat, visualizing like an athlete before a big game.

Mary couldn't doubt her instincts again.

She had to rely on her gut.

She'd ignored it when it told her they should leave the island, deferring to Desmond and her daughter.

No more. Never again.

She had to listen to her gut. Trust her training. Now it was time to act.

Mary looked down at the Glock. When she'd first started shooting, it had felt heavy in her hand.

Now it felt perfect.

She flushed the toilet, pretended to wash her hands, then stared in the mirror a final time to steel herself for what she needed to do.

You can do this.

Mary turned out the light, then returned to the bed with her right hand behind her back, watching Desmond's shape in the light coming through the crack in the curtains.

She kneeled onto the bed, breathed in and out slowly and deliberately, then raised the pistol and aimed it at his head.

Desmond's eyes opened, but didn't seem the least bit surprised.

"You are going to take me to my daughter now, or I'll blow your goddamned alien head off your fucking body. Nod if you understand me."

The monster nodded.

* * * *

CHAPTER 17
BORICIO WOLFE

Boricio stared down at Luca, pressing on his wound, watching as his chest rose and fell with ragged breaths.

Come on, man, don't you die on me, too.

Even though this was another Luca, not the one who had "fixed" him, Boricio couldn't help but feel an affection for the boy now trapped in a young man's body. Bits of memory flitted by, of the other Boricio and the other Luca, how they'd been adopted brothers, raised by Will Bishop. Perhaps that was why the kid had risked his life to heal Boricio and bring back his memory.

Not many people put their own asses on the line for Boricio. That shit was meat on the grill and sauce on the pasta.

Boricio looked up the stairs at the chunks of Rose on the wall and felt more of his stomach sour. There was no way Luca could bring her back, even if he wasn't hovering near death.

He turned back down to Luca.

Focus on the boy. Don't look up there. Nothing there but regrets. Team Boricio don't have time for fucking regrets.

Where the hell is Keenan?

Some prick yelled, "Hands in the air!"

Boricio looked down the stairs to see some government agent dressed like G.I. Fucking Joe aiming a shotgun at Boricio like he was Cobra Commander.

"Sorry, pal, I'm not putting my hands anywhere, or this kid's gonna die."

The agent, with his strong jaw, close-cropped red hair, and pockmarked face, didn't look like he was used to hearing *no.*

"It's OK," Keenan said, finally appearing, "he's with me. Are the paramedics here?"

"Is the place secure?" the agent asked.

"Yeah," Keenan answered, "get someone in here for this young man."

The agent went out the front door. Boricio glanced up to see Keenan holding a black metal box.

"Find what you're looking for?" Boricio asked.

"Yeah," Keenan said. "And you don't know anything about the vials?"

"I don't know shit about any vials. I was in a coma up until a couple of days ago. Seems that Rose, or whatever she'd become, had plans for me, but the Boy Wonder healed me and was going to help me get the fuck outta Dodge when this old fucker came in shooting the goddamned place to cheese." He paused, then added, "I hope the vials were worth all this."

"I'm sorry about Rose," Keenan said. "But the old man, Acevedo, had already killed her, and she wasn't coming back. The alien was trying to leave her mouth, likely looking to infect you next."

Boricio said nothing. He could argue that Luca could've saved her, if they'd only had enough pieces left, but saw no point in arguing, particularly when he wasn't even certain Luca would live.

A pair of paramedics rushed in with a stretcher, pushing Boricio aside. One of the medics, a young woman with brown hair in a tight ponytail, pulled the cloth back, checking Luca's wound, then returned it, keeping pressure on it. She said something about a "GSW" into her radio while the other paramedic, an older bald man with giant hands, lifted Luca's eyelids and flashed a light into them.

Luca gasped again, eyes wild as he looked around, trying to say something.

"It's OK," the woman said, trying to calm him.

They lifted Luca onto the stretcher and rushed him out of the house.

Boricio followed them out to a medical helicopter, but was pushed back by the woman.

"I need you to stay here," she said.

"He's my brother," Boricio lied, yelling over the chopper's whirring blades.

"I still need you to wait here." The woman climbed into the copter and closed the door in Boricio's face.

Keenan pulled Boricio back, as the chopper began to ascend. "Come on."

Boricio turned on him, "Where the fuck they takin' him?"

"To Mercy Memorial. He's in good hands."

"I want to go."

"Why?" Keenan asked. "There's nothing you can do for him. He'll be under professional care, after which he'll be brought to Black Island."

"Black Island?"

"Yes," Keenan said, "and I need you to come with me."

"Um, I dunno about that, Boss Hog. This Duke's got shit to do."

Keenan put his hands on Boricio's shoulders. "I'm giving you the courtesy of *asking* you to come with me, Boricio. My boss won't be quite as courteous."

"So what, you gonna arrest me?"

Keenan sighed. "Don't you want to see Mary and Paola?"

"What? The Olson twins are there?"

"Yes," Keenan said.

"Well, why the fuck didn't you lead with that?"

A car pulled up to the house, and a familiar-looking woman with long blonde hair got out with another agent. They headed over to Keenan and Boricio.

"Did you stop him?" the woman asked.

"Not in time. He shot Luca and killed two other people."

"Oh, God." The woman's hand found her cheek.

Boricio noticed that she was stealing glances at him as she spoke to Keenan. He was about to say something when she turned to him and asked, "Do we know each other?"

Boricio shook his head no even as memories from the other Boricio, an infected Boricio, swirled through his head. Her name was Marina Harmon, the rich bitch daughter of J.L. Harmon, that freaky cult leader.

As Keenan introduced them, Boricio feigned like he hadn't seen her show already.

"We need to get to the airport," Keenan said.

Boricio nodded, staring back at the house.

His Rosebud was gone, but at least he could still see Mary and her little lamb.

* * * *

CHAPTER 18
BRENT FOSTER

"I want to go home," Ben whined as they waited in the dilapidated stone house in the woods on the island's west end. The old home's furniture looked like it had been abandoned in the 1950s, the downstairs windows had been boarded over, and the floors were littered with dust and debris. The refugees were making do in the only clear spot they could find in what was once a kitchen area, sitting around a small table.

A wind-up lantern teased light into the room. Brent figured it was better to stay in the darkness than venture upstairs where morning sun illuminated the rooms, but the children might be more likely to wander in front of an open and uncovered window.

The plan was simple in the plotting stages, but the execution had holes. They were supposed to sit tight until Paola was able to send Brent another telepathic message, assuming she was still alive and that she and Mary weren't killed by Desmond. But sitting tight with a two-year-old and a five-year-old was a lot simpler on paper than in practice.

The kids had been antsy all morning, and Brent couldn't blame them. The trek through the woods as they searched for a place to hide out had been a bear, though Teagan had done her best to turn their misadventure into a game. They were, ostensibly, playing hide and seek with Mary and Paola.

But the ruse was thinning as they sat in the two-story house without power, running water, or a single creature comfort.

Teagan was doing surprisingly well managing both kids and pretending she wasn't scared, even though Brent imagined that he could practically hear her pounding heart.

"We've got to wait for the girls to find us," Teagan said, pinching Ben's nose.

He giggled, like always, gobbling whatever attention Teagan was willing to give him. Sometimes Brent worried that his son was too competitive with Becca. But Teagan was doing an excellent job of managing Ben's expectations, understanding that he'd only lost his mother a few weeks ago and was in an almost desperately needy time.

"I'm hungry," Becca cried.

"Me, too," Ben said.

Teagan's smile looked like it hurt. "We'll have lunch in a little bit."

They'd packed enough snacks, water, and peanut butter sandwiches to last a few days, but boredom was likely to fuel their hunger.

Brent stood, pacing in front of the sink, trying not to show his creeping unease. He felt trapped in the house and wanted to go somewhere else even though they had nowhere to go.

Teagan reached into her bag and brought out a *Piggie and Elephant* book and handed it to Ben. "Why don't you read to Becca? She likes when you do the elephant and pig voices."

Ben was particularly proud of his reading ability and jumped on every chance to impress the girls.

"OK." Ben smiled and sat beside Becca at the table.

As Ben read and Becca giggled, Teagan stood, joined Brent by the sink, and whispered, "Any word from Paola?"

He shook his head no.

"What if they start looking for us? I mean there's not a lot of places on the island to hide."

"I dunno," Brent said. "I've got another idea, though I'm not sure if it's a good one."

"What?"

"I was thinking maybe I could swim to Paddock Island. If I can get there, I can call Ed and tell him what's going on."

"Do you know Ed's number?" Teagan asked.

"Yeah, I memorized it. But ... there's a good chance they blocked his phone from receiving calls except for a few approved numbers. If that's the case, I'm not sure what to do. Besides, I hate to leave you alone with the kids."

"I'm not going to lie — I don't want you to leave either. But if you decide to go, I'll watch Ben like he was my own."

"Thank you," Brent said.

He paced, weighing his options. Brent wasn't as worried about swimming toward the other island, even though the water would likely be freezing, as he was about abandoning Teagan and the kids. Not that his being on Black Island would make that big a difference. It wasn't like he was a kick-ass warrior like Ed. But he did have a Glock, and was a decent shot, whereas Teagan was terrified to hold a gun, much less learn to use one. Brent figured he might be able to take out a solo Guardsman or two, but was no match for an entire unit if one was dispatched to bring them in.

He hated feeling helpless.

Hated waiting on someone else.

Hated not being able to help Mary execute her plan against Desmond.

He wondered if she'd been able to do it, or if the monster had caught her. If so, she may be dead already. If that were the case, there was a damned good chance that Desmond was already searching for Brent, Teagan, and the kids.

His stomach churned and made him feel hollow.

Brent watched Ben reading to Becca and despite his nerves couldn't help but smile at how his son ate every one of her giggles.

Look at them, happily oblivious to our danger.

The longer Brent stood there watching the children and feeling his helplessness grow, the more he wished he'd stayed at Mary's and shot Desmond. Of course that wouldn't have helped Mary get Paola back, but it might have meant his own child would be safe a while longer.

Ben laughed again and looked up to see if his daddy was watching him entertain Becca.

"Good job," Brent said.

Ben returned to the page, and Brent had to leave the room before emotions claimed him.

He headed upstairs and into a room that looked out over a clearing to the east, the most likely place a search party, or assault team, would come from.

He watched the area, wondering how long they'd be safe for.

Brent spotted someone standing just beyond the tree line. The man, wearing a black Guardsman uniform, seemed to be staring straight at the house.

Brent fell to the ground beneath the window, heart hammering.

Did he see me?

Shit.

He debated whether he should peer out the window again, to be sure his eyes weren't lying. Instead, Brent decided to run to another window, in a room to the right along the same wall, in case the man was watching the other window, waiting to see if his own eyes were telling the truth.

Brent slowly approached the open window, hands shaking as he crawled along the floor, wishing there were curtains to conceal him. He'd already told Teagan and the kids to stay away from the windows downstairs, and had left them in the kitchen, where windows had all been boarded long ago. And yet he might have stupidly allowed himself to get caught.

The Guardsman could already be on his radio calling for backup.

Brent rose just high enough to peek over the windowsill.

He saw The Guardsman still standing and staring at the house.

He *had* to do something.

* * * *

CHAPTER 19
MARY OLSON

Desmond was surprisingly cooperative as Mary led him into the facility with a gun at his back.

"You might want to hide that thing as we approach the elevator," he said. "There are cameras all over this place, and I can't be responsible if someone else sees you as a threat to eliminate."

"I bet you'd like that." Mary shoved the gun inside her jacket pocket, then thrust it into the small of Desmond's back.

"I'm not your enemy, Mary. No more than Paola is your enemy."

"What are you talking about?" she asked as they stepped into the elevator.

"I just find it interesting that you all refer to Paola as having 'The Light' inside her, when in fact it is an alien, no different than myself. Yet you are no doubt thinking of me as 'infected with The Darkness,' am I correct?"

"I don't give a good goddamn what anyone calls anything. I just want my daughter back, so stop stalling and bring me to her."

Desmond placed his palm on the elevator's security panel. The elevator bumped then descended. Mary kept the gun trained on him from inside her jacket pocket.

Desmond stared at her, as a parent might stare at an unruly child.

"What are you looking at so smugly?"

"Just wondering what's going on in that tiny little brain of yours. What do you plan to do with me once you get Paola? Shoot me? Report me to the superiors? What is it you hope to gain with this little stunt?"

"I just want my daughter back," Mary repeated, "now shut the hell up. I'm tired of your lying mouth."

"Fair enough." Desmond crossed his arms and leaned against the elevator wall. When the box stopped, he pressed his fingers on the seven and zero buttons. The elevator lowered another floor then Desmond placed his palm against the panel again, and the doors slid open.

"More guards ahead," he whispered, "act like you're happy to be with me."

Mary pushed him forward through the doors and plastered a fake smile onto her angry face.

One of the guards looked at Mary and seemed like he was about to say something or perhaps ask for credentials, but must've thought twice, due either to Desmond's rank or the rage in her eyes.

Or maybe they're infected, too.

How the hell am I going to get out of here?

Mary couldn't afford to consider that now. If she lingered too long, doubt would settle, and she was sure the alien would use it against her.

Desmond led her through more doors, down hallways to a final doorway.

"She's in here," he said stopping outside of it. "But before I let you in, I need to consider an offer."

"Fuck you; open the door."

"OK," Desmond said with faux exasperation, like a game show host warning a contestant not to choose door number three. She had no time for alien head games.

Mary's pulse quickened as she stepped inside the huge room and saw two rows of four glass chambers along walls to her left and right. A light was on in the last chamber, where she saw her daughter lying on a cot.

The door closed behind them.

Paola looked up, eyes wide at the sight of her mother. Her mouth opened to say "Mom," though Mary heard no sound.

"Open her door." Mary pulled the gun from her jacket and aimed it at Desmond.

"OK," Desmond said. "Computer. Cut the oxygen to cell four, and drain the remaining amount."

Mary's stomach dropped.

What?

She looked at Paola in her cell as the girl looked up at the ceiling.

Desmond turned to Mary. "You have exactly one minute before all the oxygen is sucked from Paola's chamber. And then, depending on her lungs, maybe another minute, minute and a half before she runs out of air and drops dead to the floor."

Mary shoved the gun in his face.

"Let her out!"

Desmond smiled, "Ah, Mary, Mary, do you really think your gun scares me? Shoot me, and I'll trade this form for yours." He looked her up and down, "And it is quite a nice form to be inside."

"Open the door!" Mary shouted.

She looked back at Paola's cell. Her daughter was gasping for air, eyes wide and scared.

"Ah, she really should've grabbed a good lungful before," Desmond said. "Maybe she *won't* last another minute."

Mary swallowed.

"Open the fucking door!" Mary screamed and shot him in the chest.

Desmond fell back against the wall, still smiling, but not mortally wounded.

Mary yelled and motioned for Paola to get down to the ground.

Paola did as instructed.

She turned and fired a shot, then another at the glass.

Bullets ricocheted off the glass, whizzing around the room, one getting lost in the far wall, then another coming back at her, hitting and chipping the floor about four feet to her right.

Paola looked up at her mother, crying out, though Mary couldn't hear her.

But in her head, Paola's voice suddenly cried out, "Kill him. Shoot him in the head."

Mary turned the gun on Desmond, aiming straight at the alien's face, pistol shaking in her hand.

"Your choice, Mary, but only my voice will open the door and return the air to your daughter's room."

Mary looked back at Paola, shaking her head and continuing to scream inside Mary's mind, "Kill him! Kill him now!"

Mary's finger circled tighter around the trigger, the gun shaking wildly in her hand. "Open the door!"

Desmond kept smiling. "Put down the gun, Mary, or your daughter will die. I will take your body, become you, then go kill Brent, Teagan, and the children. Five seconds."

"Five."

Paola's voice screamed in her ear, "Kill him, Mom, kill him!"

"Four."

Mary shoved the gun hard against his head and growled in his face. "Open it!"

"Three."

"Open it, you cocksucker!"

Desmond said, "Computer. Speakers on."

The sound of Paola's gasping filled the chamber.

"Two. Do you really want to *hear* your daughter die?"

Mary looked back to see Paola's face turning crimson through her gasps. She looked, bug eyed, at her mother, shaking her head no.

Mary looked at Desmond. His mouth opened to say "One."

She handed him the gun. "Turn on the air!"

"Computer. Turn the oxygen back on."

Paola gasped, drawing deep breaths as she collapsed against the glass, momentarily saved.

Desmond turned to Mary, said, "About time you started thinking smart," then took the pistol's butt and hit her hard across the head.

* * * *

CHAPTER 20
BRENT FOSTER

Brent pulled his shirt over the gun holster as he went downstairs and whispered into Teagan's ear. "Keep the kids quiet. I'm going to check on something."

"What is it?" she whispered back.

"Don't worry." Brent didn't want to alarm her and thus unintentionally scare the kids. The last thing he needed was crying children with a Guardsman right outside the house.

"I'm going to make a phone call; I'll be right back." Brent kissed Ben on the head.

"I want to go outside," Ben whined.

"Me too," Becca joined in.

Shit. I really don't need this.

"We can all go out later. Right now, I need to make a call, and I promise we'll go outside later, OK?"

Teagan stepped in. "Who wants some pudding?"

"I do, I do!" Ben yelled.

Brent cringed as he imagined his son's voice traveling toward the tree line and alerting the suspicious Guardsman who may or may not have already seen Brent in the window.

Teagan seemed to notice the fear on his face.

"OK," Teagan said, "let's play the quiet game, and I'll give you each a pudding cup."

"OK!" Ben yelled, possibly louder.

Teagan pressed a finger to her lips.

"OK," Ben whispered.

"Thank you," Brent said to Teagan.

She was surprisingly adept at this parenting thing for such a young girl. Sometimes Teagan seemed better equipped than Brent, at least when it came to keeping Ben from a meltdown. Caught by emotion, Brent gave her a hug and immediately felt awkwardly emotional, hoping he wasn't broadcasting his fear that they'd been discovered.

She smiled. "Sure thing."

"I'll be right back."

He turned from Teagan and went outside, almost expecting the Guardsman, or even multiple Guardsmen, to be waiting to take them in — or kill them.

Brent was relieved to see no one outside. He grabbed his gun and headed toward the home's rear where he'd seen the man just outside the clearing.

As Brent made his way toward the back yard, it dawned on him that he had no idea what the hell he'd do once he found the Guardsman. Would he shoot the man? Brent had no idea if the Guardsman was even compromised or sleeping with the enemy. He might be a regular guy earning his paycheck, clueless he was working for an alien. Maybe he hadn't even seen Brent in the window. Perhaps he was working a regular patrol and not looking for anyone.

Or, Brent feared, he could be part of a squad, already informed about the man in the window.

Brent couldn't just sit in the house. He was sick of doing nothing, of having his hands tied by circumstance or his child, unable to help anyone. He wondered what Ed Keenan would've done earlier that morning with Mary. Would he have agreed to let her handle the situation herself? *Hell, no.* Keenan would've taken over. He would've waited for Desmond to come home, put a gun in the guy's mouth, and demanded that Dez bring him to Paola right now, dammit.

But Brent *hadn't* done that.

He'd let Mary convince him to get the kids away from the house, to tuck his tail between his legs and hide.

He'd agreed at the time because he *was* thinking about the kids' safety as well as Teagan's. Mary had made a good argument that the kids' welfare was priority one, and that Mary was well trained and could handle herself just fine with Desmond. But now Brent wondered if he, Teagan, and the kids were really any safer hiding out in some abandoned house like rats waiting for Guardsmen to stomp them. Even if they were, that did nothing to protect Mary or Paola.

Brent was sick of waiting for the bad guys to win.

He'd played it safe his entire life, and look where it led him. A day didn't pass without Brent wishing he'd done more to convince Gina that he wasn't nuts, and that the events of October 15 had actually happened.

Things had gotten out of hand and ugly. He lost his temper, rather than finding a smart way to prove his sanity. If he'd been smarter or bolder, Gina might still be alive. Brent might have his entire family still with him.

But no, he'd allowed fear to push him into stupid decisions — Allowed the fear that he'd get locked up and never see them again to keep him from them.

What good had that fear done?

Gina was dead, and he was on some godforsaken island with an alien intent on destroying the world.

It was time to stop being afraid.

Time to take action and do what he could to seize victory, secure the safety of Teagan and the kids. They were counting on him, and he couldn't let them down.

Brent spotted the Guardsman still standing just past the tree line. The brown-haired man, tall, thin, and in his early thirties, wasn't wearing a helmet, just a Guardsman's black beret. He had a pistol in a belt holster, and a flashlight that doubled as a baton on the other side of his belt.

The man had yet to spot Brent outside.

What the hell is he doing out here?

The Guardsman was standing still, staring at his tablet. Had he already called reinforcements? Was he studying blueprints of the old house and planning an attack?

Brent had to move fast.

He decided to cut through the woods and flank the man, hoping he was alone as he appeared. Brent raced as fast as he dared until he drew close enough for his footfalls to reach the Guardsman, then slowed down until he saw the man about ninety yards ahead.

Brent drew the gun, taking aim, and slowly approached from behind, his heart slamming against the walls of his chest.

He walked slowly, carefully, avoiding branches and dead leaves as best he could, pistol trained on the back of the man's head as he went.

Brent misstepped and cracked a branch.

The Guardsman spun around and dropped the tablet, hand reaching for his gun.

"No!" Brent yelled, firing a shot that echoed through the woods.

He hoped the kids didn't hear it, but couldn't imagine that they hadn't. He hoped Teagan could keep them calm, keep Ben from freaking out, having flashbacks of his mother shot dead in front of his eyes.

The Guardsman froze, hand inches from his gun.

"Hands up!" Brent said.

"OK, OK, no need to shoot," the man said, voice calm.

"What are you doing out here?" Brent asked.

"A survey of the property, that's all. Who are you? You living here?"

"I'm asking the questions," Brent said sharply. Better to show no fear with the Guardsman. "Give me your radio, and the tablet ... and your gun."

"You're making a big mistake." The man bent down to retrieve his tablet.

"Keep your fingers away from the screen!" Brent demanded with his gun.

The Guardsman put the radio, and the weapon, on top of the tablet and shakily started to hand them to Brent.

Brent's heart raced faster as he looked up from the man's shaking hand to his eyes: cold, calculated, fearless. The man was planning something.

Brent backed away, now holding his gun with both hands. "No, put them on the ground, slowly, and back away."

The man did as instructed, eyes on Brent the entire time as if he controlled the situation. His cocky look made Brent want to squeeze the trigger.

"Who else knows you're here?"

"Everyone. I'm part of a four-man unit surveying the island's neighboring properties. If I don't meet up with them, they'll come looking for me. Why don't you let me go, and I'll pretend I never saw you."

Instead of responding to the offer, Brent ordered the man to back up, then went and picked up his radio, gun, and tablet. Brent put the man's gun in his own holster, shoved the tablet under his arm, then looked at the radio. It was a phone radio, similar to the one Brent had before he ditched it earlier to avoid tracking. He wondered if the communications of this one was also limited to the island.

He decided to call Ed.

"What are you doing?" the Guardsman asked.

"Shut up," Brent said, dialing.

He listened as the phone rang.

Hope swelled in his chest as the phone continued to ring. If he could reach Ed, tell him what was going on, he'd feel a million times better about their odds of safely fleeing the island. As the phone continued to ring, Brent was faced with a new quandary — should he tell Ed about Jade?

Ed needed to know, and Brent had wanted to tell him since the moment the man's daughter was killed. But might that knowledge cloud his thinking? Make him less likely to help them defeat Desmond?

The phone continued to ring.

A new fear crept into his mind. What if they'd taken care of Ed already?

The line then went dead.

Brent dialed again, to be certain he called the right number, then waited through too many rings.

The Guardsman stared at Brent with that icy glare that made Brent want to shoot him in the face.

The ring again fell into silence. Brent sighed.

Dammit.

If Ed's dead, we're screwed.

Brent wondered if he should try to call Mary, see if there was any update on her situation. But if he called her, especially from this Guardsman's phone, and she hadn't yet acted, and Desmond picked up the phone, the jig would be up.

The Guardsman continued to glare at Brent as Brent racked his brain trying to figure out what to do next. He couldn't take this Guardsman hostage, could he? And if not, what were his options? Kill him? The man had done nothing to him, and didn't seem infected.

Everything inside Brent felt tight as the world narrowed around him, thinning his choices, and chances to do the right thing.

"Dammit!"

"You OK?" the Guardsman asked.

Brent looked up at the man to see his same infuriating expression of calm.

"No, I'm *not* OK."

"I'm not sure what's wrong, but you ought to consider coming with me to the facility. We can get you some help, sir."

"No," Brent said, "we're not going anywhere."

"You can't hold me forever. And if you shoot me, they'll find you. Our uniforms are fitted with a biometric system that pings headquarters if something happens to me, or ... if you attempt to circumvent it."

Shit.

Brent hadn't considered that. In his efforts to try and take matters into his own hands, he'd screwed himself, Teagan, and the kids.

Brent suddenly had an idea he was surprised he'd not thought of before. Yes, Desmond was infected, but he wasn't in charge of the island.

"Get me Director Bolton on the radio."

Incredulous, the Guardsman said, "What? Why?"

"We're all in danger. Are you familiar with the alien infection?"

"Of course."

"One of your top men is infected," Brent said. "I need to tell the director. Do you have a direct line? Not to his office, but to him?"

"Yes," the man said.

"OK, I want you to call him. And don't say anything about where you are or who you're with."

"I don't even know your name, sir."

Brent returned the Guardsman's radio and waited while he dialed. "Director Bolton? I've got someone who needs to speak with you."

Brent kept his pistol on the man as he took the phone and put it to his ear. "Hello, Director?"

"Yes?" Bolton asked, "Who is this?"

"My name is Brent Foster. I'm one of the people brought in by Desmond Armstrong, along with Ed Keenan to help you all."

"OK," the director said, clearly perturbed by the interruption. "How can I help you?"

"I need to tell you about an infection in your ranks."

"What are you talking about?"

Brent wasn't sure if he should tell him now or ask to see him in person. If he told him now, there was a chance it could get to Desmond.

"Well?" Director Bolton pushed Brent to spill it.

"Desmond Armstrong is infected with The Darkness. He's kidnapped a child and is holding her on the facility's eighth level."

"Armstrong is infected? How do you know this? Do you have proof?"

"Yes," Brent lied, "but I need to meet with you. I'm not sure if he's infected anyone else, but you could have a coup on your hands, sir. You need to be careful who you trust."

"Where can I pick you up?"

"It has to be you and someone you can trust." Brent handed the radio to the Guardsman to tell Bolton the coordinates.

The Guardsman hung up. "Armstrong's infected?"

Brent looked at the man, uncertain if he could be trusted. Desmond could have infected him. Brent held onto his radio, tablet, and weapon. For now, the man was his prisoner.

"Come on." Brent ignored the Guardsman's question and led him at gunpoint to the house.

**

A black van arrived outside in less than twenty minutes.

Brent stood by the second-story window, watching as the passenger-side door opened and Director Bolton stepped out.

Brent turned to the hostage Guardsman and pointed his gun. "Looks like our ride is here."

They headed downstairs where Teagan and the kids were waiting. Brent kept the gun behind him, so the kids wouldn't see it.

He said, "OK, we ready to go for a ride?"

"Where are we going?" Ben asked.

"I told you, we're going to meet with a man."

"So are we done playing hide and seek with Mary and Paola?" Ben asked.

"For now." Brent couldn't meet his son's eyes.

Ben ran up to Brent. "Pick me up, Daddy."

"Not now," Brent couldn't risk dropping his guard just in case his captive turned out to be infected.

"Will you hold Becca's hand?" Teagan stepped in to save the day.

"OK," Ben said, smiling.

They headed outside, the Guardsman in front.

Director Bolton approached, wearing a charcoal suit, offering his hand, "Mr. Foster?"

Brent shifted the gun from his right hand to his left behind his back, then reached forward and shook Bolton's hand.

"Yes, good to meet you, Mr. Bolton." Though Brent had seen the man a few times in person, they'd never talked.

The van's driver's side door opened, and a Guardsman stepped out, wearing a thick, full black uniform and dark-visored helmet, carrying a black duffel and a shotgun — likely Bolton's driver and security.

Brent felt anxious as the man approached.

"Don't worry, he's just going to collect your guns, a security precaution."

"You sure you can trust him?" Brent asked.

"I've had the same inner core for years," Bolton said. "We've had two breaches, Sullivan and now Desmond Armstrong, both from that damned other world. But my inner core, four people, have never been alone with Sullivan or Armstrong. I believe we're safe."

Brent hoped so as he retrieved both his gun and the one he liberated from the Guardsman and dropped them into the duffle.

The helmeted Guardsman took the bag back to the van and climbed into the driver's side. Bolton led the rest of them to the van.

As the Guardsman attempted to get in first, Bolton put a hand on his shoulder. "Your unit will come get you."

"Can I at least get my stuff back, sir?"

"Sorry, I put your gun in the duffle bag." Brent handed the man his radio and tablet.

"I'll see to it that your gun is returned, son," Bolton said. "Go ahead and finish whatever you were doing here."

"Yes, sir." The Guardsman turned and headed toward the backyard, carrying his tablet.

"After you." Bolton smiled and waved a hand toward the van's open side panel.

Teagan, Becca, and Ben climbed into the van's rear. Brent followed, sitting in the middle row of seats with the kids between himself and Teagan.

Bolton slid the side door closed then climbed into the front passenger side.

Nobody spoke as the van cut through the woods, not even the kids, who were looking nervously up front.

Brent wondered if Bolton was saving conversation for when Teagan and the kids weren't in the same close space, then grew nervous when he realized they were headed to the facility. He imagined them passing Desmond as they got out of the van. He'd be dangerous if already on to Mary's knowledge of his infection. He might attack them, Bolton included, there in the open. It wasn't as if anyone could stop him after he unleashed the aliens' full potential.

"Sir," Brent said, "are we headed to the facility?"

"Yes, Mr. Foster. We're going to my headquarters."

"Did you have someone pick up Desmond?"

"Mr. Armstrong is in custody, yes," Bolton said.

"And what about Mary, and Paola?"

"They're fine, sir."

Brent sighed, hoping this ordeal was nearing its finish. If Bolton had managed to capture Desmond, and Keenan had secured the vials, perhaps the Black Island Research Facility could stop the aliens before they destroyed another planet. Perhaps he and Ben could live something resembling a normal life.

For the first time in as long as he could remember, Brent felt hopeful.

Teagan looked over at Brent and smiled. Surprisingly, the kids had yet to ask any questions.

The van dipped into a parking garage on the facility's ground level, and a large steel door clanged closed behind them. They drove until they reached a large elevator where two Guardsmen with rifles stood sentry. The van came to a stop, and Bolton got out, sliding the side door open.

Bolton nodded at the guards, one of whom held his hand over a security pad beside the elevator.

They entered the elevator, Ben reaching up and grabbing his father's hand, tight. Teagan carried Becca, staring back and forth between Bolton and her mother, likely trying to figure out the man's identity.

The driver followed them into the elevator, and the doors slid shut behind him. He'd left the bag of weapons in the van.

The elevator hitched, a hiccup to startle Ben before its descent.

"It's OK, buddy." Brent looked down, bent over, scooped up his son, and carried him against his chest. Brent looked his son in the eyes and smiled. "I promise everything will be OK."

Ben leaned close to Brent's ear and whispered, though probably too loud, "The man in the helmet is scary."

Brent turned and saw his reflection in the man's visor and figured the helmet probably *was* scary to a little kid. Hell, Brent would be frightened of an intimidating man in a helmet and black Guardsman uniform.

The Guardsman said, "Yeah, the helmet is a bit scary, Ben," then reached up to remove it.

Brent stared in horror as Desmond smiled back.

"Hello, Brent. You didn't think I'd infect Desmond and not the Director, did you?"

Before Brent could move, he felt a gun in his side, Bolton pressing it into his ribs.

As the elevator held its descent, Brent felt certain that they were plummeting to their deaths, and he was responsible.

He'd failed them all.

Desmond smiled, pulling his own holstered gun on Teagan. "Don't even think about doing anything stupid."

* * * *

CHAPTER 21
MARY OLSON

Mary woke to darkness, confusion, and a thousand nails hammering into her skull.

She reached up, felt a large, egg-sized lump on her forehead, then remembered Desmond hitting her with the gun.

Paola!

She sat up, blood rushing to her head, adding to the intense pain.

Dim amber lights in the cavernous room reflected off just enough of the glass surface to let her know she was in a cell like Paola's.

She looked around, hoping to be sharing a cell with her daughter, but Mary was alone.

She stared through the glass and saw that of the room's eight cells, six others were filled, though it was too dark to make out their occupants, or see if any were Paola.

I'm OK, Mom, her daughter's voice spoke in her head. *I'm in the cell next to you. Think your thoughts. Don't speak them. They're listening, and I don't want them to know we can communicate.*

Mary looked up to see Paola pressing her hand against the glass wall.

Mary put her own palm to the wall, crying.

I'm so sorry. Are you OK?

I'm OK. You should have killed Desmond and let me die.

No, don't talk like that. I wasn't going to let him kill you.

He's going to kill us anyway.

We don't know that. If he wanted us dead, he could've already killed us.

You're right, Paola thought. *He's planning something that will make us wish we were dead.*

What are you talking about? How do you know?

I've seen his dreams. He has the vials ... all of them. There's nothing stopping him from doing whatever he wants.

What does he want? To do what they did to the other world?

Worse.

What could be worse?

Paola's silence sounded like a scream.

Mary asked again, *What could be worse?*

I don't want to think about it, Mom. Please don't ask.

Mary looked around at the other shapes beneath the red light.

Who else is in here with us?

Hold on.

The amber lights turned up their intensity enough for Mary to make out the others. At first, she was surprised that Paola could control the lights by thought. But her wonder quickly withered to horror when she saw Desmond's prisoners.

Mary gasped.

Oh God. No.

He has us all.

In the cell to her right Mary saw Boricio standing, staring at her, shrugging his shoulders.

Beyond him, she saw Brent and his son in another cell, sleeping on the bed.

Across from Paola, Teagan was rocking Becca, who appeared to be crying. Keenan sat on the floor in the next cell, knees to his chest as he stared at her. Beside him was Marina, the head of the Church of Original Design, the woman whose house they'd gone to, hoping to cure Paola. She was lying on her mat, turned toward the back wall, possibly sleeping. The final cell was empty.

Where's Rose? Mary asked her daughter.

She got infected with The Darkness, and then she died.

Oh God, Mary thought, looking back at Boricio, wanting to hug him, console him. *He must be so messed up. First person he ever opened his heart to.*

He's hurt bad, yes.

Can you talk to the others? Mary thought.

Yes. Everyone but Marina. For some reason, I can't reach her. Maybe because she's the only one of us The Light is not part of.

Mary glanced at Keenan again, saw him staring at the glass, and suddenly realized why.

Does he know about Jade?

Yes.

Oh God.

She wanted to cry, to hug him, too.

Mary began to pace. *We've got to get out of here. Dammit.*

She racked her brain, trying to think of anyone who could possibly help. But everyone she could possibly turn to was sharing her boat, including Boricio.

She looked back at him again. He looked like a caged panther, itching to get free as badly as she.

Mary's mind flashed back to something Desmond had said — about he and Paola being no different. They were both infected by the aliens, the only difference being that his alien was deemed bad while Paola's was good.

Mary had an idea.

* * * *

CHAPTER 22
PAOLA OLSON

Paola stared at her mother, listening to the plan as she thought it.

Paola nodded. It was a bold scheme, reliant on a hunch that someone other than Desmond was watching them on the security cameras. And that whoever was watching had been instructed to keep them alive.

Paola reached into the minds of the others, all except Marina and the children, and relayed the plan, as they'd need to be prepared for movement the moment she did what had to be done.

She told them all to remain in their present positions. Brent had to pretend he was sleeping, as did Teagan.

Once everyone agreed, Paola reached into Boricio's mind.

I'm going to need your guidance. Can you help me?

You know it, Paola. Boricio thought, in what felt like a growl. *Let's give these fuckers some nightmares.*

Paola positioned herself so she faced the camera in the cell's rear corner and began rolling her eyes into the back of her head. She cried out, gasping as if choking, and brought her hands to her throat.

Paola fell to the ground, hard, thrashing around as if in a seizure.

She could hear her mother banging on the glass, screaming for someone to help her daughter.

Come on.

No one was coming.

Was the show for naught? Was nobody watching?

Paola kept thrashing, and added a gurgling as if she were choking on her saliva or something she imagined might convince a guard to run in and help her.

The main lights turned on, drowning the room in bright white.

Paola continued her act, not looking to see if anyone was coming. She had to keep selling it.

Her mom, and now the others, were all screaming for help. She couldn't hear them through the glass, but their thoughts were screams in her mind.

She heard her door open.

A Black Island Guardsman rushed in, no helmet, and dropped to the ground. Another man stood behind him, shotgun in hand.

"What's wrong?" the first man asked.

Paola kept shaking, then tried to whisper something urgently to him to bring him closer.

He leaned in.

Showtime.

Now!, she thought.

Everyone in their cells played their part, distracting the other Guardsman by pounding on their cell walls at once.

* * * *

CHAPTER 23
THE LIGHT

The Light leapt from Paola's throat, rushing into the Guardsman's mouth before he could stop it.

The Light, equal parts Luca and the alien species, took immediate control of the Guardsman, Joseph Calloway.

"Knock it the fuck off!" the other Guardsman yelled, smacking the butt of his shotgun on Keenan's cell.

The Light reached down, grabbed the pistol hanging from Calloway's holster.

Raise it and shoot right in the back of the skull, just like I taught you, Boricio thought.

Boricio hadn't taught Luca or The Light, but The Light had enough of Paola's memories to remember her training.

Calloway raised the gun, aimed at the back of the other Guardsman's skull, and pulled the trigger.

The shot instantly killed him.

"Woo-whee!" Boricio yelled, clapping. "You're blinding me with science!"

The Light sent Calloway to Boricio's cell first. He placed his palm on the door and opened it.

Boricio popped out of the cell, grabbed the shotgun from the dead Guardsman on the ground, and turned back to The Light. "Time to get this team on the field."

The Light went to the other cells and released the others, Paola last.

It was odd seeing Paola from outside her body. The Light wanted to reenter as she was more vulnerable without *It* inside her. But The Light had to stay inside Calloway until they left the facility. His palms and retina scans were their passage.

The Light searched Calloway's memories: There were another two Guardsmen stationed just outside the elevator. They would have to take the elevator to the main floor and flee the facility after that. From there, The Light wasn't sure where Mary and Boricio would want to go next — leave the island or kill Desmond. The Light guessed the latter, but first they had to take out the guards.

Calloway turned to Boricio. "OK, there are two guards stationed at the elevator. I'll go and distract them. You follow behind and take them, OK?"

Boricio laughed. "Man, I knew you and me would get together and kill some fuckers, little lamb, but I didn't think you'd be so goddamned ugly."

Paola said, "Hah-hah!"

Boricio turned to her and winked. "Just kiddin', sweetie. Hold on while Uncle Boricio kills some fuckers with your alien self."

The Light led the way, stepping through the double sliding doors by himself, holding them open.

One of the two Guardsmen, a man named Hollings, asked, "What are you doing away from your station, Calloway? Something wrong?"

Boricio appeared seconds later and turned Hollings's face to gore with the shotgun.

Kent, the other Guardsman, went to fire his weapon, but Calloway raised his and fired a trio of shots. The first two missed, but the third pierced his helmet, dropping the man a moment after his gun went off.

The Light turned and saw a blast in the wall, inches from Boricio.

"Damn, little lamb, try not to miss so much next time?"

"Sorry," said The Light.

They returned to the others. Boricio handed Mary and Keenan shotguns from the two fallen Guardsmen.

Boricio smiled. "So who's ready to get the fuck outta here?"

* * * *

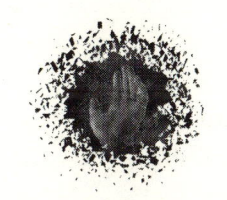

CHAPTER 24
MARY OLSON

Mary hugged her daughter close as they stepped into the elevators. The puppet Guardsman pressed his palm against the security panel and hit a series of buttons to send the elevator back to the surface.

"I thought I lost you, baby," she said, her eyes welling with tears.

"It's OK, Mom, we're together now. I'm sorry I couldn't reach you. I think Desmond was keeping me from talking to you, so I had to reach out to Brent."

"No, you did the right thing."

Mary looked at Brent, who was holding Ben in his hands. He smiled nervously. They'd escaped the cells, but not yet the facility. Brent was doing his best to present a calm face.

Ben, sleepy eyed, said, "We found you, Paola."

"Yes, you did," Paola smiled.

Brent said, "We were 'playing' hide 'n' seek with you both while we hid in a house on the west side of the island."

"Ah, OK." Mary smiled and waved at Ben.

Teagan and Becca stood beside Brent, Becca still crying, rubbing her ruby eyes.

"We're going home, soon." Teagan kissed her daughter on the cheek.

Boricio and Keenan headed toward the elevator doors, guns aimed out as they arrived at the top floor. Marina followed like a nervous bird behind them.

"How many Guardsmen'll be waiting?" Boricio asked the puppet.

"Should be five on duty, but likely just one in the area immediately outside the elevator. Take him out quietly, and you won't attract attention."

Boricio looked at Keenan. "Silence isn't exactly my forte, you wanna handle this?"

Keenan nodded.

The doors opened.

A Guardsman was standing about twenty feet from the elevator, staring at the exit doors on the other side of the lobby.

Keenan raised his hand, telling the others to stay back as he rushed, light footed, toward the Guardsman.

Mary was surprised how quickly, gracefully, and silently he moved.

The Guardsman turned when Keenan was about ten feet away. He saw Keenan, then everyone else at the elevator.

Too late, he raised his M-16.

Keenan punched the man in the throat, sending him to the floor.

He then dropped on top of him, quickly slamming the butt of the shotgun into the man's face three times.

Keenan grabbed the assault rifle and waved them forward.

They ran to join Keenan in the lobby. Keenan handed Brent the shotgun as he held onto the M-16. "Here ya go, buddy."

Brent put Ben down, telling him to hold Teagan's hand and don't let go.

Mary could hardly believe their luck: The space between the lobby and front doors was surprisingly empty. Beyond the lobby was a large expanse of paved area that would have held a parking lot if the island's inhabitants drove to work instead of walked. She wondered why they didn't head to the parking garage and take one of the vehicles, but figured they'd have to cross more Guardsmen, and were likely better off on foot until they figured out their next move.

As they approached the front doors, Mary asked Boricio, "What next? Do we leave the island or go find Desmond?"

Boricio stepped out the front doors and into the night then turned to Mary. "We find Desmond Do-Right and kill the fucker dead."

A pair of gunshots cracked the cold night air and stopped them in their tracks.

Paola collapsed to the ground.

Mary screamed as she looked down and saw her daughter's face destroyed, blood gushing from her head. Mary fell beside her, holding Paola, looking down at her dead body, trying to wish life back inside her.

Mary's heart froze in her chest. Time stopped.

No, no, no, no!

Boricio screamed out, "Up there!"

Along the facility's first-story roof, four Guardsman were lined along the top, sniper rifles aimed.

"You fuckers!" Boricio fired his shotgun at the roof, hitting nobody.

"Back inside!" Keenan yelled, firing his rifle and laying down cover to run.

As the others ran, Mary stayed frozen, cradling her daughter's body, not wanting, or able, to move.

Just seconds ago, they'd been talking, holding one another. They were almost free.

And now ... this.

"Come on!" Boricio grabbed her shoulder.

"No!" Mary yelled. "No more running!"

Keenan kept firing shots. Lights appeared behind them — vehicles pulling up.

Desmond's voice hit the loudspeaker. "Put down your guns!"

Keenan kept firing at the Guardsmen on the roof. "Tangos at twelve o' clock down. Got many Tangos at six o'clock. Let's go!"

Mary stood, grabbed the shotgun, and fired at the five vans, not knowing which held Desmond.

She emptied the shotgun, not hitting anything, as they were out of range, and screamed.

Guardsmen opened fire.

Desmond's voice returned to the speakers. "Put down your guns, and I'll let you live."

"Fuck you!" Mary screamed.

She dropped the empty shotgun and ran toward Desmond, fingers clenched in claws, eager to tear the flesh from his face.

"No!" Boricio yelled, catching up to Mary and grabbing her around her waist, yanking her backward as Keenan emptied his gun at the Guardsmen in front of them.

"Come on!" Boricio screamed into Mary's ear, dragging her back into the facility, leaving Paola's still-warm body behind.

"Let me go!" she yelled, clawing, trying to break free.

Boricio held her tight, refusing her wishes.

"What now?" Brent asked.

Someone inside the lobby yelled at them to lay down their weapons.

Mary barely registered the other Guardsmen closing in from behind.

Everything was happening behind a gauze through which Mary could barely hear. Movements seemed slow and underwater.

Mary looked down and realized she was bleeding.

She pulled up her shirt and saw the hole in her abdomen.

Again, time quit.

Mary looked up to see the lobby Guardsmen approaching.

Outside, more Guardsmen.

They were trapped.

She looked to see Ben and Becca screaming as Teagan cowered on the lobby floor, holding them down.

Paola was dead.

The kids would be next.

They were all dead already.

Gunshots shook Mary from her daze and kicked time back into motion.

Calloway, the Guardsman occupied by The Light, fired and took down one of the Guardsmen approaching from the lobby.

The Light was still alive.

Maybe I can get it to heal Paola!

They had to survive. Had to get back outside and to Paola.

Brent and Keenan fired several shots, taking out the other lobby Guardsmen.

"Come on!" Calloway said, "let's hit the elevators."

"The elevators?" Keenan repeated.

"We'll go back downstairs. I may be able to hack the elevator to keep them from following us down."

"And then what?" Boricio asked.

"I don't know," Calloway admitted.

"Wait," Mary said, "we've gotta get Paola. The Light can heal her. Bring her back."

Calloway shook his head. "I don't know if I can save her, Mary. I need to save you all first."

"Please!" she cried. She looked outside to see Desmond and at least twenty other Guardsmen approaching the front doors. It would be impossible to reach her daughter's body without an army.

Part of Mary wanted to go out and just let Desmond kill her. End the pain.

But as Ben and Becca's cries cut through her pain, Mary knew she had to do everything possible to keep them alive. Then, she hoped, they could return to Paola in time.

"Let's go," Mary cried as she followed them to the elevators.

Calloway opened the elevator doors, and they stepped inside.

She couldn't believe they were heading back down.

The children's cries were chaotic within the elevator, killing her focus as she tried to conjure an escape from certain death.

* * * *

CHAPTER 25
LUCA HARDING

Luca's skin was burning. He opened his eyes and ended the dream where Mommy was making eggs on his arm.

But he was still too hot. The sun outside was brighter than it was supposed to be.

Luca got up from his bed, surprised to be back in his old house. No, not his house. This was Will's.

"Hello?" he called out. "Is anyone home? Will? Boricio?"

Neither his adopted father nor brother was home.

Luca had the oddest sensation of déjà vu, as if he'd been here before. The sensation coalesced with another — that he wasn't supposed to be here at all.

Something was off in the world.

But Luca's mind was foggy, and his skin itchy.

Suddenly, he wasn't home, but outside on the beach. He could hear gulls crying, feel the salt on the cool breeze blowing through his hair, but couldn't see anyone as far as he looked up and down the shore. He'd never been to a completely empty beach, nor seen a shore so empty with the sun sitting so high in the sky.

Luca wondered if he was in a dream, but something in his surroundings felt peculiar. Something insisted it wasn't a dream.

And yet Luca was sure he wasn't awake.

He was somewhere in between.

Luca looked out over the water, noticing the many birds dipping and diving, grabbing fish before returning to the sky.

Except it didn't look like fish. Luca walked closer to the sea for a better look and noticed bits of white stuff bobbing up and down in the tide, some even washing up on the shore before getting dragged back to sea.

The ocean roared as Luca kept moving toward it, trying to see what the birds might be eating.

Warm water rushed over his feet as the tide washed his ankles. Something bumped against his skin, and Luca looked down, finally getting a look at the bird's meal.

The piece of white got caught against his leg as the foamy tide withdrew, leaving the piece of meat behind.

Luca bent over and saw that it wasn't meat, but rather a finger.

His stomach turned as Luca realized that the floating white things dotting the tide weren't fish, but rather thousands of corpses, getting pecked apart as they floated.

Luca screamed, turned, and ran from the shore, straight toward the abandoned boardwalk.

He kept running, not daring to look behind him.

Luca found himself under the boardwalk, suddenly cold and shivering in the dark.

He heard a whining, and saw a pair of blue eyes watching him. A husky, standing there, tail wagging.

"Come here, boy," Luca said, feeling like he'd seen the dog before, though he couldn't remember where.

Above him, he heard someone calling out, "Lobster tacos! Get your fresh lobster tacos!"

Lobster tacos?

The voice sounded familiar.

The dog ran toward the voice.

Luca followed, running up the stairs to the boardwalk, eager to place the voice. He saw the dog, then the little lobster taco stand and an old man behind the cart.

Will!

Luca raced up to his dad, and threw his arms around him.

The dog barked, circling the two of them like a long-lost pet.

"Daddy!"

Luca hugged Will tight. It felt like forever since he'd last seen him.

"Luca!" Will pat the boy on his head. "Oh God, it's been so long. How are you?"

"I dunno." Luca shrugged, looking out at the sea of dead bodies again. "Nothing's right. I can't remember anything."

"That's because you're in the hospital. They're operating on you, and you're under some powerful sedatives."

"What happened to me?"

"You've been shot."

"I was?" Luca couldn't remember being shot.

Flashes of memory swirled through his head, things that didn't make sense. A burning compound, a dead girl, and Luca healing her. Paola. He remembered her before another memory came, this one confusing: Will shooting him.

Luca turned his head sideways trying to make sense of the memory. "Did you shoot me?"

"You need to go back now. Your friends need you. Your brother needs you."

"Brother? Boricio?"

"Yes," Will said. He pointed to an open elevator where they all stood, facing off against Desmond and an army of armed Guardsmen.

Will waved to Luca. "Go to them, Luca."

"Wait," Luca tried to call out, but Will and the dog were already fading into a bright light.

Luca woke in surgery.

"He's waking up," said a man in the distance.

A nurse shouted to administer some drug he'd never heard of.

Luca struggled to hang on, to focus on where he needed to go. Struggled to connect with his friends in the elevator as the drug made its home in his bloodstream.

* * * *

CHAPTER 26
BORICIO WOLFE

The elevator was heading down to the eighth level when it suddenly lurched to a full stop on the fourth.

"The fuck?" Boricio said.

"He must've overridden the controls." Keenan aimed his rifle at the elevator doors, waiting for them to open.

Boricio asked, "How many cock swallowers are there in this damned place?"

"Armed? At least forty," Keenan said.

"And how many have the alien Ebola?" Boricio asked.

"No idea," Keenan said.

Calloway spoke. "I can't feel how many. Most of them are likely working under Desmond and Bolton, and don't know that their leaders have been compromised."

"Still deadly just the same," Brent said.

Boricio looked at Mary, chewing on her bottom lip and staring at the doors, fists clenched, looking like she could murder the world, or at least every Ebolafied fucker inside it.

A voice crackled to life from overhead speakers.

"Hello, friends," Desmond's voice said, "I really hate this unfortunate turn of events. I had tremendous plans for us all. You don't have to die."

"Fuck you, Desmondo!" Boricio yelled, hoping the fucker could hear him.

"Ah, Boricio the Great. I would think that you of all people would recognize an opportunity when offered. Don't you want to live forever?"

"Not like that," Boricio yelled.

Desmond continued, "Don't you all want to be something better than you are? I can give you a life that's superior to anything you've ever imagined. Join me and be a part of humanity's evolution. We are looking for the best of your species, to bring you with us, and rule the world. No more petty wars. No more murder. No starvation. Enough for all. We can live forever in a paradise of our making. Or ... you can stay and die in the old world with the animals. Perish or thrive. Your choice. You have until the elevator reaches the lobby to decide. I suggest you choose wisely."

Boricio looked around at everyone.

Ben cried, "I don't wanna die, Daddy."

Brent hugged his boy, picking him up, tears wetting his eyes. The girl, Teagan, scooped up her crying daughter.

Boricio would rather die than get an anal tentacle probe from these fuckers.

He looked at Calloway. "Tell us, should we take this offer? Will he let us live? What will life be like?"

"I think he will let us live. Though I'm not sure what your lives will be like. He could conceivably coexist with you as I did with Luca and then with Paola. It *is* possible. But it's also possible he will consume your bodies and minds ... I don't know."

Boricio turned to Brent and Teagan. "Hey, I won't blame you all if you take the offer. Life is life, and I suppose any chance at breathing might be better than a dance with the devil. But I'm not going out like that."

"I don't know what to do," Brent said, his face pale, eyes wide.

Ben cried, "I don't wanna die, Daddy."

Boricio turned to Mary. Tears soaked the sides of her face, but she didn't say a word, nor meet a single eye.

The elevator began to ascend.

Third level.

Ben cried and brought Becca to tears. Teagan choked back her own and said, "I don't know what to do."

Second level.

"Tick tock," Desmond's voice crackled through the speakers. "Time to decide. Live or die, die or live? By the way, Mary, I can bring Paola back. She doesn't have to die."

Mary's anger faded as her eyes welled up again. She turned to Boricio. "He can bring her back?"

"He's a liar, Mary. Don't believe him."

Mary stared at the elevator doors, looking every bit as torn as Boricio imagined she must be.

Boricio glanced at Keenan who returned his stare with the same stony expression. He, like Boricio, had nothing left to lose, and was willing to go out firing. But was it fair to throw the Brady Bunch into the fray?

The elevator hit the first level, and Desmond came on the radio. "Ding. First level, ladies' apparel and death. Time to decide."

The elevator doors began to open.

Boricio met Brent's eyes. He shook his head no, and Boricio understood immediately. He didn't want to live, not like that.

Boricio brought his gun to the back of Ben's head, figuring the least he could do was end the kid's misery.

Brent caught Boricio's intention and pulled his son away, shaking his head no.

The elevator doors opened.

Desmond stood behind a line of armored Guardsmen, his head barely visible, using them as a shield. There were at least twenty in a line, each holding a machine gun, all aimed into the elevator's interior.

Standing in front of them, Paola, her face healed, even though her shirt was stained with blood.

"Please, Mommy, come with us."

Mary cried out and looked at Boricio, as if seeking permission to do what every bit of her wanted to do.

"Don't believe it," he said. "It's not your daughter."

Mary closed her eyes, turning away from Paola, crying.

"You don't have to die. You can all come and be truly free," Desmond said. "Just step off the elevator and join us."

Boricio surveyed the line of men who waited for either surrender or war. Of the three with guns, Boricio figured he would have the best shot at killing Desmond, but doing so would likely get everyone in the elevator killed.

Desmond said, "Whoever wants to live step off the elevator."

Boricio looked at Brent and Teagan.

Neither flinched.

Their children cried, and they hugged them closer.

Boricio swallowed, staring at Ben's bloodshot eyes. The child cried, "I don't wanna die."

Boricio couldn't believe both parents were willing to choose death over the alien's offer.

He wasn't sure he could do the same if he were a father.

"Nobody?" Desmond asked.

Mary turned back and looked at Brent and Teagan, back at Desmond, and then Mary.

"Fuck you, Desmond!" she cried.

"Sorry to hear that." Desmond shook his head. "OK, gentlemen, open fire."

Gunfire erupted from the Guardsmen's assault rifles.

Keenan and Boricio fired back.

Calloway leaped in front of the open doors, his body riddled with bullets from both sides as the doors slammed suddenly shut.

Calloway fell to the ground, bloody and shredded.

Boricio heard screaming from Teagan behind. He turned to see her huddled on the ground covering her daughter. She was looking at Brent, also huddled, Ben under his body, blood pouring from one or both.

Marina lay against the wall behind them, struggling to keep her eyes open as her stomach bled out.

Bullets continued to thunk into the elevator doors, dinging dents by the hundred.

"It won't hold long." Keenan raced to the buttons and pressed the 7 over and over. The elevator didn't budge.

Boricio wasn't sure how the doors were pulled shut. It must've been Calloway, or The Light.

But the doors wouldn't last long.

The first bullet ripped through the doors and pierced the wall behind them.

"Shit!" Keenan shouted, slamming his palm on the buttons again.

Mary stood frozen, staring at the elevator door as if waiting to die.

She wasn't looking at the doors, but rather the midnight-colored spire pluming from Calloway's corpse. The Light, searching for a new host.

It floated toward Mary and looked as if it might enter her open mouth, before it blinked from existence.

* * * *

CHAPTER 27
LUCA HARDING

Luca stood in the elevator, an astral projection of himself staring at the bullets ripping through the door.

They're all going to die soon.

"Stop!" Luca cried out when a bullet hit Ben. Another two found Teagan's ribs and back as she struggled to cover her daughter.

Two more hit Keenan in the chest. He stumbled back and dropped his rifle.

Stop!!

But there was no one to stop this.

No one to help him.

He was on his own.

Then Luca saw The Light rising from Calloway's body.

The Light hovered in front of Mary, and turned to the boy.

"Luca?" The Light said, then blinked inside him.

* * * *

CHAPTER 28
MARY OLSON

Mary watched the bullets tear the doors to shreds. Sounds had bled into one another forming a relentless cacophony, all still underwater.

She was ready to die.

Prepared to end her pain.

Mary saw Paola, or the corruption of her body, through holes in the doors.

That isn't her. Don't look.

Luca appeared in the elevator, hovering where Calloway had been.

She had to be seeing things. No one else seemed to see him.

Luca looked at Mary, then down behind her.

She turned to see Brent holding his bleeding son, crying out to the heavens.

Teagan was crying out, eyes rolling into the back of her head as she lay on top of her daughter, blood seeping from Teagan's side.

Bullets continued to pierce the elevator.

One slammed into Mary's back.

She fell to the ground, crying out.

Another three bullets tore into Keenan, ripping his chest open.

Marina looked like she was already dead.

Boricio turned and widened his eyes.

"Luca?"

More bullets ripped through the elevator door.

She heard a loud thunking and turned as someone fired a grenade into the elevator.

Mary closed her eyes, waiting to die.

And then there was silence.

* * * *

CHAPTER 29
LUCA HARDING

Luca stood in the elevator, watching his friends fall in a hail of bullets and felt a merging of memories, his own, the other Luca's, and now Paola's melting into his brain's soup.

Another memory surged forward — October 15, 2011, when he'd seen what had been unleashed after Luca had given the vial to his adopted brother, Boricio Bishop.

Luca had reached out and collected these souls, ushering them into his world in an attempt to fix what he'd been responsible for breaking.

Little did Luca know he'd only broken things more by bringing future friends to a dead world.

He could never make things right. Nearly all of his world's population had perished on October 15. He couldn't bring them back.

But he *could* try to help these survivors.

Luca wasn't sure how he'd done it the first time, or even how to do it again. He turned to The Light inside him and surrendered, begging *It* to help.

And then, in a blink, they were all gone.

He turned to see Desmond, the carrier of The Darkness, who now possessed all of the unopened vials.

Desmond glared at Luca as the Guardsmen emptied their guns into *Its* burning brightness.

But Desmond could not kill him any more than he could kill The Darkness.

Not now anyway. Another clash, like the one on Black Island on the other world would unleash more destruction. Better to run — and live to fight another day.

Luca blinked, and was back inside his own body on the operating table as surgeons sewed his wounds and stabilized his body.

Luca could hear them talking even as he was still under, remarking on how different he looked now — how they could swear he'd aged on the table.

Little did they know where he'd gone or what he'd done with the survivors of October 15.

* * * *

CHAPTER 30
BRENT FOSTER

One moment Brent was screaming and cradling his dying son in a hail of gunfire. The next he was holding Ben in a wide-open field of tall grass swaying in a gentle breeze beneath a nearly full moon.

He looked down to see Ben crying and looking around.

He pulled at his boy's bloody shirt, to find the wounds on his stomach.

They were gone.

He was healed.

How is this possible?

"Daddy! Where are we? What happened?"

"I don't know." Brent looked around trying to make sense of things. He heard Becca's sobs just seconds before he saw her and Teagan materialize beside him.

What the hell?

Moments later, they heard Keenan screaming, and gunshots before he appeared, his rifle blasting into the empty night.

Keenan stopped, realizing he was no longer in the elevator, turning with rifle in hand, searching for whatever enemy was to be found, whoever had somehow brought them here.

And then the woman, Marina, appeared, standing there, looking as confused as Brent felt.

They all stood in the darkness, staring at one another.

"Where are we?" Marina asked, confused.

"We're back," Keenan said. "We're on the other world."

"We are?" Teagan asked. "How do you know?"

He pointed at the distance, at dark shapes reaching into the pure black sky. "That's a city. Not a single light is on."

"No," Teagan cried out. "No, no, no!"

"Shh!" Keenan rushed over to Teagan and put a hand on her mouth.

Becca cried out, "I'm scared, Mommy!"

"Don't be scared," Brent soothed. "He wouldn't have sent us here if it weren't safe."

"Who wouldn't have?" Marina asked.

Brent suddenly remembered, and things were starting to make sense.

"Luca. I saw him in the elevator just before we vanished. He must've healed Ben, too."

Marina had started to say something, maybe ask who Luca was, but was interrupted by Keenan.

"And me," Keenan said, looking down, patting his chest. Holes in his uniform showed where he'd been shot, but his skin, like Ben's, was no longer marred.

Marina looked down at herself and saw a large bloodstained hole gaping in her shirt. She reached down, tearing at the hole, making it wider, feeling around.

"I'm healed, too!"

Tears stung Brent's burning eyes. "He did it. He saved us. Again."

Keenan shook his head. "Wait a second. Where's Mary? And Boricio?"

Brent looked around, seeing no sign of anyone else.

"Hello?" Brent called out, his voice echoing in the night.

"Keep it down! We don't know what's left on this world. Might be full of them aliens." Ed said.

"Maybe Mary and Boricio are still being healed?" Ben suggested.

"Maybe," Brent said, though that didn't feel right.

"What do we do? Where do we go?" Teagan asked, voice high pitched with worry, rocking Becca in her arms. "How will we survive? Do y'all think those aliens are still here?"

Ben clutched Brent's leg. "I'm scared, Daddy."

The last sound any of them wanted to hear filled the air — the awful, alien clicking somewhere in the distance.

"Oh God," Teagan cried. "No. Not again."

Keenan lifted the rifle, turning it, searching for the source.

Brent searched for his shotgun, but realized it must not have accompanied his crossing. He was holding his son, not a weapon, when Luca teleported them out of the elevator.

The clicking grew louder and more abundant. Another horrible sound joined the brutal symphony — hundreds of running somethings, like a herd of buffalo.

"There!" Marina whispered, pointing toward the tree line a couple of hundred feet to their left.

Shadows within shadows, moving fast, quickly closing in.

Keenan raised the rifle and fired. There was no way he had enough ammo, even if he had enough time, to take them all down.

Shrill screams as one, or perhaps a pair of creatures fell; it was tough to see clearly even with the bright moon bathing the swaying field. But what he could see — hundreds of shapes coming from the trees — rattled Brent's body with raw fear.

He grabbed Ben and Becca. "Come on!" he said, running with Teagan at his side.

The children screamed in his ear, high-pitched cries, shrill to match the aliens' intensity.

Brent kept running forward, unsure where he was headed, heart pounding so hard he felt certain it would either explode or surrender its beating. His legs were fire, his back aching with the exhausting weight as he raced across the uneven ground, praying he wouldn't trip and kill the kids.

Come on, Ed! Take these fuckers out!

Keenan's shots suddenly stopped.

Icy fear splashed his insides.

Oh God, Brent's dead!

He didn't dare look back. Stopping to do so would slow or trip him.

He heard Teagan at his side, barely keeping pace, her breath so ragged it sounded like torn.

Brent couldn't tell if either Ed or Marina was also behind them, had taken off in another direction, or were already dead in the grass.

"No!" he heard Teagan cry out, followed by a thumping.

Brent peeked back, though still running forward, to see she'd fallen to the ground, half concealed by flowing grass.

His ankle twisted, and pain pierced his leg, sending him, and the children, flying forward to the ground.

No!!

The galloping, along with the aliens' awful clicking, grew louder, closer.

Brent looked up, searching for his son.

"Ben! Becca!" he cried out.

Thunderous movement, clicks, and shrieks were all Brent could hear.

He had to find them, grab them, and keep running.

He stood, but collapsed as pain screamed through his ankle.

No, no, no, no! Fuck, I can't walk!

Brent turned, looking for Teagan, to see if she'd gotten up and tell her to take Ben and run. He'd serve as a distraction, take as many of the fuckers out as he could.

But Brent couldn't see Teagan through all the tall grass.

He saw only darkness.

And then, a blinding light came from above — a helicopter.

Brent heard shrieks all around him, and chaos — running, ground being torn from the Earth, alien screams, and a different kind of clicking as tracer fire ripped into the aliens, sending them scurrying back toward the tree line.

Brent sat up, staring in shock. The helicopter hovered above, firing until the aliens had all turned away.

Ben stumbled forward through the grass, holding Becca's hand, both faces dirty and each of them crying.

"Come here." Brent opened his arms and hugged them, watching the helicopter land. The thing was huge, like a military chopper, though Brent wasn't familiar enough to know a Blackhawk from a Chinook.

He heard movement behind him, and turned to see Keenan approaching, gun over his shoulder, Marina by his side.

"Shit, I thought you were dead."

"Not yet, old friend," Keenan said.

They both looked at the helicopter as two people outfitted in black uniforms hopped out. They wore all black, like the Black Island Guardsmen, but their uniforms were slightly different. Different but familiar, though Brent couldn't place it at first.

The two soldiers approached, and Brent was surprised to see that one was a woman as she lifted the dark visor.

The woman looked at them, smiling. "Well, holy fucking shit, where the hell have you two scumbags been?"

It took Brent a moment before he recognized her as the Black Mountain Guardsman who had taken him and Keenan hostage before teaming with them at the battle for Black Island.

"Lisa?" Keenan said. "What the hell are you doing here?"

"We were making a routine sweep of the area, searching for a stolen supply truck. We saw you all pop up on the radar, and came out here."

"Did you see anyone else? We came with two other people."

"Nobody else. Came from where?" Lisa asked.

"Back on our world," Brent said. "It's a long story."

"OK, well, tell me on the way to the chopper. We're heading back."

"Back where?" Keenan asked. "Black Mountain?"

"No. We have another base."

"Where the hell are we?" Keenan asked.

"Montana," she said. "Camp's a few miles away."

"How many of you are there?" Marina asked.

"Twenty-five," she said, "down from fifty-one."

"You tell us your story; we'll tell you ours," Brent said, following Lisa and the other Guardsmen to the chopper.

* * * *

EPILOGUE

Three years later ...

Ed Keenan bumped along in the van's passenger seat as they raced down the ghost town's street, pursuing one of the thieving bandits on motorcycle who'd stupidly tried robbing their truck.

"You got a shot on 'em yet?" Harry asked as he attempted to keep pace with the bastard.

"Not yet," Ed said, attempting to aim with the AR-15.

The motorcycle was weaving back and forth, and the van was jostling hard on the broken roads, rendering every shot impossible.

They had to catch this bastard to find out where the raiding party was holed up before they struck again. By Ed's estimation, there were ten, maybe twenty of the bandits nearby. If there were more, they would've already attempted a more direct attack and tried to take over their compound rather than coming after their trucks when they went out to find supplies. They'd already lost five drivers in the last six months, and Ed wanted to end it before winter threw the compound into lockdown again.

The cyclist turned down an alley between two large warehouses, speeding up, and taking the turn too fast.

The bike and driver went down, sliding along the road.

"He's ours now!" Harry turned into the alley and slammed on the brakes.

Ed prepared to hop out of the van, gun in hand, and chase the guy on foot — assuming he wasn't too injured, or dead, from the crash.

But Ed stopped with his hand on the door handle as he looked straight out the window at the thing that shouldn't be.

Hovering in the middle of the road was a violet square of light about ten feet by ten. The bike lay on the ground in front of the light, but the cyclist was nowhere to be seen.

"What the fuck is that?" Harry asked.

Ed didn't like the looks of it.

He stepped out of the van and raised his rifle, carefully approaching the light.

He saw something move from within it. A dark shape coming closer.

Ed took aim, readying himself to open fire on whatever the hell emerged from the light.

Harry was out of the still-running van, also aiming his shotgun at the temporal disturbance.

Suddenly, the cyclist's body came flying from the light, landing ten feet in front of Ed.

Harry took two shots at the cyclist, but missed both times.

The man's face and arms was scraped to hell from his wreck, but he was still alive, barely.

"You really shouldn't go leaving your garbage all over the place," a man's voice said from inside the light.

The voice was familiar.

Another dark shape drew closer, and then the man stepped through the portal.

"Boricio?" Ed said, dumbfounded.

"The one and only, at no man's service but happy to see you," Boricio said with a shit-eating grin. He had two pistols hanging from holsters at his side and a sword's hilt sticking up from behind his black leather jacket: a cowboy ninja on meth.

"How?" Ed asked. "Where the hell have you been?"

Another figure stepped through the portal — a man who looked around forty, with dark curly hair and a thick beard. Something about his eyes looked familiar.

Ed realized he was looking at an older version of the kid, Luca.

"Luca?"

"Hi," the man said, soft spoken.

"You know these people?" Harry asked, his gun still on them.

"Yeah," Ed said. "They're OK. You question this scumbag while I catch up."

Ed walked over and shook their hands. "Where have you two been?"

Luca said, "Preparing."

"For what?" Ed asked.

"It would be easier to show you," Luca said, nodding toward the portal.

"How do I know I can trust you?" Ed asked. "How do I know you're not infected?"

"You'd already be deader than dead, Double-O Dipshit," Boricio quipped. "Come on, we ain't gonna cornhole yer pucker."

Ed followed them into the light.

As he stepped through, he felt his body vibrating, and a loud hum filled his ears. For a long moment, Ed felt like he was stuck in time or space, everything a blur around him.

And then he was out, on the other side, in what looked to be a long, dark studio apartment with brick walls. Black curtains were drawn tight over the far wall. The portal hummed and glowed behind him.

"Where are we? Are we … back on Earth?"

"Yes," a woman's voice said from his right.

Ed turned to see Mary, her hair cut short, dark circles under her eyes. A black tank top revealed ripped biceps, as if she'd spent the past three years pumping iron in a prison yard.

"Mary," he said, offering his hand to shake, "how are you?"

She shook his hand firmly, "Welcome home, Keenan."

He noticed the tattoo on Mary's left bicep: Paola's name in a heart. Beneath that, another heart with no name.

"We've gotta go back and get Brent and the others," Ed said. "They'll be glad to know you're alive."

"In time," Boricio said. "First we need to see how you're gonna take this."

"Take what?" Ed asked.

Nobody answered. Mary, Boricio, and Luca exchanged glances as if they were trying to decide whether to share their secret with Ed.

There were two other people Ed didn't recognize, a young blonde in her twenties, sitting at a table working on some sort of large black circular contraption. Perhaps a camera. Beside her was a thin black guy who looked around forty, working on a large gun that look like nothing Ed had ever seen.

"What's going on?" he asked.

"We're getting ready," Mary said.

"Ready for what?"

She walked toward the curtains at the far end of the apartment and pulled them aside.

Brightness flooded the room. Ed drew closer to the windows and gasped at the city's skyline, filled with large hovering black spaceships cutting through a thick smog.

"What the hell is this?"

"They took over. They turned this world into something you ain't gonna believe. Enslaved a lot of us, killed even more."

Ed felt sick to his stomach, scanning the skyline before he looked down to the streets below at the perverse abominations walking the streets — a cross between infected and aliens.

Boricio asked, "So, Keenan, you ready?"

"Ready for what?"

"To join Team Boricio and take this big, blue marble back?"

Keenan thought of Jade. He'd lost the only thing that meant a damn to him. He had nothing to lose, and three years of imprisoned rage to unleash.

He met Mary's eyes, a partner in loss.

"Hell yeah, I'm ready."

TO BE CONCLUDED
IN
YESTERDAY'S GONE: SEASON SIX

WANT TO KNOW WHAT HAPPENS NEXT?

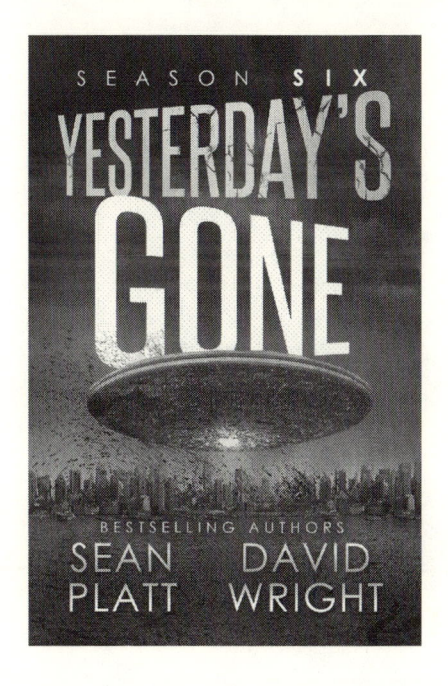

The story continues in *Yesterday's Gone: Season Six*
SterlingandStone.net/book/yesterdays-gone-season-six

AUTHOR'S NOTE

Phew, the season is over!

While *Season Three* remains the most difficult season we've written to date, this was the season that intimidated us the most as we were preparing to write it. I'm using this author's note to give you our mindset and concerns both going into the season and as we wrote it.

Obviously, if you haven't read *Season Five*, you should stop reading as there ARE spoilers ahead. That's why we put it AFTER the season! You didn't just jump to the Author's Note first, did you?!

Don't worry, I used to do that, too.

From very early on in the first season of *Yesterday's Gone*, we knew the war between the Light and Darkness would come home, and it would be an all out alien invasion. No, scratch that — an alien *occupation*.

And we knew bits and pieces of the things that would lead us to the sixth season and the ending we have in mind. But a lot of the in-between stuff wasn't clear. We needed to pave the road to *the ending we want to tell*.

Given that YG is our flagship series with the greatest number of fans, there's also that pressure to deliver a story that makes you glad this went six seasons rather than wrapping in three. And we want you to finish wishing we wrote ten more! (Not that we have any plans for that.)

This season's tasks:
Tell an awesome big story
Bridge the gap between Seasons Four and Six

Continue to develop and surprise you with Collective Inkwell's brand of deep, complex characters.

Because while *Yesterday's Gone* is a big action-packed spectacle, we always put our characters at the front of everything we do. And this season we needed to really put our favorite characters in some uncomfortable spots — especially Mary and Boricio.

On the subject of Mary, I noticed a few comments from people who thought that our female characters weren't very strong in *Yesterday's Gone* — something to the effect of the female characters suffering a lot of torment, and relying on men to save them.

This wasn't a frequent comment, but even a few mentions will get us to look at what we've written and see if maybe there's something we overlooked. It's hard to see your own stuff objectively, particularly so close to publication.

So do I think our women are too weak?

No, I don't.

Why?

Because we don't subscribe to the current fad of creating super women (or men) who can do anything and kick all kinds of ass with a machine gun even if prior to the story they'd never handled a weapon.

I think there *should* be strong female role models in fiction, and that women in books shouldn't be relegated to cliched "women in distress" roles or used *solely as* romantic interests, or props for men. However, I think that when you go too far in the other direction, you wind up being patronizing, and creating a wholly unrealistic character that nobody identifies with!

And here's the thing — everyone suffers in our books. Men, women, children — *everyone*.

If you're a lead character in a Collective Inkwell book, you're going to have a rough time. Your hopes will be dashed, your fears will be realized, and ... you might just get killed off.

Happy endings are a guarantee for no one.

I happen to think Mary is a very strong character, particularly given the shit she's been through. But she's not military trained, a secret agent, or a serial killer. She's a mother pushed to the extremes in pursuit of protecting her child. But she still worries whether she's doing the right thing. She still second guesses herself. Because she is NOT a super hero. She is human – like all our characters.

There's a scene we wrote for Season Four where Mary and Boricio were attacked by the infected in the motel parking lot. Boricio told Mary to stay back while he took on the enemies.

Now, I can see how that might make Mary look like she's letting the man take over, but you have to consider two things. One: Boricio told her to stay put. Boricio is pretty damned convincing when he tells you to do something. Second, even if Mary can kick ass (and she's had weapons training), she still has to consider one thing: if she dies, her daughter is on her own. In other words, just because she can do something doesn't mean it's an easy decision to put herself at risk. Sometimes running or hiding is the wisest move.

While that might be seen as Mary being weak, many of our other characters (except maybe Ed Keenan) would've done the same thing in that position.

Hell, one of our weakest characters in the book is Brent Foster. If he were a female character, I imagine we'd catch all sorts of hell for all the fretting he does in the series. Hell, we *have* gotten flack for Brent being too whiney. But here's the thing – he's not unlike many men I know. Guys who aren't fighters. Who aren't skilled killers. Guys with more book smarts than street smarts, who tend to overanalyze themselves into analysis paralysis.

Like I said, we write human characters — warts and all.

But most of our characters *aren't* warriors. They're regular people put into difficult positions, fighting for their lives.

Boricio was another character we thought a lot about this season. Last season, a minority of readers felt that he'd been neutered a bit. "Boricio finds love and is hanging out with Mary and Paola? What a pussy!"

But I don't think I'd want to read a series where the main characters were the exact same in *Season Five* as they were in *Season One*. We don't want Boricio to be a one note character. We love the complexity of him having to reconcile his killer side with the now "fixed" part of himself.

He's not a good guy by any means. But he's also not the psychopath from the first season.

This season, we were tempted to push Boricio back in the other direction. But then, as the story unfolded, we said no, fuck that noise. We're going to break him down even more.

Last season he faced his past in the form of a father of a young woman he'd killed. This season he faced his greatest weakness — the death of a love he'd finally allowed to flourish inside him.

Losing Rose (again) has done something to Boricio which turns him into the force he'll be in the final season. It was a necessary journey, and one we enjoyed writing as much as Mary's.

Lastly, this season saw us exploring Luca more. He's still a kid, but a bit wiser for all he's been through.

He's also not the Luca we first started with (that boy had become The Light at the end of Season Three.) This Luca is even more complex, riddled with guilt, and struggling with the power growing inside him and The Darkness' plans for domination — something Luca doesn't think he can stop.

We originally planned to make Luca the embodiment of The Darkness. We were going to take our most innocent character, Luca, and turn him into the big bad guy while making our baddest character, Boricio, into the main good guy.

But as we were writing the story, it just didn't feel right — at all.

Luca didn't WANT to become the main bad guy. While he'd suffered at the hands of bullies, and had a few rough spots, it hadn't changed his core. And in fact, the alien inside him responded as much to his kindness as anything — preventing Rose's Darkness from carrying out It's plan.

When we decided that Luca wasn't going to be the main bad guy, and Desmond was instead, we briefly considered killing Luca off. However, we had plans for him in the sixth season. Paola wasn't so lucky.

Given where the story was going, and what she (and her mother) had already endured, it felt like we'd be cheating if she *had* made it out of this season alive.

It was tough killing her. She was a resilient kid and we particularly loved writing the scenes with her and Boricio.

I think the only regret in killing her now is that we didn't give her more point of view chapters. We considered upping her chapter counts this season but thought that doing so might give away our plan to kill her off. We've all seen the TV shows where a secondary character is killed off and you can see it a mile away because all of a sudden that character starts getting plenty of screen time.

We didn't want to telegraph Paola's death.

I admit to quite a bit of glee when we planned this out. First pretending to kill her when Desmond hid her away. And then we returned her to Mary, only to have her die almost out of the blue during their escape.

George R.R. Martin has nothing on us when it comes to killing main characters!

All of this is to say that we love our characters, and hope that it shows — even when we kill them off.

And here's the thing about readers' opinions: remember how I said that some people thought Mary was too weak, Brent was too whiney, and Boricio had been neutered? Well, they're perfectly entitled to think those things. There *are no* perfect characters, just as there are no perfect people.

Our characters are all flawed in some way, just like us.

These are as much your characters as they are ours. And we're honored that you care enough about the people in our world to develop strong feelings — good and bad.

We hope you enjoyed this season as much as we did writing it. Thank you for continuing this journey and inviting us into your lives — it's an honor that continues to humble us.

We can't wait to show you what's in store in the final season, which you'll see early next year.

As always, thank you for reading,
Dave (and Sean)
October 4, 2014

FIND OUT WHY READERS CAN'T GET ENOUGH
COLLECTIVE INKWELL

To see all our of our books, visit:
www.SterlingandStone.net/collective-inkwell

ABOUT THE AUTHORS

Sean Platt is the bestselling co-author of over 60 books, including breakout post-apocalyptic horror serial *Yesterday's Gone*, literary mind-bender *Axis of Aaron*, and the blockbuster sci-fi series, *Invasion*. Never one for staying inside a single box for long, he also writes smart stories for children under the pen name Guy Incognito, and laugh out loud comedies which are absolutely *not* for children.

He is also the founder of the Sterling & Stone Story Studio and along with partners Johnny B. Truant and David W. Wright hosts the weekly Self-Publishing Podcast, openly sharing his journey as an author-entrepreneur and publisher.

Sean is often spotted taking long walks, eating brisket with his fingers, or watching movies with his family in Austin, Texas. You can find him at sean@sterlingandstone.net.

David W Wright is the co-author of several horror series, including the bestselling *Yesterday's Gone* and *WhiteSpace*, as well as the disturbing standalone books, *12* and *Crash*.

Dave is also the curmudgeon co-host of the weekly Self-Publishing Podcast, he invites listeners along on his journey toward better health on the strikingly personal The Walking Dave podcast, and regularly rants about his many pet-peeves on the ridiculous podcast Worst. Show. Ever. (which should never be listened to by anyone, ever).

Dave is an accomplished and intermittent cartoonist who lives in [LOCATION REDACTED] with his wife and son [NAMES REDACTED]. Dave cultivates the perfect level of paranoia and always carries a decoy wallet in case he gets mugged. You can stalk him at dave@sterlingandstone.net or visit his personal blog at www.davidwwright.com.

For any questions about Sterling & Stone books or products, or help with anything at all, please send an email to help@sterlingandstone.net, or contact us at sterlingandstone.net/contact. Thank you for reading.